"Silena, Come Here."

She shook her head as he tried to pull her back against him, but she didn't fight him. Not yet.

"I don't want you to hold me, Sam. I don't want to feel that way about you."

"What way?" he asked, holding her anyway.

She forced herself to step back again. "Any way. I don't . . . I can't fall in love with you."

"*Are* you falling in love with me?"

"No!" She took three steps back, putting ample distance between them. "You're just as much a lie as everything else in my life, Sam. I don't need any more lies."

Also by Terri Herrington

Her Father's Daughter

Available from
HarperPaperbacks

TERRI HERRINGTON

HarperPaperbacks
A Division of HarperCollins*Publishers*

HarperPaperbacks *A Division of* HarperCollins*Publishers*
10 East 53rd Street, New York, N.Y. 10022

Cover illustration by Jim Griffin

First printing: January 1993

Printed in the United States of America

HarperPaperbacks, HarperMonogram, and colophon are trademarks of HarperCollins*Publishers*

❖ 10 9 8 7 6 5 4 3 2 1

This book is dedicated to all those who showed me how to be thankful for adversity, and taught me to use it as an instrument for growth, a tool for strength, and a path toward happiness. The way can never be lonely with friends like you.

Silena

Prologue

1873

The day-old infant's anguished cry pierced the night as its mother's arms relaxed their desperate hold and fell limply to the bloody sheets. Jim McCosky dropped to the floor beside the bed and, trembling, reached across the baby to turn the woman's bruised face to his. All life was gone from her expression, but her tears were still warm.

"I never meant to hurt you," he whispered, his voice wavering.

The baby's wail grew louder, more urgent. Beneath its swaddling blanket, it kicked its hands and feet with angry force, as if, already, it sensed the danger that hovered near. Jim got to his feet and turned away, rubbing his face with leather-tough hands. The need for vengeance tore through him, but that baby's cry overpowered it.

Through the open window, he heard the old shepherd dog begin to bark at some approaching danger. Every muscle in his road-weary body tensed. There would be trouble for certain if anyone discovered him there. Instinctively, he drew his Colt with a sweaty hand and, with the other, scooped up the screaming child, carefully balancing its small head in the crook of his elbow. Miraculously, the baby hushed.

From the distance, came the sound of a horse galloping toward the house at breakneck speed, and Jim looked one last time at the woman lying on the bed, mentally beseeching her to awaken and take the baby from his arms, to free him to destroy the man who had destroyed him. But he knew it was too late for that. Reverently, he pulled the sheet over her face. He tried to recall what she had looked like before, without the bruises and the cut across her swollen lip, without the whites of her eyes spotted with blood, but nothing could erase the image that the last hour had implanted on his mind. He would never forget, no matter how long he lived.

The horse outside stopped in front of the house. Still holding the baby, Jim crept down the stairs toward the backdoor, praying to a God he only believed in when he was in a fix that he could find a way out of this one without getting the baby killed. If the Colonel had not seen his palomino tethered in the trees at the side of the house, he might have the chance to run for it. But if the baby cried before they had made their escape . . .

Quickly, he pushed the fear from his mind. As quietly as his years of scouting had taught him to be, he slipped out the backdoor. Clutching the baby to his chest, he started toward the trees, where he could barely see his horse moving in the dim moonlight. He cursed the darkness, but then realized that, perhaps, it would be his salvation.

The front door slammed against the wall, and footsteps bounded up the stairs. A thunderous roar came from inside, and Jim heard his own name being shouted in venomous rage. The Colonel had found his dead wife, and he knew Jim had taken the baby.

Holding the infant tighter, Jim broke into a run. Grabbing the horse's reins with the hand that held his gun, he slung his leg over the worn saddle and quietly guided the horse around the back of the house. If he was lucky, he thought, the Colonel would light out in search of him. Then, when his pursuer was gone, Jim could get away.

The front door crashed open again, and Jim heard the Colonel mount his horse. Sitting still in the darkness, he held his breath.

The baby began to cry, a piercing wail that echoed in the darkness.

Jim drove his spurs home, and his horse lurched forward with all its might. A gunshot whizzed inches from his head, and he could hear the Colonel's horse galloping close behind him. Crouching forward in his saddle, he switched the reins to the hand resting under the baby's bottom and looked over his shoulder, trying to aim. The Colonel was gaining on him, and one well-aimed bullet grazed the wrist of Jim's right hand. His pistol fell to the ground.

Grinding his teeth in pain, Jim spurred the horse again. The baby screamed louder, and he tried to hold it closer.

If he could just make it two more miles to the river, he thought, he was sure he could make an escape. No one knew the markings along the bank as well as he. Not even the Colonel.

Another bullet shot over his head. Cursing, he tried to reach the rifle hanging from the scabbard on his saddle.

But hampered by the pain in his right hand, and the kicking baby in his left, he couldn't free it.

The river babbled up ahead, beyond the clay-and-rock formations that were covered by thick sanctuaries of trees. At exactly the right moment he cut his horse hard to the left and disappeared into the blackness of the brush. The baby quietened, as if the new speed and direction offered some degree of comfort.

Pulling the horse to a stop he freed his rifle with his bloody hand and listened for the sound of the Colonel's horse. It passed him by, though it had slowed somewhat. Only yards away, the river bucked and billowed over the rocks, threatening anyone who dared cross it there, but the threat was greater from the man who was now threading through the woods, in silent search. All it would take was one cry from the baby.

Sweat trickled down Jim's temples, and he tried to steady his breath, hoping to hear the Colonel's as he came closer. The smell of sweat assailed him, and a twig snapped. He poised his rifle to fire, but felt the baby rooting against his coat, nuzzling for its mother's breast. *Don't cry,* he pleaded silently. *Please don't cry.*

A horse whinnied. Quickly, he moved his gun toward the sound. The blood was beginning to soak into his sleeve, and the pain made his fingers less nimble than usual, but he managed to hold his finger over the trigger, ready to fire the instant he saw movement.

But before he could make out the Colonel's form, the baby wailed again. Another bullet whizzed by Jim. Without waiting to return fire, he dug his heels into the horse's flanks and launched down the path he had memorized, heading through the trees, straight to the bank of the river rolling and spitting in callous invitation.

He could hear more shots behind him, and the

Colonel's vicious cursing. The baby's muffled cry crescendoed. Holding it tightly, Jim turned his mount along the river and galloped for his life.

But the Colonel narrowed the distance between them, and a lucky shot hit the Palomino. The mare's leg buckled. Wildly, the horse turned to the river, stumbled down the bank toward it, and fell into the rushing water. Instantly, the water foamed up to devour both horse and rider.

On the bank above, the colonel pulled up his sweating horse. Where McCosky had disappeared, there was now only swirling water, but the Colonel wasn't satisfied. Raising his six-shooter, he opened fire, and shot at the water until he had no bullets left. Then he dismounted, and stood on the shore, listening, waiting for the cry of a newborn child. . . .

But all that could be heard was the deadly peaceful sound of the unmerciful river, and the fury of his own heart pounding in his ears.

1890

The family Bible landed with a rustling, ripping thump on the puncheon floor, and Silena fell to her knees to gather up the crumpled book and smooth its torn pages. Pa hadn't meant to throw it, she told herself, forcing back the tears stinging her eyes. It had just been handy, lying there on the checked tablecloth where they read of it each night.

"Pa," she whispered, desperate to keep her voice even, "it's torn . . . the page with Mama's note to you . . ."

Jake Rivers jerked the Bible from her hand and, crumpling the pages between the covers, slammed it on the table. Bracing his hands on either side of it, he hung his head. Silena held her breath, waiting to see what harsh act would come next.

But none came. Instead, Jake opened the Bible with trembling hands, found the inscription, and set his mouth in a grim, unsteady line as he smoothed out the wrinkled page. Silena wondered if the rip on the page tore at his heart, just as it tore at hers. Long ago, before she had even learned to read, she had memorized the words on the page, the words that her aged housekeeper, now long dead, had read to her when her father wouldn't. *No matter what, I'll always love you.* It was signed simply, *Eva.*

The love was a given, something she read in her father's eyes, but she never stopped wondering what the "no matter what" referred to. Had her mother known that she would die before her milk had even come in? Had she prepared for that? Or was there something else, some dark secret that Silena could add to the others her father kept locked in his heart, away from her?

Still sitting on the floor where the Bible had been, Silena gaped up at her father, knowing her tears were going to fall, knowing she couldn't stop them. She was usually so good at blinking them back, or at least hiding them from him, but tonight his inexplicable anger at her simple request that he take her to Omaha had come as such a frightening surprise.

"Pa . . . I'm sorry," she whispered, worried that some wrong movement might trigger his rage again.

He closed the Bible and set one hard, callused hand on its leather binding. He shut his eyes tightly, and she saw him swallow. Deep, labored breaths racked his shoulders as he struggled with some emotion that threatened to master him. As always, Silena sought to soothe him and relieve the pain in his eyes, the pain she had never fully understood.

"We don't have to go to the Wild West show," she said quickly. Her voice broke and slipped into a raspy high pitch, and she pushed a silky, limp strand of flaxen hair back from her damp cheek as traitorous tears began to fall. "It's just that Omaha isn't that far away, and I thought you'd want to see Wild Willy as much as I do."

"Don't cry." Jake pushed away from the table and bent over her, his gentle command only making her tears fall harder. Silena rubbed her hands over her face and summoned all her energy to do as he said, but it was to no avail. Jake laid his hands on her head. "Aw, Silena, you know I hate it when you cry."

"And I hate it when you shut me out," she said, looking up at him again. "When you won't give me reasons for the way you feel. When you hide things, and I feel how important they are."

"I ain't hidin' nothin'," Jake said, the hard edge returning to his voice. "I just don't need to see Will Hawkins stampedin' through a crowd o' city gawkers shootin' at targets just to refresh my memory about days that are gone forever. Ain't no use dredgin' up the past."

Jake went to the shelf where he kept a bottle of whiskey. He rarely touched it, for he'd always said it didn't pay to have a muddled mind, that one never knew when he'd have to react quickly.

But tonight was clearly different. Silena slid her fingers down her face and watched him open it, toss down the cork as if he wouldn't be needing it again, and take a long swig from its murky contents. When he turned back to her, she could have sworn she saw the slightest trace of fear in his eyes.

Slowly, she rose to her feet, straightened her blue calico dress, and tried not to look so distraught. Idly, she picked up the cork and turned it over in her hand, but she kept her misty emerald eyes fixed on the bearded face of the man who'd almost always harbored a calm spirit where she was concerned.

"But you said he was your best friend," she pressed, knowing even as she spoke that she would regret it.

"That you saved him from drowning. You weren't just fooling, were you, Pa?"

Jake slammed the bottle down on the counter, spilling some of the contents. "Are you calling me a liar, girl?"

"No!" she cried. "I *always* believe your stories, Pa. That's why I don't understand. He was your friend. . . ."

"I got all the friends I'll ever need right here in Hayton," he said, pointing his finger down at a stain on the tablecloth, as if it represented the tiny little world he had created for her, with all its boundaries and limitations. "There's almost a hundred people right in this town. Don't need nobody else, and neither do you."

She turned away and smeared her tears across her face. How could she explain that it wasn't friendship she sought outside the town of Hayton, but answers to questions that had plagued her since she was old enough to wonder about her mother? Forbidden questions that occasionally sent her father into grief-filled drinking binges. On the rare occasions when she had risked his sinking spirits and his raving refusals to discuss the woman he had loved, she had ultimately despised her own hunger to know what the woman had looked like, what color her eyes were, how she'd worn her hair, where she'd been raised . . . *anything* more than that tiny note her mother had scrawled in the front of Jake's Bible, or the one possession she had left behind—an amethyst ring carved in the shape of a horseshoe, surrounded by a circle of pearls, that Jake kept in a tiny box beneath his bed.

But Willy would know about her, Silena thought. He would have known her mother, for if her father's stories were true—and she'd never doubted otherwise—Willy had been closer than anyone to Jake before Silena was born. He could give her the answers she couldn't get from her father. All she had to do was go to Omaha to see him.

"It's not just Willy," she lied, setting the cork back on the shelf where the whiskey bottle had been. "I just wanted the chance to get outside of Hayton for once."

She turned back to her father, saw that his gray eyes were fixed on her. There were ghosts in those weathered eyes, she thought. And for the life of her, she didn't understand where they came from.

"I want to see what it's like, Pa," she said, her own troubled eyes meeting his with more urgency than fear. "I'm the only one I know who's never left Hayton. I want to see more than this dusty little town and these sod walls and the same tired old faces I see every day of my life."

The color in her father's face deepened as his teeth clamped together, and Silena knew she'd pushed him too far.

"These sod walls have protected you for seventeen years, girl, and so has *this* tired old face!" He reached out as if to shake her, but formed his hand into a fist instead and dropped it to his side. Then, backing away from her, as if to put some desperately needed distance between them, he took another gulp of the whiskey, wincing at its potency.

He looked back up at her, and for a second she saw a fine mist in his eyes. Her own desperation softened at the sight, and instinctively, she went to him and slid her arms around him. His arms closed around her, crushing her in an embrace that seemed almost tragic in its urgency.

"There are things you don't understand, Silena," he whispered harshly. "Things you never will. Sometimes you just got to let things be."

Silena pulled back and looked into her father's eyes for a long moment. "But that's not the way you raised me."

Jake's face distorted in deeper pain, and he opened his mouth to speak. But no words escaped his lips, for there was nothing more he could say.

Quietly, he let her go, went to the backdoor, and still clutching the bottle like a weapon against the secret threatening his life—her life—he disappeared into the night.

The autumn breeze was brisk as Jake stepped out into the night. Kicking a rusted bucket out of his way, he headed for the big oak tree near the barn where he kept the surplus goods he didn't have room to stock in his store.

His bones popped as he bent over and found the spot against the trunk, where he could lean back, drink, look at the stars, and think. He could see the blurred image of Silena's mother, and as he closed his eyes the edges of her face sharpened. Taking another swig, he felt the picture coming more into focus. Blond silken hair, eyes the color of a spring grassland, skin as pink and blushing as the loveliest of sunsets.

He opened his eyes and gazed up at the stars. The Big Dipper was clear and expansive tonight, reminding him of younger days spent out in the prairie and the mountains and the brush. It hadn't been easy transforming himself from a wanderer into a settler, from a loner into a father. But his plight had not been given to him as a choice, but a necessity. He'd done his best, and it made him proud that he'd done it so well.

Not even Eva would have found fault with the way he'd brought up her daughter.

The sound of the piano from the saloon a few doors down and across the street drifted on the wind, and he heard Nell Plumer's laughter lilting through the night. No doubt about it, he thought, taking another sour gulp as his head rested back on the tree trunk. Nell liked her job. Being the only whore in town, she had her work cut out for her, but she never seemed to get tired. Jake had thought of seeing her a time or two himself, but he'd had the best, and saw no point in settling for anything less. Jake supposed his urges had numbed over the years, along with the ache in his heart that only stirred back to life when Silena started with questions he couldn't—or wouldn't—answer.

How could he explain that he would be risking both their lives if he was seen outside of Hayton? How could he make her understand that showing himself to Willy Hawkins, after all these years, could turn into a fiasco he didn't have the wherewithal to fight?

He couldn't tell her those things, for they would require explanation. All he could do was refuse to take her, and hope she got over her own anger and confusion.

He held the bottle to his mouth and, pouring half of it down his throat, rejoiced as the razor-sharp memories began to blur again. They were best handled when blurry, he thought. They were best dealt with when he couldn't feel.

Thick darkness washed over him in warm, even waves, and before he'd given the matter much more thought, he had surrendered entirely to the whiskey-scented night.

The morning was so young when Silena arose the next day that the sun had not yet offered its first signs of rising. She got out of bed quietly, trying not to dwell on her distress at having to deceive her father. It had to be done. For her own peace of mind, she had to go to Omaha. She would make it up to him later, she vowed to herself.

Quickly, she prepared to meet the friends she had rounded up last night to go with her. She had slipped out through her father's mercantile, which was attached to the house, while he was still sulking and drinking out back, and had found what she was looking for easily enough. Any number of young men in town were anxious to take Silena Rivers anywhere she pleased. Hitch Calhoun was the one she chose, because he seemed the least harmful and the easiest to hold at bay. She also invited Margaret and Caleb Plumer, because their mother Nell—the "lady" who worked the saloon—left her children to their own resources. No one would care if they left town for a day.

They had set their meeting time for before dawn, and then, with butterflies fluttering deep in her stomach, Silena had hurried home, determined to keep her secret from her father until she was long gone. But her secret had been safe, for she found Jake asleep on his thin mattress, fully clothed, with the empty whiskey bottle clutched in his hand.

Careful not to wake him now, Silena began dressing in the clothes she had saved for an occasion such as this one. She tied her stiff, rarely worn corset as best she could without help, then stepped into the starched white petticoats made by Caldonia Hall, the town's dressmaker, doctor, midwife, and the woman who had taken both Silena and Margaret—"Hayton's little motherless girls"—under her wing. No one ever bothered to remind her that Margaret's mother was still alive and active at Murdock Smith's Liquor Emporium, for Miss Caldonia preferred to think of the girl as an orphan rather than the daughter of a whore. Since they were children, Miss Caldonia had schooled them in "seamstressing," spinning, and dyeing, to the point that if she'd wanted to, Silena could have put together the most elaborate of dresses. Problem was, she didn't want to. Why should she sew, she'd asked herself a thousand times, when her father was more than willing to let her order her dresses from the Sears Roebuck catalog? Besides, there was nothing like the feeling of watching the Wells Fargo wagon pull up to her pa's store and unload a box of things she had waited months for.

She pulled on the sage-green cashmere dress she'd gotten that way, and watched the way the silk braid around the bottom of the circular skirt glistened in the candlelight. The corset was worth it, she thought, smoothing her hands over the tight silk yoke at her waist. She hoped Wild Willy would be proud that his friend had raised such a polished young woman.

For the first time since the idea of going to Omaha without Jake had occurred to her, she allowed herself to consider what she would do if her father's stories about Willy *were* a lie. What if they hadn't been close friends? she thought. What if her father had only exaggerated to impress her? Heaven knew, his other stories of his scouting days were rife with inconsistencies, but something told her there was truth in the ones he'd told her of Willy. Willy would remember Jake, she thought. He had to. And if he did, he must remember her mother.

Just in case, she stole into her father's tiny bedroom, knelt down beside his bed, and lifted the blanket hanging over the side. Peering beneath it, she reached for the small box he kept hidden there.

Her heart hammered in her chest, threatening to be overheard, as she fumbled with the clasp, then finally pulled the lid open. Her mother's ring lay wrapped in a virgin cut of black velvet, just as it had been the last time she'd sneaked a look. Her father had caught her trying it on, and his wrath had rivaled that of last night.

"This ring is too precious to be worn around," he had said, pulling it from her finger and wrapping it carefully back in the velvet. "It has to stay put away, Silena. It belonged to . . . it was hers. . . ."

"But when I'm older, can I have it, Pa?" she had asked. "If I take good care of it?"

He had cleared his throat and gazed down at the ring, as if a world of memories were contained in the stones. "We'll see," he'd whispered. "When you're older."

Well, now she was older, and even though her father still guarded it as if it were some secret treasure that might vanish when the first rays of light were cast upon it, she was going to wear it today. Whatever mystery it possessed might be unraveled when Willy saw it. Maybe it would jog some memory in his mind.

She slipped it over the ring finger on her right hand, closed her hand into a fist to keep it from falling off, though there was little chance since it was a perfect fit, and pushed the box back under the bed.

Her father stirred, and she knelt upright, a flush of guilt burning her cheeks. Cramming her hand into her pocket, she prayed he would turn over and go back to sleep.

His eyes opened, and he squinted at his daughter, kneeling on the floor beside him. "Silena," he said, rising up on an elbow and bringing a hand to his head as though to steady it. "What are you doing?"

"I'm . . ." She struggled with the lie forming so readily on her lips, the lie she had prepared about helping Maude Akins birth her baby, but it wouldn't come. Instead, she altered the truth enough to appease him. "I was coming to tell you I'm going to meet Margaret. She . . . she needs me. . . ."

"Margaret?" He dropped back down to his flat pillow and closed his eyes again. "Is she sick? Where's her ma?"

"At the saloon," Silena said, not correcting his assumption. "I have to hurry, Pa. She's waiting."

She pressed a soft kiss just above his beard, and his big hand moved to stroke her cheek. "Silena," he whispered, his voice hoarse as it rose above a whisper. "I'm sorry about last night."

Silena sat back on the heels of her worn leather boots, folded her hands in the lap of her skirt, and tried to harden her resolve to go through with this deception. "Me too, Pa," she whispered. "There's a lot of stubbornness in both of us."

Her voice cracked with the words, and fearing he'd see the tears crowding her eyes, she came to her feet. "I love you, Pa. Don't worry about me."

"Will you be back in time to open the store?" Jake asked, rubbing his temples and turning back over in his bed.

"I might be a little late," she whispered.

When he didn't protest, she hurried out of his bedroom, thankful he hadn't noticed her clothes in the darkness, and went to the living room—the room Jake had allowed her to decorate with furnishings from another catalog. It always pleased her to step onto the carpet she had chosen so carefully from samples Jake had gotten from William Pollock Company in Philadelphia. The finely arranged furniture had also been selected with painstaking care, and Silena was confident that nothing cluttered the room that didn't have a sound reason for being there.

Because the room was small, only the sofa boasted upholstered cushions, for Miss Caldonia had driven the point home that upholstery and cushioning were bad for the health and didn't leave enough air to breathe in rooms as small as this. For that reason, the rest of the furnishings—a chair, a table, a piano, and a bookcase—were all made of the finest wood and hand-carved by Slam Whitmire, whose establishment was right next door to the Rivers's Mercantile.

But despite how the room pleased Silena, today it made those guilty pangs dig more sharply into her, for she realized Jake had always been more than lenient with her in most things, even to the point of spoiling her. He didn't deserve to be deceived or defied.

But as she stood in front of the gold-leafed mirror hanging on the wall beside the door, Silena told herself she had no choice. The plans had all been made, and nothing would keep her from going through with them. Last night, she had taken great pains to twist her hair into coils with bits of cloth tied into knots, and now it hung in long curls to her shoulders. She swept the sides up and pinned them properly, then turned sideways and checked her profile in the mirror. Satisfied that she looked her best, she pulled on her poke bonnet, tied the ribbons beneath her chin, and scanned the room for anything she may have forgotten.

Quickly, before Jake could get out of bed and stop her, she slipped out of their house and into the store attached to the front of it. The scent of lye soap—made by several of the women in town and traded for staple goods or bolts of cloth—mingled with the scents of dry coffee, kerosene, and tobacco. Hurrying to the front door, she unlocked it and stole out into the predawn darkness.

"It's about time you got out here."

The voice came out of the blackness, and Silena swung around and saw Hitch Calhoun lurking between the mercantile and the Whitmire Carpentry Shop, grinning like a mischievous boy. Despite the fact that he was nineteen, two years older than Silena, she couldn't help *thinking* of him as a boy. His Stetson always rode the back part of his head more than the top, and his brown shaggy hair, no matter how hard he worked on it, always looked a little too curly to be taken seriously. "I was gettin' ready to come in after you," he said.

"My pa would've shot your head off, Hitch," Silena whispered. "Now let's go before he wakes up. Where's the wagon?"

Hitch grabbed her hand with a little more possession than she liked, and she unceremoniously pulled it free. "Hitch, we're just going as friends, okay? I didn't ask you to come for any other reason."

"I know why you asked me," he said. "Because I have a rig, that's why. One o' these days I'm gonna find me a gal who appreciates me." Trying not to look hurt, the skinny rancher started up the clay street toward where the wagon was waiting, and Silena lifted her skirts and followed him.

"Not in this town, you won't, Hitch. Don't you ever just want to get out? Don't you want to see other places, meet other people?"

Hitch breathed a hard laugh and shook his head. "If it weren't for that pneumonia, I'd be in Kansas buying cattle with my pa right now. 'Course, Kansas ain't much. Not what you think. I seen other places, Silena. They ain't so much better."

His step picked up as they passed the sheriff's office and barbershop, which stood side by side since one man held both jobs. The town joke was that the outlaws stayed out of Hayton for fear that if they got caught in Sheriff Hollister's jail, he might try to give them a haircut and shave. Most of Sheriff Hollister's patrons would rather have taken their chances with a noose than with his dull razor blade skimming across their throats.

They passed the livery stable, then slowed at the saloon, where Jared and Adam Grady lay unconscious in the street, probably right where Murdock Smith, the saloon owner, had thrown them last night. Murdock was known for being a generous proprietor, but along about three every morning, it was said, he developed a mean streak toward those too drunk to stagger home.

Shaking her head in disgust, Silena stepped delicately over them, but her traitorous thoughts drifted back to her pa. Except when she spoke of her mother, she had never seen him drink more than a shot or two. It was strange that last night's request, which had nothing to do with her mother—at least as far as Jake knew—should have sent him into such a state. Another pang of regret struck her heart. She hoped he wouldn't worry too much when he found her gone.

"There's the wagon," Hitch said, pointing to the corner beside the saloon.

She looked up and saw her two other coconspirators were already at the wagon. Margaret and Caleb Plumer waved and scurried to the wagon bed.

"Hurry," Caleb said. "The sun'll be up soon."

Margaret, smaller of stature than Silena and two years younger, stood up as Silena approached and swept awestruck eyes over her new dress and bonnet. "Oh, Silena, look at you. You always make me feel so drab."

"Don't be silly," Silena said. "You look fine. Before we get to Omaha, I'll fix your hair if you'll help me with mine."

Margaret's brown eyes brightened at once. "Do you think you can do anything with mine?"

"Of course I can," Silena said. "Now, come on, Hitch. We have to hurry."

Hitch put his hands on Silena's waist to help her into the wagon. "We're doin' okay," he said. "The way it looks, we'll get there a good hour or two before the show starts. I hear tell they got Injuns ever'where, and a gal who can outshoot most men, and a slew of wild animals—"

"And Wild Willy," Silena said, her guilt and worry already abating as she climbed up onto the front of the wagon. "Fastest gunslinger in the West. The handbill said he'd killed two hundred Indians single-handedly, and when he was a boy, my pa saved him from drowning."

"The handbill said that?" Hitch asked, grinning as he climbed up beside her. He flicked the reins at the horses and sent them into a noisy trot.

"Not exactly," Silena said. "But my pa said it."

Hitch breathed a skeptical laugh. "Your pa claims to've knowed ever'body from Dan'l Boone to George Washington, and he ain't even that old."

Silena's eyes whiplashed him in the darkness. "Are you calling my pa a liar?"

"I'm just sayin' that you can't believe everthin' you hear. You go to Omaha actin' like you're Willy's long-lost kinfolk, and you're gonna wind up real disappointed."

Silena glared at Hitch, then looked over her shoulder to see that Margaret and Caleb were watching her with awkward quiet, as if they, too, doubted her father's word. Swallowing back her anger, she bit her lip and told herself she'd show them all soon enough.

The wagon seemed to rattle louder and the horse's hooves clomped up a greater racket as they neared the Rivers's Mercantile. She caught her breath when she saw that one of the lamps inside was lit. Was her father up? Had it occurred to him that Margaret could have reached her ma quicker than Silena, and that Caleb could have helped her with whatever she needed?

"Hitch, we need to go faster," she said, her voice quavering as they grew closer to the store. "Please—"

But before she could get the words out, the door to Jake's store crashed open and her father came storming out. "Silena! For God's sake, you come back here!"

Without waiting for Hitch to react, for she feared he'd hand her right over to her ranting father, she grabbed the reins from his hands and whipped the team into a gallop. "I'll be back by sundown, Pa!" she called over her shoulder.

Hitch almost fell back into the wagon bed. "Gall dang it, Silena! What in blazes are you doin'?"

"I'm going to Omaha," Silena said as they left her gaping father behind. "And nobody is going to stop me."

The white stallion's star-studded hooves hammered up a cloud of dust as Sam Hawkins shoved the reins between his teeth and slipped his feet free of the silver stirrups. Deftly, he tightened his legs and slid sideways on the saddle until his shoulder slipped into the horsehair sling braided from Duke's white mane. Slipping his boot under the saddle, he dropped upside down. His hat fell off and was left behind as the horse ran faster toward the whiskey bottles he had carefully assembled that morning, and suddenly Sam opened fire from under the horse, alternating hands and six-shooters until all twelve bullets were spent, and all twelve bottles had shattered.

Then, as if it were part of the act, Duke reared once in victory, as if he'd done the shooting, then swung back around so Sam could scoop his hat up off the ground, drop it on his shaggy brown hair, and slide back to an upright position on the saddle. Slowing Duke to a trot, Sam eyed the broken bottles and decided to try it again, this time with smaller targets.

"A few more times, Duke," he muttered, stroking the horse's mane. "We can do it faster. I know we can." The stallion whinnied and pranced, as if agreeing with his rider.

"Hey, Sam!"

Sam turned around and saw the show's manager—a small, bald man who always found more things to worry about than he had time to fix—running toward him, waving his hands urgently. "What is it, Jessup?"

"It's your pa. He's drunk again and shootin' up ever-thin' in sight. Folks are startin' to pull in for the show, and somebody's liable to get hurt!"

"Aw, hell." Sam dismounted and tossed the reins to Jessup while he dusted off his buckskins. "Didn't I tell you not to let Willy have his gun when he's drunk?"

"I can't keep it from him," Jessup said. "Hurry, Sam."

Sam broke into a run toward his father's tent, the one marked WILD WILLY—LIVING LEGEND, and saw the legendary hero of the Wild West show sitting outside in a chair tilted back on two legs, shooting his pistol up at some invisible enemies in the sky.

"Damn flies!" Willy shouted, and the gun went off again without particular aim. Everyone within bullet's reach had vanished, to Willy's dismay, for there was nothing he loved better than an audience.

"Give me the gun, Willy!" Sam shouted, not breaking his stride even when a bullet ricocheted off the ground near his foot. "Damn it, Willy, you're going to kill somebody!"

"Gotta get rid of these stinkin' flies," the overweight, gray-haired hero bellowed, and raised his pistol at one that dared to buzz in front of his face. The gun went off again.

More annoyed than worried, Sam moved in behind his father and grabbed the pistol. Wrenching it out of Willy's hand, he shoved it into his belt, since his own holsters were both full. "Now, come on, Willy. You need to go sleep this off."

"I need a drink's what I need," Willy slurred, allowing his son to pull him to his feet and guide him back into the tent. "Damn flies. I'll kill every last one of 'em. You go on back out there and kill me a few, will ya?"

"I will," Sam said, dropping his father's heavy frame

onto the cot that rarely got slept on, since Willy usually only rested wherever he happened to be when he passed out—a bar, a town street, a whore's bed. "Now try to get some sleep, Willy. We have a show in three hours."

"Sleep," Willy said, his eyes shutting. "Can't sleep. Damn flies."

Sam watched as Willy fell still, his breathing lapsing into a deep, grunting snore. Quietly, so as not to rouse him, Sam gathered all the guns—rifles and pistols of all models and sizes—that his father might decide to use after he'd gone, then quickly slipped out of the tent.

"It's okay," he told the troupe members, who were just beginning to relax again. "He's sleeping. Don't anybody give the man a gun until he's sober. When you're sure he's thinking straight, I'll have them in my tent."

"What if the press wants to see him?" Jessup hurried to match Sam's long, determined stride. "They're gonna be here today, you know. They'll want to see him."

"Send them to me," Sam said. "I can handle them."

"And what about the stagecoach?" Jessup threw in. "The wheel broke off this mornin', and they ain't fixed it yet."

"Then I'll go fix it," Sam said, stopping and looking down at Jessup with irritation. "Is there anything else?"

"Naw, sir," the small man said, backing away with a yellow grin. "Reckon that's all."

"Good." Sam started to enter his tent, but Jessup stopped him again.

"You reckon Willy'll be performin' today?"

"God only knows." Sam went into his tent and laid his father's guns on his cot. He looked over his shoulder, saw Jessup standing under the tent flap, waiting for a definitive answer. "Don't worry about him, Jessup. He just needs a good rest. All we have to do is get through these last few shows."

"You know, Sam," Jessup said, coming further into the tent with that worried look that always rubbed Sam the wrong way. "Even sober, Willy's aim is gettin' worse all the time. And when he rides, he gets all outta breath. . . ."

Sam pulled the fly-killing pistol out of his belt, emptied the chamber, and dropped it onto the bed with the others. Heaving a deep sigh, he pulled off his hat and went to the tent flap. Scratching his hair back with the hand that held the Stetson, he stared out on all the bustling activity of the troupers and the spectators beginning to mill curiously around the grounds. Deserving or not, Willy was the nucleus around which all the chaos revolved.

"Doesn't matter," he said, glancing back at Jessup. "He's the one they come here to see."

"I'm just sayin' that maybe it wouldn't be so bad if he slept through the show today, seein' how the press is gonna be coverin' it and all."

Sam fixed his eyes on the little man who had been his father's right hand for years. He didn't like seeing Jessup turn on him now. He pulled his hat back on, letting it ride low on his forehead as his brown eyes narrowed with contempt. "And I'm just saying that if Willy wakes up and has a mind to ride in the show today, neither one of us is going to stop him. Got that?"

Jessup hesitated a moment, spat at the dirt floor, then brought his dull, resigned eyes back to Sam's. "Yeah, Sam. Reckon I do."

"Matter of fact," Sam added, "I aim to do my damnedest to see that he does wake up."

Jessup turned morosely away. Satisfied that he'd made his intentions clear, Sam started out of his tent.

"Where you goin'?" Jessup asked.

"To fix the stagecoach wheel," Sam said. "And whatever the hell else needs doing."

The last fifteen minutes of the twenty-mile trip from Hayton were the longest of Silena's life. As the sun had risen over the plains, bathing the earth in warm rose tones, she had constantly watched behind them, waiting for her father to come galloping after them, determined to hog-tie her and force her back to Hayton. So far, she hadn't seen a sign of him.

She had long ago convinced Hitch that he had to run the team to avoid her father's wrath, and since he dreaded the moment of confrontation with Jake, he had obliged, leaving her to climb into the wagon bed to work on Margaret's long, wiry black hair. In a matter of minutes, she had realized that the ride back there was considerably rougher than it had been in front. It was impossible, she thought, for a lady in a corset to sit flat on a rickety wagon bed, moving faster than it probably ever had before. Instead, she pulled up her skirts and knelt, trying not to fall as the wagon bounced and bumped. It was disgraceful that Hitch hadn't provided for better seating arrangements, she thought. Even an old crate or a box from Pa's store would have served better than nothing. And it wouldn't have killed him to sweep out the dirt and hay.

"By the time we get there," she muttered in a voice too low for Hitch to hear, "we're going to be filthy. Look at all this dust."

"You could ask him to slow down," Margaret whispered. "That way the horses wouldn't kick up so much dust."

"Heavens no!" Silena let her eyes stray behind them again, and seeing nothing threatening, she pivoted on her knees and wrenched her neck to look ahead, anxious to catch the first glimpse of the Wild West show, which she knew was camped just outside of Omaha where the train had left it.

"I just wish Hitch would show a little more consideration," Silena whispered, "But I guess I shouldn't complain."

Silena swept Margaret's braid under and sacrificed one of the pins from her own hair to hold it in place.

"He never notices me when you're around," Margaret said, her voice barely audible over the commotion of the horses' hooves and the rickety wheels and the wind whistling in their ears.

"Who doesn't?" Silena asked, forcing her eyes back to Margaret's hair.

"You know." Margaret cupped a hand over her mouth to make sure that the driver wouldn't hear. "Hitch."

A surprised smile curled over Silena's lips, and she turned her friend around and met her eyes. "You're sweet on Hitch? Why haven't you told me?"

Margaret blushed and turned her face away. "Well, first I thought you might be, too."

"Me?" Silena shook her head and smoothed her hand

over the flyaway wisps in Margaret's hair. "Goodness, no. Hitch is nice, but he's not for me."

"Then who is?" Margaret asked. "You're even older than me, Silena. Time's creepin' by, you know."

"So let it creep. I don't reckon I'll shrivel up and die if I turn eighteen without a husband." Silena dropped her brush into her lap and turned Margaret back around to have a look at her work. "That's nice. You look real pretty."

Margaret's thick black brows drew together in concern. "Silena, sometimes a girl can't be so picky. Especially when there ain't that many to choose from."

Not daunted, Silena pulled her handkerchief from a pocket and tried to rid her face of some of the dust it had caught. "So what are you saying?" she asked. "That I should marry Hitch Calhoun?"

"No!" Margaret glanced up at the men in front, engaged in quiet conversation between themselves, and tempered her voice. "Somebody else, but not him."

"Well, it won't be anybody from Hayton," Silena said. "I can promise you that."

"Then who?" Margaret asked.

Silena took off her bonnet and handed it to Margaret to hold. "Nobody you know," she said, pulling her wind-tangled hair over her shoulder and gliding the brush through it. "Nobody I know, either. At least not yet. But when I meet him, I'll know. He'll be somebody unpredictable . . . but not mysterious. Somebody who can surprise me without keeping secrets from me."

Her eyes glistened as she sat back on her heels and gazed at the fields of bluestem and goldenrod waving in the cool breeze, and she wondered if Willy would, indeed, unravel some of her father's mysteries today. "I won't abide secrets," she whispered. "If a man loves me, he'll tell me the truth about everything."

"They all tell lies," Margaret said, her resigned tone falling to a soft, sad note. "You should hear some of the ones my ma hears at the saloon. Long as you don't believe 'em, I reckon they don't hurt nothin'."

Sighing at Margaret's dejected view of the world, Silena took her bonnet back, pulled it on, and retied the wide green ribbons at her throat. "You can accept that if you want to, Margaret. But I'd just as soon be a sour old spinster than marry a man who lies."

Her own words caught in her heart, reminding her of the lie she had told just this morning. She touched the ring on her finger, and traced the shape of the jeweled horseshoe. She wondered if Jake had discovered it missing yet.

Pensively, she let her gaze drift to the dusty road behind them, straining to make out any sign of her father. Several other wagons flecked the horizon, but none seemed to be on an urgent mission. Still, she watched them, waiting.

"Silena, you reckon that's it up yonder?" Hitch called back, and Silena turned around and saw the flags waving in the distance, and the tents and tepees staked around the grounds. She almost fell out of the wagon trying to get to the front. "Hurry, Caleb. Trade places with me!"

Realizing he had no choice against her stubborn will, Caleb surrendered his seat and climbed in back. "Hurry, Hitch," she cried, "and when we get there, I'll introduce you to Wild Willy!"

"Fine," Hitch said, ignoring her command to speed up his team. "After that, you can introduce me to President McKinley and Queen Victoria."

"Don't tease, Hitch," Silena warned as her hair flapped behind her in the wind. "I'm gonna make you eat your words as soon as we meet Wild Willy!"

* * *

"Where's Wild Willy?

The reporter's question, reasonable though it seemed to Sam, made Jessup bristle. "He's restin' before the show," the manager said. "Ain't he, Sam?"

The reporter's eyes moved to Sam Hawkins, sitting tall and proud atop Duke, the white stallion that was as much a showstopper as the son of the legend himself.

"That's right," Sam said, chewing on a piece of straw. He tipped his hat down at the reporter, who was dressed in a black broadcloth suit. It seemed dreadfully out of place in the rugged setting. "You can talk to him after the show. Have you met Chief Running Horse yet?"

The reporter's attention instantly shifted toward the Indian tepees set up across the campgrounds. His smug expression altered as he moved his doubtful eyes back up to Sam. "No. Is he dangerous?"

"Only if you make him mad," Sam said with a grin.

"I just mean . . . I heard stories. . . ."

"About him and his warriors scalping Dugan's infantry?" Sam asked. He knew the story in detail, since he had created it himself for the handbills. "Ask him to show you the scalps. He's right proud of them."

"But . . . I don't know how to sign. . . ."

"Doesn't matter," Sam said. "Running Horse speaks English well enough. Take him on over to the chief, Jessup."

He watched, the lines of his grin cutting into his tanned face, when the frightened reporter tried to look unworried as Jessup escorted him to the Indian chief, who was already adorned for the show in his colorful bonnet and war paint. Undoubtedly the chief had scalped a few white men in his day, but not as many as legend said. The truth was that Sam had found Running Horse's tribe living in poverty, and had offered him fair wages to join the show.

The Indian father of eleven, who'd seen the destruction and waste of the prairie at the white man's hand, held responsibility for his family and his tribe above his own pride, so he had agreed to join the troupe for a year. Ticket sales had tripled the first month he rode in what the show called the "Stagecoach Robbery," for people actually imagined that the hatred they saw in the Indians' faces was real, and that the murders they inflicted on the stagecoach driver and passengers was as authentic as the squaws and Indian children camped on the edge of the compound.

Sam looked away from the nervous reporter approaching Chief Running Horse and let his eyes stray from one area of the compound to another, watching for any problems that might need to be taken care of as the early-arriving spectators roamed around the grounds, marveling at the sights of the buffalo grazing on the outskirts of the camp, of the bear trapped in a circus cage, of Indian women laundering their clothes and preparing their meals, of Indian children, wearing only breechclouts and moccasins, engaged in a game of "stickball" in imitation of the older Indians, who took the game as seriously as a raid on a gang of marauding bandits.

He watched with amusement as two white girls approached an Indian boy, one with vibrant curiosity, the other with wilting timidity and, perhaps, a little fear. It was the curious one that his eyes followed, the one with hair the color of corn silk and eyes like the endless miles of grama grass that had colored the plains when he was a boy, before railroad men and miners and settlers had claimed the land for themselves.

She wore that same untainted innocence, he mused

as he watched her step into the circle of Pawnee children and take one of their proffered sticks with a hoop at the end laced with rawhide. She swung to hit the ball, and when it made contact, her laughter reached his ears over all the music, and milling, and racket of the crowd. She looked up and their eyes met, and he realized that he was laughing with her, sharing the excitement that thousands of spectators shared every show. But something about her was different.

Her youthful, innocent smile faded, and Sam became vividly aware that it was a woman, not a girl, who gazed back at him. For a moment Sam forgot there was work to be done, details to be attended to, catastrophes to be avoided. A growing awareness of the tightness in his groin made his own smile fade away as his eyes made a slow sweep to her mouth, down her chin, down the delicate column of her throat, to the swell of her breasts above her dress.

She blushed, the soft rose color spreading over her cheeks, and her right hand came up to stroke a strand of hair back from her face. Her ring caught his eye, an amethyst in the shape of a horseshoe, surrounded by a circle of pearls, and some long-forgotten memory began to stir in his mind. He had seen that ring before, when he was a boy, but the foundation of that memory seemed lost beneath a thousand others.

Her gaze strayed off into the crowd, and he saw her smile fade. Sam followed her eyes, but couldn't see what—or who—had stolen her attention away. When he looked back at her, she had abandoned the Indian children and disappeared into the crowd.

He waited for a moment, scanning the crowd for that green bonnet or those enchanting eyes, but when he was sure he had lost her, he forced his thoughts back to the show. Reining Duke around, he headed for his father's tent, hoping to find Willy awake and capable of riding a horse, let alone shooting—and hitting—the glass balls thrown twenty-one feet into the air for his targets. But when he dismounted and slipped into the tent, he saw his father still lying where he'd left him on the bed, the stench of whiskey reeking from his sweat-stained clothes.

"Damn," he whispered, knowing how angry Willy would be if he woke and realized he'd slept through the opening in Omaha. Willy clearly couldn't ride in the "Stagecoach Robbery," which came early in the show, but it was still a good four hours before the finale. Maybe he'd wake up in time for that.

As he left the tent and swung back onto his stallion, his eyes strayed back to the game among the Indian children, seeking out the shimmer of flaxen hair beneath that bonnet. Idly, he swept the faces of the growing crowd, past the Mexican vaqueros squatting around a fire engaged in storytelling for the spectators, past Quick Shot Lucy, flirting with a cluster of wranglers, past the small herd of buffalo and mountain elk where they grazed.

And then he saw her, sitting on the ground opposite Running Horse, engaging the Sioux chief in reluctant conversation. Sam wondered at that, for the Indian rarely spoke to any of the spectators who milled past him, pointing and whispering, as if he were a statue rather than a man. He saw her throw back her head and laugh with delight, and for a moment he could have sworn that the solemn old Indian cracked the slightest hint of a smile. He watched her bid good day in Indian sign language—sweeping her hand to sign "good," then ending with a flourish of both hands for "day"—and saw that Running Horse returned the sign and watched her walk away, as if experiencing his own bit of admiration for the exuberant young woman.

Sam's own curiosity drew him to ride through the thick crowd, tipping his hat to the ladies who ogled him, and make his way to Running Horse, who sat cross-legged in front of his tepee.

"Morning, Chief," Sam said, not bothering to dismount.

The chief, a man of few words, nodded.

"That woman who was here," Sam said. "She was talking to you. What did she say?"

"Asked about Willy," Running Horse said. His voice was a thick monotone, though it was noticeably devoid of accent.

Sam frowned and looked in the direction she had gone. "What did she want to know?"

"Where his tent is," the chief answered. The hint of a smile tugged at his hard mouth, and he followed Sam's searching gaze. "Asked me to dinner if I ever go through her town."

Sam's eyes flashed back to the old Indian. "She invited you to *dinner*? Are you sure?"

Running Horse's smile transformed his granite features as he looked up at Sam. "You bet I go, too, if I get to Hayton."

Sam's slow smile traveled across his face. "Tell you what, Chief. If you go, take me with you."

Running Horse laughed aloud, something Sam had only seen on the rare occasions when the chief had bent his elbow a few too many times. "Running Horse has a woman already. You find her, go yourself."

"I reckon I will, Chief," Sam said.

Guiding his horse back through the crowd, he spotted her again, ambling among the cowboys lassoing calves in the corral. They, too, noticed the striking young woman. Two of them whistled, and he saw the secret pleasure on her face, though she turned away and pretended not to notice.

And then he watched her stroll toward Wild Willy's tent, and her face was transformed in awe, as if she pictured some mythical giant who would stalk out at any moment, save a few damsels, scalp a few Indians, then throw himself on his horse and dash off for a three-hundred-mile jaunt for the famed pony express. Sam supposed in his younger days his father had done all that, but not these days.

A man approached her from behind, grabbed her arm, and she swung around, startled at the sight of him. Sam sat stiffer in his saddle as he saw the man pointing to the gates of the compound, trying to drag her with him.

The woman jerked free again and tried to walk away. But the man wouldn't let her go.

A growing sense of uneasiness tightened inside Sam, something close to anger, and that protective instinct he'd cursed for the last three years swelled up inside him again. Sitting taller on his horse and straightening his Stetson, he signaled his horse to turn around and retreat a few yards.

The lady looked like she needed an escape, he thought, and he was just the one to give it to her.

Silena jerked her arm from Zane Barlow's grip and tried to walk away from him. "Leave me alone, Zane. I'm not going back!"

Zane, who kept the livery stable two doors down from her pa's store, moaned as if she'd ruined his day. "Come on, Silena. Your pa paid me to fetch you. I cain't go back without you."

"Why didn't he come himself?" she asked. "Did you ask him that?"

"Yeah," Zane said. "He tole me I was a faster rider, and that he figgered I'd catch up to you before you got here."

"Well, you didn't, and I'm here, so just leave me be!"

She started to walk away, but he grabbed her arm again. "Please, Silena. I need that money. I got a busted carriage needs fixin', and the girls need new shoes—"

"Let go of me!" she said. "I'm not leaving here until I've done what I came to do."

"Aw, hell," Zane said. "Does it have anything to do with talkin' to Wild Willy? 'Cause if it does, your pa told me he'd give me double if I kept you from it."

"Double! He was willing to pay you double to keep me away from Willy?"

Just as Zane took her other arm, forcing her to look at him, the sound of a horse's galloping hooves distracted them. Silena looked to her right and saw a magnificent white horse barreling toward her, carrying the cowboy in white buckskins who had made her shiver with awareness earlier. Now she shivered in fear.

"Look out!" Zane cried.

Silena screamed as the rider bent down, scooped her around the waist, and pulled her up on the horse in front of him.

It took a moment of her heart thundering in time with the horse's pounding hooves for her to realize that she wasn't in danger. The cowboy held her tightly with a strong arm, and his chuckling against her ear made her catch her breath.

"Hope I didn't scare you, ma'am," he said. "You looked like you needed rescuing."

Silena stole a wide-eyed look at him over her shoulder. Laugh lines crinkled out from his eyes, put there from hard years of squinting in the sunlight and enduring the wind and the sun and the grime of the outdoors. For a second she wondered if she would have been safer with Zane, but that thought fled her mind as the cowboy's strong arms held her against him. In a raspy voice, she murmured, "Yes . . ."

He tipped his hat and grinned. "Then I'm happy to oblige, ma'am."

Silena felt that stinging blush creep over her cheekbones again.

Tightening his arms around her waist, he spurred his horse and sent it flying even faster.

Silena fell back against her captor, encased in his strong arms, as he galloped with her from the campground.

By the time he brought Silena back around to her friends a few moments later, a chattering crowd had gathered to watch.

"Silena Rivers, come down from there!" someone shouted, and Silena looked down to see Zane Barlow, looking a little whiter than he had before, waving his lanky arms frantically. "Your pa's gonna skin me alive!"

"Oh, no." Silena looked back at the cowboy over her shoulder. "Please, don't let me off here."

"Wouldn't think of it," he said, and she felt his breath against her face. He smelled of clove, and she couldn't help letting her gaze drop to his lips, full and moist and smiling. "So you know him?" he asked as he spurred his horse past the crowd.

"Yes," she whispered, distracted by the way his stubble felt when his face gently, and ever so innocently, brushed hers. "He's harmless, but he wants to take me home, and I just got here. I've got to avoid him if I can."

His horse slowed to a stop well past the crowd, and she moved her gaze from his face to the saddle horn her hand clutched at her hip.

She felt the need to slide down the horse's side and put her feet firmly back on the ground, but the cowboy didn't loosen his arm at her waist. Instead, he held her against him, offering no escape from the whirlwind of feeling he had created within her.

"He called you Silena," he said, his voice a deep rumble against her ear. "I'm from a town in Kansas called Salina."

"My father's from Kansas," she said, "and he named me after that town. Spelled it wrong, though."

Sam's chuckle vibrated against her hair again, and his hand moved to lift hers from the pommel. His big hand, rough and callused and warm, encompassed hers completely, and his thumb brushed over her ring.

"Your ring . . . it's unusual. Seems like I've seen it before."

His intimate touch shook her to her core, but she didn't have the strength to pull away. In an attempt to cool the sizzling emotions scorching her heart, she swallowed and tried to speak. "Really? Where?"

"I don't know," he said.

She heaved in a shaky breath and wondered if he could see in her eyes that she wasn't supposed to be wearing that ring, that it belonged in a box under her father's bed, that she had as good as stolen it this morning.

"It . . . it was my mother's before she died," she whispered.

"And she left it to you?" he asked.

Her face fell again. Struggling with the fading truths and pieces that didn't fit, she tried to find some reason why her father kept this precious possession from her. "No . . . I just wear it sometimes."

As if the cowboy sensed her falling spirits, he laid her hand back on the horn and covered it with his own. She looked up at him and tried not to seem so shaken. "What do you do in the show besides frighten women half to death?" she asked, breathless.

The cowboy's evasive grin seemed permanently etched in his face. "You name it, I do it."

Her eyes widened even more. "Then I guess you know Wild Willy?"

His grin faded slightly, as if the question disappointed him, and he moved his hand from hers and loosened his hold on her waist. "Everybody knows Wild Willy."

She swallowed again and noticed the black flecks in the depths of his eyes. They lent him a tough edge of wildness, as if he'd just ridden in from a cattle drive after days of sleeping under the stars and cooking over an open fire. She wondered if a man like that could be tamed.

"But I mean . . . do you know him *well?* Well enough to introduce him to a person?"

The gentleness in his eyes suddenly turned hard, and she felt strangely as if she'd lost something that had never been hers. "Maybe," he said, his voice taking on a chilly edge. "Depends on the person, I reckon. Who you got in mind?"

Silena blushed and studied her ring. "Who do you think?"

The cowboy drew in a long, heavy breath, as though her confession didn't surprise him at all. Gently, he lowered her to the ground, and steadying herself, she stared up at him, urgently trying to hide the disappointment on her flushed face.

His eyes strayed off with dull indifference. "Well,

now, I reckon I could take you to Willy's tent after the show. He has a weakness for the ladies . . . the younger the better. Especially when they're star struck."

Silena's eyes flashed sudden alarm. "Oh, no! I didn't mean—" As if she couldn't finish the thought, she brought both hands to her warm cheeks. "You see, Willy grew up with my pa. I've heard about him all my life, and I'd just like to say hello and . . . ask him about my mother. I think he knew her."

Slowly, the cowboy's icy glare melted. He looked at her for a long moment, as if turning her words over in his mind. Finally, just when she thought he would ride off without a look back, he leaned down until his face was daringly close to hers, and crooked a finger under her chin. His grin was more defined in his eyes than it was on his lips.

"I'll tell you what," he said softly, his voice as deep as rich velvet. "Any gal who can make Running Horse smile ought to be allowed to say hello to anybody she wants. Meet me back here after the show. If Willy's free, I'll take you to him. Just . . . don't be disappointed if he's not, okay?"

Silena bit her lip and tried not to look too hopeful. "I won't," she said on a raspy rush of breath. "I know how busy he must be."

"Yeah," the cowboy said, his smile faltering again. "Real busy." Then, sitting up straight on his horse, he nicked it with his reins and flashed her that smile again. "Enjoy the show, okay? And if that moron harasses you again, grab one of the troupe members and send them for me. I'll take care of him for you."

"I will." Silena's whispered words were too soft for him to hear as she watched the cowboy ride away. He was out of sight before she realized she hadn't even asked his name.

3

Silena spent a few minutes searching for Hitch, Margaret, and Caleb, and finally saw them standing near the gates being opened to the arena. Lifting her skirts, she grabbed Margaret's hand and nodded toward Hitch and Caleb. "Come on, let's get our seats."

"Silena! Was that you up there with that cowboy?"

"Yes," Silena said. "He rescued me from Zane Barlow. My pa paid him to take me back to Hayton."

"Rescued you?" Hitch laughed out loud. "Don't nobody need rescuin' from Zane."

"Well, I did," she said. "I'm telling you, he's determined to get me out of here. Now let's sit down before it's too late."

And before the others had time to object, Silena led them into the arena.

They found seats near the front and directly in the center of the arena, and while they waited for the show to begin Silena pored over the more detailed handbill she'd gotten at the gate.

"Which one's your cowboy?" Margaret asked.

"I'm not sure," she said. "He didn't tell me his name. I guess I'll know when he comes out."

"He's probably one of them guys who gets killed by an Injun," Hitch said, his voice dull and brooding. "He probably rides out, gets shot, and spends the rest of the day laying out on the dirt."

Caleb laughed at the image, but Silena wasn't daunted. "You'll see," she said. "He's somebody real important. One of the stars, even. He promised to take me to meet Wild Willy after the show."

"Right," Hitch said. "If he can find you in this crowd. And even if he did, you ain't still considerin' walking into some strange man's tent, are you?"

"He isn't strange," Silena said, vexation sharpening her tone. "He's my pa's old friend."

"Yeah, yeah," Hitch said. "Just the same, I'm goin' with you."

"If you can find me, you're welcome to it," Silena mumbled under her breath, and Margaret nudged her and giggled.

The Wild West Cornet Band began to play and the announcer, dressed in a black frock coat and beaded moccasins, rode out on a tall roan, and in a voice that reached every ear in the arena thundered, "Welcome, Omaha, to the Wild West show!"

As the music crescendoed the twenty-piece band marched out for the opening parade. Chief Running Horse followed on horseback, and behind him were a half-dozen Pawnee squaws with their papooses, their horses led by their bucks. Then came forty or more Sioux and Pawnee braves, whooping and yelling, then a huge band of cowboys, a string of elk and some buffalo, dog teams and goat teams driven by

Indian boys, and the stagecoach driven by six mules.

"There he is!" Silena shouted through the roaring crowd as the mounted stars rode out in all their glory, waving into the stands and making their horses prance and rear. Sam was among them, grinning and twirling his pistols, flirting with the crowd.

"See, I told you he was one of the stars!" Silena told Hitch. "I just have to figure out which one."

Hitch didn't say a word. Brooding, he kept his eyes fastened to the arena as the parade cleared and the first event began—an exhibition of the pony-express rider's method of carrying the mail and changing horses and riders with startling quickness.

"Where was Wild Willy?" Caleb asked after a moment. "Shouldn't he have been in the opening parade?"

Silena shrugged and applauded as the pony-express riders changed. "Guess they're saving the best for last."

"Who's gonna take Willy's place in the Stagecoach Robbery?" Jessup asked in a panic when Sam came out of Willy's tent shaking his head, a sign that he'd been unable to wake his father.

"I will," Sam said, stepping into his stirrup and slinging his leg over his horse. "I know the routine."

"But if you do his part, who'll do yours? If the right person ain't drivin' the stage, it could tip over with the mayor in it. Wouldn't that be a story for the newspapers tomorrow?"

"Get Buck Lawson to drive the stage," Sam said, guiding his horse back toward the arena. "He can handle it as well as I can. We can't spare anybody else." He started back to the gates, then turned back, making the white stallion prance with the desire to run. "Be sure to tell Bo I'm riding instead of Willy. We don't want him announcing it wrong and getting the crowd all excited. I still aim to get Willy up before the finale."

Jessup nodded and headed off toward the troupe, his chagrin apparent in every line of his face.

Silena's eyes shone with exhilaration as the Pawnee braves rounded up all their Indian ponies in a mad half-mile dash. As soon as they had cleared the arena, amid cheers and whistles from the excited audience, the gold-gilded stagecoach appeared, led by six mules and a waving driver. The anouncer named the dignitaries in attendance—the mayor of Omaha and his city councilmen—who were introduced one by one and applauded as they waved and stepped into the coach to round the half-mile track.

The mock agent warned the driver of the danger he faced from Indians and bandits, and swearing he could handle the job, the driver, perched on the high seat, drove his horses around the arena three times, the mayor waving to the spectators as if he were the star of the show.

Suddenly a band of fifty Indians led by Running Horse burst out of nowhere, shrilling and whooping and firing blank cartridges and whizzing arrows at the coach. The mules bolted forward as some of the Indians left their horses to climb inside the stage. And just as the driver was shot and the mayor was about to be scalped, Sam and his rescue party dashed out to the rescue.

"It's him!" Silena cried, clutching Margaret's hand. "Look at him!"

She watched, stunned with admiration, as Sam Hawkins bounded across the arena, shooting the Indians and driving them back. When all had either "died" or retreated, he and his band launched into what seemed an authentic "scalping" of them, followed by another Indian attack with more shooting and war play. Until finally Sam Hawkins and his men stood victorious, and the mayor and his men emerged, unscathed, out of the stagecoach.

The cowboys galloped one last time around the arena, shooting their pistols and waving at the crowd, and finally the announcer called out their names, to which each responded with a flourish.

"Sam Hawkins," Silena said, scanning the brochure until she came to his name. "Right here! Sam Hawkins, son of the famed Wild Willy Hawkins—" She caught her breath and looked up at Margaret. "Oh, my gosh. He didn't even tell me! Willy's his *father!*"

And before she could read more about his exploits across the West, Sam Hawkins was barreling back across the arena at full speed, hanging upside down from his horse and shooting at a row of little glass bottles!

The show was nearing the finale when Sam decided to get Willy up, no matter what it took. Too many people were expecting to see him, and he didn't aim to disappoint them.

He went into his father's tent and saw Willy hadn't stirred since he'd laid him on the cot. He'd have a powerful headache when he woke, Sam thought, and he probably wouldn't be able to shoot a wounded buffalo breathing down on him. But sometimes all it took was Willy riding out on his prancing mare to bring the crowd to their feet. Maybe they would forgive a few mistakes.

He shook his father, and Willy stirred and mumbled something.

"Willy, wake up. It's time for you to ride. The show's almost over."

"Gotta ride," Willy muttered, trying to lie back down. "Show's over."

Sam ruthlessly pulled his father back up. "Come on, Willy. Stand up. We've got to get you in costume."

Willy opened his eyes and squinted around the dim tent, his face a twisted portrait of pain and irritation. Finally, he focused his bloodshot eyes on his son. His breath would have killed that wounded buffalo if his bullets couldn't, Sam mused.

"What the hell are you doin' here?" Willy asked, and Sam knew he was relatively more sober than he had been a few hours ago. "Why ain't you out there ridin'?"

"I already rode." Sam grabbed his father's black shirt and white kerchief and thrust them at him. "We've got to get you ready. The crowd's going crazy out there."

Willy stumbled across the room to grab his buckskins, then stopped a moment and clutched his head. "What the hell did I drink?"

"Everything in sight," Sam muttered. "Now here. Put on your shirt, and I'll go get your guns."

"My guns? Where are they?"

"In my tent," Sam said. "I hid them from you so you wouldn't kill anybody."

Ignoring Willy's mumbled expletive, Sam left the tent and walked down to his own. Behind him, he could hear the crowd cheering for Quick Shot Lucy as she shot at the ticket stuck between her husband's teeth. Sam grinned and thanked his stars that Lucy didn't drink.

He gathered his father's guns, loaded the double-action six-shooters and the rifle, and started back to the tent. Jessup was waiting outside, afraid to go in. "Is he up? Is he gonna ride?"

"He'll be there," Sam said. "Just signal Lucy to hold them a little longer. Send the clowns back out if you have to."

Jessup gave Sam a beseeching look, as if he'd just gotten the worst news he'd had all week. "But he'll miss his targets, Sam. He won't be able to hit nothin'!"

"Don't worry about it," Sam ordered, his voice losing its patience. "I'll take care of everything."

"You gonna take care of him making a fool of hisself in front of the whole Omaha press? You gonna take care of him ruining the reputation of the whole show?"

With lightning quickness, Sam grabbed Jessup's dirty collar and shoved his face into his. "Yeah, Jessup," he said through his teeth. "That's what I'm gonna do."

The small man fell back as Sam released him. Straightening his shirt and tie, he muttered, "Okay, Sam. Whatever you say."

Sam went back into his father's tent and found Willy dressed, but already he held a new bottle of whiskey in his shaky hand. His father took a long drink, set the bottle down, and looked up at his son. He looked so old, Sam thought, so used up.

"You don't need that, Willy." Sam took the bottle and recorked it. "You need your wits."

Willy snatched the bottle out of Sam's hand and pulled the cork back off with his teeth, then spat it out. Some of the bottle's amber liquid sloshed onto his shirt. "I got enough wits to knock you back to Kansas!" he said through his teeth. "Don't you touch my whiskey, boy, and don't you ever touch my guns again."

Sam compressed his lips and laid the guns on the cot.

"You were shooting at flies, Willy. Folks were afraid to stand out in the open."

Willy pulled on his holster, belted it, and found the pistols he needed for his act. "The day ain't come when I can't hit what I aim at. If I aimed at flies, then by God, that's what I hit."

"Now that's really something to be proud of, isn't it?" Sam watched his father take another swig, and shook his head with disgust. "Willy, there are thousands of people out there waiting to see you ride and shoot. Don't you think you can stay sober long enough to give them their money's worth?"

Willy set the bottle down and checked his repeating rifle. "I ain't drinkin'," he said. "I was just tryin' to get rid of this poundin' in my head, and steady my hands."

"They steady now?" Sam asked sarcastically.

Willy twirled his pistol and aimed at his son. "What do you think?" he asked with a cocky grin.

Sam shook his head. "I think you'd better holster those guns and mount your horse before that crowd gives up and goes home."

Willy holstered his guns and wiped his nose on the back of his sleeve. "I'll give 'em their money's worth, all right," he said. "How many'd you say are out there?"

"About three thousand," Sam said.

"That many." Willy staggered to his tent flap, and Sam followed, poised to catch him if he fell. "All to see me."

"That's right," Sam said, though a frown drew his thick brows together. "Came to see the legend. The Wild Man himself."

He followed Willy out of the tent, saw his father squint in the sunlight and look around helplessly for his horse.

"I tethered her in back," Sam said before Willy had the chance to ask.

From the distance, came the sound of the cheering crowd, and the pop of Lucy's gun. Willy looked toward the arena, then back to his son. "Lucy's already on. Who took my place in the 'Stagecoach Robbery'?"

"I did," Sam said.

His father spat at the ground. "I reckon that put 'em all to sleep."

Sam tried to ignore the scathing remark, for his father had been flinging them for years. "We drew some applause, Willy."

"Did you now?" Willy asked, his voice thick with skepticism. "If I'da been out there, they'da been beggin' for a encore."

For a moment Sam stood watching his father, quietly suppressing the bitterness that stemmed back to his childhood. He'd never been big enough or strong enough or fast enough or skilled enough to earn his father's respect. He was smart, his father had always conceded as if that were some shameful affliction that made him less of a man, but *smart* didn't make your aim any better, and it didn't keep you alive in a fix. Funny thing was, Sam had long ago surpassed his father in his skills with a gun, but Willy still didn't see it.

"But you *weren't* out there," Sam pointed out, his voice sharpening. "So we had to make do."

"Yeah, well." Willy struggled to get his foot in the stirrup, but he couldn't quite manage it. "Give me a hand."

Sam shoved back his bitterness, for there was only time now for concern that the wobbly hero wouldn't be able to mount his horse. Steadying the stirrup, he helped his father climb up on his horse, patted the mare's rump, and said, "Give them hell, Willy. I'll go tell Jessup you're ready."

He watched his father sit taller in his saddle, almost matching the image of the legendary hero—the image that even he had believed in as a kid. It would be all right, Sam thought, as long as his father could stay in the saddle. He'd see to it that everything else went smoothly.

Mounting Duke, Sam galloped up to the arena and signaled Jessup that Willy was on his way. Jessup shot him another doubtful look, then reluctantly gestured to Lucy to end her performance.

The crowd went wild with anticipation as Lucy left the arena, and the band began to play the theme song that preceded Wild Willy's appearance. Six cowgirls rode out and circled the arena, and a team of "wild" Indians came hollering from the other direction to take them hostage. And just as it looked as if all hope was lost, the music crescendoed, the gates opened, and Wild Willy came riding in, shooting his pistols in the air and "killing" the Indians to rescue the distressed damsels.

The crowd came to their feet, three thousand voices all cheering and whistling. They watched as Wild Willy rode off stage to change guns and came back with a Winchester repeating rifle and four holstered six-shooters, promising more stunts that would stun the expectant crowd.

In the stands, Silena's mood changed from starry-eyed ecstasy to annoyed worry when she saw Zane Barlow standing a few yards away, scanning the faces of the spectators, searching for her. He was desperate to foil her plans to meet Willy, she thought, but she was just as desperate not to let him.

When the crowd came to their feet, she decided it

was the perfect time to get away. Slipping past Hitch, Margaret, and Caleb, she made her way to the aisle.

"Where you goin'?" Hitch asked.

"I have to do something," she said evasively. "I'll be right back."

"But you'll miss Willy's shootin'."

Silena peered between two heads and saw Zane ambling closer to her section of seats. "But I won't miss talking to him, and that's really what I came for."

Hitch grabbed her arm. "What are you up to?"

"Nothing!" she whispered harshly. "I just saw Zane Barlow, so I'm slipping out for a minute. I *told* you I'll be right back."

Moaning, Hitch dropped her arm, but before he had the presence of mind to follow her, she had run down the steps toward the back of the stands and vanished.

Sam heard the crowd cheering wildly at Willy's stunts, but he knew it would be a different story once Willy traded his blank cartridges for real ammunition. He dismounted, left his horse to graze in the grass "backstage," and ambled to a side of the grandstands, where he had a clear view of the arena as Willy prepared for the glass-ball-breaking exhibition. He told himself that it would be difficult for Willy to miss the glass balls, for not only would they be thrown more slowly in the air than they would for the other trick shooters, but Sam had loaded Willy's gun with twenty grains of black powder and one-quarter ounce of chilled shot. This had a wider range and should ensure Willy hitting his target, but Sam had seen Willy miss more than he hit on many occasions, and he feared today would be the worst yet.

He held his breath as the crowd hushed, and he heard

his father signal the release of the trap. The first group of balls shot up one by one, and Willy opened fire.

Each of the balls fell back to the dirt, unscarred. The announcer, who customarily counted the few remaining balls to impress the crowd, only looked up at Willy in horror.

Sam could feel the tension and disappointment in the crowd, but moreover, he saw the humiliation on his father's wizened face. And Sam knew that Willy no longer had what it took to get himself out of this fix.

Stepping behind a wall where no one could see him, Sam drew his double-action revolvers, aimed, and waited for the balls to launch into the air again. Even from this distance, he could see the sweat trickling down his father's face, staining the white kerchief around his neck, and he knew the old man's hands were shaking as he aimed his pistols.

The balls went up, and Willy began to fire. From his corner of the grandstands, Sam fired, too, rapidly shattering the balls one at a time with split-second timing, until all had been demolished in midair. The crowd went wild. Sam saw Willy's surprise, then his sudden ecstasy as he took off his hat and waved to the spectators.

Getting braver, Willy signaled for the announcer to reload the trap. Fine beads of sweat broke out over Sam's lip as he hurried to reload his six-shooters and aim again.

The balls shot into the air, and Sam opened fire simultaneously with his father. The crowd was cheering too loudly for anyone to realize that most of the gunshots were coming from a different direction, and one by one the balls shattered in midair, until there were none left for the announcer to count.

Still unaware that it wasn't his own aim destroying

the balls, Willy drew up as proud and cocky in the saddle as he had in his heyday when he really had been capable of such shooting, but his new confidence only made Sam's job tougher.

Sweat trickled down his chin as he waited to see what Willy would attempt next. Silently, he uttered a prayer that he'd be able to keep up with his father's new temerity and give these people their money's worth, Willy his pride, and the show an unhampered reputation.

"What are you doing?"

Sam swung around like a bank robber caught in the act and saw Silena watching him, her eyes filled with surprise. And he wondered just how the hell he was going to explain his way out of this, without bursting her inflated image of the Wild West hero she had come so far to see.

4

"You're not supposed to be here," Sam said, looking over Silena's shoulder to see if anyone had sneaked back here with her. "Get on back in the stands. You'll miss the show."

"You're shooting for him, aren't you?"

He stared at her, unable to speak, searching his mind for some suitable explanation, when suddenly he heard his father shooting again. "Damn it all, woman!" he said, turning around and aiming his gun toward the center of the arena again. "Just stay back and be quiet!"

Silena stepped back and watched, dumbfounded, as Sam shot at the balls his father was getting the applause for. When that round was finished, he quickly reloaded, watched his father's next move, and fired again the moment Willy's gun went off.

Her heart sank like those first glass balls Willy hadn't been able to hit, shattering in the pit of her stomach. The big hero, the Wild West star, the celebrated gunslinger, couldn't even shoot his own targets!

It was a few minutes after Willy stopped firing, after his second encore, when it was clear the star wouldn't fire again, before Sam turned around and faced her. His eyes were hooded, and she saw the guilt hiding behind them.

"You didn't see that."

"Yes, I did," she said defiantly. "I saw all of it." Her voice shook. "Tell me. Do you do the shootin' for everybody, or just Willy?"

"I don't do the shooting for anybody but myself . . . usually," he said. He glanced back over his shoulder, saw his father come back into the arena with a rifle with blank cartridges, and begin his next stunt.

"Willy's been drinking too much. That's why he wasn't in the show until now. I had to wake him up and practically throw him on his horse, and I knew he couldn't shoot. This is the only time I've ever done this."

"I thought he was supposed to be the best gunslinger in the world," she said. "The handbill said he could shoot upside down, right side up, backward, and every which-a-way. They said he had single-handedly gunned down a whole tribe of Cheyenne with arrows coming at him from everywhere. Now you're telling me that a few drinks and he can't shoot at all?"

"Not a few drinks," he said. "A lot of drinks. He *is* the best gunslinger in the world, and he damn well did do all those things. We wouldn't say it if it wasn't true." The lie didn't alter his face at all, for he'd told it so many times. "Fact is, he had a real bad day, and got dirt-slobbering drunk. Even I couldn't shoot if I was that drunk, and I'm the next best gunslinger in the show."

The disappointment Silena felt in Wild Willy began to give way to her admiration of the man who had helped him with such skill, and she wondered if, indeed, he was only "next best." "You're good," she acknowledged, glancing down at his guns, one still in each hand. "I've never seen anybody shoot like that before."

He smiled and holstered one pistol, then tipped his Stetson. "I appreciate that."

Studying him further, she cocked her head and narrowed her eyes. "It's no wonder you're so good," she said. "Being his son and all. You didn't tell me he was your father, you know."

"Yeah, well . . ." He looked down again at the guns still smoking in his hands, and holstered them. "Look, I need your help on this. Don't let on you saw this, okay? Willy doesn't know I helped him. He thinks he did it all himself. And that's fine, because he could have. You should come see another show, when he's himself. You'll see that he's the best shooter that ever lived."

"I believe he's one of the best," she said with a half smile, trying to disguise the awe in her voice. "But I can't believe he's better than you."

He matched her grin, and she noticed the tiny clefts in each cheek when he did. "He taught me everything I know," he admitted.

She sighed and stepped up next to him, watching Wild Willy dazzle the crowd further. "For a minute I thought maybe the handbill had been lying about him. If he couldn't do his own shooting . . . I'm glad to know this isn't the usual thing."

"It's not." Sam looked down at her, and the soft scent of a foreign perfume drifted up to him. "When Willy drinks . . ."

"I understand," she said. "My pa drinks sometimes, too." Quickly qualifying her confession, she added, "Not much, but sometimes."

That haunted look drifted back to her eyes, and Sam

remembered what she'd said about wanting to ask Willy about her dead mother. He wished he could distract her from that mission now, for he knew that Willy would be in no mood for reminiscences. His headiness over his shooting, mingled with his irritability from his hangover, would be a combination that Sam could barely control. Silena was too pretty to take around his father at a time like that; he hated to see her leered at and propositioned.

He heard the theme music that indicated it was time for him to line up for the grand finale, and grabbing his horse's reins, he made ready to mount. "You won't tell, will you? It could ruin Willy . . . and me too. It's real important that you keep quiet."

"On one condition," she said, seizing the opportunity in a way that took him by surprise.

He smiled at that determined look in her eye, and asked, "What condition?"

"You keep your word and take me back to meet Willy."

His face paled, but rallying, he took her hand and ran his thumb softly over a knuckle. Her heart jolted, but she didn't take her eyes from his.

"How about we skip that and I take you for another ride? I could show you some real pretty country. . . ."

She felt her face reddening with the invitation, but she had staved off such offers before. None from anyone quite so exciting and charming, she had to admit, but she wasn't one to be won over quite that easily.

"Willy," she said. "I want to meet Willy. I *need* to ask him about my mother. It's real important."

Sam saw the importance glistening in her green eyes, eyes that didn't back down or give up. Something in the way she said it touched his heart, and for a moment he hoped that Willy could give her the answers she needed.

Flicking her chin with a callused finger, he smiled. A thrill shot through her at the contact. "Well, I might not ever get over the disappointment that you'd rather be with him than me," he said, "but I'll take you. Meet me right here after the show." He started to mount his horse.

"I can't."

He looked down at her from his mount. "Why not?"

"Because . . . Zane is still after me, and he'll do anything to keep me from seeing Willy. When the show's over and the folks start coming out, he could find me. Is there a better place? Someplace away from the crowd?"

Sam grinned. "You're a real determined lady, aren't you?"

She answered his smile. "That's what my pa always says."

He reached down to take her hand. "Come on up here with me. I'll let you off backstage, and after the finale, we'll go to Willy's tent."

Putting her hand in his, she smiled as he pulled her up in front of him. And as he ran his horse around the back of the stands to the area where all the Wild West stars were preparing for the grand finale, the "Cabin Burning," she knew that everything was going to be fine. What could go wrong, after all, when she was in the presence of such a powerful man, who seemed to have all the answers?

The excitement backstage was even keener than that in the stands, and when Sam let her down in what he said was a "safe place where you won't get stampeded or shot," she marveled at the flurry of activity. So many heroes gathered into one place, up close, she thought. So many courageous men and women.

She watched as the Sioux Indians galloped out on horseback and raided a cabin, dragging the family out and setting their home on fire. Just as they began to kill the woman and her children she saw Wild Willy swagger through the showmen backstage, throw himself onto his horse, and look around to see if everyone was ready.

He gave the signal, and he and the other stars burst into the arena, where the audience screamed and applauded with delight. Sam was among the "saviors" who rescued the woman and her children, murdered the Indians, and saved the day.

From her position where Sam had put her, Silena stood on tiptoes and applauded with all her might, wishing the show could go on and on, that she could stay here amid this excitement and heroism forever, that she could know these people and be at home with them, as they seemed to be with each other. She thought of their travels, of the world they had seen, and she envied all of them. She had seen nothing except what Hayton, Nebraska—population ninety-seven—had shown her.

And then her thoughts returned to her father, standing out in front of his store that morning, pleading with her to come back. She had lied to him and disobeyed him, and she would have to pay later. Not in a physical way, for her father had never lifted a hand to her, but he would load lectures, anger, and guilt on her. Still, she thought, he wouldn't make her regret what she had done.

Especially not if she got what she had come for.

The stars waved to the crowd, and the Indians "miraculously" came back to life for their bows. The audience went crazy with exhilaration as the music swelled and the show ended.

The stars galloped off the field in a cloud of dust, and something in Silena's heart flipped as she singled out Sam, smiling at the crowd with his showman's charm. When he was backstage and started toward her, her heart flipped again.

"So what'd you think?"

Unable to hide her complete adoration, she smiled up at him. "It was just . . . just wonderful . . . so exciting. I almost believed it was all really happening."

He slipped off his horse, still breathless from the ride, and took her hand. She knew it was trembling, and that he felt it, and she wondered how many other women he reduced to shivers and stutters after they'd seen him in action. "I'm glad you liked it," he said. "I put a little extra into it today just for you."

She bit her lip as he dropped a kiss on her hand, and felt her face growing hot. Did he know his power? she wondered. Did he know how confused and helpless he made her feel, as if she were feather light and at the mercy of a fickle wind? Then quickly, she told herself that of course he did, that he probably picked out one or two women each show, charmed them, and made them think they had inspired him. Determined not to be just another of them, she withdrew her hand and hid it in the folds of her skirt.

"So . . . can I go meet Willy now?"

Sam's smile faded a little at her slight retreat, and he looked around. "Yeah. Looks like he already went back."

He handed Duke over to someone in the troupe and, taking her hand, led her through the cast. With wide eyes, she watched for the stars she could single out, Quick Shot Lucy, and Running Horse, and Bad Boy Jacob, and Bronco Bob. They cut through the lady riders, or cowgirls—not quite as pretty up close as they had been from a distance—and several of them called out, "Good show, Sam."

Sam grinned and winked as they passed, and a surge of jealousy shot through Silena. Was there a woman among them who was special to Sam? One he spent his evenings with, wooing and charming, the way he had charmed her today?

They went around the burlap flaps that separated the backstage from public view, and made their way into the crowd already beginning to come out of the arena. "You sure you want to do this?" he asked, grinning down at her.

"Positive."

"Okay," he said, "but you'll have to be prepared. He'll probably make some lewd and ungentlemanly advances, if he doesn't throw us out. And if he starts cussing, well, just cover your ears."

"I've heard cussing," she said, "and as for those advances, I did just fine with you, didn't I?"

His grin broadened. "You did at that." Then the smile faded, and a serious look defined the worry in his eyes, making him appear deeper than the shallowness of all fun and stunts. He was a thinker, she thought instantly, for eyes like that reached further than grins and gunslinging. "Just don't be disappointed. Sometimes people blow their heroes up in their heads, thinking they're perfect and good. It's a letdown when they turn out to be human."

She felt as if he was warning her about something, and the thought put her on her guard. There was a strange sobriety in his voice, where before he had spoken with a sexy, rugged drawl.

"And whatever you do, don't tell him what you saw

today. No matter how mad he makes you. And say something flattering to him, something about how good he shot."

She frowned and slowed her step, and looked up at him. "He *is* your pa, isn't he? That is what the handbill said."

"Yeah, why?"

"Because you sound like one of his troopers afraid to cross him, instead of a son."

"Nobody wants to cross Willy when he's been drinking," he said somberly. "I can handle him just fine, but if I can help it, I'd rather you didn't have to."

"I can take care of myself," she said. "I've been protected all my life, and now I'm ready to find out what I've been protected from. Besides, he looked just fine backstage, and he was wonderful in the last part of the show."

Sam shrugged. "I guess. Just . . . don't be disappointed, that's all. He gets a lot of people trying to meet him. He's not friendly to all of them."

"He'll be friendly to me," she said with certainty. "Soon as I tell him who I am."

Heaving a deep, reluctant sigh, Sam smiled again. "All right. But after this, you owe me. I still want to take you on that ride."

His gaze dropped to her lips, then climbed back to her eyes, and she felt her throat going dry once more. She thought of being back in his saddle, leaning against him, warm in his arms, breathing his male scent. . . . She thought of those lips as his tongue ran across them, of how they might feel against hers, of how decadent and defiant and utterly out of her character it would be to ride off with him. It would shock her friends. It would shock her father. And it would even shock herself.

"I . . . I don't know," she said. "My friends are . . .

well, they'll be waiting for me." The stuttering again, she thought. The trembling.

"Well, maybe I can talk you into it," he whispered. He took her hand again, turned it over, and ran the pad of his thumb across her palm. Her cheeks blazed, and slowly, she slipped her hand from his.

"No," she said breathlessly, realizing that if he could make her knees weak just touching her hand, he could melt her completely if he ever kissed her. Besides, these feelings weren't ladylike. Miss Caldonia would have frowned on it, and Miss Belle—who ran Miss Belle's School of Manners, Poise, and Domesticity—would have choked at the very thought. "I don't think so."

"I'll still try," he promised. Giving her a last wink, he pulled back the flap of the tent and preceded her in. "Willy?"

"What'd you do with my whiskey?" Willy bellowed out at the sight of him. "You better not have hid it!"

Silena hesitated at the flap, suddenly afraid to enter.

"I didn't hide it, Willy," Sam threw back. "You probably drank it all."

"Then get me some more! My head feels like Lightning's been gallopin' on it. I shoulda let Running Horse scalp me for real and be done with it."

"But it was a great show," Sam said.

Silena could hear Willy's voice change at that. "Did you see how many balls I shot up, Sam? Damn near every one. Don't let nobody tell you I'm losin' my touch."

"No, Willy, you won't ever lose your touch."

Silena saw Sam look back at her over his shoulder, and he crooked his finger for her to come inside. Reluctant at first to enter the dark tent, she slowly ducked under his arm, with which he held the flap back. Wild

Willy was sitting on a cot, his shirt unbuttoned, revealing a hairy, fat paunch rolling out over his belt. His hair was dirty, and he smelled, and his glassy eyes were bloodshot.

"Willy, I got somebody I want you to meet. She says you know her pa."

Willy squinted up at her, and a lascivious grin broke out over his face. "Well, what we got here? Pretty little thing like you wanted to come back and meet the star, did you?"

Silena tried to smile, and stepped toward him, extending her hand. "Yes. You were wonderful. I've never seen such shooting."

"Well, then," he said, flashing her a yellow-toothed smile, "why don't you come over here and sit right down for a spell?" He patted his leg, inviting her to sit on his lap. Silena's smile faded instantly, but Willy didn't notice. "You just look perty enough to eat."

"Uh . . . no, thank you. I'm fine standing."

"She didn't come here for that, Willy," Sam said, his voice flat. "Tell him who your pa is, ma'am."

Silena tried to rally her strength. "I . . . I'm Silena Rivers. Jake Rivers's daughter."

"That's nice, honey," Willy said, reaching for her hand.

She recoiled, and Sam stepped up beside her. "Willy, I told you, she didn't come here for that. Do you know her pa or don't you?"

Willy's face distorted with disgust at Sam's interference. "Well, I don't know! What's his name?"

"Jake Rivers," Sam repeated. "Can't you hear?"

"Yeah, I can hear," Willy shouted back. Spitting on the ground, he turned back to Silena. "Don't know nobody named Rivers."

Silena's face fell by degrees, and Sam watched as she tried to pull up her pride and try again.

"Are you sure?" she asked. "I mean . . . he told me you were best friends."

Willy cleared his throat, spat again, and shook his head. "Lots of folks say they know me to impress each other. Don't mean nothin'."

"Anybody ever tell you you have a talent for tact?" Sam asked his father, disgusted.

Willy grunted. "This little lady didn't come here for tact, did you, honey?" He reached for her again, but her face only distorted more as she backed away. For a moment Sam thought she might burst into tears. He touched her elbow and started to urge her out. "Come on, Silena. It's all right. He probably just forgot."

"He wouldn't forget!" she said, jerking away from his touch and spinning around to face Willy squarely. "How could you forget somebody who saved you from drowning?"

Willy moved his bloodshot gaze up to her and rubbed at his temples. "Gall dang it, girl, if your daddy told you he saved my life when I never even heard of the man, then he's a liar."

Tears sprang to her eyes. "Well then . . . my mother. Eva Rivers. Do you remember her?"

Willy twisted his face, as if trying to remember. "Was she a whore?"

Sam felt the last strand of his patience snap, and he kicked the chair beside him. "Damn it, Willy, does this look like the daughter of a whore?" He didn't wait for an answer, but turned his red face to Silena. "What was her name before she married your pa?"

Silena's face changed from an expression of startled surprise to one of utter helplessness. "I . . . I don't know." She swallowed and tried not to look so devastated. "Guess I'd hoped Mr. Hawkins could tell me." Her voice cracked, but she lifted her chin and went on. "I don't know much about her, but I do know that she was not a . . . a . . ."

The word wouldn't come out, but more tears did. "My mother was a lady," she said finally, with absolute certainty.

"Then I wouldn't have knowed her." Willy threw back his head and let out a bawdy guffaw, but no one joined him. "Don't know no *ladies* by the name o' Rivers, either."

Defeated, Silena looked down at her hands. Smoothing her skirt, she swallowed and started to leave. But at the flap of the tent, she turned back.

"My pa said you had a sister named Fanny who could lasso a calf in half the time you could."

For a fraction of a second Willy's expression seemed to clear. He looked at her again, surprise in his eyes. Slowly, he came to his feet. "What did you say his name was?"

"Rivers," she said, life returning to her eyes. "Jake Rivers."

"I swear to God I don't know nobody named Rivers."

Her heart fell further, but that flicker of surprise in his eyes left the tiniest hope in her heart. He knew her father, she told herself, but maybe it was true that, in spite of their long friendship, he had forgotten.

Pulling herself up straighter, she took a bold step toward him, holding out her hand. "Then I'm sorry I bothered you," she said. "And I thank you for your time."

Awkwardly, Willy took her hand and glanced down

at it. She saw his eyes sweep over the ring she wore, and suddenly his grip was tighter. He looked at it for a second too long before he brought his eyes back to hers and in that instant, she knew she saw recognition in his eyes.

"Anytime," he said vacantly.

Avoiding Sam's sympathetic gaze, Silena pushed past him and left the darkened tent.

Sam watched her push through the crowd to the friends who had probably been looking for her. Still standing at the tent flap, he muttered, "Damn you, Willy. Why'd you have to be so hard on her? It's a shame to see tears in eyes as pretty as those."

Willy didn't answer with the stream of curses that he usually gave vent to at the slightest criticism. Looking back inside the tent, Sam saw him staring off into space. He was frowning, and his fingers were stroking his hard lips, the way they always did when he tried to sort something out.

"What is it, Willy?"

"Nothin'."

Something about his father's sudden quiet shook Sam, and stepping closer, he sat down on the cot across from him. "She was pretty, wasn't she?"

"Yeah," Willy said, still distracted. "Real purty."

Sam watched with a rising sense of suspicion as Willy continued to stare off. "So, Willy. *Can* Fanny lasso a calf in half the time you can?"

The question shook Willy out of his reverie, and a slow grin crossed his face. "Fanny don't lasso calves no more. She turned into a lady, after all. Used to get my gall real bad that she was quicker'n me. She could shoot, too. I tried to keep it secret. Not many folks know."

Sam laughed at the picture of the aunt he'd only seen

in pictures roping and tying a calf, and competing with her brother in marksmanship. But his laughter died as it occurred to him that Silena had known something significant, something that, perhaps, only someone from Willy's past could have told her.

"What about that drowning stuff, Willy?" he asked, fixing his eyes on his father.

Willy rubbed the gray stubble on his chin again, and his frown returned as he looked at his son. "That's the thing," he said. "I did almost drown once, when I was no more'n ten."

Sam's eyes brightened. "All right, then," he said. "Who saved you? Did you know his name?"

"Hell yes, I knew his name." Willy sprang up and went to the tent flap, peered out. Silena was no longer in sight. "It was a friend named Jim McCosky. And he died seventeen years ago."

"I remember hearing you talk about Jim," Sam said, disappointment flattening his voice. "And I remember when he died. Really shook you up."

Willy let the flap go and turned back to Sam. "Did you see that ring she was wearin'?"

"Yeah," Sam said. "It looked familiar to me, but I couldn't think where—"

"The insignia," Willy said, stepping back toward Sam. "Don't you remember that insignia me and Jim came up with back when we started that ranch in Kansas?"

Sam's eyebrows rose. "Yeah. That was it, wasn't it?"

"Couldn't be," Willy said.

"Naw," Sam agreed. "Couldn't be. Unless . . ."

"Unless what?"

"Well, she said something to me about wanting to know about her ma. Said her ma left her that ring. Maybe her ma knew Jim somehow."

"Maybe," Willy said. "But I never knew Jim to give fancy trinkets like that to a lady. You think?"

"Could be," Sam said. "'Course, that's not what she said. She *said* you knew her pa."

"But I don't," Willy said with less conviction, waving his hand in the direction Silena had disappeared and swaggering back to his cot. "Damn fool probably just told her that to impress her."

"Probably," Sam said. "Still, I wish we could have given her something. I hate to disappoint somebody that pretty."

Willy pulled his boots off and plopped down on his cot. "Quit moanin' over her and go get one of the cowgirls if you're hurtin'," he said. "That itch can be easily scratched."

Deciding not to dignify Willy's advice with a response, Sam left his father's tent.

Smiling and tipping his hat to the well-wishers and fans, he pushed through the crowd to the side of the compound where the carriages parked. Scanning the heads, he searched for Silena's green bonnet.

It was a few moments before he found her, but when he did, he could see that she was arguing with the friends she had presumably come here with. He supposed she was all right now. Her fear had been to miss meeting Willy. Now that she had, her pursuer wasn't a threat.

It was a damned shame, too, he thought. For he had enjoyed rescuing her.

5

Silena tried to climb up on the wagon, despite the fact that Zane and Hitch still chided her for disappearing the way she had.

"Dang it all, Silena, you scared me half to death," Hitch cried. "Do you know what your pa would do to me if he found out I'd let you go in Wild Willy's tent?"

"Probably no more than he'll do to you for bringing me in the first place," Silena said. "Are you coming or not?"

Hitch threw up his hands and looked helplessly at Zane.

"Silena, just ride back with me so your pa'll *think* I done my job," Zane said. "Please."

"What did he say?" Margaret asked, working her way into the conversation. "You did meet him, didn't you? I knew you would, even though they said you wouldn't. Did he know your pa like you thought?"

Silena fixed her eyes straight ahead and sat with her back stiff. She felt the tears stinging her eyes, but she held them back. "Are we going or not?"

"Silena, I need that money!" Zane said. "I spent the whole durn day chasin' you around—"

"Well, you *shouldn't* have," she said. "I told you to go home. Besides, you probably had a better time than you've had all your life, so stop whining. My pa knew when he sent you that you couldn't catch me."

Punching a harmless fist at the air, Zane stormed off to his own wagon.

"Did you meet him or not?" Margaret demanded. "Silena!"

"Yes, I met him. All right?"

"What about that gunslinger?"

"I was with him, too," she said, though she could see the indignation on Hitch's face. "I went backstage and saw the whole finale from there."

"Really? Oh, Silena! You're so lucky!"

Silena smiled slightly at Margaret's enthusiasm, but she still felt those tears threatening her. Softening her voice, she leaned down to Hitch. "Please, Hitch. Let's just go."

"He didn't know your pa, did he?"

Snapping her chin up, she said, "He did so."

"Did not. You'da been braggin' to the stars and back if he'da knowed him. He probably said just what I told you he'd say."

"Well, he didn't," she said with less conviction, but this time she couldn't stop the tears. A big one dropped over her lashes and rolled down her cheek.

Caleb shoved Hitch. "Look at 'er, Hitch. You made her cry. Are you happy?"

Hitch looked like he'd just been caught setting fire to a neighbor's barn. "Aw, Silena, don't cry. I didn't mean it. It don't matter to me whether your pa knew Wild Willy or not. That ain't why I like you."

Silena wiped her tear and looked back toward the

compound. Sam was standing a few yards away, near the fence, watching her. Quickly, she averted her eyes. She looked down at Margaret, saw that her face had fallen at Hitch's words, and climbed over the backboard into the wagon.

"I'll ride back here," she said. "Come on, Margaret. You sit up front this time."

Margaret hesitated at the prospect of sitting next to Hitch, but she climbed up next to him.

"What the hell," Caleb muttered as he stepped up into the wagon bed. "I got bruises on my bruises from the ride over, but I reckon I can handle it if you can. Wonder if it's any more comfortable layin' down."

He swept the hay and dirt around with his hand and stretched out, hands behind his head, a sight that would have been comical if Silena's heart hadn't felt so heavy. As they pulled out of the compound Silena let her eyes stray back to the fence, where Sam still waited. He tipped his hat to her and offered her a soft, apologetic smile again. Something in her heart stirred, but she didn't acknowledge it.

Instead, she closed her eyes and tried not to look at him again until they were too far out of sight for him to see her.

Sam watched the wagon fall into the line of other rigs, carriages, and horses, and disappear in the cloud of dust they stirred up. She had come here with such stars in her eyes, and all of those stars had been shot down. First she had discovered that the legend was a drunk who couldn't shoot straight, and then she had stood there like a lady while that same legend called her father a liar and her mother a whore.

Feeling as if something important had been taken

from him, Sam ambled back through the people, ignoring the smiles from the pretty ladies who surrounded him after each show, ignoring the questions from the troupe members, ignoring even Jessup when he saw him coming out of Willy's tent, again in a temper.

He reached his own tent, went in, dragged off his boots, and lay down on his cot, his hat riding low over his head. In a moment Jessup was at his tent flap, ducking his head inside. "Guess we did it," he said.

"Yep. We did it."

"Again."

Sam didn't answer, so Jessup came further inside. "I seen what you done today, Sam. And it ain't the first time, is it?"

"What I did about what?" Sam asked, keeping his eyes closed and his hat over the top half of his face.

"Shootin' for your pa," Jessup said.

Sam pulled his hat back and angled his eyes toward the manager.

"Don't worry," Jessup said. "I'm glad you done it. If you hadn't, well, I don't know what we woulda done. He wasn't hittin' a single ball."

"He was unsteady. It won't happen again."

"Yes, it will, and you know it. He's drunk every show, and his aim gets worse and worse. And I can't help thinkin' that makin' him think he's still got it is doin' him more harm than good."

"You leave that up to me," Sam said.

"And that girl," Jessup went on. "The one who was standin' there with ya. I saw her. How do you know she won't talk?"

"She won't."

"How do you know!" Jessup demanded. "She could go right to the press."

"I said she won't talk," Sam said, sitting up slowly and fixing his hard eyes on Jessup. "She won't. So just don't give it another thought."

"Who was she, anyway, that you'd trust her like that?"

"It isn't a matter of trust," he said. "It's a matter of just knowing. And don't worry about Willy. He's going to be fine."

"I've heard that before," Jessup said. Heaving one last sigh, he ducked back under the flap, leaving Sam alone.

Sam closed his eyes again, and realized that he had said it before, many times. He had made excuses to all of the troupe members, had apologized to each of the stars separately and together dozens of times, after Willy had berated them and sent them packing. He had covered for his father on countless occasions, and had done the shooting for him, as he had today, at least three times before.

Willy was getting old, he realized, and he needed to rest. He'd led a long, hard life, and now he found it hard to keep the pace. Especially since Stella died.

Sam's thoughts drifted back to his sister, so small and frail, so unfit for the road life that had been thrust upon her. And then he thought back further, to a time when they had been happy, to a time when Stella had been a three-year-old rascal ducking in and out of their mother's skirts, giggling and teasing him. He had been the man of the house while his father worked as a scout for the cavalry. His head tightened as he remembered the few times in his life that Willy had drifted home, stayed a few weeks, then left again. Sam had believed in him then, and no one could have told him one bad thing against his father. He was a hero in the boy's eyes, a larger-than-life figure who was treated more like a celebrity than family when he was home. When he'd started the Wild West show, his star had risen even higher, and suddenly everyone seemed to have heard of the legend. And Sam saw him even less.

But Sam hadn't minded, for the role of man of the house suited him fine. He was the protector of his mother and sister, and he liked having them need him. He hunted when they needed food. He worked jobs when they needed money. He guarded them when they were afraid.

But the year he'd turned twelve, his mother had grown sick of consumption and died, despite his desperate efforts to save her. It was then that he had found life to be out of his control.

Riding into town like the hero come to save the day, Willy had sold the farm and taken Sam and Stella on the road with him. And suddenly Sam and Stella had been thrust from the predictable, stable, happy life their mother had given them into a fast-paced, wild, roving life in the family of showpeople who seemed closer to Willy than his own kin.

Since Willy hadn't a clue how to raise children, and didn't much care to learn, Stella had become Sam's exclusive charge. He had loved her and nurtured her as much as a twelve-year-old boy could, and as much as his father allowed, since Willy fancied that tenderness and exhibitions of love proved him somehow weak. Stella never adjusted fully to her life on the road, and Sam had grieved over the death of her childhood spirit, and tried to get it back for her. But it was long gone.

It had been two years now since she'd gotten pneumonia on the road in an early Wyoming winter, and despite Sam keeping vigil by her bed and performing every bit of medical and superstitious magic he knew, she had died on her twentieth birthday last year.

He had let her down, just as he had let down his mother. He had always tried to be their hero. But he wasn't heroic enough.

Now Willy was a declining drunk who insulted pretty young girls and made them cry. But Sam couldn't put much blame on the old man who'd taken Stella's death so hard. He hadn't been the same since she died. And neither had Sam.

It was Sam's lot, now, to take care of his father, he thought, and the other troupe members who depended on him. He would do what had to be done.

The heroism written of Willy on the handbills might be a lie, he mused, but that didn't mean he had to stop trying. Someday, perhaps, he would bring Willy back from his own ruin, save the show that was in deep financial trouble, and win the appreciation and respect of the father who never paid him more than passing heed.

Either that, or he'd wind up just like Willy, divided and steeped in regrets, miserable and angry. But he doubted it, he thought, because one of these days, he might just get tired of pretending to be a hero.

Jake was waiting on the front porch of his mercantile, pacing like a foaming tiger, when Hitch's wagon rounded the corner into Main Street.

"Brace yourselves, brothers and sisters," Caleb said in the voice of one of those traveling evangelists who sold holy water for a penny. "We're in for a storm tonight."

Silena didn't answer as the wagon slowed to a halt in

front of the store. Deciding there was nothing to do but get it over with, she stood up and faced her father.

"Pa?"

Jake didn't say anything, but he stopped his pacing and fixed her with a look that froze her straight through to her bones.

Feeling shakier than she'd expected, Silena let Caleb help her out of the wagon, Hitch stood up, still holding the reins. "Uh . . . Mr. Rivers, it's my fault. I kinda talked Silena into going. . . ."

"It's all right, Hitch," Silena cut in softly. "He knows nothing could have stopped me."

At Jake's continued silence, Hitch sat back down next to Margaret and waited for Silena to say something more. Instead, she just stared at her father, tears glistening in her eyes.

"Well . . . I'll stop by tomorrow . . . or the next day," Hitch mumbled.

Silena shook free of her father's stare and turned her pale face toward her friends. "Yes. Thanks for the ride."

Margaret offered her a half wave and Caleb muttered something about "great wailing and gnashing of teeth" as the wagon started to pull. Silena turned back to her father.

"I met him, Pa," she said, her voice shaking. "I met Willy."

Her father's face didn't alter as he kept his eyes on hers. "And?"

"And . . . he told me he'd never heard of Jake Rivers."

For a moment he stared at her, his face dull and expressionless, and unsurprised. Then, as if the conversation was over, Jake turned and walked into the store.

"Pa, did you hear me?" Silena demanded, following him in. "He said he didn't know you! That you'd lied!"

"Then let it be!" He swung around, his face a brilliant shade of red. Quickly, he slammed the door shut and flipped the sign to "Closed." "Just let it be! He says he don't know me, so leave it at that! I'm a liar. I made it all up."

Silena stood stunned, watching him, as he faced her. "No, you didn't. You didn't make it up."

Jake's face distorted in a mixture of pain and desperation, and he stepped closer to her. "What?"

"I said, you didn't make it up. None of it makes sense, but I don't think you lied."

"Why not? He *told* you, didn't he? He's a big hero, a legend, and he said it. It must be true!"

"It was the ring." The words were out of her mouth before she realized it, and she caught her breath and slipped her hand behind her back.

Jake's eyes seemed to turn smoky as he took in her words. "What ring?" he asked in a whisper.

"The ring." Her words came out in a weak whisper, but she swallowed and went on. "Mama's ring. When I shook his hand, he saw it, and I know he recognized it. The look on his face—"

In an instant Jake crossed the distance between them and shook her shoulders. "Damn it, girl, what did he say? What did he say about the ring?"

Surprised at the sudden reaction, Silena shook her head. "Nothing! It was just a feeling!"

He let her go, and she stumbled back. He held out a hand, and she saw that it was trembling. "Give it to me," he said. "Give me the ring."

"It's mine," she said, her lips shaking. "Please, pa, it's all I have of her."

"Give it to me," he repeated in a steely, dangerous voice. "Now!"

Jerking it off her finger, she threw it at him, and he bent over to pick it up. When he stood back up, his hair had fallen forward over his forehead, lending him the look of someone to be feared. But the tears glistening in his eyes belied that.

He shook his head slowly. "You don't know what you've done, Silena. You don't know what you've done."

"That's right," she said. "What *have* I done? Tell me! I don't understand any of this!"

"This ring." He held it up, then closed it in his fist. "It could mean big trouble for us. It could open up a whole mess of trouble."

"Why? It's just a ring, Pa. Who cares about it, anyway?"

Jake shook his head and, turning away, covered his face. She could see that he was perspiring and could hear his heavy, labored breathing.

She stepped closer to him, touched his back, and whispered, "Tell me, Pa. Please."

Slowly, he turned around and pulled her into a hug, and she clung to him with all her might. Instantly, she felt the security, the protection, the love he'd offered her all her life. For a moment the secrets didn't seem so important. But she couldn't ignore the desperation, the almost fearful urgency, with which he held her.

"There's nothin' to tell," he said finally. "Nothin' at all. And the ring . . . it's just so expensive. I worry about you wearin' it out in public. You don't know how valuable it is. Somebody could hurt you to steal it."

As if the explanation sounded better as he went along, he continued with it. "That's prob'ly why Willy looked funny. Prob'ly ain't often he sees a young girl like you wearin' such a expensive ring. I—I'll just keep it put up, where nobody can find it. Just in case . . . "

She backed away, releasing herself from his embrace, and searched his eyes for some sign of honesty. But he didn't look at her, and she knew there was a lie hidden in those words.

"Pa, the show was good, and there'll be others before they close down. It isn't too late for you to go. Maybe if he saw you, he'd remember. Maybe if—"

"I don't know him, Silena," he said, too loudly. "Can't you get it through your skull that sometimes I say things I don't mean? Sometimes I make up things."

"All right," she clipped, blinking back her tears. "All right."

She started through the store, to the kitchen, taking off her bonnet as she went. "I'll start supper now," she said. "It'll be ready soon."

But by the time supper was ready, Jake was out back again, nursing a new bottle of whiskey.

The sky was hazy tonight, and a brisk north wind chilled him, but not as much as the chill his fears caused within him. Willy had seen the ring, and there was no doubt in Jake's mind that he had recognized the emblem.

Throwing back a swig of liquor, Jake cursed himself for ever telling Silena about his friendship with Willy. But he had never dreamed that she'd have the chance to meet him, hidden away here in Hayton. That was his mistake, he supposed. He had never counted on her growing up so fast, developing such a mind of her own, and cultivating a curiosity which wouldn't be quelled with lies and evasions. He should have known the day of reckoning would come.

The backdoor of the house opened, letting out a

soft ray of lamplight from within. He looked up to see Silena—so small, so pretty, so fragile—coming toward him. The thought of her fragility, her vulnerability, which she didn't even know she wore like a red cloak wrapped around her, frightened him to death.

"Pa?" she said in a tentative voice. "Supper's ready. Aren't you hungry?"

"Nope." He took another swig and turned his bleary eyes on her. "You done it, you know. You done it today."

"What, Pa? What did I do, besides make a fool out of myself with a star? I went to Omaha, had a good time, and nothing all that bad came out of it."

"You don't know," he slurred. "You just don't know. There are things. . . ."

His eyes seemed to haze over with thought, and he stared into space. She would have given everything she owned to see what he saw for just a few seconds. "What things, Pa?" she asked, kneeling down beside him.

His eyes took on a look of pain and distress, and with a shaky hand, he reached up to touch her hair, which now fell around her shoulders in soft flaxen tendrils. "People want you . . . besides me," he said. "People who would hurt you."

"What people?"

He took another drink, felt it burn through his stomach, then settle warmly, numbly, in the pit of his stomach. "There are things you don't know," he said as his eyelids grew as heavy as his heart. "Dangerous. You just don't know. . . ."

His eyes closed, and she shook him, desperately trying to wake him. "Pa, what? Tell me."

"Go on in, girl," he slurred, wishing he hadn't said as much as he had. "Tired."

"Pa, what were you saying?"

"Go on," he said again.

He hung his head, and Silena got to her feet and stared down at him, lying drunk and incoherent against the tree, still clutching that whiskey bottle in his hand.

Angry tears rose to her eyes. Leaving him there, she stormed inside, went to his bed, and pulled out the box where he'd always hidden the ring before. It was gone, and she knew he had found a better hiding place for it. A place where even she could never find it.

Angrily brushing her tears away, she went to the torn Bible and opened it to the note from her mother. *No matter what, I'll always love you.* No matter what.

There were no more answers today than there had been yesterday, she thought miserably. Only more questions. And more ghosts in her father's eyes.

She undressed and brushed her teeth with castile soap, then washed out her brush in the basin of water in her room. Taking the basin outside, she dumped the water on the dirt and made her final trip of the night to the outhouse. Jake still slept against the tree, that bottle of whiskey balanced on his stomach.

Jake didn't like for her to come out here alone at night, she reflected as she closed herself in the small building. Not since she'd encountered a rattlesnake that had come too close to biting her. Ever since, he had insisted on checking the outhouse thoroughly before she used it. Beyond that, he had put in an order for the first water closet in the town so that Silena's life would be easier. It hadn't arrived yet, but Silena looked forward to the day it did.

When she had finished preparing for bed, Silena sat down on her bed and, closing her eyes, tried to give in to her fatigue and relax, but all she kept seeing was

Willy's eyes as he'd looked at the ring, and Jake's eyes when she'd told him.

Something important was being kept from her, she thought, but it wasn't in her power to find out what. At least not yet. But the time would come soon enough. She'd just have to wait, and listen, and seek. . . .

She heard a knock at the door to the storefront. Quickly pulling on her robe and lighting a lamp, she made her way through the mercantile. Through the glass, she saw Margaret.

"Margaret!" she said, opening the door. "What are you doing here? It's late!"

"I just wanted to see if you were all right," Margaret said, coming inside. "Your pa looked so mad, and I didn't want to think he'd hurt you or somethin'."

"Hurt me? My pa would never raise a hand to me, Margaret. I'm just fine."

She started back through the store and led Margaret into the house. "Do you want some tea? I could put a pot on."

"No, that's okay," Margaret said, still keeping her voice low and looking around. "Where is he, anyway? Your pa, I mean."

"Out back," Silena said, putting on the kettle anyway. "He always goes out back when he's mad at me. Was your ma mad?"

Margaret laughed, but the sound held little mirth. "My ma? She didn't even know we were gone."

Silena turned back and noted the girl's pale face. Her heart swelled, for she knew how Margaret's mother's indifference affected her. It was the common link between them—the absent mother, the inability to understand, the injustice of it all. It hurt them both equally, though Silena had to admit that Margaret's case was harder. Nell's profession had made an outcast of Margaret as well, for the people of the town would never see her as anything but the daughter of the town whore.

"So did you and Hitch have a lot to talk about ridin' back today?" she asked.

"Didn't you hear?"

Silena shook her head. "Caleb about talked my ear off, and with that and the sound of the wagon creaking, and the horses and the wind, not to mention my concentrating on how uncomfortable it was back there . . ."

"You coulda come up. I woulda traded places."

"No," Silena said, taking the kettle off of the stove and pouring the boiling water into the teapot. "I wanted you up there with Hitch. Something tells me you two are good for each other."

"Wish somethin' would tell him," Margaret said. "He spent the whole time rantin' and ravin' about you. Said he couldn't believe you kept cavortin' with that Hawkins fella, and that you didn't have no business goin' in Wild Willy's tent like some harlot."

Silena flung around. "Harlot? He called me a harlot?"

"I told him you didn't mean to act like a harlot, that you just wanted to meet him so bad."

Silena caught her breath. "You think I acted like a harlot?"

"No, Silena," Margaret said with a genuine smile. "It was wonderful. That fella whiskin' you up on his horse like that, and takin' you backstage, and showin' you to the star of the show . . . I admire, you Silena. I wouldn'ta had the guts."

Silena sank down onto her chair and poured the tea into two cups. "Oh, Margaret. It wasn't a question of guts. It was a question of desperation."

"But things like that happen to you, Silena. Nobody never sweeps me off my feet. Nobody never cares if I cavort or flirt or act like a harlot. That's what they expect of me."

Silena slammed her hand down on the mahogany table top. "I did not act like a harlot! Just because Hitch Calhoun said it doesn't make it true. I was a perfect lady, *despite* Willy's advances—"

"He made advances?" Margaret said with a gasp. "What did he do? What did *you* do?"

"Nothing," Silena said, wishing she'd never mentioned it. "As soon as I told him why I wanted to meet him, he let up."

"Was Hitch right, Silena? About him not knowing your pa?"

"No, he wasn't right," Silena said, her voice falling flat. "Hitch doesn't know everything."

"Then why were you so quiet coming home?"

Silena stood up and went to the stove. "Because I was thinking about my pa, that's why. Dreading coming home."

"Yeah, I know." Margaret pulled up out of her chair. "I guess I better be goin'. I'm tired, and Caleb's prob'ly wonderin' where I am."

"Yeah. Thanks for coming to see about me."

She followed Margaret back through the store, unlocked the front door, and stepped out front with her. The night was dark, with only a few darkened clouds visible in the sky, and the wind was cool and brisk as it swept across the plain. Down at the corner, the music of the saloon piano could be heard faintly, and outside it stood two or three clusters of men in loud conversation.

Margaret turned back to her, lingering before mounting her mule. "You think Hitch'll ever like me, Silena?"

Silena smiled. "I think so. Just don't give up."

"But I ain't like you," Margaret said. "I didn't go to Miss Belle's school like you did. I don't know the proper ways to do things, the proper way to act. Hitch sees that, and he compares me to you. I feel so, so dumb and ugly when I'm with him."

Silena took Margaret's hand and squeezed. "Those are things that can be learned easy enough, Margaret. You just need somebody to teach you, like I had. I can teach you in no time. Besides, Miss Caldonia has taken you under her wing. She says you have a real talent for dyeing threads and fabrics. She wouldn't let anyone else do that for her. Me, I can't do anything except stock shelves and count money. If you can learn all that, you can learn how to act like a lady."

"Really? You think?"

"I know," Silena said. "If my pa hadn't sent me to Miss Belle's, I wouldn't know how to hold my teacup or how to fix my hair, either. It's just something that needs to be taught. And one of the first lessons is that young ladies shouldn't be out this late alone."

Margaret giggled. "They probably shouldn't sneak out before dawn and leave town, either."

Silena smiled. "No, you're right. I guess no amount of learning is guaranteed to stick. I abide by the manners and rules that work for me, but the ones that don't, well, I just ignore them."

"Well, whatever you teach me, I won't ignore," Margaret promised. She was reaching for her old mare's reins, when down the street the door to the saloon crashed open and two men fell out, wrestling and kicking and cursing. A few others spilled out behind them, and Silena saw Nell, Margaret's mother, run toward the men to stop the fight.

"Damn you, Seth, stop it. I told you I'd go with you, didn't I?"

Two stronger men pulled the fighters apart, and the one Nell addressed wiped a smear of blood across his face. "When I'm here, she's mine!" he shouted to the still-struggling cowboy across from him.

"She ain't got your name tattooed on her ass, and I don't see no weddin' ring on her finger."

Nell went to Seth and began blotting the blood with her fingertips.

"Oh, stop it. Both of you. J.D., I told you to come back tomorrow night, and I'll be here. I don't like folks fightin' over me like a coupla dogs."

Margaret gave Silena a meaningful look, as if to say that her mother actually thrived on having men fight over her, but she didn't say anything. They watched as Nell expertly appeased both men, then escorted one of them back into the saloon, probably to one of the upstairs rooms, as the other man hobbled off.

"Mama's always been real pretty," Margaret whispered before getting back on her horse.

"Yeah," Silena said, not knowing what else to say.

"Men always fight over her. They really like her."

Silena thought of telling Margaret that the kind of popularity her mother had was not something to be coveted, but she suspected the girl already knew.

"You know, I don't think Mama ever set out to be a . . . a saloon girl," Margaret said quietly, still gazing in the direction her mother had disappeared. "Men just liked her. Lots of them. And I reckon she liked them, too."

Silena was quiet as Margaret climbed up on her horse, and finally she whispered, "Be careful, Margaret. Don't go past the saloon. Go the back way, and don't stop for anything. And for heaven's sake, next time you have to come out at night, make Caleb come with you. Drunk men love pretty young girls. Even better than your mother."

"I know," Margaret said, waving a hand as she kicked her horse and disappeared around the bank.

Silena went back in and slipped out of her robe. Lying down, she stared at the ceiling. Margaret's words played through her mind, and unsummoned, Willy's fleeted through her mind, as well. *Was your ma a whore?*

Tears filled her eyes as she realized that anything was possible. The truth was, there were still too many secrets, secrets she was determined to understand.

And the longer those secrets were kept from her, the worse she would imagine them to be.

Willy's aim at the spittoon was far more accurate than his aim with a gun, Sam mused as he sat across from his father in the Omaha saloon Wheeler's Point. He watched his father wipe the back of his hand across his mouth and take another swig of his whiskey. Across from them, Caldwell Jones, the drummer who'd known his father since their cavalry days, tossed down a pair of kings.

"Gall dang it, Caldwell," Willy said, spitting again. "I never shoulda sat down with you."

"I always could outplay you," Caldwell said around the cigar in his dry lips. "I remember back in Kansas, that time we was playin' with them scouts from Wyoming. You remember that? You was gettin' to be a high roller, and you made a bet bigger than you was."

Willy threw back his head and laughed. "And Jim McCosky was there, and he helped bail me out when I was just gettin' ready to run for it."

"D'you ever pay 'im back?" Caldwell asked.

Willy's grin faded. "Never got the chance. He died just a year later."

Sam finished off his glass and leaned his elbows on the table. "McCosky. Is that the one we were talking about the other day, Willy? The one that girl Silena was talking about?"

Willy's eyes hazed over, as they had done several times since that day. "Nope. That was a fella named Rivers, remember? I didn't know him." He turned to Caldwell with a lecherous grin. "You shoulda seen her, Caldwell. Come right into my tent, prettiest little gal you ever saw. Practically plopped down on my lap."

Sam felt his backbone stiffening as he listened to his father's lies, and unlike the other times he'd sat quiet as his father lied through his teeth about his conquests of fans, he grabbed up the cards and began stacking them. "She didn't sit on your lap, Willy. She said no. She was a lady."

"He knows 'cause he tried her before he brought her to me," Willy explained to Caldwell. "But I don't think he had much luck, 'cause he's been in a foul mood ever since."

"I'm not in a foul mood," Sam said through his teeth. "She was a lady, and she came to your tent to ask you about her pa. You saw the ring, and you admitted it looked familiar—"

"You done lost me," Caldwell said, taking a swig of his drink. "What ring?"

Willy's expression clouded over again. "Nothin'. Just . . . she mentioned a near-drownin' incident back when I was a boy. Jim McCosky was there, nobody else knew. And then she had on this ring that looked like the insignia me and Jim had for that ranch we started. . . . But her name was Rivers."

"Couldn't be Jim," Caldwell said, waving to the bartender for another refill. "Jim's dead."

"I know that," Willy said. "It was just sorta odd, her askin' about things Jim did, and wearin' that ring."

Sam waited for the bartender to bring them their drinks and turned his frown on Caldwell, who was watching a red-haired Terpsichore dancing with a wrangler. "Hey, Caldwell. What do you remember about McCosky's death?"

"Not much," Caldwell said. "Me and Jim never knew each other that well. All I know's what I heard."

"What was that?"

"That McCosky kidnapped that cavalry colonel's baby. Tried to get ransom—"

"Naw, that can't be true," Willy cut in, waving off the man's words. "I heard that story, too, but it's hogwash. McCosky didn't have a dishonest bone in his body, and he sure as hell wouldn't go around kidnappin' babies."

"Just the same, that's what the story was. They said the Colonel had killed some Injuns McCosky traded with, and he did it to get revenge."

"I knew McCosky all his life," Willy said, irritated, "and he never met a Injun he liked. He sure as hell wouldn't kidnap nobody's baby over a Injun. I can say that for sure."

"A lot of people said it was so," Caldwell argued. "And McCosky and the baby both drowned in the Platte River."

Sam frowned down at his glass, trying to put the pieces together. "How long ago was that?"

"Back in Seventy-two or Seventy-three, wasn't it, Willy?"

"Seventy-three," Willy confirmed, his face as sober as Sam had seen it in weeks, despite the amount he'd had to drink tonight. "I'll never forget it. I was ridin' in the cavalry when I got word."

"Seventeen years ago," Sam muttered, staring at Caldwell. "Tell me something. The baby . . . was it a boy or a girl?"

"Hell, I don't know. You, Willy?"

"Never did think to ask," Willy said. "Why?"

Sam leaned back in his chair and stared at the mirror over the bar, thinking. "I don't know. It's just . . . that's about how old that girl was. About seventeen."

"You don't think . . .?"

Sam looked at his father, his eyes more full of questions than assumptions, and Willy shook his head. "Naw. That gal couldn't have been the baby. That's too farfetched. McCosky wouldn't kidnap some baby and hide out til she was grown. That's crazy."

Sam couldn't deny the madness of the idea, and he had to wonder if his imagination hadn't taken flight on the wings of all the alcohol he'd put away himself tonight. "Yeah, I guess."

Caldwell didn't let it go that easily, though. Leaning forward, he frowned, the deep, dirty lines of his face making him look somber. "You know, if that was the baby, and the Colonel found out she was alive, he'd prob'ly offer a fortune to get her back."

Sam looked up at the avaricious man who made his living bargaining for wares. "We're speculating, Caldwell. Don't go running off your mouth where you could start trouble, all right? This girl didn't do anything wrong."

"Colonel Rafferty's a rich man," Caldwell said, his eyes still brightening at the ideas forming in his mind. "A real rich man. Mean son of a bitch, but that never bothered me much."

"Mean son of a bitch is right," Willy said. "Every time I heard those stories about Jim, I wondered why he didn't just kill the bastard if he was aimin' to get revenge. Hell of a lot more trouble to steal a baby. None of it ever made no sense."

Caldwell threw back his drink and scraped his chair back. "Well, if you two are done talkin' about ghosts risen from the dead, I'm goin' to grab me a little redhead and do me some dancin'."

Willy laughed as his friend left the table, grabbed one of the girls standing at the bar, and began whirling her around. Sam didn't watch, for he was remembering the sadness in Silena's eyes, and hoping to God that his questions about her hadn't brought more trouble into her life.

Trouble was a common occurrence on Saturdays at Rivers's Mercantile. It was the day when farmers and ranchers from far outside of Hayton came to town to make their purchases. There was no pause in her work on Saturdays, Silena knew, but still the steady stream of customers expected her to smile, as she always did, stop for small talk, and direct them to the purchases they considered buying but needed to be talked into.

Sometimes on Saturdays as well, Margaret brought her home-dyed cloth and threads to sell in the store. She often stayed to help out when so much had to be done that confusion and chaos abounded, but today Silena found that Margaret's "help" slowed her down, for she couldn't stop talking about Hitch and his lack of attention to her, and the ideas she had for catching his eye.

"You can't be so obvious," Silena said in a quiet voice as she wrapped a bolt of cloth and set it back on the table. "You need to just be yourself."

Margaret shrugged. "Ma says when a gal likes a man, she oughta just go up to him and let him know it."

Silena turned back to Margaret and, smiling sadly, said, "Do you really want to attract men the way your ma does, Margaret?"

"Well . . . no. But I don't know no other way."

"It's not a trick, Margaret. It's just something that happens."

"But it won't happen," Margaret argued, "as long as Hitch is sweet on you. Can't you try to be a little uglier around him, or not fix your hair so pretty, or something?"

Silena grinned and went back around the counter to straighten the corset stays that a customer had just rifled through. "Margaret, Hitch will notice you soon enough. I promise. We just need to make a few adjustments."

The door opened, letting in a chilly breeze, and Silena turned and saw three ruddy, dirty cowboys striding into the store. Because it wasn't unusual for traveling parties to stop through Hayton on their way to Omaha, she closed the glass door and smiled helpfully at them.

One of the men ambled toward her, the heels of his boots shaking the planks of the floor as his spurs jingled. His hair was as dirty as the chaps he wore, and his face was ruddy and filthy. A three-day-old beard shaded his jaw, and Silena could see that one of his teeth was rotted as he offered her a false smile that made her shiver.

"May I help you, gentlemen?" she asked.

"Maybe," the man said. He looked around him, to the few other shoppers in the store, then winked at his companions and gestured for them to join him. "We're lookin' for somebody."

"Oh? I can probably help you then. I know everybody in Hayton."

"Jim McCosky."

Silena didn't recognize the name. She looked over at Margaret, who seemed to have shrunk back against the counter. "I don't know a McCosky. Do you, Margaret?"

Margaret's wide eyes were on the other two men, who were closing in. Two women, browsing through the button drawers, looked up and, intimidated, quickly abandoned their shopping and pushed out of the store.

"Uh . . ." Margaret stopped, cleared her throat. "McCosky? No, nobody here named McCosky."

"Jim McCosky," the first man said. "We were told he owns this store. That him and his daughter run the place."

Silena breathed a half laugh. "Well, that's impossible. My father owns this store. His name's Jake Rivers, not Jim McCosky."

A slow, frightening smile inched across the man's face. He turned to the other two men and gave them a nod. "Well, now, that sounds mighty coincidental to me. Don't it to you, fellas?"

"They told us he might be usin' another name," one of the other cowboys said around a piece of straw in his mouth. "Let's see now. What was it they said he called hisself?"

The first man made great ceremony of taking off his hat and scratching his greasy head, pretending to think. "You know, Buck, I do believe it was Rivers. How 'bout that?"

Silena frowned and faced the man squarely. "I don't know who you are or what you want," she said, "but my pa isn't 'using' another name. That's his real name, and if you don't believe me—"

"Where is he?" the man cut in.

"He took some feed over to the Miller farm. He'll be back shortly, but . . ."

The last of the customers quickly scurried out of the store. Silena swallowed and inched closer to Margaret.

"Well, now. Ain't this interestin'?" the rotten-toothed man asked. "Looks like we're all alone here, boys. All alone with these two pretty young ladies."

Silena began to back away, but the man started toward her. The other two were now close behind him.

"I have a gun," she said. "Don't you come near me."

"Where's your gun?" the man asked, grabbing her arm and jerking her against him. He touched her hip, and she tried to pull away. "Is it here?"

"Let go of me!" she shouted.

Margaret was inching toward the door, but when she broke into a run, one of the other men started after her. "Silena!" Margaret cried.

The rotten-toothed man tightened his grip on Silena and pushed her against a counter, knocking over and breaking a bottle of kerosene. The smell floated up over the air, mingling with the scent of whiskey and days-old sweat. He groped at the top buttons of her shirtwaist, tore it open, and shoved his grimy hand inside. "Is it in here, honey? You got your gun hid in here?"

Silena reached behind her. Grabbing what was left of the broken bottle, she shoved it in his face. "Let go of me right now!"

She heard Margaret scream in the corner, and a hand plow propped near the door fell crashing to the ground.

"Can't go yet, honey," the man said. "We gotta wait for your pa to come back. But meanwhile, a man's gotta make use of his time."

He laughed harshly, and Silena shoved the bottle out farther. Its edge cut into her thumb, drawing blood, but she didn't feel it.

"Get away from me or I'll cut that smile off of your face," she said through her teeth. "I swear, I will."

But the man only laughed again. Summoning all her strength, Silena closed her eyes and grazed the glass across one of his stubbly cheeks. Blood instantly welled up, and the man fell back. Fire filled his eyes, and he knocked the glass from her hand.

She screamed as he threw her against a corner of the counter, where her back hit and scraped as she slid to the floor. He was on her instantly, and as she struggled with all her might she could hear Margaret doing the same across the store.

Suddenly a gunshot deafened them. The man attacking Silena went stiff, his weight anchoring her. Screaming again, she slid out from under him, and saw the blood oozing from his back.

Another shot rang out, and she turned and saw her father at the door, face-to-face with the man who'd been attacking Margaret. The third man was bent double in the corner, clutching the arm that Jake had hit with his second shot.

"I don't know who the hell you are, but by God, nobody messes with my daughter—"

"She ain't your daughter!" the wrangler with the gun said. "We know who you are, McCosky, and the Colonel sent us."

Silena had gotten to her feet and was inching toward Margaret, still trembling on the floor. She turned her confused, terrified eyes on her father. His face was white, and she saw the gun trembling in his hand.

"I don't know who you're talkin' about," he said. "But if you don't drop that gun by the count o' three, I'm gonna blow your brains clear to Omaha."

The one with the wounded arm reached for his gun,

and Jake shot again, the bullet making him draw back, abandoning the gun. "Let's go, Buck. This ain't that important."

The man called Buck continued to stare Jake down, and Jake's grip on his pistol grew steadier. "One . . . Silena, you and Margaret get on out o' here."

Silena grabbed the shaking girl, and they started to inch toward the front door. "Pa . . ."

"Two," Jake said, clicking the hammer back. "Now, Silena."

Silena reached the door and pulled it open. Margaret dashed out, but Silena hung back. "Pa, please be—"

"Three!" A gunshot cracked with the word, and Silena ran as fast as she could, as far as she could, down the wide stretch of dirt that made up the main road. More gunshots exploded in the store, and she heard crashing and cursing. One of the men hobbled out to his horse, threw a bloody leg over it, and started a mad ride out of town.

Silena raced to the sheriff's office, gasping for breath. Stumbling in, she shouted, "Sheriff! Help!"

Miss Mattie Aberson, the little woman who ran the post office and occasionally cleaned the sheriff's office, appeared with a broom from around the corner. "Did I hear shootin'?"

"Where's the sheriff?" Silena cried.

"Next door cuttin' the mayor's hair," the woman said. "Silena!"

Silena ran back out of the office as another gunshot sounded from her father's store. Covering her face with her hands, she screamed as the other cowboy ran out, still clutching his wounded arm and firing behind him. Mounting his horse, he galloped away as fast as he could.

Behind her, the sheriff ran up with a pair of scissors in his hand. "What the hell is goin' on over there?"

Silena couldn't seem to say a word. Instead, she started running, again back toward the store, back to her father, back to the blood and death that would confront her there.

Jake Rivers lay twisted on the floor in a pool of blood, but he still clutched the gun in his hand.

7

By the time Silena had stopped screaming, the sheriff had abandoned his scissors, loaded his pistol, and made his way, much too cautiously, to the doorway of the mercantile. With the barber's cape still thrown around his shoulders, the mayor—his hair trimmed neatly on one side and still shaggy on the other—peered in behind the sheriff.

"What the hell—"

"*Do* something!" Silena shouted, falling to her knees and pulling her father's head up onto her lap. "Go after them! Get Miss Caldonia! Wire for a doctor! Hurry!"

The sheriff stood still for a moment, taking in the sight of the dead man across the room, and Jake Rivers bleeding on his daughter's lap.

"I'll get Caldonia," the mayor shouted, taking control. "She'll know what to do. Matt, you get on your horse and get after them outlaws."

"But I don't have a posse," the sheriff argued. "I don't have a—"

"Please, hurry!" Silena screamed. "He's dying!"

She tried to lift her father, but he was too heavy. Her dress stuck to her legs where the blood had soaked her, and she felt life bleeding out of him with every moment that passed. A few other men who had run up the street pushed in past the dumbfounded sheriff and lifted Jake, who began to stir as he was moved.

A scream tore from the doorway. Silena, still shaking, looked up to see Margaret, tattered and scratched. "Is he . . . is he dead?" she quavered.

"No," Silena said quickly, not letting go of her father's head as the men carried him through the door. "He's fine. He'll be just fine."

A crowd had begun to form outside the store, and Hitch pushed through. "Silena! What happened? Are you all right?"

Silena shook her head as he started to reach for her. "Help Margaret, Hitch. She might be hurt, and she's had a scare."

He turned and saw the battered girl standing in the doorway, her clothes torn and bloody scratches on her neck and face. "You all right, Margaret? You need to see Miss Caldonia, too?"

Silena didn't turn to see what Margaret said. All she knew was that her father's blood left a dark trail as they carried him up the steps to the door of the closest thing they had to a doctor in town.

Jake came to as the two men carrying him dropped him a little too roughly on the hard bed in Miss Caldonia's guest room. In a hazy blur of clarity, he told himself that as soon as he had the chance, he would see to it that Hayton got itself a bona fide doctor. Miss Caldonia was good for croup and childbirth, but he doubted she'd had much experience patching up a man who'd just confronted the bullets from the ghosts of his past.

But Caldonia was all he had, and he reckoned he'd accept anything she could do to relieve the pain crushing him. Besides, her daddy had been a doctor back east, and most of the people of Hayton figured that had given her more of an apprenticeship than most modern doctors could boast. Caldonia claimed to have "read" enough medicine to hold her own with any school-educated physician, and since the nearest real doctor was as far away as Omaha, she was good enough for most emergencies.

The truth was that the town of Hayton was lucky to have anybody who knew medicine at all, considering that most of the residents here were people who'd gotten here by accident and never had the means or the intelligence to move on. It wasn't exactly a lucrative place for a doctor to practice. Most of Caldonia's medical care was paid for in eggs or chickens, a nice hot Sunday meal, a jug of cider, or a bushel of corn.

Through the hazy stream of his fragmented thoughts, Jake heard weeping. Cracking open his eyes, he saw Silena standing over him, grieving as though he was ready to be lowered into his grave.

"Stop that cryin', girl," he grumbled. "I ain't dead yet." He looked up at her, trying not to wince at the pain shooting down his leg and burning on his shoulder. "You all right?"

"Me?" Silena wiped her tears away with a trembling hand and nodded. Her face was the ashen color of panic, and her clothes were torn open, revealing the chemise beneath it. She hadn't yet noticed that she wasn't decent. "I'm fine. But look at you. They shot you, Pa!"

"I been shot before, didn't kill me. Get Caldonia to give you somethin' to put on over that dress before one o' these boys gets the wrong idea."

Silena glanced down at her dress and realized that it was still torn open. Clutching it around her, she looked up, noting the way the two other men averted their eyes.

"Where is Caldonia?" she asked sharply. "Pa's losing a lot of blood."

"She was out at the Hutchins place, helping Amanda put together her weddin' dress. The mayor went after her. They'll be here shortly."

"Damn dressmaker doctor. She'll let a man bleed to death in the name of straight seams," Jake muttered.

Judd, one of the men who'd brought him in, grinned. "Ain't like she expected a gunfight today, Jake."

"Nobody did." Jake winced at the pain and looked over at the other man, who was watching him helplessly. "Carlson, get over to the saloon and get me a bottle of rye, will ya?"

"You bet, Jake. I'll be right back."

Jake watched him go, then forced himself to talk again. "Silena, get my knife outta my pocket there, and cut my shirt and pants around the wounds." His voice grew gruffer, but weaker, as he spoke.

"We need to put some pressure on them wounds," Judd said. "It'll stop the bleedin'."

"Glad to hear you say that," Jake muttered weakly. "For a minute I thought you might just stand there with your thumb up your ass while I bleed to death."

Silena pulled out his knife and, still trembling, cut open his pants leg and peeled the cloth off of his wound. "This one's in the knee, Pa."

"Got one in the shoulder, too," Jake muttered. Perspiration broke out over his forehead as Judd found some bandages, grabbed his arm, and pressed the compress into the open wound.

"Here, Silena," he said, nodding toward the other bandages he'd found. "You do the knee."

Fresh tears spilled from Silena's eyes as she pressed the wound with all her strength, but the blood soaked the bandages, seeped through her fingers, and dripped into the mattress in minutes.

The door was flung open and Carlson came back in with a jug of whiskey. "Here you go, Jake," he said. "Take a swig of this, and we'll have the pain dulled in no time."

"We can't stop the bleeding!" Silena cried.

"Caldonia's on her way," Carlson said. "I seen the wagon comin' over the hill."

Jake just nodded painfully and took one deep swig of whiskey, then another.

True to Carlson's words, Caldonia was there moments later, taking control the second she walked in. Miss Caldonia was a small, plump woman who'd been widowed for years. Most folks of the town joked that her husband had died of exhaustion from watching his wife work, for Caldonia's schedule would have worn out even the most robust man in town. And when Miss Caldonia started barking orders like a cavalry captain, well, no one around her dared to argue.

"Well, well," she said after she had dug the bullets out of Jake and had covered the wounds with a mixture of tea dust and tanned leather scrapings. "This seems right familiar. Brings back a few memories, it does."

From his drunken stupor, Jake moaned.

"What do you mean?" Silena asked. "Has my pa been shot before?"

"Didn't he ever tell ya how we met?" Caldonia asked

as she bound the wounds. "Come to me with a gunshot in his wrist. You was a tiny little thing, just born."

"Who shot him?" Silena asked.

"Injuns," the woman said. "'Course the wrist healed, but this leg looks right bad. Bone's shattered. He might lose it."

Silena wiped her father's brow and looked down at him. If he'd heard, he was too drunk to care. "What about the shoulder?"

"Flesh wound," she said. "It'll heal all right, long as infection don't set in. He'll be in bed for a while. Might be best if he stays here where I can watch him. 'Course, if you think those outlaws'll be back . . ."

Silena looked up at the woman, her own face tight with fear. "They were asking for someone else. Somebody named Jim McCosky. They said that was pa's real name."

Caldonia looked up at her, frowning. "I've known Jake seventeen years. I never knowed him to go by any other name. Did you tell them that?"

"Yes, but they had been told that he ran the store here." She paused and tried to get past the feeling of nausea in her stomach. "What if they do come back, Miss Caldonia? He killed one of 'em. Injured another. And they seemed bound and determined to get him. They could come back now that he's weak and finish him off."

Miss Caldonia took a deep, long breath and gave Judd and Carlson a questioning look. "You got a point there," she told Silena after a moment. "Your pa needs rest and quiet. And if he needs to be hid, well, I guess we'll find him a place to hide."

"But where?" Silena asked. "The town's so small. They could find him anywhere if they really looked."

"How 'bout Hitch's ranch? His daddy and most of their boys are gone to Kansas to buy livestock, so there'd be room for him."

"And Hitch could help protect him if anyone came looking," Silena said, thinking aloud. "And I could stay there some."

"We'll keep it secret, though," Miss Caldonia said, turning stern eyes to the two men, "because we don't know who might talk once they have a gun pointed to their head. Everybody agree?"

Judd nodded his head, and Carlson muttered, "Yes, ma'am."

"We'll move him tonight in my wagon," Caldonia went on. "You stay here with your pa for now, Silena, and I'll ride out and clear it with Hitch and his mama."

Silena followed Miss Caldonia and the two men to the door, bolted it behind them, then went back in to her father. He seemed to be half-asleep, but then his eyes slitted open. "Pa," she whispered, "Pa? Did you know those men?"

"Colonel," Jake slurred, closing his eyes again. "Colonel."

"Colonel?" she asked. "One of them was a colonel?"

"It's you they want," he said, his words blending together. "You gotta hide."

"Me? They don't want me, Pa. It was all a mistake. They wanted somebody else. Jim McCosky. They musta gotten us mixed up with him."

"Hide, Silena," he whispered. "Hide, for God's sake. They'll tell him . . . now that they found me . . . he'll send 'em back . . . or come from Kansas hisself. . . ." His eyes closed, and Silena shook him.

"Pa! What do you mean, now that they found you? They weren't looking for you. It was somebody else! Pa!"

He lay unconscious, in a drink-induced, wound-weary sleep, and Silena knew that he wouldn't tell her more. Not now, anyway.

Her hands still hadn't stopped trembling. Hugging herself, she sat down next to her father and listened with all her might for the sound of horses galloping, guns shooting, women screaming, or outlaws cursing. But the town was dreadfully still, and nothing seemed to stir.

It was quietest before a storm, Silena knew, and mentally, she tried to prepare herself for what was to come. But it wasn't easy when she hadn't a clue where this nightmare had been born.

The one-room sod house where Margaret and Caleb lived with their mother—when she bothered to come home—never seemed quite clean, though Margaret managed to keep it uncluttered and neat. The dirt floor was the culprit, for no amount of sweeping ever rid the room of its dirt smell or the black dust that seemed to soil everything.

Some things weren't meant to stay clean, Margaret had theorized long ago. And today she felt like one of those things.

She led Hitch into the house and avoided meeting his eyes, for she knew that he wondered just how far the outlaws' attack on her had gone. He closed the door behind them and stared at her, quietly assessing the damage.

Her hand gravitated to the bruises on her legs, which were growing more and more tender, and she tried not to limp as she went to her bed to sit down.

"Are you sure you're all right?" Hitch asked. "I could fetch your ma . . . or Caleb."

"No." She felt tears coming to her eyes and tried desperately to hold them back. "Ma's no doubt sleepin' in over at the saloon. And Caleb's out with his sheep. I'm okay." She stared mournfully at Hitch for a moment, then quickly drew her thoughts back. "Uh . . . could I get you somethin'? Some cider, or . . ."

Hitch cleared his throat and spoke softly. "I don't need nothin', Margaret. Why don't you just go change outta them torn clothes and relax? I'll stay for a minute."

She nodded, but made no move to go behind the curtain that was strung up to offer her privacy from Caleb when she dressed. Her eyes filled with tears suddenly, and she focused on the dirt floor. "Hitch . . . I'm not like my mama," she whispered. "I mean . . . I didn't want . . . "

Hitch's eyes were fully on her when she looked back up. "He hurt you, didn't he?"

She shook her head. "No, I'm fine. Really."

Hitch held her gaze for an eternity longer, and she knew that he saw right into her, to the ugliness the outlaw had planted there.

"Is there anything I can do?"

Margaret wiped her eyes and shook her head. "No. Really, I'm just fine."

Their eyes met and held for a long time, and Margaret felt a crackling tension in the room that was both terrifying and confusing. Finally, he spoke again.

"Silena looked a little roughed up, too. Did they . . .?"

Margaret's heart crashed, for even the small bit of sympathy she had garnered from him was fleeting. "I don't know. I think Jake came in time."

"That's good," he said.

Margaret stood up and started to go behind the blanket. Before disappearing behind it, she turned back to him.

"I ain't like my mama," she said again through trembling lips. "No matter what happened today, I ain't like her. Folks'll say I am."

"Not to me, they won't." Hitch slid his fingers into his front pockets.

She looked at him for another sad, lonely moment, wishing from her soul that he would take her in his arms, hold her, and make her believe what she needed for him to believe. But that wasn't about to happen.

Silently, she slipped behind the blanket and began to change her dress.

Hitch was still with Margaret when he heard the sound of horses outside, and Margaret jumped and seemed to wilt. Touching her arm and moving her protectively behind him, Hitch inched to the window to see who was there. Caleb and Nell were heading for the house, their faces stricken, and Margaret knew they had heard about the incident.

Caleb was the first inside the door. Tearing across the room, he took Margaret's shoulders. "What did they do to you?"

Margaret shook her head, unable to speak.

"Did they hurt you?" Caleb shouted. "Did they—"

"No, I'm fine," Margaret lied. Hitch caught Caleb's eye and, with a tiny shake of his head, indicated that Margaret wasn't telling everything.

"Jake came in in time."

"Thank God!" Nell cried, bursting in, still clad in a crimson saloon dress cut too low on bosoms that bounced when she walked. She wrenched her daughter out of

Caleb's arms and crushed her against her. "Honey, when I heard what happened . . ." She jerked Margaret back to look at her. "How many of them took you?"

Tears welled up in Margaret's eyes. She tried to step out of her mother's smothering embrace and shot Hitch a self-conscious look. "None. I'm fine, Mama. They didn't do anything."

Caleb looked around and saw her soiled, bloody dress lying on the bed. Snatching it up, he wheeled around. "Did they do *this?*"

Margaret covered her face and nodded, and Caleb strode toward her.

"You've got a bruise," he said, his voice lowering slightly, though a tornado whirled behind each word. "Did they hit you?"

"I . . . I fell . . . and I hit the table."

"He knocked you down?" Caleb shouted.

Margaret's face twisted in shame. "Oh, Caleb. Please don't look at me like that! Jake came in and shot him—"

"Is he dead?" Caleb demanded.

"No. He hit him in the arm, but he got away."

Caleb swung around and took down his rifle from the place where it hung on the wall. Without slowing his step, he started for the door.

"Caleb, where the hell are you going?" Nell demanded.

"To find that bastard and kill him!"

"No!" Hitch stopped him. "Caleb, you cain't go off blind into the night after him. The bald truth is that he'll prob'ly be back. You'll get your chance then."

"Why do you think they'll be back?" Nell asked, turning her heavily painted eyes on him.

"Because Jake killed one o' their men, and they're likely mad. And the rumor in town is that they're after somethin' specific. Somethin' to do with Jake." He turned back to Caleb, still standing at the door, his face as red and raging as Hitch had ever seen it.

"I have to get home now. But Margaret needs you here, Caleb. I'll let you know if anything happens."

"I won't wait long," Caleb said. "Those bastards have an appointment with their destiny, and I aim to be it."

"Don't worry, Caleb," Hitch said. "We'll need everybody we can get if they come back. You won't be left out."

The night was long for Silena, as Jake's fever deepened with the infection that had set into his leg, keeping him in a delirium that only grew worse by the first light. She hadn't slept at all, except for a few winks, sitting in the chair beside the bed that Hitch's mother had arranged for Jake in the attic. Hitch had been in and out all night, catering to Silena like she was royalty lighting in his home, but the attention only drained her more.

It was quiet out here at the ranch, too quiet. But Hitch had said the same was true in town. The saloon had been empty last night, he said, and the piano player had chosen to stay in his room. Even Nell had opted to take the night off, for the men in town had other things on their minds. Silena hadn't been back to the store since the gunfight, but Hitch had assured her that he had locked it up for her, adding that he would help her clean it up as soon as she was ready.

She couldn't face the idea of her father's store being shot up, of jars broken and barrels turned over, of blood coating the plank floor. But someone would have to take care of things there, and it didn't look like it was going to be Jake.

She had to be strong, she told herself, whether she

wanted to or not. But sometimes strength was a curse, for it forced people to do things they didn't want to do. It had forced Jake, yesterday, to kill a man. It had forced him to stop two bullets at the risk of his own life. It had forced him to endure what must have been ungodly pain, until he had quietly slipped out of consciousness.

Now it was her turn to be strong.

She heard a horse galloping toward the house, and her stomach knotted. Terror shivered through her, and she went to the window.

Caleb was tearing toward them in a cloud of dust, and Hitch ran out to meet him, his mother close on his heels. She saw Caleb untie his rifle from his horse's saddle, and they both disappeared into the house.

There was news. Something was happening in town. She stepped back from the window and waited as she heard Hitch's footsteps bounding up the steps to the attic.

"They're back," he said, breathless.

Silena's hand flew to her mouth. "Oh, my God. What are we going to do? What if they come here?"

She ran back to the window and peered out, but the town was too far away to see from here.

"They might, Silena," Hitch said, setting comforting, but shaky hands on her shoulders.

She heard Caleb's steps and turned around. "Caleb, did you see how many there were?"

Caleb cocked his rifle and went to the window. His face was red from the brisk ride. "At least five of 'em, and they're shootin' up everythin' in sight, lookin' for Jake."

"Why?" Silena cried. "What do they want with him? It doesn't make sense!"

"Don't have to make sense," Hitch said.

Caleb was busy loading three guns as he spoke rapidly. "I'm pretty sure I saw the son of a bitch who attacked my sister," he said. "She said Jake hit him in the arm, and this one had a bandage on his arm. I'm gonna splatter his ass all the way to Wyoming if it's the last thing I do."

The calm vow silenced Silena and Hitch for a moment. Finally, Silena wiped the tears from her eyes. "Maybe . . . maybe they won't come this far. Maybe they won't find us."

"Well, if they do, I think we can hold 'em off," Hitch said.

"How?" Silena's question was racked with panic. "How can you hold off five hardened gunfighters bent on getting to my father? You're nineteen years old, and Caleb's only sixteen. I don't even have a gun—"

"We can do it," Hitch said, his face reddening with the challenge.

"Damn right, we can," Caleb added. "I have a personal stake in this now, and that bastard's gonna pay."

"No one has a greater stake in this than I do," she said. "Hitch, I need a gun."

Hitch gave her an incredulous look. "What?"

"Give me a gun. I can shoot a little."

"I ain't givin' you no gun, Silena. Just stay put—"

"I said to give me a gun! I can hold them off if they get this far."

Hitch's shoulders drooped. Sighing, he surrendered his rifle. "Look, Silena, they likely won't even come this far. Maybe the sheriff can take 'em before they head this way."

"The sheriff?" Silena cried. "He's a *barber*, Hitch! He knows how to handle a razor, but when it comes to protecting a town, we're lucky if his gun happens to be loaded. He's no help."

"Don't matter," Hitch argued. "We have a lot of capable men in this town."

"No, we don't," she said, lifting her chin as her anger rose, as if it were their own fault that the town wasn't better armed. "We have a bunch of farmers—half of them old as the hills—and women and little children. We're defenseless!"

Hitch looked nervously out the window, trying not to show his own fear. "All I can do is what I can do, Silena. It may not be good enough, but it's the best you got." He nodded to Caleb, who was looking out that window with murderous intent in his eyes.

"We need a plan," Caleb said. "Come on, Hitch. We got to make a plan before I go after 'em."

Silena watched, numb, as they went downstairs, leaving her alone in the attic with her father. A slow wave of horror washed over her. Blood was going to be shed. Maybe more of Jake's, maybe her own this time. And these two young men, so innocent for all their tough talk, would be thrown into a tempest of killing and bleeding, and no one even knew why.

No one except Jake.

What they needed right now were some real heroes. A couple of bona fide gunslingers who could scare the gang out of town, scare them so far that they'd never come back again. A couple of people like the stars she'd seen in the Wild West show.

An idea grew in her mind as she stood staring out the window, clutching the gun as if it was her last grip to life. The Wild West show. Heroes. Wild Willy. Sam Hawkins. She could ride there in a couple of hours, bring them back. . . .

Wild Willy had claimed he didn't know her pa, and she supposed he wouldn't feel any obligation to help him. But there had been something about their conversation that made her feel differently. The way Willy had looked at the ring . . . She turned back to Jake and studied him for a long time, wondering what lay beneath the facade she'd known all her life. What secrets? What horrible sins?

It could mean big trouble for us. It could open up a whole mess of trouble. . . .

And trouble had come, and now Jake lay feverish and wounded in a dusty attic, hidden from a band of outlaws determined to kill him.

Jim McCosky. Why had the outlaws said they were looking for Jim McCosky? Was it possible they really did know who they were after?.

Maybe she was the one who was confused.

She turned back to the window, and as a wind swept toward her from the town she thought she heard gunshots again. Panic swept over her, and she cocked the rifle.

Jim McCosky.

What was it they said he called hisself?

You know, Buck, I do believe it was Rivers.

Silena stared out the window for what felt like a long time, the rifle held ready and her thoughts whirling. Finally, when no more shots sounded, she went back to her father's bed, leaned over him, and touched his burning forehead. He had drifted in and out of consciousness all night, and occasionally the bleeding had resumed. The pain in his leg was probably the worst, she thought, and already she could see the red stripes starting to shoot up from the swelling around the bandage.

Jake stirred and muttered something incoherent, and she bent over to hear. But he fell still again. Taking a wet compress, she wiped his forehead.

"Pa?" she asked softly. "Those men, Pa. They were after Jim McCosky. Is that you?"

Her father moaned, and she knew it was futile.

Willy hadn't recognized the name Jake Rivers, but he'd recognized the ring, and the story about Fanny. Could it be that he hadn't recognized the name because Rivers *wasn't* her father's real name? Could it be that Jake Rivers really was Jim McCosky, and that they'd stayed hidden in this no-account little town for all these years because he was hiding from something?

If that was the case, she thought, then Wild Willy might recognize the name McCosky to be that of his old friend. Maybe he would want to help, if he knew someone was out to kill him. She knew that in her panic she was building far too much on far too little. She had no real reason to think Jake was really Jim McCosky, or that Willy would help even if he was. But she couldn't help hoping. Maybe all she had to do was ask, and he and his other gunslingers, far better shooters than anyone she'd ever known, could come back and save the town from the flying bullets of the outlaws before they found her father.

Looking out the window again, she saw Caleb's horse reined near the barn, still saddled and ready to run. Opening the latch to the attic, she climbed down.

Hitch saw her the minute she cut through the parlor.

"Where you goin', Silena? It ain't the time to make a trip to the outhouse."

Seizing the excuse, she brandished the gun. "I'll hurry," she said. "I just can't wait."

Breathing a long-suffering sigh, he left his post by the window. "All right, but I'm comin' with you."

"No!" she said quickly. "A girl needs privacy. It's bad enough I have to sleep in an attic for fear of somebody killing me, but I will not take company with me to the outhouse!"

Hitch moaned as Silena started out of the house.

She broke into a run the minute she was out of sight. Within seconds she had reached Caleb's horse, untethered it, and mounted it, still clutching the rifle. Quietly, so as not to draw Hitch's attention, she walked it around the back of the barn, out of Caleb and Hitch's hearing, before she kicked it into a gallop toward Omaha.

Willy would help her, she told herself, as soon as she asked him. He had to, because he was her only hope. And whatever it took, she was going to save her father and her town from the criminals that stalked them.

If Willy wrought hell when he was drunk, he ruled it when he was sober. Sam watched his father scowl and bark some obscenity to one of the Indian squaws who had dared to talk back to him, and he questioned his own wisdom at forcing his father to dry up for a couple of days.

But it had to be done. He couldn't go on like this, covering for his father, taking the burden of the show on his own back. It was time Willy took some of his responsibility back and got himself in shape.

"You going to shoot again, Willy?" he asked his father, who sat like a diseased man atop his mount.

Willy sneered at the bottles set up for his target practice. "I ain't practiced with bottles since I was fourteen. I'm a professional. I don't need no practice, anyway."

Sam grinned and moved Duke closer to his father's horse. "Willy, when I started riding with you, you told me that a man can never get *enough* practice."

"I was referrin' to the whores," Willy said.

Sam tried not to humor him by showing his own amusement, so he pulled his hat low down on his forehead and studied his pommel. "You were also talking about shooting, and you know it. It won't hurt to sharpen your aim a little."

"I could shoot lint off your shirt, boy, and not tear the fabric, so don't tell me about sharpening my aim."

Sam shook his head and peered at the bottles again. "You wouldn't be scared of missing, would you, Willy? Your hands a little shaky? Your vision a little blurry?"

Willy spat at the dirt and turned his hard face to his son. "I ain't scared o' nothin'. Least of all your smart theories about me."

"Then just shoot," Sam said, his voice taking on an annoyed edge. "If you aren't scared, shoot."

As if to shut his son up once and for all, Willy belligerently jerked out his six-shooter and aimed. The gun shook in his hand, but Sam told himself that it shook more when he was drunk. He pulled the trigger six consecutive times and hit three of the six bottles.

Sam's backbone went rigid. Holding his breath, he looked at Willy, waiting for the inevitable explosion.

"I need a drink," Willy said. "If I had a drink, I could relax and hit everythin' I aimed at. But I can't do nothin' with you breathin' down my neck, actin' like my keeper."

"I'm not your keeper, Willy," Sam said. "I just wanted you to see that maybe things aren't the way you think they are. Maybe the whiskey's affecting you more than you think. Maybe you need to rest, and dry up all the way, and practice. You could be good as you used to be if you'd just take a little time—"

Willy thrust his hand out and grabbed Sam's collar, jerking him almost off his horse. "I'm as good as I ever was, and don't you forget it. It's *my* name on them banners. It's *my* name that draws them crowds. And it's *my* gun that pops them skeets, no matter how fast or how high they shoot 'em."

Sam pried Willy's hand off his collar. His own hand curled involuntarily into a fist, but he settled stiffly back into his saddle. His jaw tensed as he thought of telling his father just whose bullets had really been saving the show each day, but there didn't seem much point. It would only make Willy harder to live with. And for the life of him, he didn't want to hurt him.

"'Course, a little practice wouldn't hurt *you* none," Willy said.

Sam straightened his hat and guided Duke away. "You better watch it, Willy, or someday I'm going to be shooting lint off your shirts. I just might be able to already."

Willy gave a phlegmy laugh. "Still a dreamer," he told his son.

Sam stopped Duke and looked at his father over his shoulder. "A dreamer who saw that you only hit three out of six bottles."

Familiar rage transformed the older man's face. Quickly drawing his other pistol, Willy turned around and shot at the three remaining bottles. In six shots, he managed to demolish them.

Sam stared, incredulous, wondering if that bullish pride on his father's face was really genuine. Didn't he realize that if it took twelve shots to destroy six bottles, his aim was worse than a twelve-year-old boy's who'd just picked up a gun for the first time? Didn't he see the significance in the fact that he could shoot the hardest targets when he was in front of an audience, but couldn't even hit a glass bottle here, sitting dead still and as sober as he'd been all month?

"All's I need is a drink," Willy said.

"Then go get one, Willy. But don't expect it to improve your aim any. Or your disposition."

Willy had already kicked his mount when they heard

the sound of a galloping horse from the north coming toward them. Sam pushed his hat up slightly and squinted toward the form riding toward them, urgency in every motion of the horse's sweating body.

It was a woman riding the horse, a woman with long, flowing, tangled flaxen hair, a bloodstained dress that wasn't meant for riding, a rifle clutched in her hand, and a look of pure terror and exhaustion on her face.

Quickly, he dismounted and waited. As the figure came closer he realized who she was. The horse slithered to a stop, and Silena Rivers slid off and fell into Sam's arms.

"You've got to help me!"

Silena knew even as she said it that the words sounded crazy, but standing here with her father's blood on her dress, panting from her wild ride, she didn't give much thought to censoring them.

"What is it?" Sam asked.

"It's my father," she grasped, and the tears began to spill. Her lips quivered, and she covered her mouth with a trembling hand. "You've got to help me. They'll kill him, and they'll kill me, and the town is so frightened. . . ."

"Would you back up and start over?" Willy snapped, still perched on his horse. "What in the hell—"

"You remember her, Willy," Sam said, cutting into his father's annoyed rambling. "Silena Rivers. Remember she was here a few weeks ago?"

Willy didn't answer, but the confusion on his face seemed to diminish a little. "What happened, girl? Calm down and just say it straight out."

"A gang," Silena said. "Yesterday I was in our store, and three men came in asking for Jim McCosky." She watched Willy's face for some sign of recognition.

He frowned and sat up straighter in his saddle. "Jim McCosky?" he repeated.

"They said that was my pa's real name. That they'd been told he was using an alias."

She paused a moment, and the look on Willy's face frightened her. Slowly, she stepped toward him. "You know Jim McCosky, don't you?"

Willy looked at Sam, and Silena caught the message being passed between them. Sam took her arm and gently turned her around. "What happened, Silena? What did they do?"

She swallowed, but the tears began to come harder. "First they came after Margaret and me—" Her voice broke, and she tried again. "Then Pa came in, and there was a gunfight. Pa was shot . . . and he killed one of them."

Willy climbed off his horse and stepped toward her. "Your pa . . . is he dead?"

"No! But he's real bad. And the other two got away, but this morning they came back, and now there are five of them, and they're tearing up the town looking for Pa . . . and I know they'll kill him and anybody in their way! You've got to help me! You've got to!"

"Hold on now," Willy said, holding out a hand to stem her demand. "What do you mean, we've got to help you?"

"You *have* to," she cried. "Our sheriff is the barber, and half the time he can't remember where he keeps his bullets! We don't have anyone who would be able to fight this. Please . . . you're the only ones I know who could outshoot those outlaws."

Willy's face turned noticeably pale, and he turned a stricken look on Sam. "You must be crazy, girl! I ain't goin' to get into a shoot-out with a bunch of murderers!"

"But you've done it before. More. You've killed hundreds of Indians, both of you, and those must be worse than five drunk outlaws. I read your handbill. I know what you're both capable of!"

Sam dropped her arm. Taking off his hat, he scratched his fingers through his hair and pulled it back on. "See, honey, the thing is . . . a lot of what you read in those handbills . . ."

"It's for publicity," Willy blurted. "Some of it's a little . . . exaggerated."

"No!" Silena turned to Sam and took both his arms, shaking him. "I saw you. I saw you shoot!"

"But it's a show, Silena. It's just a show. You need the marshall . . . or somebody who can—"

"You're all there is!" she shouted. "The marshal's too far away!"

"I ain't goin' nowhere," Willy said. "I'm a performer, and yes, I can shoot. But I don't aim to risk my life for a town I ain't never even visited."

"But my father!" She turned on Willy, her eyes desperate. "He's lying there burning up with fever, in and out of consciousness. He could die anyway, or lose his leg, but he can't fight back if they find him. There aren't that many places to look for him. It's only so long before they'll figure out where we've hidden him. Meanwhile, who knows how many others in town will have to die? Don't you even care?"

Willy dropped his troubled gaze to the ground, but he shook his head. "I can't help you."

"What if he *is* Jim McCosky? Would you do it then?"

Willy looked up at her, his dull, yellowed eyes boring into hers. "Jim McCosky's dead."

"Maybe not," Sam argued.

Willy shot him a look. "You don't really think . . .?"

"A lot doesn't make sense about that story, Willy. We considered it ourselves. Maybe it's him."

Silena's eyes rounded in hope, and she turned her eyes to Sam. "Then you do know him? This Jim McCosky?"

"I don't, not really," Sam said. "But Willy does . . . did."

Silena backed away a few steps, holding her head as if it would burst. "If you knew him," she said, "if he was your friend when you were a boy, if he was the one who saved you from drowning, don't you owe it to him to help him?"

"Owe it to him?" Willy repeated. "Honey, even if I did owe it to him, don't mean I could go up against those men. If he *is* Jim McCosky—and I ain't sayin' he is—then the Colonel sent those men. I'm a performer, not a gunfighter, and neither is Sam. We can trick-shoot and hunt, but when it comes to fightin' real men with guns aimed back at us, that ain't quite somethin' that appeals to me."

"Then you're a bigger coward than you are a star!" she cried. "And worse, you're a fraud. None of it is true! None of it!"

She started back to her horse, whose breathing had not yet returned to normal.

"No!" Sam stopped her before she mounted. "You need a fresh horse. You need to rest—"

"Let me go!" she cried. "My father may be dying right now! I don't have any time to waste! I never should have come here!"

Sam wrestled her away from the horse and shook her. "Let me get you a fresh horse at least. This one won't make another mile."

Willy remounted his horse. "I'll get her one, Sam. Hand me the reins."

Sam handed over the reins to Caleb's horse, and Silena watched, hot tears still burning down her face. "I need to hurry."

"He will," Sam said. "But you shouldn't be going back there alone. You should stay here, out of danger—"

"And let them kill my father and destroy my town? *I'm* not a coward! I can't do that!"

"I'm not a coward, either," Sam said, his neck growing hot. "I'm realistic."

"You're a coward *and* a liar," she said.

The redness rose to his face, and he glared down at her. "What are you talking about?"

"I'm talking about your claim that you couldn't take those outlaws. I saw you shoot for Willy. I know what you can do."

Sam flung around, guiltily looking for anyone who might have heard. "Would you please not say that out loud? Someone could hear!"

A new sense of power filtered through Silena, and she lifted her chin. The fear and panic fled momentarily. "Come with me," she said, "and I'll keep my mouth shut about your shooting for Willy."

"What?" he asked, disgusted. "I can't go with you, Silena. I told you, I'm not what you think I am. Besides, I've got responsibility here. People depend on me!"

"This is life or death, Sam!" she cried. "I'll do whatever it takes to save my town and my father. Even if it means telling Willy your secret!"

Sam opened his mouth to react, but Willy was already heading back with a fresh, saddled horse.

"Please," he said, his own panic beginning to strain his voice. "Please don't do this."

Silena's lips trembled as Willy grew closer, and she looked up at him. "Mr. Hawkins," she began. "There's something I think you should know about your son."

"What's that?"

Sam grabbed her arm. Silencing her with a squeeze and a desperate, beseeching look, he spoke before she could. "I'm going with her, Willy."

"The hell you are!" Willy shouted. "You can't just ride off—"

"I'm going, Willy," Sam cut in, giving Silena a quelling look. "She's right. I can outshoot almost anybody. I can help."

"But you ain't never killed a man in your life! What you gonna do when you're kissin' the barrel of some mean son of a bitch's shotgun?"

"I reckon I'll do whatever I have to," he said. He took the reins to the horse Willy had brought and handed them to Silena. "I'll stop by my tent for some more guns and things I might need."

Silena nodded. "Thank you, Sam."

Sam breathed a bitter laugh as he started to walk away. "Ain't like I got a choice, is it?"

"What do you mean, you ain't got a choice?" Willy asked.

Sam stopped and gave Silena one last meaningful look. For a moment she was certain he would call her bluff.

She was wrong.

"The lady needs rescuing, Willy," he said. "And I figure I'm the only one can do it."

They rode as fast as their horses would carry them, Silena in the lead, and Sam just behind. As they rode he squinted at her in the wind. She had stopped crying, but terror still reigned on her face. The sight softened his anger at the way she had manipulated him, and he couldn't help wondering just how bad it had gotten yesterday.

The bloodstains on her skirt beckoned his eyes, and he remembered what she'd said about the outlaws. *First they came after me. . . .*

Had they hurt her?

The thought of what they might have done sent a chill of fear coursing through him, and he told himself that even without her threats he'd like to kill every last one of them for laying a hand on her. He held no allegiance to her father, but there was something about her . . . something he couldn't explain.

The fact that she needed him in some real way—some desperate way—unlike the way the show needed him, gave him a new sense of purpose. He would fight the best he could, and if his skill with a gun was any help, he would be able at least to frighten off the outlaws. Maybe she had exaggerated the danger.

Halfway to Hayton, the sky opened up, and a bolt of lightning in the distance shot down. Thunder quaked around them, but Silena kept riding. Her hair was soaked, and her clothes where dripping and pressed against her, just as his were. He looked over at her, saw that she wouldn't be daunted by the change in the weather.

The lightning came closer.

"We've got to stop," he yelled across to her. "We're riding right into the storm."

"We *can't* stop," she said. "*They* won't stop."

Another bolt of lightning hit within five hundred yards of them.

"There's a cave up there," Sam said, pointing to a jut of cliffs half a mile up to the right. "We can stop there until it passes."

"No!" she shouted. "We have to hurry. I'm not afraid!"

"Well, I am, damn it!" He reached across and grabbed her reins out of her hand. She tried to wrestle them back, but he was more experienced on horseback than she. Before she knew it, her horse was headed for the cave he had indicated earlier.

They reached it just as a series of lightning bolts danced across the plains. Silena slid off the horse, fighting mad, as Sam walked the horses into the opening of the rock's overhang.

"You coward!" she shouted, shoving her wet hair out of her face. "How can you go back there and face five gunfighters if you can't even face a little bad weather?"

"A little bad weather?" Sam asked. "Are you trying

to tell me you didn't see those lightning bolts? Are you trying to tell me you could stand up to that?"

"Yes!" she said. "This is urgent. I don't have time for a storm!"

"Well, you don't have any choice. Just like I don't!"

She started to cry again, and he saw her shiver. The blood on her skirt had begun to run, and not realizing she had touched it, she smeared some across her cheek. Sam let go of the horses and went toward her.

He reached up to wipe the blood from her face, but she recoiled. "There's blood on your face," he whispered. "You must have touched your skirt."

Swallowing, with the tears still coursing down her wet face, she let him wipe the blood away.

"Where'd it come from?" he asked.

"What?"

"The blood?" Pain filled his face, but he forced himself to ask. "Is it yours?"

"No," she said, looking quickly away from him to the storm still flashing across the plains. "I changed clothes after . . . This is Pa's blood. His wounds kept bleeding through the night. Just when I'd think they'd stopped, they'd start again. It got on my dress."

Sam could see that not a mark marred the smooth, porcelain flesh of her face. But lower down, on her chest, just above the neckline of her dress, he saw a bruise and a scratch. He wondered what she hid beneath her clothes.

"Did they hurt you?"

She looked away again, and jumped when a flash of lightning seemed to strike just outside the cave. "They shot Pa."

"You didn't answer my question," he said. When she still looked away, he touched her face and turned her to look at him. "Did they hurt you?"

The tears in her eyes seemed to multiply with the question, and her lips trembled as she kept them tightly compressed. "They tried," she whispered. "But he came just in time. Killed the one who . . . who was . . ."

"The one who was hurting you?"

"Yes," she said. "I've never seen a man dead before, but I was so glad. . . ." She threw her hands over her face, and Sam drew her into his arms.

She collapsed against him, sobs racking her small body. For a moment she let him hold her, let him rest his chin against her hair, let him crush her in his strong embrace. She felt so small, so helpless, but he couldn't escape the memory of her riding into the camp today, all determination and purpose, intent on getting what she came for.

No, she wasn't helpless, but still she wept like a child who'd had her world snatched out from under her. He wondered just how much of it had been, and suddenly he was angry, and the fight became his, not just hers alone.

"I won't let them get to you again," he said. "I swear it."

Bewildered, she looked up at him. "How can you say that, when I forced you to come? When you wouldn't have if I hadn't?"

His jaw popped as he bit back his own rising anger and looked down into her tear-reddened eyes. "I'm coming, and that's the main thing," he said. "Nobody can outshoot me. I may not be a gunfighter, and I'm not crazy about the idea of a shoot-out. But I'm not a coward. And I'll kill any man who ever tries to put his hands on you again."

Stricken by the intensity of his intimate vow, she stared up at him. Her eyelashes were wet and webbed together, but the tears had stopped. Beneath his hands, he felt her still shaking, and he wondered if it was from the cold or the way he held her.

His hand came up to gently wipe the tears from her cheek, and then he settled his palm against her jaw, stroked it with the roughness of his fingertips. She kept looking at him, that tiny frown between her brows revealing her confusion. He wondered what would happen if he dipped his face, just a little, and kissed her.

If she had been any other woman, he wouldn't have given it a moment of consideration. He would have assumed that she would allow it, that she hoped for it. . . .

But Silena was different.

Still, she didn't pull out of his arms, didn't recoil from his hand sliding through the warm tears and cool raindrops glistening on her face.

Before he had the presence of mind to stop himself, he lowered his face to hers and grazed her lips with his. Her eyes closed, and he felt a quick breath escape her lips. He pulled back slightly to determine if it was another sob, but she didn't move. Her eyes remained closed, and her hands remained curled on his chest between them. Her lips were parted ever so slightly, and her breath came harder, warmer.

He took her mouth again, and felt her hands sliding up to his shoulders, felt her rising on her toes, felt her lips parting. His tongue found hers, and something deep within him stirred, something that had been stirred many times before . . . but something else as well.

The kiss was almost desperate, but it was sweet as well, and it tasted of her tears. The taste reminded him that she was not someone with whom he could fulfill his desires right here and now. She was a frightened bird who would flit away if he pushed her too far. Something deep inside him didn't want her to withdraw from him.

So he withdrew instead. He released their embrace, stepped back, and breathed, "I'm sorry."

Silena sucked in a deep breath, let out a shaky sigh. Nervously, she turned to the opening of the cave. "The rain hasn't quit, but the lightning has," she whispered. "Can we go now?"

Sam went to the edge of the cave and looked out. The lightning seemed to have played itself out, so he reached for the horses again. "Come on," he said. "I'll help you up."

He held out his hand for her, and she looked at it for a moment. Finally, she took it, and let him help her back into the saddle.

The wind whistled through her ears and the rain pricked her skin. Silena leaned forward in the saddle and tried to move the horse faster. Sam was right beside her, the brim of his hat shielding his eyes from the rain.

She hunkered her arms in closer to her body, trying to stop the chill, but her clothes were soaked clear through. Up ahead, it looked as if the clouds were breaking up, and the rain was about to stop.

She wished she'd had a coat to wear today, or brought a change of clothes. But there hadn't been time.

She glanced over at Sam, looking so natural and calm atop his big horse, and felt a quick stirring of shame at what had happened between them. She hadn't expected to react to him the way she had, but something had stirred in her when he'd vowed to protect her. For a moment she had felt secure.

But now she told herself that Sam was smooth with his words, and she had no reason to believe them. She had forced him to come, and she wondered if he was afraid. He was walking into a battlefield, and so was she. And she knew enough to be frightened to death.

If he is Jim McCosky, and I ain't sayin' he is, then the Colonel sent those men.

A sick feeling, the same that had overcome her yesterday when she'd stood beside her father's bed, swelled within her. There was a secret, something that her father was keeping from her, something that others knew.

A fresh tear fell to her cheek, to mingle with the raindrops beating down on her. Still, she wiped it away.

Sam caught her movement and looked over at her. "You okay?"

She nodded.

"Cold?"

She didn't answer, so he slowed his horse and reached for hers, pulling back on the reins.

"What?" she asked, when they had slowed to a walk. "We don't have time for—"

He slipped out of his coat even as she protested, and handed it across to her. "Put this on."

She didn't take it. "My clothes are soaked. If I wear your coat, I'll get it all wet."

"If you don't, you'll catch pneumonia and you won't do your father any good."

Sullenly, she took his coat, slipped it on, and felt the warmth still there from his own body heat warming her. The arms were too long and the shoulders drooped off of hers, but it was sweet relief.

"Thank you," she said.

He tipped his wet hat, gave her a one-sided grin, and they started on their way again.

* * *

An hour later a smoke plume rising in the distance caught their eye before they even saw the town of Hayton. Silena stopped her horse and stared at the thin column.

"Something's burning. They're destroying the town."

Sam squinted in the direction of the smoke and scanned the horizon, trying to see any sign of hostile riders. But all was quiet.

"We'll go around the town so they don't see us, and come up from the east to the Calhoun ranch. That's where I left Pa." She wrapped her arms around herself, pulling Sam's coat tighter, and shivered. "I hope he's all right."

"He will be," he said, but he knew it was an empty promise.

She looked over at him, her wet face still glistening in the sunshine just beginning to peek through the clouds. "Are you sure I'm not overestimating your skill with a gun? Like for instance, that you've never shot a real bullet in your life, only blanks, or that your shooting for Willy the other day was only another trick?"

"It was no trick," he said. "I only do my tricks in front of crowds. And as for my shooting, I already told you. I can outshoot any man I've ever met."

"But can you shoot *at* him?" she asked. "Especially when he's shooting at you?"

"I can do my best," he said, chagrined by her lack of confidence in him. "And I didn't notice any interviews before you threatened me."

"I was in a panic. Still am."

"Well, I'm not exactly about to doze off, myself." He heaved a deep sigh. "I'll need help, you know. And I think it would be best if you didn't tell the whole town what Willy told you about our just being showmen, instead of real gunslingers. They'll need confidence in me if they're going to help me. More than you have."

"I don't know who you'll find," she said. "Hitch and Caleb, maybe the sheriff, Zane Barlow, and a few of the farmers . . . Nobody very heroic or courageous. Truth is, you're the best we've got. That's why I came for you."

"Then you'll keep it a secret?"

She looked back toward the town and the blackish-gray smoke cloud still rising into the sky. "Yes, I'll keep your secret. For now. I guess if it'll make our men stand up and fight, maybe it's worth it."

Sam followed her on the route that she seemed to know so well, and prayed that they wouldn't encounter the outlaws on the way. He could take them himself, if he had to, he thought, but he didn't want her to get caught in the cross fire. He should have left her back in Omaha. He should have insisted that she stay.

But if what he suspected was true, the outlaws would have come for her there, anyway.

They reached the Calhoun ranch, which was a few miles out from the town, minutes later. The moment they rode in, Hitch came barreling out, half-frantic. "Where in blazes have you been, Silena? We've been out of our minds worried about you!"

"I went to Omaha," she said. "To get Wild Willy to help us. Willy couldn't come, so Sam Hawkins came instead."

Hitch gave Sam a guarded, untrusting look and held Silena's horse while she slid off. "Silena, do you know how stupid it was to run out like that? They could have caught you–"

"How's my pa?" she cut in breathlessly. "Is he all right?"

"He's feverish," Hitch said. "But I haven't had much time to watch him. Ma's been seeing to him, but we didn't know what to tell him about you if he woke up—"

"What about the outlaws?" Sam asked. "Have they been out here yet?"

"No," Hitch said grudgingly. "But Caleb's been sneakin' in and outta town. He says they've set the livery on fire, shot out every window down Main Street, and they been goin' door-to-door tearin' up houses lookin' for whoever's hidin' Jake."

"Jake?" Sam asked. "I thought they were looking for McCosky."

"They are," Hitch said. "They claim Jake Rivers *is* Jim McCosky. Seem dead sure of it."

Sam looked down at Silena, standing pale and cold beneath the coat that made her look even smaller.

"It's just a matter of time before they get here," she said. "That's why I brought Sam. You saw him shoot. He's the only one who can save us."

"I coulda held 'em off," Hitch said belligerently. "You didn't have to bring him here."

Sam dismounted and began hostering his guns—two on his hips, two more in shoulder holsters, and another two in his boots. Hanging his rifle by a strap on his back, he asked, "How long will it take you to round up all the townsmen?"

"Too long," Hitch said. "Besides, most of 'em don't want to leave their families."

"What about the men who can? Aren't there any?"

"Maybe half a dozen," Hitch said. "Maybe not that many."

"Then let's get them," Sam ordered. "The faster the better."

"What for?" Hitch asked. "What'll I tell 'em?"

"That we're going to town," he said. "And we're going to run those outlaws out."

"Hell, no, we ain't," Hitch said. "I ain't goin' in there."

"Somebody has to!" Silena cried. "Hitch, if we don't run them out, there's no telling what they'll do."

"It's all right," Sam said, still checking the barrel of his shotgun. "If I have to, I'll do it by myself."

Silena looked at Sam, knowing that he was testing Hitch's pride, and she pulled his coat tighter around her. "All right, Sam. It looks like you're all we've got."

"Okay, I'll go," Hitch said. "I wasn't sayin' no 'cause I was afraid. I'm not afraid. I just didn't see the sense in it, that's all. But if it's the only way."

The door to the house opened, and Caleb dashed out, with Margaret and Nell behind him.

"Silena, did you take my horse?"

"Yes, I took it," she said, wincing, "but I didn't come back with it. It's still in Omaha. I'm sorry, Caleb, but I needed a fresh one."

Caleb eyed the horse she was sitting on suspiciously. "Omaha? You went all the way to Omaha? On my horse?"

"We'll get it later," Sam cut in. "It's being well cared for. Meanwhile, you can use this one. It's used to gunfire, so it might do better, anyway."

"Sam's going to help us," Silena said, getting off the horse and surrendering the reins to Caleb. "We have to hurry."

Caleb grabbed the horse and mounted it quickly, then pulled his mother up behind him. "First, I got to hide Ma and Margaret. I didn't want 'em home alone, but they cain't sit around in this powder keg without me."

"Powder keg?" Silena felt her face redden.

"My house ain't a powder keg," Hitch said.

"It is with Jake layin' in it. Ain't that why you didn't want your ma stayin' here?"

"I thought she'd feel safer with the Phillipses, is all."

Silena's heart jolted, and she felt a shiver pulse

through her. *Had* they turned Hitch's home into a powder keg?

"It ain't that bad, but you should come, too, Silena," Hitch said, pulling Margaret up behind him. "We could hide you—"

"No!" she said. "I'm staying with Pa."

"Hurry up, you two," Sam said. "We've got to get organized. No time to waste."

"We know how urgent it is," Hitch said through his teeth. "We been here all along, remember? Ain't like we just blew into town like the conquerin' hero."

Caleb sent Hitch a quelling frown. "Dang it, Hitch, we oughta be thankin' him, not insultin' him. Now come on. We got work to do."

Silena watched, the newly familiar terror rising inside her, as her friends rode away.

"They're gone now, but I reckon they'll be back long about sundown," Murdock Smith, the town's saloon owner, announced to the three other men Hitch and Caleb had rounded up to meet in the Simpson barn, five miles outside of town. "They drank everythin' in sight, then blew outta town, sayin' when they come back they'd find Jake. They been goin' at this all day. I 'spect they're sleepin' it off, so that oughta buy us a little time."

Sam swept a somber look over the men perched nervously in various positions of readiness, and thought it was a shame that this was all the town could offer him in the way of help. He took off his hat, tapped his thumb against the brim, and repositioned it on his head as he sought some inspiring words that might rally spirit into these men.

"That gives us a few hours to make a plan," he said. "And when they come back, we can give them the fight they're looking for."

"Give 'em a fight?" the mayor barked. "I tell ya what

we ought to give 'em. We oughta just give 'em Jake Rivers and that daughter of his so they'll ride out and leave us the hell alone."

Hitch turned on the mayor, his face reddening. "Silena doesn't have anything to do with this."

"The hell she don't," Sheriff Hollister threw in. "They been askin' for her all over town, too. Seems they might even want her worse than her pa."

Sam's backbone went rigid. Frowning, he stepped forward and looked at Caleb, the only one in town who had really kept up with what the gangsters were doing, rather than hiding out. Sam didn't know if that indicated bravery or just plain stupidity. "Is that right, Caleb? Are they really after her, too?"

"Appear to be," Caleb said.

"Well, hell, if it's a woman they want," Zane Barlow cut in, his long face looking more troubled with each passing moment, "then let's give 'em Nell. What do you think, boy?" he asked Caleb. "You think your ma might help us out?"

Caleb's eyes dulled over. "My ma ain't outlaw bait," he said belligerently.

"Besides," Murdock added, "they can have her whenever they want her. Ain't the same as a fresh young virgin."

Sam curled his hands into white-knuckled fists, telling himself that crashing the man's nose through the back of his skull wouldn't solve the matter at hand.

"Our job is to protect the women, not debate over which one would satisfy the outlaws the most," he bit out. "They can't ride in here and demand whatever they want without a hell of a fight. We've got to scare them out so they won't come back. Ever."

"Yeah? Well, what do you care?" Hitch asked, his voice rising in pitch. "You'll shoot 'em up for a coupla hours, scare 'em outta town for a day or so, and then you'll be gone. It'll be us who have to stay and fight it out. We're the ones who have to wait and wonder if they're coming back. It ain't like we got a competent sheriff or nothin'."

"Hey now, boy," Sheriff Hollister said, his face growing red. "I don't see nobody else rushin' forward to volunteer for this job."

"That's enough!" Sam's voice shook with finality, and he looked from man to man, realizing dismally that "the real world" wasn't all that different from the world inside the Wild West show. Men still acted like boys, and logical thoughts rarely entered their minds. "We don't have time for all this old-maidish bickering. There are lives at stake."

"Where *is* Jake, anyhow?" the mayor asked, turning to Sam.

"He's well hidden," Sam said. "That's all you need to know."

"So let me get this straight." Mayor Malone hooked his thumbs in his pockets and studied the floor, his large, pompous paunch creating a comical profile. "I'm supposed to go out there and fight a bunch of gunslingers to keep 'em from gettin' to somebody when I don't even know where he is?"

"You catch on fast," Sam said. "No wonder you're mayor."

Not certain if he'd been insulted, the mayor bristled. "Well, I got a little bit of a problem with that. I'm not sure I should *be* fightin' for Jake. How do I know they ain't got a good reason for wantin' him?"

"Nobody has a good reason for shooting up a town, killing citizens, and raping its women," Sam said.

The men grew quiet, and Sam walked around them,

looking at each of them in turn. Hitch, still pouting over the fact that the Wild West hero had come back here with Silena, Caleb, brooding and angry, and ready to wreak vengeance on the man who'd attacked his sister,Mayor Malone, whose hair was still lopsided from his half haircut the day before, Sheriff Hollister, who wore his white barber's coat, but had at least remembered to put on his holster and his badge, Murdock Smith, the saloon owner, who'd spent most of the day hidden himself while the gang had ransacked his bar. And Zane Barlow, deep in thought, as if trying to think of a face-saving way out of this mess. It wasn't much to work with, Sam thought, but he'd made heroes out of nobodies before.

The way to do it, he thought, was to win their confidence completely and make them think that they could do no wrong if he was with them, the way he did with the newcomers to the troupe.

"It's going to take a little bit of ingenuity," he said, his voice quiet, but decisive. "But I can outshoot any of them bastards, and while I'm doing that you all can be hammering them home with your own bullets. The trick is going to be to plant the right men in the right places so's to surprise them when they ride in. It won't be easy, believe me, but I've been through worse."

He slid his hat far down his forehead as he uttered the lie, and went on. "There was a time when I went up against a whole tribe of Navajo, just me and a couple of forty-fives, and I wiped out the whole lot of them. All I need is enough guns and enough ammunition, and I'll have them dancin' the cancan all the way to the jail . . . or into their graves."

The men—all except for Hitch—watched Sam with grudging interest.

"It's true," Caleb said, turning back to the others. "Says all that in his handbill. I got one at the house. You shoulda seen him shootin' in the show. All them Injuns he killed when they tried to rob that stagecoach."

"That was actin', you moron," Hitch said. "They didn't really kill nobody."

"But it wasn't actin' when he was hangin' upside down shootin' at them bottles, or them targets up in the air," Caleb said. "And it says right there in the handbills all the stuff he did. Didn't you read it?"

"Wasn't that interested," Hitch said. He gave Sam a brooding look, then forced himself to ask. "Well, are you gonna tell us your plan or not? You do *have* one, don't you?"

Sam bristled, but he knew the young man's hostility came from his attraction to Silena. He couldn't blame him for not welcoming another man as competition. He didn't much like the idea himself.

He also didn't much like the notion that he was the lone leader of these gossipers who carried guns they probably didn't even know how to use. Each of them was either too green or too soft, and the futility of what he was trying to do with them washed over him.

"To tell you the truth," he admitted, "I don't know if any of my original plans will work with you. None of you wants to cooperate, you don't seem loyal to Jake in a way that'll save his life, and frankly, I don't get the feeling that any of you plans to put your life in much risk if the need comes up."

"So what're you gonna do?" Hitch asked, standing up and facing off with Sam. "Take 'em all by yourself?"

"Maybe," Sam said. "Or maybe I ought to just go back home and let you handle it."

Hitch didn't back down. "Wouldn't bother me none."

The sheriff stood up with a start, knowing that if Sam left, the responsibility fell to him. "Hitch Calhoun, you shut your trap. He's all we got."

Sullenly, Hitch plopped back into his chair.

Still not sure whether any of this was worth it, Sam began to outline his plan. An hour later, after everyone had been briefed and was set to get into position to wait for the next attack, Sam began to wonder if he was risking his life for a townful of people who didn't have the good sense to light a stick of dynamite. Leaving the other men still sitting in the barn, he wandered outside. It was hopeless, he thought. Hopeless and futile. If he couldn't hold the outlaws off all by himself, there was every chance that they'd stampede right over him and leave nothing in town but a few hundred bullet holes and a hundred cowering corpses.

But his wouldn't be among them.

Willy was right, he thought. He was no real hero, and he didn't feel up to catching a barrel of bullets in the name of honor or of impressing Silena. Not even if he had the promise of her naked body against his, sliding his hands and lips over her skin, tasting her flesh . . .

Well, maybe that *would* make it worth it, after all, he mused.

Idly patting his horse where it stood tied with the others, he pondered that thought for a moment, trying to decide if the possibility was enough to make him stay, but then he told himself that the thought was as farfetched as Sheriff Hollister's stopping the outlaws single-handedly. Silena wasn't offering him her body. Just her gratitude.

And that wasn't enough.

Making his decision, he mounted his horse and took one last look at the town. It probably wouldn't even be standing tomorrow, but he would. And he'd be in one piece.

His conscience might be a little wounded, but he supposed he could live with that.

Jake Rivers's fever rose as afternoon turned to evening, and his body convulsed violently as he thrashed in his bed. Silena fed him as much whiskey as she could make him swallow and changed his bandages every time the bleeding started again. The red lines that meant blood poisoning were shooting all the way up his thigh now, and Miss Caldonia had said more than once that he might lose the leg.

Each time he came to and focused his myopic vision on Silena, he would ask for his gun and call her Eva, mumbling something about how he wouldn't let the Colonel get away with this.

The Colonel. He seemed to be the key to this whole mess, someone who was menacing and frightening, someone who might have sent these outlaws to kill her father and do who knew what with her. But if that was true, if Jake knew of him, as Willy had, didn't that mean that her father really was Jim McCosky?

She shuddered and backed away from his bed. Exhausted, she dropped into the chair beside the window. Picking up Hitch's rifle and setting it across her lap, she stared out into the dusk falling over the town.

What did it mean if her father wasn't who she had known him to be all these years? If he was someone else, then who was *she?* Her name would have been manufactured, too, and she wasn't just the daughter of a store owner, but the daughter of a man whose past she knew nothing about, a past so volatile that it still haunted him seventeen years later, threatening to kill him and destroy his town.

But why?

She tried not to concentrate on the despair that must lurk behind the answers to those questions, for there wasn't time. Any minute now, the outlaws could be back. They had already been through three fourths of the town, and this trip, she feared, they would discover Hitch's farm and her father lying in a stupor.

She heard a horse coming toward the house and her stomach knotted. She raised her gun, aimed, and waited.

She recognized Sam's horse first, then his hat and the shirt he wore. Lowering her rifle in relief, she burst out of the attic, ran down the stairs and out the front door.

"Sam! Are they back yet? Have they come?"

"Not yet." Sam got off his horse and stalked into the house, where earlier he'd unloaded the supplies he'd brought with him. "But I don't intend to wait around."

"What?" The word came out on a breath of horror.

Sam tried to avoid looking at her. "This is hopeless, Silena," he said. "And believe me, I know hopeless when I see it. The town has been shot to kingdom come, windows are broken, some of the shops are burning. Half the houses in town have been ransacked. Who knows how many women they've raped along the way, and now I have to face running them out when all I got to help me is a bunch of kids and cowards? No, thank you."

Silena's eyes rounded in terror. "But you *have* to! You can't leave me here! My father—"

"I don't intend to," Sam said, loading his things back into his saddlebag. "I'll take you with me. It's you they're after, and—"

She grabbed the saddlebag from him and made him look at her. "What do you mean, it's me they're after? What do you *mean?*"

"Just that . . . well . . . isn't that what they said?"

"No, that isn't what they said." Her voice quavered as it rose in pitch. "Do you know something I don't know?"

Sam looked away, shrugged, and struggled to find the words that would appease her, without telling her what he'd learned from Willy. It was more than apparent to him now that his father's curiosity had caused this mess to start. Jim McCosky had supposedly been killed in the Platte River, along with the baby he had stolen. It had taken his father's questions to dredge him up.

"Caleb and the saloon owner, they said they heard the outlaws were looking for you, too. Said they wanted you. Now, I told you, you can come with me, but—"

The shock on Silena's face stopped him. "*Why* do they want me?"

"Same reason they want your pa, I reckon," he said. "But if we're going, we have to get—"

"No!" She raised the rifle she still clutched at him, her finger over the trigger. "I'm not going anywhere. I won't leave my father to the mercy of those murderers, and I won't leave the town to be destroyed by them. And neither will you."

Sam's amusement wrinkled the corners of his eyes. "Put that gun down, Silena. This isn't even my town. I have nothing to do with this."

"Then it would be an awful shame if I had to kill you over it," she said.

It didn't take a lightning bolt to convince Sam she was serious, and that her finger was a little too ready to pull that trigger. "What's killing me going to serve?"

"It'll make me feel better," she said through her

teeth. "And it'll give me some practice that I'm probably going to need."

His grin faded, and he glanced toward the stairs. "Look, what if I figure a way to take Jake with us? What if I can sneak him out of town?"

"You can't!" she cried. "He's burning with fever, he's unconscious, he's probably going to lose his leg if he doesn't die or get killed first. There's no way he can ride a horse, and if we tried to take him in a wagon, they'd find us. It won't work! We have to stay and fight."

Tears of rage formed in her eyes, and she stepped closer to Sam, her finger still poised to pull that trigger. "Don't you ever want to be anything more than a showman? There's nothing courageous about twirling pistols for applause, Sam. If you saved Hayton, you'd have something *real* to put in your handbills! I didn't figure you for a coward."

"I'm not a coward. I just know my limitations, is all. And that includes a bunch of idiots who probably don't know the barrel of a gun from the hammer." Sam heaved a heavy sigh and turned back to the door, peering out. Darkness was beginning to settle over the town. "They'll be here anytime now, and all I have to work with is a bunch of kids and cowards."

"They're braver than you are," she challenged. "At least they aren't turning tail and running."

"It's *their* town!" he shouted, swinging back around. "It's their home! It's even their lives. But it's not mine!"

"Oh, yes, it is," she said. "If you don't do what you promised to do, I'll blow you away myself."

He stared her down for a long moment, and finally, he spoke, his voice tense but calm. "I know you will."

"Do you?" she asked. "Because I'm not so sure you do."

It was the desperation in her eyes, not the gun aimed on him, that changed his mind. He knew she hadn't even cocked the rifle, probably didn't know how. It would be easy enough to appease her, pretend to be going back for town, but he didn't think he'd feel too good about himself if he did.

Besides, Willy would be expecting him to do just that, and she was right. It was time he had something real to put on his handbills. Either that or his tombstone.

"I saw you shoot for him," she whispered as tears burned down her cheeks. "I saw you do the impossible. You're the best, Sam, and you know it. I need you now, and I'm not gonna let you go."

He swallowed and issued a deep breath. "All right," he said finally. "I'll stay. I wouldn't have gone without you, anyway."

"Yes, you would have. You'd have gone in a minute."

"That's not true. My plan was to take you with me, get you out of danger, but since you won't come—"

"You mean, since you don't want a hole through your stomach."

He grinned slightly. "That too." He looked at the stuff in his saddlebag, gestured toward it. "I'll leave that here to let you know I'm telling the truth. I'm going back to town to work on our strategy. And when they come, when you hear the shots starting, you go back up to the attic and stay there. Don't come out until I come for you. And if one of them gets to you, you use that gun." Grinning, he leaned over and took it from her. "By the way, you have to cock it like this before it'll shoot. Keep that in mind."

Silena only stared at him as he handed the rifle back to her and she realized he hadn't been the least bit afraid of her as he ambled back out to his horse and mounted it. Slowly, she followed him.

"If you run," she said, though she knew the threat seemed weightless, "I'll come to Omaha myself and shoot you down."

He slid his hat low on his forehead and peered at her from under the brim. The amusement in his eyes was barely discernible as he bent down and dropped a startling kiss on her lips. "Stay hidden, Silena," he said seriously. "I'll be back when it's all over."

Lowering her gun, Silena touched her still-tingling lips, and as he started back toward town she called, "Be careful, Sam."

But she doubted he had heard. And in light of the threats she had made against him, and the way her heart pounded now, she decided it was best that he hadn't heard, after all.

The moon was high in the sky when the sound of galloping horses, war whoops, and gunshots sporadically fired into the air swept through the wounded town. Sam peered out from behind the charred remains of the livery stable, checking the positions of the men he had strategically placed.

Hitch, who seemed to be the best marksman among the bunch—and didn't mind saying so—had ridden out to his ranch to protect Silena and Jake, just in case Sam and the others didn't get all of the outlaws. That left him with Sheriff Hollister, Mayor Malone, Murdock Smith, Zane Barlow, and Caleb.

He looked up on the roof of the saloon and saw Zane squatting, his rifle aimed, but he wondered if the man would have the presence of mind to use it when the time came. Caleb was the only one in place who looked as if he had remembered to load his gun. Quickly, Sam scanned the rooftops of Jake Rivers's store and the bank, but the sheriff, if he was there, was carefully hidden, and the mayor, too, was nowhere to be seen. He hoped to God they hadn't abandoned their posts.

The noise of the gang grew louder as they approached the town. Sam swallowed and set his hands on his six-shooters. This wasn't like the show, he told himself. There wouldn't be applause at the end. There wouldn't be Indians who got up when it was all over, shook his hand, and had a drink with him in his tent. Whoever he shot would likely shoot back at him, and when he hit them, they wouldn't get up. At least, not if he was worth his salt.

Gunshots sounded from too close by. Peering around the wall, Sam saw that they came from the five outlaws racing along the street, not from the sheriff or the mayor. In fact, there was no gunfire at all from the roofs where he had posted them.

Slowly, he inched out from behind his barricade, crouched behind a water trough, and aimed.

His first shot hit its mark, and one of the gunmen fell off his horse. As the horses scattered and their riders looked around for the source of the bullets, the others opened fire.

In the midst of the danger, his fears fled, and Sam rose slightly to get a clearer view of the men coming toward him. With star-quality precision, he sprayed the scrambling men with the eleven remaining bullets in his pistols.

He saw Caleb on the roof of the saloon, silhouetted against the moonlit sky. The boy was shouting, "I'll kill you, you son of a bitch!" One of the outlaws flicked a gun in his direction, and Sam saw Caleb's body jar with the impact of a bullet. Without preamble, he dropped to the ground with a bone-crashing thud. Sam's heart jolted. He'd seen men fall in gunfights before, but they were never really dead. Now the irrational idea occurred to him that Caleb might not be either.

All of the outlaws had dismounted and had pulled their horses up onto the walkways in front of the shops, out of the way of the flying bullets. The men were hiding in various locations. Most were wounded in one way or another from Sam's fire, but all were still dangerous. Quickly, he reloaded, looked at Caleb again, and waited for the boy to move.

But it appeared there was no life left in his body.

Sweat beaded over Sam's brow, and he wiped it away. If he left him there, the outlaws were likely to shoot at him again. Already the boy's blood was soaking into the dirt, leaving little hope of any life remaining.

And yet . . .

Holding his pistols poised, Sam rose slowly, shielding himself behind the one wall of the livery stable. Suddenly he opened fire, spraying his bullets for cover as he ran out into the street, grabbed Caleb's arm, and dragged him toward the saloon.

The gangsters fired back, their bullets whistling past his ears. One nicked the toe of his boot, but none hit its mark, for the sheriff and mayor finally started shooting, along with Jared Grady and Zane, making it impossible for the outlaws to get a good enough view of him to do him any real damage.

Sam got Caleb inside the door. Laying the boy out, he tore his shirt open. Only a small bullet hole showed on the front of his chest, but his back bore a gaping wound from which blood gushed. Shaking, Sam felt his pulse, realized there was none, and shook the boy, as if the very action could make him wake up.

"Damn it," he said, panic rising to his voice. "You can't die. You're not supposed to die!"

Some filament of control snapped inside him, and when he heard a crash behind him, he flung around, ready to murder the first person he saw. Through the open door, he saw one of the outlaws sneaking from barrel to barrel outside the store, inching his way toward the saloon. Again, he reloaded his six-shooters as fast as he could and readied the rifle strapped over his shoulder.

The man's gunfire preceded him, but Sam was well out of the way, and his return shot hit the outlaw between the eyes with the first bullet. Sam sucked in a breath as the man fell, his eyes still open, pinned on Sam as he died.

"Three more of you bastards," Sam said under his breath, as if the dead man could hear. "And I'm gonna get every last one of you."

He heard a horse whinny, and looked across to the walkway, where he could see feet beneath a gelding. Quickly, Sam aimed and fired, and hit the man in the ankle.

"Shit!" the outlaw screamed, then hobbled inside the door of the barbershop to escape more fire.

He heard the sheriff's laughter from his perch over the bank, and thought of telling the idiot to shut up. But it was too late.

Another bullet whizzed overhead, silencing him.

"He's dead! Oh God, Sam, he's dead!" the mayor screamed.

Another bullet whistled overhead, but the mayor escaped it.

There was no time for grief or thought. Only instincts had a place in this fight. And Sam gave in to his.

Shielding himself behind the saloon wall, he went to

the broken out window and cupped his hand over his mouth.

"That's two of ours for two of yours," Sam called out into the silence. "But there's more of us than there are of you. And I can pick off every last one of you myself."

For a moment no one answered. Finally, he heard a voice coming out of a shadow only yards away. "It's only McCosky and his girl we want," the outlaw shouted. "Nobody else has to get hurt. Tell us where they are, and this town'll never see us again."

A burning fury raged in Sam's stomach. Wiping the sweat out of his eyes, he pulled his extra pistols out of his boots and readied them for the fight. "They left town!" he called. "You've already searched every house in town; can't you figure that out?"

"Naw, we ain't searched every house," the voice said. "There's still some we ain't searched. And we ain't stoppin' till we've torn every standin' structure apart."

He heard the sound of the hoofbeats, and knew in his gut that something was about to break. Suddenly a riderless horse galloped into his view. Knowing that a good rider could crouch above the stirrup, hiding himself behind the horse's torso as he ran by, Sam shot at the horse. It rolled over exposing its rider. Opening fire again, Sam hit him.

"Any more tricks?" Sam shouted. "There's only two of you left."

For a while there was no answer, but Sam knew better than to feel secure. They were waiting, watching, listening, just as he was.

Half an hour went by as he stood at the window, his guns poised and every sense in his body alert to any movement.

He looked up and down the moonlit street and the

shadowed walkway, realizing that he could see only two horses still tethered. A third lay in the street, but the other two had disappeared.

And then he heard the sound of horses galloping behind the buildings. The outlaws must have taken them through the store and out the backdoor. By evil chance, they were headed in the direction of Hitch's ranch!

Taking the chance that he had been tricked, he ran out, guns still poised, and grabbed Duke from where he'd reined him in the remains of the livery stable. No one fired.

Quickly mounting, he spurred the horse and shot out down the main street of town, determined to stop them before they reached Hitch's ranch. Before they got to Jake Rivers. Before they found Silena.

From her dark place in Hitch's attic, Silena sat huddled beside the window, gun in her lap, listening for more gunshots. It had gotten quiet over half an hour ago, too quiet, and she covered her mouth now and tried to stop the tears flooding down her face. Where had those shots hit? Had someone died?

Her body trembled, and she pulled her knees up beneath her dress and tried to hug herself, and still hold on to the gun Sam had given her. Was he all right? Had she gotten him killed?

Jake moaned from the bed behind her, and she uttered a silent prayer that he'd make it through this so that Caldonia could do what was necessary tomorrow to save his life. She also prayed that his delirious shouts wouldn't get too loud, wouldn't give their hiding place away in the event that the outlaws got this far.

The sound of steps beneath her alerted her. Lifting the hatch of the attic, she saw Hitch coming up the stairs.

"Somebody's comin'," he cried. "I heard a gunshot over the ridge and horses headin' this way. Stay put, Silena, and don't make a sound."

Closing the hatch, she caught her breath and raised the rifle, but it wouldn't hold still, for her hands trembled too violently.

She heard the hammer of horses' hooves coming closer, and tears stung her eyes, blurring her vision. Maybe it was Sam, she thought. Maybe he had killed them all, and he was coming with the news.

But those flimsy hopes were dashed when she heard another exchange of gunfire, and she scooted back against the wall, crumpled down, and prayed with all her might.

Sam saw the outlaws the moment he topped the ridge, and then he heard the shots coming from Hitch's ranch. He wondered if Silena had sense enough to stay out of the way, if she was well hidden, if she was all right.

Digging his spurs into Duke's flanks, he shot forward and tore through the night. Gunfire broke out, and he prayed that Hitch could hold the bandits off until he reached them.

He saw the two horsemen flank the house. One of them grabbed hold of the roof, flung himself up, and began to crawl across it. Deciding to keep his own presence quiet, Sam rounded the perimeter of the ranch, came up from the back, and reached the roof himself. He saw the man's shadow, but his body was crouched on the downslope of the roof, and Sam wasn't able to aim at him.

Below him, he heard the gunfire as Hitch went after

the man still on horseback. It was a trick, he wanted to tell him, a distraction so that the other one could get inside the house, but all he could do was get there first.

In the moonlight, he slid along the roof on his belly, guns poised, as he watched the outlaw looking for a window to slip into. He held his breath and prayed the man would stay on the side of the house he'd chosen, for he knew the attic Silena and Jake were in opened on the other side.

The man found an open window. Quietly, he pulled down from the eaves and swung himself to the sill.

Quickly, Sam crawled to the next window and did the same. In seconds, he was inside the house. Holding his breath, he made his way as quietly as possible to the hallway. Checking it, he saw that the man was on his way to the other side of the house, having seen the attic stairs.

Outside, he heard a crash, and then Hitch screaming, "I been hit! Damn it!"

Another gunshot cracked, and Hitch shouted, "I got 'im!"

The outlaw found the stairs and started up them, each rung creaking with his weight.

Sam raised his gun. "Take one more step and I'll blow you all the way back to the hellhole you crawled out of," he said.

The man turned around, pistol in hand, and sent a bullet ricocheting off the floor at Sam's feet. Sam dodged it, but when he started to shoot, the man had leaped down from the ladder and disappeared into the shadows of the hall.

From her hiding place, Silena covered her ears and tried to stop trembling. She had heard Sam's voice outside the door, then the gunshots, and she knew it was just a matter of seconds before one of them reached her.

Her teeth chattered in fear, and she shivered and held herself tighter.

Below her, she heard a voice, one she did not recognize.

"All I want is to take Jake's body back to the Colonel," the outlaw said. "And I want to take the girl back alive. You can kill me, but the Colonel will send more. They'll keep comin' till he has what he wants."

Silena looked in the direction of the hatch, her face stricken with terror. Why did they want Jake dead? And even more pressing, what did they want with her?

"He can send them," Sam said. "But I'll keep killing them."

She heard footsteps, then the greater terror of silence, and waited, holding her breath. An eternity of quiet stretched around her. She trembled more and picked her rifle back up, held it toward the door, ready to destroy anyone who came through it.

And suddenly there was another, final gunshot that shattered her courage. She heard a thud on the floor just below the attic. Sucking in a deep, terrified sob, she pushed closer back against the corner, holding the rifle with all her might.

The hatch creaked open, and she cocked the rifle.

And just as she put her finger on the trigger Sam stepped into the room.

She only stared at him in shock, still holding the gun on him. He took a step closer.

"It's over, Silena," he whispered. "It's all right."

Sucking in a sob, she allowed him to take the rifle from her hands, and when he reached for her, she fell into his arms, weeping out all the fear and terror she had felt for the last few hours.

He held her close, allowing her tears to soak the front of his shirt, allowing her to cling to him the way no one had ever clung before.

"I thought . . . you were . . . dead."

"I'm not," he whispered, stroking her hair. "I'm not."

The stairs creaked, and Hitch appeared in the entrance, clutching his bloody shoulder and sweating beads the size of pearls. "Silena, you okay?"

Silena wiped her face. "Hitch! Were you shot?"

"I'm okay," he grunted. Sam let go of Silena and went to examine Hitch's arm.

"He's bad. I need to get him some help."

"I told you I'm okay," Hitch groaned again. "Caleb can take me to Miss Caldonia's when he gets here."

Sam stood still for a moment, recalling Caleb's body doubling over with the force of that outlaw's bullet, then tumbling to the ground. Somehow, he didn't have the strength to break that news to either of them now. "I don't think you ought to wait. Just let me take you."

"It's all right. I can still ride. You stay with her and her pa."

"No," Silena whispered. "I'll . . . I'll be all right, Sam. Take care of Hitch."

"I'm goin' alone," Hitch repeated.

"All right," Sam said. "If you're sure . . ."

Hitch nodded. Still pressing his fist against his wound, he started for the stairs. Before he went through it, he turned back, hesitating. "Uh, Sam . . . before Silena comes out, you'll want to move the body."

"Yeah," Sam cut in. "I will."

Hitch creaked down the stairs, leaving them alone. Silena looked up at Sam, her face bright with fear. "Do you . . . do you expect more of them to come?"

"There were five. We got them all, Silena."

"But . . . they said he would send more. Who is he, Sam? Who is the Colonel?"

"I don't know," he whispered, stroking her hair. "I don't know."

"Yes, you do!" A tremor rippled through her voice. "I heard your father mention him today. You know why they want my father, and you know why they want me. Tell me, Sam. Please tell me."

"I would if I could," he whispered, setting his hands on her shoulders. "I swear to God. But I don't know any more than you do."

She dropped her head to his chest, and sliding his

arms around her, he pulled her so close that he could feel her trembling right through to her core. She felt so small against him, so fragile, and that old protective instinct swelled inside him.

Not knowing the right thing to do, but following his instincts as he had done two other times that day, he leaned down and dropped a kiss on the corner of her mouth. She looked up at him, her wet, tear-reddened eyes so innocent, so pained. Something stirred deep inside him, and he kissed her again.

Slowly, he felt her trembling subside, and when she stood on tip toe and brought his lips back to hers, he felt a sweet melting of all the coldness he'd felt for the last few years.

His mouth opened at her urging, and their tongues moved together in a sweet ritual. Outside, he could hear Hitch beginning to ride away, and he knew they were alone, except for her father, unconscious on the bed.

The kiss became deeper, and her hands slowly slid up his arms, to his neck, to the heavy stubble on his face. She took off his hat, dropped it to the floor, and ran her fingers through his hair.

The kiss broke, and they looked at each other for a fragment of eternity. Her eyes conveyed new fear, but it was a fear of what wouldn't happen as much as of what would.

And then that fear changed to shame, and she pulled back.

"I'm sorry," she whispered.

With smoky, confused eyes, he studied her face. "For what?"

"For . . . for that. I was scared . . . I wasn't thinking."

"This isn't about thinking," he breathed. "It has nothing to do with thinking."

She stepped back and looked at her father, as if he

would wake up and reprimand her. "I know . . . but I can't. . . ."

He crossed the floor and set his hands on her waist, and looked down into her eyes. As she looked back he saw the clarity of her confusion, the blur of her convictions. The time would come for loving her in that way, he thought, but now was not it.

"You're tired," he whispered. "You need to rest."

She nodded, and started toward the stairs.

"I want you to lie down," he said. "But wait until I come back for you. I have to move the . . ." His voice trailed off before he could say the word "body," and Silena cringed and hugged herself.

She turned away as he went down the stairs, and heard him sliding the corpse across the floor. Trying not to dwell on it, she checked her father again and saw that he was breathing normally. Fatigue washed over her, the deepest, sickest fatigue she had ever felt in her life, but she struggled not to let it overtake her.

Sam came back up the stairs. "Come on now," he said quietly.

Wearily, she followed him down, unaware, in the darkness, of the bloodstains on the floor. Sam led her into Hitch's parents' bedroom. She stepped in and looked longingly toward the bed. "Sam, I can't sleep here. I can't leave Pa that long."

"You have to sleep," he said. "You won't do your father any good if you're sick yourself."

"Then I'll sleep up there with him," she said. "I can make a pallet on the floor, and lie there beside him. That way I can hear his breathing, and be there if he wakes up."

Sam studied her for a long moment, realizing that he wasn't going to convince her to climb onto that bed, no matter how tired she was. A woman who would suffer a personal assault, her father's near death, a battle within earshot, all in forty-eight hours, all the while keeping an unceasing vigil beside her father except for when she'd ridden to Omaha for help, never once stopping to eat or change her clothes, wouldn't be convinced to get a good night's sleep.

"All right," he said quietly. "I'll find some blankets."

She climbed the stairs back to the attic while he looked, and when he had what he needed, he took them to her and made her a bed on the floor. "Here," he whispered. "Lie down. Go to sleep."

She knelt on the blankets and looked up at him. "Where . . . where will you be?"

"Not far," he said. "Just call if you need me."

He saw the pain on her face before the tears pushed to her eyes again. "I'm . . . I'm scared, Sam."

Without thinking, he reached for her and pulled her into his arms. "Shhh. It's all right. I'll stay with you."

He urged her down, then lay down beside her, holding her in the circle of his arms.

For a moment she lay tense, and he knew she didn't trust him to lie there with only sleep in mind. But he made no move to do anything else.

She relaxed by degrees, and finally, she fell asleep wrapped in his arms. And as he held her his heart burned. For he didn't want it to end.

Word spread slowly that the outlaws were all dead and the town was safe once again. Margaret and Nell came out of the place where Caleb had hidden them and made their way through town to see what needed to be done.

A shudder rose in Margaret's heart at the damage. Two more buildings were burning, and a group of women stood in a line passing buckets of water, trying to put out the blaze. Smoke wafted across the air, and covering her mouth, Margaret coughed.

The saloon was packed full, but through the open door, she could see that few were there for alcohol. In the center of the melancholy crowd, Miss Caldonia worked patching wounds, treating burns, and digging out bullets.

Margaret followed her mother inside and looked around. Zane Barlow leaned against the bar, his hand bloody from a stray bullet. On one table lay the mayor, groaning as Miss Caldonia dressed his wound. And then she saw Hitch, soaked in sweat and leaning back against the wall with his eyes closed, clutching a wadded old shirt against his bloody shoulder.

"Hitch! Were you shot?"

Hitch opened his eyes a crack as she took the rag from his hand. Gladly, he surrendered it. "I'm next," he groaned. "She said I'd be next."

Margaret peeled the cloth away, making Hitch wince, and studied the hole where the bullet was lodged. Pulling him toward a table, she said, "Come over here, Hitch. Lie down. I'll get you some whiskey."

Obediently, for he had no energy to fight, he let her lead him to a table.

"Come on," she said quietly. "Let's take off this shirt."

Hitch squeezed his eyes shut and groaned again as she pulled the shirt off, trying not to hurt the congealed wound any more than necessary. Blood soaked his left side, and every muscle was tensed, poised to fight the pain.

"Pour some o' this on that wound, Margaret," Miss Caldonia called across the room. "I'll get that bullet out soon as I get finished with the mayor."

Margaret took the bottle of whiskey that Miss Caldonia referred to and poured some onto Hitch's wound. He bit his fist to muffle his moans, then sat up, furiously, and jerked the bottle out of Margaret's hand. "Hitch, you have to let me—"

Before she could protest, he had brought the bottle to his lips and was gulping it down. When he brought it back down, it was almost empty.

"Now," he said, handing it back to her. "I'm ready for you to try that again."

Margaret took it and poured again. This time, he managed to hold still.

"You ready to get that bullet out, Hitch?" Miss Caldonia asked boisterously from across the room.

Hitch didn't bother to open his eyes. "Couple more bottles o' that, Miss Cal, and you can dig my liver out for all I care."

Caldonia laughed and started toward him.

It didn't take long for Miss Caldonia to clean Hitch's wound and bandage it properly, but by the time she'd finished, he was close to drunkenness.

Margaret helped him off the table and pulled his arm around her shoulders. She had helped him make his way to the door when, out on the street, they heard a scream. Looking out, Margaret saw her mother fall to her knees in the dirt.

"No!" the woman wailed at the top of her lungs. "Nooo!"

Hitch caught a post in front of the saloon. "What the hell?"

Margaret let him go and rushed to her mother's side. "Ma, what is it? What's wrong?"

"Caleb!" The word came out as an agonized shriek, and Margaret looked around for her brother.

"He ain't here, Ma. He must be helpin' with one o' the fires."

Nell shook her head violently. "My baby's dead! They killed him!"

"What!" Margaret let go of her mother and stumbled back. "That's a lie, Mama. Caleb's fine. He's . . . he's probably just—"

"He's *dead!*" Nell screamed, getting to her feet. "My baby is dead!"

"No!" Margaret backed away, her eyes burning with fury. "They're lyin', whoever told you that. It ain't true."

She backed into Hitch, who suddenly seemed more sober than he had moments before. Setting his hand on her shoulder, he faced her mother, fear of his own tightening the lines of his young face. "Who told you Caleb was dead?"

"Zane and Murdock!" she cried. "They said his body's behind the sheriff's office with the others, but I can't . . . I can't . . ."

Slowly, Hitch slid down the post until he sat on the porch of the saloon. His breathing came harder, and he felt his heartbeat running away, threatening to stampede him.

"It ain't true, Hitch," Margaret said, shaking her head. "Please . . . it ain't true."

"Oh, my God." Hitch took her trembling hand and pulled her down beside him. Closing her into the circle of the arm that wasn't in a sling, he buried his face in her hair. "Oh God, no."

Margaret's refusal to believe broke down slowly as she felt the grief overtaking Hitch, but she struggled to hold that belief at bay. Somehow, believing seemed to be a huge betrayal of her brother, as if her acceptance that he was dead would make it so. The fact that Hitch believed her mother's hysterical wails made it seem even more true, however, so she pulled away from him, refusing to share in his grief, and turned back to her mother.

"It's a lie, Ma! You have to believe me. Caleb ain't dead!"

Hitch's voice was broken when he whispered, "Margaret."

She flung herself around as tears stung her eyes. "I'll prove it!"

She started to run, and Hitch pulled himself up and shouted, "Margaret! Where are you going?"

"I'll show you!" she screamed as she raced toward the sheriff's office. "He can't be dead! He's my brother!"

Abandoning the support of the post, Hitch stumbled after her. "Margaret, don't!"

But she kept running until she reached the sheriff's office, and she burst in. Hitch followed her in, wavering with dizziness from too much alcohol and loss of blood. "Margaret!"

Margaret tore through the office to the backdoor, which lay open on its hinges. A cool, foreboding wind swept into the room, but she didn't slow her step.

"Margaret, wait!"

Hitch was almost behind her when she tripped out the door and saw the bodies stretched out in a line behind the building.

"See?" Margaret asked, her voice shaking. "He ain't here."

Hitch leaned against the wall and wiped the sweat from his brow as he tried to focus on the vacant faces of the men on the ground. As if she'd proven her point, Margaret turned to go back inside.

That was when he saw the boy turned on his side, a bloody circle coating his back. Somehow, he knew it was Caleb.

Feeling a wave of vicious nausea climbing inside him, he stumbled toward his friend's body. "Aw, noooo."

Margaret froze at the door, unable to look where Hitch stood.

"Margaret . . ."

Slowly, she turned, and watched as Hitch dropped to his knees and gently turned the body over.

A desperate, miserable, high-pitched sob tore from Margaret's throat, and she covered her face with both hands and tottered inside.

Hitch threw up in the dirt, then swatted at his stinging eyes as he staggered in. He found Margaret crouched on the floor in a little ball, rocking and sobbing from the deepest part of her soul.

Dropping down beside her, he pulled her against him. She dug her face into his shoulder, and as he held her he wept with her.

After a while he pulled Margaret's face up to his, wiped her tears, and whispered, "Come on. I'll take you home."

He wavered to his horse, the haze of drunkenness and blood loss still making him unsteady. He slung his foot over and reached down for Margaret's hand. She pulled up behind him, a thigh on either side of him, and laid her wet face against his back.

As they rode home neither uttered a word. For the agony reached too deep in both of them.

When they reached her front door, Margaret slid her arms tighter around Hitch's waist. "Don't leave me, Hitch," she whispered through shaky lips, red and swollen from the fierceness of her crying. "Please don't leave me here alone."

"I won't," he whispered. "I'll stay here with you for a while."

Taking her inside, he lay on the bed beside her, holding her in his arms as she wept. When sweet merciful sleep cast its spell over them, they didn't let each other go. When they woke hours later, they were still in each other's arms.

JOIN THE TIMELESS ROMANCE READER SERVICE AND GET FOUR OF TODAY'S MOST EXCITING HISTORICAL ROMANCES FREE, WITHOUT OBLIGATION!

Imagine getting today's very best historical romances sent directly to your home – at a total savings of at least $2.00 a month. Now you can be among the first to be swept away by the latest from Candace Camp, Constance O'Banyon, Patricia Hagan, Parris Afton Bonds or Susan Wiggs. You get all that – and that's just the beginning.

PREVIEW AT HOME WITHOUT OBLIGATION AND SAVE.

Each month, you'll receive four new romances to preview without obligation for 10 days. You'll pay the low subscriber price of just $4.00 per title – a total savings of at least $2.00 a month!

Postage and handling is absolutely free and there is no minimum number of books you must buy. You may cancel your subscription at any time with no obligation.

* * *

Sam held Silena while she slept, wishing there was some way to break through her barriers and make her acknowledge the attraction he knew she felt for him. It had been in her eyes and her smile that first day he met her. He had felt her shiver of awareness as he'd held her in his saddle, had recognized the awe she'd felt for the hero she'd believed him to be.

And that kiss in the cave . . . when she'd stood on her toes and curled into him. She had been as mesmerized with desire as he, no matter what she wanted him to think. Then last night, when she had melted, then apologized for feeling what he had felt. But a lot had happened in the last day. People were dead. Others were dying. And the scars left behind might never be healed.

He closed his eyes, but all he saw was Caleb's body being shaken by bullets, then tumbling from the roof. Once again, he saw the boy's blood gushing the life right out of him, and panic rose inside him again.

He wondered if he should have told Silena, but decided it was better that he'd waited. She wasn't ready to face it. And he wasn't ready to add more pain to her already wounded heart.

She needed him, he thought, and somehow that need filled a need in his own soul. He hadn't felt this connected to anyone since his sister, Stella, died. He hadn't been able to save Stella, but by God, he was going to save Silena. He'd lost both the women in his life who'd ever meant anything to him, the ones he'd been supposed to protect.

Silena was his final chance, he thought, and he wouldn't let her down. Not even if it meant giving his own life.

13

It was some time before dawn when Silena woke and found herself entangled in Sam Hawkins's arms. At first she just lay there, basking in the warmth, letting her eyes roam over his stubbled face, his tousled hair, his strong chest. . . .

Then shame swept over her. She had fallen asleep in his arms and slept with him all night. Where was Hitch? Had he come home and found her this way? Close on the shame followed fear. Yesterday, Sam had saved her life and the life of her father, but what would come today?

Quickly, she jumped from the nest of blankets they slept on and tried to straighten her rumpled clothes. She needed the outhouse, she thought, and a mirror before Sam woke. It had been two days since she'd changed her clothes, two days since she'd had the chance to consider how she looked.

Walking quietly so as not to wake Sam, she left the attic and climbed down the steps into the hall. For the first time she saw the blood spot on the floor, where the outlaw had been shot. A long path of blood led to one of the other rooms, where Sam had dragged him to protect her from the sight.

Now the thought of the body drew her. It was morbid, she realized, but something about the horror of it forced her to the door. Avoiding the blood spot, she went slowly to the door and peered in.

The man lay on his stomach, facedown, and the smell of blood and death wafted over the room, choking her. Covering her mouth, she backed out. Her foot slipped on the half-congealed puddle, and she fell forward. When she stood up, her skirt and one hand were smeared in blood.

Muffling a sob with her clean hand, she climbed the stairs back to the attic, unable to go on with her mission. Stepping over Sam and the blankets, she went to her father. The smell of death stagnated in the air around him, along with a stench of rotting flesh on a man who still lived.

He was still breathing, and she felt his head and saw that the fever still raged.

Feeling a sudden urgency that time was running out, she cried, "Sam!"

Sam was up in a second. "What happened?"

"We need to get some ice for Pa's fever, or get him to Miss Caldonia's," she said. "His fever's higher, and those red lines up his leg are worse."

Bare from his waist up, but carrying his pistol in one hand, Sam stepped forward and examined the leg. "Honey, that leg's going to have to come off. It looks bad."

"Let's take him now, Sam."

He nodded and looked down at her, saw how she was shaking, how frazzled she appeared, and when he lifted her hand, he saw the smeared blood.

"What's this?" he asked.

"I fell," she said. "In that . . . that man's blood."

She started to turn away, but he turned her face back up to his. "Are you all right?"

She nodded quickly and wiped her hand on a clean spot on her skirt. "We have to get him to town."

"But are *you* all right?"

"I've never seen a dead man so close up before," she cried. "I've never slipped in his blood, and—"

"Neither have I," he said.

She looked at him then, and remembered how she had caught him trying to escape yesterday. Was there a man alive who had honor anymore? Was there a man alive who told the truth? Did every woman in the world walk around in a daze, trying desperately to separate truth from all the lies the men concocted—lies that caused murders and rapes and devastation? She honestly didn't know.

Pulling back, she asked, "Can you carry him?"

Sam nodded. "Did Hitch leave a wagon?"

"Yes," she said. "I think he only took his horse."

"Good. I'll go hitch the horses, and I'll be back in a few minutes."

He started down the stairs, but turned back before leaving. "Silena?"

She looked up at him, unable to meet his eyes completely. "Don't go out there until I get back, okay? You're too pretty to be all smeared with blood."

"I . . . I just want to wash some of it off. And I need to change Pa's clothes before we take him out."

"I'll bring you a pail of water and some of Hitch's clothes," he said. "Just stay put. No need to face ghosts if you don't have to."

Trying to hide her relief, Silena nodded and went back to working on her father.

* * *

There was a different mood in the town when Sam and Silena rode in with Jake lying in the back of the wagon. The smell of the burned livery stable and the post office still wafted over the air, and all around windows were broken, walls were burned, and the look of devastation was everywhere.

Feeling as if she rode through the worst nightmare of her life, Silena looked around her at the faces of the people who'd lost loved ones when the outlaws had terrorized the town before the final shoot-out. She didn't yet know for sure who had died and who hadn't, but from the faces, she could see that lives had been lost, and the fear of the night had marked the rest.

As they rode through, their wheels creaking on the dirt road, breaking the silence that death and destruction had left in its wake, Silena noted the way that some of the men tipped their hats to Sam, and how the women smiled up at him. A few were bold enough to call out words of thanks for his part in saving the town. But a strange sense of alienation washed over Silena, for none spoke to her. Instead, they seemed to regard her with icy distaste, before turning their eyes to Sam.

They reached Miss Caldonia's and Sam went in to get help carrying Jake inside. Silena climbed into the back of the wagon and checked her father's fever.

Miss Caldonia rushed out behind the men to supervise. When she'd directed them to the proper room in the house, she turned back to Silena. "What would we have done without Sam? He saved the town, you know. There'd be a lot more people dead if it wasn't for him. He's so brave."

Silena let her pensive eyes drift to the door, and the memory of her catching him trying to leave yesterday flitted through her mind. He *had* saved the town, she was forced to admit, and he had saved her. But she couldn't forget that he would rather have run as fast and as far as he could. "Yeah," she whispered. "He's brave, all right."

"The town is talking about making him the new sheriff," Caldonia said. "You know, Sheriff Hollister didn't make it."

"What?" Silena jerked a look back at the woman. "The sheriff is dead?"

"Got shot last night," she said. "And this ain't exactly a good time to be without the law. We got to find a new one."

Silena felt her face going pale. "But Sam? He doesn't even live here. He just came to help this once. Besides, he isn't qualified to be sheriff."

"And Hollister was? Let's face it, Silena. He was a barber. Sam has a lot more experience with outlaws and gunfights."

Silena's eyes glazed over again as she remembered how Willy had said just yesterday that it was all publicity, that none of what people read about them was true. Did Sam really have more experience than Matt Hollister? She doubted it.

Silently following Miss Caldonia in, and fighting the urge to ask who else had been killed, Silena found the room where they had taken her father.

One of the men who had carried him in was reaching across the bed they had laid him on to shake Sam's hand. "There's going to be a town meeting at sundown," he said. "Sam, we'd like for you to be there, if you can."

Sam looked from the man to Silena and noted the solemnity on her face. She looked down at the floor.

"All right. I'll be there," he said.

"So will I," Silena added.

The man gave her a cool look, then shrugged. "If you want to, guess there's no harm."

She frowned and tried again. "No harm? What do you mean? Is it just for men?"

"Don't think so," the man said, evasively. "Sundown in the saloon. Okay, Sam?"

"Yeah," Sam said.

He looked at Silena when the man had left. "We'll go together," he said.

Silena was still staring at the door. "Something isn't right here," she said. "Something funny's going on."

"Well, there's no time to worry about it now. Miss Caldonia wants to take your pa's leg. I'm going to help her."

"Does she know how? Shouldn't we wait for a real doctor?"

"There may not be time," he said.

She shuddered and looked up at him, her eyes haunted and tired and full of pain. "He'll hate us for this."

"Probably," Sam said. "But once he hears the choices we had—letting him die or saving his life—he'll come around."

"I hope so," she whispered.

But she wasn't at all sure.

They wouldn't let Silena stay in Miss Caldonia's house while they were operating on Jake, and she didn't feel ready to go back to her own home just yet. Her stomach was too weak, her emotions too frayed.

Wearily, she wandered through town, assessing the damage. The people she passed either ignored her outright or made deliberate, if subtle, shows of contempt. Ambling by the gutted post office, she stepped over the remains of the charred wall.

"Miss Lucy?" she said to the woman who, when Silena was younger, had never failed to offer her a lemon drop from the jar she kept on her counter. "Are you all right?"

The woman turned around, her eyes red and her face as pasty gray as death. "No, I'm not all right," she said. "Haven't you heard? I lost my Jonas yesterday because of your pa's enemies."

Silena sucked in a gasp. Tears filled her eyes as she whispered, "Jonas is dead?"

"Died tryin' to keep 'em out of our house," she said bitterly. "But he didn't manage to do it."

"I'm . . . I'm so sorry."

"Sorry won't bring him back," the woman said, kicking a clump of ashes, then lifting her apron to wipe her eyes. "And it won't keep more outlaws from ridin' through. Oh, Lord, what kind of hell has your father lured to our town?"

Silena stood motionless, unable to answer, for she didn't have a clue.

"We'll be buryin' folks for days," Miss Lucy went on. "Sheriff Hollister, Caleb Plumer—"

"*What?*" Silena stumbled forward. "Caleb's not dead! I just saw him yesterday!"

"And I saw my Jonas yesterday, too."

"But . . . but Caleb? It couldn't be!"

"Is though," the woman said wearily. "That boy died during the worst of the fight. I'm surprised Sam Hawkins didn't tell you. Folks said he almost got killed hisself tryin' to save him."

A wave of dizziness crashed over her, and she shook her head. "He didn't tell me."

Tears burned her eyes, and through trembling lips, she whispered, "I have to go to Margaret. I'm sorry about Jonas, Miss Lucy. So, so sorry."

She stepped over the debris and out into the cool

sunshine, and before she realized what was happening, she was running with tears burning down her face.

Caleb couldn't be dead. It was a lie. A cruel, malicious joke. She would reach his and Margaret's house, and he'd come running out, teasing her in his traveling-preacher voice, and she would laugh. . . .

But the house was still when she reached it. Breathless, she slowed and stared at it. Something in the way the clouds hid the sun, something in the way the wind stopped blowing, something in her heart told her that Caleb wouldn't be there.

She knocked on the door, and Margaret opened it, revealing darkness inside. Her eyes were raw and swollen, and her hair hung, unbrushed, over her shoulders.

"Margaret . . . I just heard."

Margaret fell weeping into her arms before Silena had gotten the words out, and Silena knew it was true. The horror that had invaded their lives had killed Caleb.

Silena stayed with Margaret and Nell all afternoon, helping them clean the house and prepare for the agonizing task of burying their brother and son. But the sick pain that settled over her heart at the loss didn't distract from her fears over her father's surgery.

He could die this very afternoon as Miss Caldonia—a woman who'd never had formal medical training and had likely never amputated a limb in her life—removed his leg. He had already lost too much blood, and Silena feared he had no more to lose.

She couldn't escape the thought that one mistake could cost Jake his life. If only they could have waited for a real surgeon to come from Omaha, she thought, then his chances would have been so much greater. But taking a leg was easy, Caldonia had promised. Just took a little time to do it right. It was the aftermath they should worry about. Worse than infection or gangrene, they needed to fear Jake's wrath when he woke to find he had only one leg.

It was midafternoon when Sam showed up at Margaret's. Silena ran outside to meet him.

"How is he, Sam? Did he make it?"

The anxious look in her eyes broke his heart, and Sam got off his horse and nodded. "He made it. Caldonia thinks it went even better than she expected."

Silena's relief showed in the depth of her sigh. "Can I see him?"

"He's out for a while," he said, "but I'll take you."

His face turned solemn, and he nodded toward the house. "Is this Caleb's house?"

Silena nodded and began to chafe her arms. "Yes. Why didn't you tell me, Sam?"

He looked down at the toe of his boot, kicked at the dirt. "I reckon I just didn't want to add anything to what you were already going through."

She felt her tears emerging again, and stared down at her own feet. "He was a good friend. Margaret's real torn up—"

"Can I see her?" he asked. "I . . . I'd like to tell her how he died. How brave he was. It's small comfort, but maybe it would make her proud."

"Yes, I think it would," she whispered.

And taking his hand, Silena led him inside.

Sam convinced Silena to ride to the meeting with him that night, but when they left Margaret's, she realized he had only brought Duke. Immediately, she became aware that she was expected to ride in his saddle with him. The memory of that first time, an eternity ago, flitted through her mind as he lifted her onto the saddle. And when he pulled himself up behind her, she remembered the previous night in his arms, remembered the safety and sanctity of that love he exuded. But it wasn't love, she told herself. It was just another lie. Just one more mystery.

But as if to dispel those thoughts, he put his arms around her, taking the reins with one hand. The other he laid over hers on the saddle horn.

"You look pretty," he whispered as the horse started away from Margaret's house. "I didn't want to embarrass you in front of Hitch and Margaret—especially with Hitch leering at me like he was— but you really do look pretty."

She felt herself blushing and looked at him over her shoulder. "How could I? I haven't been home yet . . . couldn't make myself . . ."

"I'll go with you tomorrow," he said, squeezing her hand. "It'll be tough the first time."

"Yeah." She swallowed and looked down at his hand over hers. His thumb idly stroked the side of her finger.

"But at least your pa will be fine."

"Hope so."

For a while they rode quietly. Occasionally, she looked back at him, her face full of pain and fear and heartache, and he wished he could wipe it all away. He remembered the happy girl he had first met, the one who played with the Indian children and made Running Horse laugh, and he wondered if the events of the past few days had chased that lightheartedness away forever. He decided he'd make it his business to find out.

They were quiet the rest of the way into town. The meeting had already begun, and the saloon was full of townspeople. Sam dismounted and looked up at Silena, putting his hands on her waist. Her eyes were on the door, apprehensive, as she set her hands on his shoulder and allowed him to lift her down.

"Are you all right?" he asked softly.

"I don't know," she said. "I think some of them blame Pa for what happened. I'm not even sure they're wrong." She watched, worried, as he tied the horse, and then, as if she needed the support that he could offer her, she took his arm and started inside.

It seemed as though a hush fell over the room the moment they appeared in the doorway, and one by one the eyes drifted to Sam. After a moment someone started to clap. The applause spread slowly, from one person to the next, until it erupted all over the room.

Confused, he looked down at Silena and saw that she was as baffled as he. Finally, for lack of anything better to do, he tipped his hat and started into the room.

"We've been waitin' fer ya, Sam," Murdock called across the applause. He seemed to have taken the helm of the meeting, since the saloon owner was naturally third in command after the mayor and the sheriff. "We all owe you a debt of thanks for savin' us last night."

Something about the adoration in the faces of the crowd, the celebration of his talent as being more than something people paid to see, something that was worthwhile, filled some void Sam hadn't known he had. He felt Silena letting go of his arm, and suddenly he was whisked forward, a hundred hands patting his back, a hundred smiles being flashed his way.

"As you know, we're a town without a sheriff," Murdock continued over the noise. "And Sam, we'd like to extend the invitation fer you to stay here and wear the badge."

Sam's grin slowly faded, and he looked around the

room. He saw that Silena had been shoved to the back. She stood against the wall, her face drawn and pale, watching him with sober interest.

"Well . . . you know that I don't live here, never planned to when I came," he began. "Truth is, I only came to help out, and now I'll have to be going back. The Wild West show needs me—"

"That's a show, Sam," someone shouted. "This is real life. We need you, too."

Sam shook his head and put his Stetson back on his head. "Surely there's someone here who can take over. Someone capable—"

"Ain't nobody capable as you," Zane Barlow said, sloshing his beer on the warped floor. "And we need powerful protectin'. Them outlaws come from somewhars, and once it gets out that they didn't get what they was after, there'll be more of 'em."

"They're after Jake Rivers, that's what they're after," a woman shouted. "I say next time they come, we just hand 'im over."

Half the townspeople raised their voices in agreement, and Sam sought Silena's eyes across the room. Her expression was one of disbelief, and slowly, she started fighting her way toward the front of the room.

"You can't do that," Sam said.

"The hell we cain't," one of the men shouted. "If they want Rivers and his girl, I say we give 'em to 'em. Ain't no sense in us losing one more life to save them."

"But that ain't Christian," Parson Evers said, popping up. "We cain't just throw them to them. I say we just ask 'em to leave town. That way the outlaws won't have no reason to come back here."

The roar of the crowd grew louder as half of the town shouted their approval of running the Riverses out of town, while the other half wanted to sacrifice them when the gang rode back through.

Sam raised a hand to hush the room. "Wait a minute!" he cried, feeling his own anger burning hot in that place in his heart where he guarded his feelings about Silena. "Hold it!"

The noise died down, and Sam took off his hat, checked the cleft in the top, and swept his angry eyes over the room. "There's no need for handing Jake and Silena over to anybody," he said. "And there's no reason to run them out of town. They're good people, from what I can tell, and they've made a real contribution to this town. The fact is, it'll probably be a while before any outlaws try to come back."

Having reached the front of the room, Silena turned around to face the crowd, her lips trembling as she tried to speak. "My father didn't ask for any of this, and neither did I. Either one of us would have risked our lives for any of you! How dare you talk about running us out of town or throwing us to those snakes?"

"People died because of your pa," someone shouted. "We don't want any more dead."

"My father lost his leg today!" Silena shouted. "He was shot twice, and he almost died. He's no different from any of you who got in the way of those outlaws. I don't even know what they want with him—"

"I'll bet *he* knows!" Winona Clement said. "But he's so busy telling those outlandish stories of his, that he don't have time for telling the real ones. Like what kind of past he must have had to have to go by an alias!"

Sam picked up a chair and slammed it down hard on the floor to stop the noise. "None of that matters!" he said, his thunderous voice echoing over the room. "All that matters is that they're citizens of this town, just like all of you, and they have a right to be here. And you don't have to worry about the outlaws coming back. As long as they know I'm here, they'll think twice."

Silena shot him a disbelieving look, but he went on, riding the tide of his anger.

"I'll accept your offer to be your temporary sheriff, just through the winter until my show needs me back, on the condition that you let Jake and Silena stay."

"But they'll draw 'em back, Sam! They'll be like lambs to a coyote."

"How dare you!" Silena cried.

Sam touched her shoulder, applying a gentle pressure to shut her up. "I said I'll be here to protect you," he said. "But only if you let Silena and Jake stay. This is their town, too."

"What's left of it," someone said.

He looked down at Silena, saw the tears raging down her crimson face as she stood facing the people she had loved and trusted all her life. The people who had turned on her.

She started to speak again, but suddenly closing her mouth, she turned and fled from the building.

Sam stood still for a moment, not sure whether to follow her, then he started for the door.

Murdock stopped him. "We got to swear you in," he said. "We got to give you a badge."

Sam looked down and saw the badge in the man's hand. He snatched it away and held up his right hand. "I swear to be the sheriff in Hayton, Nebraska," he said. "Now, if you'll excuse me . . ."

"But that ain't proper procedure," Murdock shouted.

"That's *my* procedure. Take it or leave it," Sam said. Before the protest could erupt from the crowd, he was out the door after Silena.

14

Silena ran as far and as fast as she could, not knowing where she would go. She ran from the saloon, where the townspeople who had been like family to her had just debated whether to banish her or allow her rape and death. She ran from the store, where her father had raised and loved her amid secrets and falsehoods.

And she ran from Sam, who was now embraced as the town hero . . . a man who would have fled town if she hadn't forced him back at gunpoint yesterday.

She sobbed with misery as she ran, but her legs gave out before the misery did. Reaching the small schoolhouse perched on the edge of town, the schoolhouse where she had learned to believe everything the people she loved told her, she collapsed against the wall.

"Silena!" Sam called.

With a monumental effort, she pushed herself away from the wall, tried to run again. Overtaking her, he caught her arm.

"Silena, stop! Listen to me!"

"I don't want to listen to you!" she cried, turning around and jerking her arm away. "You're the big hero now, aren't you? You saved the town. They think you're their savior! But I know better!"

"I *did* save the town," he shouted back at her. "They don't have a sheriff, and they need one. Right now I really am the best man for the job!"

"You don't even live here!" she shouted. "And yesterday when I caught you trying to leave town and escape all this, you didn't care then what the town needed!"

"I did care, Silena," he said. "I do still care."

"I held you at gunpoint!" she reminded him. "I forced you to go back."

"You didn't even know how to use that gun. I could have left anytime I wanted to."

"I would have blown you away," she cried. "And you knew it."

"I didn't know any such thing," he said. "Besides, I *did* stay and I did fight. When they shot at me, I didn't once cower away. And they're dead now, aren't they, Silena? They're gone."

"For now," she said. "But so are Caleb and Sheriff Hollister and Miss Lucy's Jonas." Fiercely, she wiped her tears away, but more trickled down in their place. Her nose ran with the force of her sobs, and she wiped at it as well. "But they'll be back, because for some reason that God only knows, they want me and my father."

"I won't let them get you," he said. "I took the job as sheriff. I'm staying for a while."

"But what about us?" she asked. "Are they going to lynch us? Throw us out to the wolves?" The horror of what the town had debated sent a chill through her, and she turned away from him and stared back through the darkness to the saloon.

"No. I won't let them."

Silena laughed mirthlessly. He was a fraud, this man, yet he was the only one who was willing or able to save her in a town full of people she had loved all her life.

"You don't understand," she said. "I've lived here all my life. These people are like my family. They've taken care of me, they've taught me, they've preached to me. They've been there to help when I was sick, and I've been there when they were. Most of those men spend all their free time sitting in pa's store, hanging on every word of his stories. And when a barn burned or a family member died, Pa and I were always there, ready to help rebuild."

Her voice broke, and she caught her breath, tried to go on. "And tonight I sit there and listen to them offering me and Pa up as a sacrifice. Hating us because we're the targets of these outlaws. How could they hate us, Sam? How could they consider turning us out? How could they feel so little?"

"They're scared," he said. "The town has been practically destroyed. They can't stand the thought of another episode like last night."

"Neither can I!" she cried. "I'm terrified that something will happen again. That next time you won't be here, and they'll get to me and Pa . . . that he won't make it . . . that I will—"

She hugged herself and crumpled up, but before she reached the ground her wrapped his arms around her. Then he was holding her, his big arms warm and secure and caring. She gripped his shirt with a fist and buried her face in his chest, and for a small eternity he stood there letting her cry.

It was something new. That feeling of being allowed to cry out all those tears, not being told to stop, and actually feeling another human being hold her while she did.

The feeling was foreign, but it filled voids she hadn't known were there, soothing wounds that had festered for so long she had learned to ignore them.

And yet something about that feeling frightened her. For it meant trusting . . . and trust was an emotion that was disintegrating around her. The walls of her world had collapsed, and one by one the structures of her soul were crumbling as well. What would she find when it all came down? When she had to look around and learn that she wasn't who she thought she was, that her life was a lie, that her father was someone with a name she'd never heard before two days ago, that nothing she had believed was true?

Would she still be leaning on Sam, who himself was a fraud? Would she be left in love with a showman pretending to be a hero?

Closing her eyes, she released herself from his arms and stepped back.

"Silena, come here."

She shook her head as he tried to pull her back against him, but she didn't fight him. Not yet.

"I don't want you to hold me, Sam. I don't want to feel that way about you."

"What way?" he asked, holding her anyway.

She forced herself to step back again. "Any way. I don't . . . I can't fall in love with you."

"*Are* you falling in love with me?"

"No!" She took three steps back, putting ample distance between them. "You're just as much a lie as everything else in my life, Sam. I don't need any more lies."

The words made him bristle, and he dropped his hands to his sides. "I know a lot of my life has been a lie, Silena, but I didn't lie about my talent with a gun. And I didn't lie about wanting to help you."

"You lied to the town," she said. "You let them think you were a capable leader who was qualified to be sheriff."

"I'm more qualified than anybody else here!" he argued. "And what's so wrong with them asking me to stay? What in blazes makes you think I can only run a show and perform for crowds?"

"Because that's who you really are!" she said. "I don't know why anyone would pretend to be something they're not, when they already know what they are. It's the ones who *don't* know who have to pretend—"

Her voice broke again. He reached for her, but she recoiled. "I have to go to Pa," she said. "I have to go to him . . . in case he wakes up and needs me."

He reached for her again, but she slipped out of his grip, and before he could stop her, she was running back up the street toward Miss Caldonia's house.

An hour later Sam watched from the schoolhouse steps as the town meeting broke up and the people dispersed. They seemed calmer now, though none were smiling, and he wondered how long it would take them to feel safe again.

In a way, he guessed, that depended on him. He was their sheriff, it seemed. Automatically, that made him a part of this town.

He watched from his solitude in the darkness as wagons creaked away and horses trotted side by side, and a deep longing grew up inside him to be a part of that. It was real life, just as someone at the meeting had said.

Not like show life, where everyone was temporary and nothing was nailed down.

His eyes strayed up the street to the lantern that Miss Caldonia always kept burning outside her house. Silena was in there, her heart broken, her spirit cracked, her trust crushed. He wished more than anything he could go in there and hold her all night, make her fears go away, love her until she stopped doubting her own worth.

He had seen a woman's spirit go before. Stella's had gone before her health, and though he had tried to help her find it again, she had died before he'd found the wisdom to save her.

But Silena was a second chance, he thought. No, she was a third chance. A fourth chance. For the truth was that he hadn't been able to save anyone he'd ever loved. But he would not fail this time. There was too much at stake.

He waited until the last wagon rolled away, until only the ones owned by patrons of the saloon were still parked on the drive. Then he got up off the step, straightened his hat, and started walking down the long, lonely street, wondering where he would stay tonight. It wasn't right, his going back to Hitch's place without Silena, especially when Hitch disliked him the way he did. And he didn't really know anyone else in town. He could go to Caldonia's and wait there with Silena all night, but he knew she needed to be alone.

He looked down at the badge he still held in his hand as he walked, tossed it in the air, caught it. It was his key into this town, he thought. It was his permission to lay his head here.

He saw the sheriff's office, sitting dark and empty. Its windows were broken out and its facade riddled with bullet holes, but he suspected it had a place to lie down, a stove to keep warm by, a little shelter from the wind.

Quietly, he stepped inside.

It was barren, and dirty, and dark, he thought, looking around. But it was something.

Kicking through the shattered glass at his feet, he walked into the back room, saw the makeshift jail that had probably rarely been used, except by drunks who got in fights in the saloon. Across from it was a cot.

He sat down on it, pulled off his boots, and leaving his hat on his head, lay down, guns still holstered to his sides. Pulling the hat over his eyes, he tried to sleep.

Loneliness invaded his heart like the darkness in the room, and like an old friend, he recognized it and tucked it inside him. It was something he'd grown to know, expect, and even feel comfortable with. But it was something that was getting harder and harder to settle for.

As thoughts of Silena in his arms relaxed and warmed him, he drifted into a light sleep and didn't wake until morning.

Jake Rivers lay on Miss Caldonia's bed, breathing in a normal rhythm, though he hadn't opened his eyes once since Silena had begun keeping vigil beside him. It was the morphine, Caldonia told her. She had kept him full of it since taking the leg, and it had caused him to sleep most of the time.

Silena felt the heaviness of involuntary sleep overpowering her, and her head began to fall to the side as she sat in the big, uncomfortable chair, the only one in the small room.

Jake moaned.

Quickly, she jumped up and went to his side. She touched his face, felt that his forehead was cool. His fever had broken. The amputation had served its purpose.

Slowly, he opened his eyes, tried to focus.

"Silena?" he whispered.

She caught her breath and smiled down at him. "Yes, Pa?"

He reached up a trembling hand and touched her face. "I . . . I'm sorry. So sorry."

"For what?" she whispered. "What are you sorry for?"

"For letting them find you . . ."

His eyes closed again, and she shook his shoulders. "Pa, wake up. What do you mean, letting them find me? Who is looking for me, Pa? Why do they want me?"

"The kidnappin'," he whispered on a frail wisp of breath. "When you were born."

"Kidnapping?" New tears sprang to her eyes, and a deep panic rose in her chest.

"Pa, what do you mean? Who was kidnapped? Me?"

"Yes, girl." His breathing was wheezy and ragged. "Now that he knows where we are, he'll stop at nothin' . . ."

His voice faded out, and his eyes closed again.

Fear quaked her heart, and confusion played havoc in her mind. "No!" she shouted, shaking him again.

There was no answer . . . only a deep, rhythmic, wet breathing.

"Pa! Wake up! Tell me—"

"What's goin' on in here?" Caldonia rushed into the room and bent over Jake, taking his pulse. Then she looked up at Silena and saw that she was the one who needed attention.

"What is it, child?"

"He has to wake up!" she cried, wiping the tears from her face. "Damn it, you wake him up!"

"He needs to rest," Caldonia said.

"But he told me something . . . he needs to tell me the rest . . . it didn't make any sense."

"It's the morphine," she said. "He's liable to say a lot of things. Don't mean they're true. If they don't make sense, don't pay 'em no mind."

"But I have to know . . . I have to wake him up."

"He'll wake up again later," she said, her voice quiet. "Just let him sleep, Silena. He needs his rest. And so do you. I'll stay with him for a while. You take my bed."

"No." Silena shook her head adamantly. "I won't. I'm staying here. If he wakes up again—"

"He might say somethin' else that don't make sense. I'm tellin' you, Silena. He's drugged, and probably hallucinatin' a little. Just keep that in mind."

Silena sucked in a deep breath and nodded. "I will. I know."

Sighing, Caldonia started to leave, then turned back. She opened her mouth to speak, but seemed to change her mind, and went on back down the hall.

Silena pulled her feet up into the chair with her, rested her elbows on her knees, and covered her face with her hands. And she wondered when her well of tears would ever empty, and if the turmoil and confusion in her life would ever find an end.

15

The first light of dawn pierced through the shutters in the room where Jake Rivers slept, and getting up out of the chair where she'd sat beside his bed, Silena gave up on trying to sleep.

She needed a change of clothes, she thought. She needed a bath. She needed to eat.

She needed to escape the trap that she felt now far more than she ever had before—the trap of this town's boundaries, the trap of her father's protectiveness, the trap of the mystery of her own life. She needed to get somewhere where she could find the truths.

She checked her father, saw that he slept soundly, and tiptoed out of the room and to the front door. Stepping out into the first hint of morning, she looked across the road to the store and its gunshot-shattered windows.

She needed to go home.

Hugging her arms around herself against the chill of the early morning, she crossed the street. At the front door of the mercantile, she hesitated, but forced herself to turn the knob.

The door came open, and she peered in at the havoc of broken bottles, knocked-over tables, cracked counters, and dry goods spilled over the floor. The smell of kerosene from broken bottles wafted through the air, along with a dozen other scents of perfumes and oils that ran together on the floor.

Forcing herself to go inside, she left the door open and stepped over the debris, intent on making her way to the house. But the sight of blood on the floor where her father had lain stopped her, jolting her heart. Her eyes strayed to the broken bottle she had used to hold off the outlaw when he'd been about to . . .

She began to tremble, and dread rose up inside her, intent on destroying her. They had come here for her . . . to take her back with them. And only her father knew the reason.

Kidnapped. The questions formed in her mind even as she stood looking at her father's blood. Her father was Jake Rivers, but she had come to believe Jake Rivers didn't exist. He was really Jim McCosky, and she knew nothing about that man.

She wondered if her mother was really named Eva, if she was really dead, or if she lived somewhere in torment, knowing that her child had been kidnapped so many years ago.

And now her home, the only one she'd ever known, was nothing more than broken glass, bullet-riddled walls, and bloodstained floors. She hugged herself tighter and tried to stop trembling, thinking, feeling. . . .

Slowly, she slid down the wall, letting despair overtake her, letting it cocoon itself around her, letting it smother and drown her.

"Silena."

A voice from the doorway pulled her back to the surface. She looked up from her misery to see Sam coming toward her.

"Go . . . go away," she muttered.

"No, I can't." He stooped down beside her and touched her hair with a gentle hand.

She recoiled. "Don't touch me. I want to be alone."

"Not in here," he said. "There's no reason for you to be in here with this all alone."

"It's my home," she said, a touch of sarcasm in her tone. "Why *shouldn't* I be here?"

"Because," he said, not sure he knew the answer. "There's no need to face this mess alone when I can face it with you."

"You?" she cried, looking away. "You want to face it with me? What have you got to offer me but more lies!"

"I'm not a lie," he said, turning her face back to his. "I'll prove it to you. I'm going to be what everyone thinks I am. You'll see."

"No," she said, shaking her head. "It's too late. You either are, or you aren't. Like me. One minute I was Silena Rivers, and the next minute I was Silena McCosky, and now I'm Silena God-knows-who, kidnapped from God-knows-who else. It's all a lie, a big, stupid fairy tale, and none of it makes any sense. Nobody's who they say they are, and everybody's pretending to be what they're not."

"Kidnapped?" The word fell softly in the quiet, chaos-ridden room, and Silena looked up at him. "Who told you that?" he asked.

He should have been surprised, but the fact that he wasn't horrified her even more, drawing her to her feet. He rose, too, and she stood staring at him, her wet, tear-reddened eyes fixed on his. "Oh, my God. You knew it, didn't you? You knew about this and didn't tell me."

"I didn't know anything," he said evasively. "I just . . . what are you talking about?"

She ground her teeth in impotent rage, and her face reddened as she bit out the words. "The kidnapping! I was kidnapped when I was a baby, and that man lying in Caldonia's house is probably not even my real father! *That's* what I'm talking about, Sam! Did you know that? Did Willy tell you?"

"No," he lied. "I didn't. Willy didn't tell me anything."

"You're lying, just like everybody else," she said, her voice suddenly dull, devoid of spirit or fight. "You're all lying."

He reached for her, but she stepped away. "Silena, don't face this by yourself. I'm here. I can help."

"With what?" she asked. "You're already committed to protecting the town, with that big badge and your big title. They need you, Sam, but I don't. They believe in you, but I know better."

"Silena, I haven't lied to you."

"You've lied to everyone," she said. "And even now you're hiding the truth away."

"That's not true," he argued. "I told you what I know. I haven't hidden anything."

With contempt, she looked at the badge glistening on his shirt. "When you took that badge, did you tell the town that you're no more an experienced gunfighter than I am? Did you tell them that *all* of your experience is in that show, and that until yesterday, you had never shot a man in your life? Did you tell them that every word on your handbills is a lie? Or that the only reason you saved Hayton was that you were afraid I'd blow your head off?"

He looked down at the badge on his shirt and shook his head. "They need to believe in me, Silena. They need to have confidence."

"We all need something to believe in," she whispered in a monotone. "Don't we, Sam?"

He looked at her for a long moment, intense longing in his eyes. "Don't stop believing in yourself, Silena. That first day I met you in Omaha, you were so confident, and so happy, and so determined. You believed in yourself that day, and so did I."

"I believed in a lot of things then," she said. "But I've grown up in the last few days."

"Growing up doesn't mean throwing off what you believe in. I've had some hard knocks in my life, too. I've had people that I was supposed to take care of, people who I loved, who I couldn't help. I know what it's like to lose control, to have your whole world slip out from under you."

His words touched a wound in her heart, and new tears mingled with the ones still wet on her face. Her mouth twisted as she tried to hold them back, and her face reddened with the fury of her misery.

This time, when Sam reached out for her, she didn't recoil. He held her, his arms tight and strong and warm, as she cried against his shirt. He buried his mouth in her hair, nuzzling her head against his chest. And as she cried he told himself that if it was the last thing he ever did in his life, he would help to cleanse that sadness from her heart.

"Trust me," he whispered, after a while. "Trust me, Silena."

Her voice was hollow, meek, lifeless. "I don't think I can ever trust anyone again."

"Then I'll make you trust me," he said. "Just give me the chance to show you how."

She looked up at him, her sobs still coming in hiccups. He touched her face and sighed as he dried her tears with his thumb.

His lips touched hers, and when she didn't pull away, he held her closer and deepened the kiss. He felt her relaxing against him, felt the pain draining away, felt her rising on her toes, meeting him halfway. . . .

Footsteps on the planked floor sent them jumping apart, but Sam didn't let her go. Silena looked up to see Hitch standing amid the chaos of the store. His arm was still in a sling, and he was staring at Sam with murderous eyes.

"Hitch," she said.

He looked from her to Sam, not bothering to hide the hurt in his eyes. "I came to see if you were all right after I heard how that meetin' turned out last night," he said. "But I see somebody beat me to it."

"I'm . . . I'm fine," she said, slipping out of Sam's arms and straightening her hair.

"You look like hell."

She offered a faint smile. "Thank you, Hitch. I appreciate that."

"No, I didn't mean that," he said, looking embarrassed. "The truth is that you're still the purtiest gal in town, even lookin' like hell."

The awkward words seemed to embarrass him even more.

"I don't think she looks like hell," Sam said. "I think she's beautiful, all tousled like this."

Silena couldn't manage to find another smile. "It's all right," she said. "I *feel* like hell. It's only right I should look like it."

"We've all been through a lot," Hitch said. "But I wanted you to know you can come back to the ranch and stay as long as you want."

She looked at Hitch, then Sam, then around her at the mess her home had become. "No, I don't think so. I have to . . . somehow I have to put this all back together . . . somehow I have to make some sense of this."

"Then I'll help you."

Silena shook her head at Hitch. "I don't feel up to it right now, Hitch. I just want a hot bath and a change of clothes. Pa's better now, so I can relax a little, at least for a while. And tonight I'll probably stay with Margaret. The funeral's tomorrow."

"Yeah. I was goin' to check on her next. She's pretty shook up."

"Do that," Silena said. "That's a good idea."

She watched as he turned and strode from the room, defeat written in every line of his stiffly held body.

When he was gone, Sam took off his hat and ran his fingers through his shaggy hair. "I don't blame him for feeling the way he does. Being so taken with you, I mean."

"He isn't taken with me."

"Yes, he is. Along with half the male population in this town."

The compliment only made her look more doleful. "I didn't hear any of them taking up for me last night when they were deciding whether to throw me out to the wolves."

"I took up for you."

She nodded wearily. "I know you did."

Their eyes met, and each remembered where they had been when Hitch had interrupted. He reached for her hand again, pulled her closer, but she held back.

"This isn't good, Sam. This . . . thing that's happening with us."

"What thing?"

"This . . . you know."

"No, I don't. Tell me."

"My hating you one minute, and the next . . ."

His face seemed to change, and he reached up and took off his hat, as if the lessened weight could help him to think and hear more clearly. "You're falling in love with me, aren't you?"

"No! That's not what I said."

He was quiet for a moment, but she could see the pleasure sparkling in his eyes, and she cursed herself for giving too much away.

"I just mean . . . it could never work for us," she said. "I'm not who I thought I was, and you're pretending to be who you never were."

"Sounds like the makings for a lot," he said.

"A lot of trouble," she whispered. "And I don't need more trouble in my life. I don't want to get involved with you, Sam. I don't want you rescuing me, any more, and I don't want you holding me. And I don't want any more long, wet kisses."

"They were long," he said, his eyes smoky. "And wet. The longest and wettest kisses I've ever had."

"And I expect you've had plenty."

He shrugged. "A man's got to keep up his reputation."

"And so does a woman."

He nodded and pushed away from the counter, set his hat back on his head, and studied the soiled floor. "So . . . you want me to stay away from you? Clear away?"

"Yes. I think that would be best."

He looked at her for a long time, as though formulating an argument. When he finally spoke, he didn't say what she expected. "Well, I don't think I can do that, Silena."

Her eyes glistened as she made herself meet his eyes. "Why not?"

"Because I wouldn't mind falling in love with you at all. And despite my background, I still think I have a lot to offer this town, and a lot to offer you. So you're just going to have to get used to me."

Before Silena could respond, he returned his hat to his head and started out of the store. At the door, he turned back to her. "I'll be back after you've had time for a bath, and we'll get started putting this mess back together."

She stood there watching him as he closed the door behind him and ambled across the street to the sheriff's office. And as she watched, the slightest hint of a smile played across her lips . . . then died in a cloud of apprehension.

Silena didn't soak in the bath for long, for an eerie sense of unease sifted through her, making her feel that evil still lurked in the chaos of her ruined home. They had come in here when she wasn't here, had ransacked the house as well as the store, had broken everything that meant something to her. And now, alone with the impact of it, she couldn't find any peace at all.

Quickly washing off, she got out of the big tub, dried off, and grabbed the first calico dress she came to. Trying not to look around too much at the devastation, she dressed, constantly feeling as if she were being watched.

The doors to her chifferobe hung open, the contents had been riffled through, and the floor was cluttered with things knocked off of tables and pulled off of shelves.

Everything was broken, she thought miserably, forcing herself to confront it. Everything.

She found her father's Bible lying open on the floor and, feeling a jolt to her heart, fell to her knees. Desperately, she turned the pages back to the first, searching for the note from her mother. But it was gone.

They had taken it.

"No!" she cried, clutching the Bible against her. "No!"

It was all she'd had of her mother, and they had taken it. But why? What could they have wanted with it?

Anger at all the mysterious forces operating in her life welled up in her, and she flung the Bible across the room. It hit the wall and fell to the floor, where it lay open, torn and battered.

She rose slowly to her feet. Smearing her tears across her face with the back of her hand, she decided that she wouldn't sit here and let her life fall around her. She would put it back together. So her home was destroyed. So her father had been crippled. So the threat of more horror hung over her like a pall. She wasn't beaten yet.

Feeling the red heat of fury raging in her face, she dipped a bucket into the bathwater, got the towel and dunked it in, and went into the store. The first thing she would do, she thought, was clean up the blood. And maybe when it was gone, when she had removed the stain, she would be able to see her life more clearly.

She knelt beside the stain on the floor—her father's blood—and began to scrub with all her might. Her wet hair fell into her eyes, and her tears dropped as she scoured the towel through the soapy water on the floor. But the stain wouldn't come up.

Desperate, she scrubbed harder, poured more water onto it, and rubbed until her fingertips bled with the force of it. She clenched her teeth as she rubbed, and put every ounce of energy she still possessed into cleaning off that stain.

And then she heard Sam at the door.

"Silena?"

"It's useless!" she cried, sitting in a puddle of blood-tinged water. "It won't come off! It's hopeless!"

"We'll get it off," he said, stooping beside her and taking her shoulders in his hands.

"No!" she cried. "It's on there. It can't be cleaned off!"

"Yes, it can," he said. "You just aren't approaching it right."

He took the towel from her hand and saw her bloody knuckles. Her body shook with the force of her misery, and she snatched the towel back and resumed her scrubbing.

"You've got to stop this," he told her, grabbing her wrists and holding them still. "You can't do it like this . . . not by yourself. Let me help you."

"*Nobody* can help me!"

"Damn it, Silena, I'm going to whether you like it or not!"

He jerked her into his arms, forcing her to drop the towel, and held her wet form against him until her rage dissipated into despair.

"I don't think it's a good idea for you to do this yourself," he said quietly when she was able to hear again. "I'll do it myself, and maybe get somebody to help me, but until I get the worst of it cleaned up, I think you should stay away from here."

"It's my home!" she said. "It's my life!"

"But you're facing it all too fast," he said. "Let me clean up the worst before you start trying to make sense of it all."

"You mean *hide* it," she said. "You want to come in here and hide all the horror from me. Clean up all the evidence so I won't find it."

"What evidence, Silena? What are you talking about?"

"The evidence . . . the clues to whatever it is I'm not

supposed to know . . . whatever it is that made this all happen."

"I won't hide any evidence," he said. "If I find anything, I'll tell you. I just don't want to see you scrubbing blood off the floor and being alone in here again. Can't you understand that?"

She got to her feet, swallowing back her tears, and pushed her hair away from her face.

"Will you let me do that, Silena? Please? To make up for the day I tried to run out on you?"

"You don't owe me anything," she said weakly. "Nobody owes me anything."

"I want to do it anyway."

She sighed and looked wearily toward the front door, her escape from the ghosts trapped in this structure. "I need to go check on Pa, anyway," she said.

"That's right. You'll get closer to the truth dealing with him than sorting through this mess."

"Yes. You're right," she said without much conviction. She turned back to him, then stared at the bloodstain again. It looked redder and fresher now than it had before, with the soap and water running over it, loosening the congealed places.

Feeling sick, she turned away and started out. "I'll be at Miss Caldonia's."

Sam watched her leave, then quietly looked down at the stain she had been working on. And for the life of him, he didn't know how he'd remove it from her floor. It would be just as hard as keeping her father's secrets from destroying her entirely.

Jake Rivers woke up when the morphine wore off, and gave an angry yell that could be heard all over the Simpson house. The first thing he felt was cold, a sweeping coldness that seemed to chill the marrow of his bones.

The second thing was pain, more intense than he'd ever felt, throbbing down his left side . . . stopping just beneath his hip.

But what was more disconcerting than the cold or the pain was the fact that he couldn't sit up. In fact, he was having trouble moving at all. His feet just lay there, still, unresponsive.

"Pa, it's okay!" Silena said, coming to his side. "The morphine's wearing off. I'll get Miss Caldonia. Just lie still."

He stopped yelling and tried to relax on the pillow, and reached down with his stiff arm to feel below his waist. A bandage was wrapped around his hips, down his leg. He reached farther, to the unresponsive limb, the one he couldn't move. . . .

"Noooo!"

Caldonia shot through the door as Jake struggled to sit up, clawing for his leg.

"You bitch! You made me a cripple!"

"Lie down, Jake," Caldonia told him. Nodding to a vial on the table, she said to Silena, "Hand me that vial. I'll give him another dose."

It took a moment of struggle for them to calm Jake down, and as he wilted back onto his pillow with tears of rage and confusion in his eyes, Caldonia tried to explain. "Jake, we tried to save the leg, but you got blood poison. If we hadn'ta took it, you'da died."

"My leg," Jake moaned as reality sank in along with the morphine. "You took my leg."

"Pa?" Silena stepped forward, and Jake focused his heavy eyes on her. "You were real sick, Pa. The bullet shattered your knee, and then the poison . . . There were red stripes up your leg, Pa, and your fever was burning."

Jake breathed out a long sigh and closed his eyes. "What about them men? They'll come back, and I won't be able to walk."

"They did come back, Pa," Silena said. "I went to Omaha to get Sam Hawkins, Willy's son, and he killed them all. Every one of them."

Jake's eyes opened again, and he frowned deeply. "Killed them? All of them?"

"Yes, Pa. And they've made him sheriff. He's going to stay in Hayton awhile."

"Was the Colonel with them? Did he kill him, too?"

Silena was stunned to silence for a moment, but she forced herself to speak. "No, I don't think so."

"Then there'll be more of 'em," Jake said miserably. "He won't give up that easy."

Silena touched Caldonia's shoulder, gently pushing

her aside so she could better lean over her father. "Who is he, Pa? When are you going to tell me the truth?"

"There is no truth," Jake said, closing his eyes again. "You stay away from this, Silena. Nothing but no good can come of it."

"Nothing but no good already *has* come of it, Pa! People are dead because of this secret. You've lost your leg. I'm scared to death. At least explain to me what's going on."

"I cain't," he whispered. "Nothin' to do with you."

"Nothing to do with me? How can you say that?" When Jake didn't answer, she shook his shoulder, forcing him to open his eyes again. "Pa, last night you told me that I was kidnapped when I was a baby. You owe me the truth, Pa. Who was I kidnapped from? And were you the one who took me? And why did you change your name from McCosky?"

"I never changed nothin'," he said, looking away from her. "And if I said I kidnapped you, then I was hallucinatin'. Nothin' like that ever happened."

"Yes, it did!" she screamed, and Caldonia touched her arms, warning her to calm down. "Pa, don't lie to me anymore. I can't take this!"

"You callin' me a liar, girl?" Jake asked.

She looked at him for a long moment, and some raging fury snapped inside of her. "Yes. Yes, I'm calling you a liar. You've been lying to me all my life. I don't even know who you are, and I especially don't know who I am! Yes, Pa. You're a liar."

He sat up then, in spite of himself, but his strength was too drained to get him far. Wearily, he dropped back onto the pillow. "Leave me be," he said. "I'm tired."

"No!" Silena cried, clutching him despite Caldonia's efforts to stop her. "No! You answer me, Pa! You tell me the truth right now! Who are you? And who am I?"

"I'm your father," he said, "and you're my daughter. And that's all you need to know."

The rage in Silena's face alerted Caldonia, and firmly, she pulled her out of the room and closed the door as the morphine drew Jake back under its spell.

Unlike the burials of the rest of the town's citizens who'd given their lives to the outlaws, Caleb's was solitary, quiet, and lonely.

One could argue that the other burials had taken too much out of the town, that everyone was too busy grieving over their own losses to grieve over all the others, but the simple fact that none at the grave site could deny was that Caleb wasn't "worthy" of the town's last respects.

Silena stood next to Margaret, who leaned on her mother. Nell was dressed for once like a schoolmarm, though her black neckline was a little too low for the taste of the common women of the town. Sam and Hitch acted as pallbearers, for there was no one else who would do the job.

Margaret grieved quietly as they lowered the coffin into the grave, and the weary preacher recited the words he'd recited too many other times that day. And then, when the first shovelful of dirt was dropped onto the coffin, Nell Plumer turned and fled up the hill to the tiny cabin that had so inadequately housed herself and her children.

Margaret stood alone, staring at the grave, facing the loss of the only person in her life who truly knew how to love her. Suddenly feeling as if, somehow, this was all her fault, though she hadn't a clue why or how she could have stopped it, Silena reached for Margaret and pulled the girl into a hug.

Margaret's tears fell silently onto Silena's dress. After a moment she looked up and saw that Hitch had stopped working and was merely staring at them, in quiet contemplation of his own. Finally, he turned back to his work.

Silena held Margaret while they finished filling the grave, and finally, Hitch came to Margaret, and placed a gentle hand on her back. Margaret looked up at him, her eyes red and her nose swollen from hours of endless weeping.

"I'm really sorry, Margaret," he whispered. "Caleb was about the best friend I ever had. I'm gonna miss 'im."

"Me too," she said.

He looked down at the flowers she gripped in her hands, flowers she had almost squeezed the life out of. "You want me to lay them on the grave for you?"

She shook her head and wiped at her tears. "He's my brother," she said. "I'll do it."

"Could . . . could I have one for myself?" he asked. "I didn't think to bring some."

Margaret nodded silently, and he took two from the bouquet. Then she went to the fresh mound of earth, knelt beside it without regard to the soil on her skirt, and laid down the bouquet. Hitch knelt beside her and laid one down as well.

When they stood up, he handed the other one to Margaret. "Keep this one for yourself," he said softly.

"Why?" she asked.

"Just because," he said with a shrug. "You don't always have to have a reason."

She stared down at the flower trembling in her hand, the lone daisy pulled up at its roots, waiting to wither and die alone. But it still had the scent of life, and its color was that of hope.

"I'll go cut you some firewood," Hitch said quietly. "I'll make sure there's enough to get you and your ma through the next few days."

She nodded and watched as he started up the hill.

Silena laid her arm across Margaret's shoulder and, not saying a word, started her up the hill as well. When they were halfway up, Silena looked back and saw Sam standing alone at the grave, his hands propped on the shovel handle, watching her climb the hill to Margaret's house.

By the time they reached the cabin, Nell had already fled to the saloon, leaving her black dress wadded on the floor where she'd stepped out of it when she donned the saloon dress. Silena looked around the unkempt house and decided that if she couldn't face the mess in her own house she could help with Margaret's, instead.

"Hitch is sweet," Margaret said softly, looking out the window at the man who had worked up a sweat chopping wood in his Sunday suit.

"You should invite him in after he's finished," Silena said. "Offer him something to drink, maybe a meal."

"He'd only come 'cause you're here," Margaret said, turning back from the window.

"He didn't give you that flower because I was here."

"No," Margaret said with a sigh, looking down at the flower she had held ever since. "But that wasn't really for me. It was for Caleb."

'He said he wanted you to have it."

Margaret looked out the window again, her wistful, sad eyes assessing him again. "I don't know, Silena. I'm not a very good cook, and I wouldn't know how to act. And I look awful. I couldn't think to fix my hair this morning, what with Caleb and all. . . . And I haven't slept in days. I look like sin."

"No, you don't. You just need a little fixing up. And since I'm here—"

"No, Silena. You've got problems of your own."

Silena turned back to her. "Margaret, it's the least I can do. If it weren't for me, Caleb might still be alive, and the others . . ."

"No, Silena. This ain't your fault. None of it. I won't listen to you take the blame."

"But you should blame me and my pa," Silena said helplessly. "Everybody else does."

"Everybody else looks at me the way they look at my ma, too," Margaret said. "Don't mean that's the way I am."

"No, it doesn't," Silena whispered. "You're right." She looked around at the small house and breathed a long sigh. "Well, if you won't let me help because I owe it to you, Margaret, then let me help for something to do. It'll keep my mind off of things."

Margaret's pale face lit up in a soft smile. "Thank you, Silena. I'll take any help I can get."

Hitch stayed busy for a long time, tending to the chores that Caleb would otherwise have done himself. Inside Margaret's house, Silena helped her with a bath, did her hair, and helped her put on a pot roast to cook so that she would have something to offer Hitch.

Quiet had settled over the house, a reverent, soul-deep quiet that Silena dared not disturb. She turned from the stove and saw Margaret holding one of Caleb's shirts in her hands, staring pensively down at it.

"He got this shirt from the parson," she said quietly. "It was all wore out, had holes in the elbows. . . . I fixed it for him, and dyed it brown so it wouldn't look so dingy." She idly stroked the worn-out fabric as she spoke. "It was a good shirt. Wonder if Hitch would want it."

"Probably would," Silena said quietly.

Tears welled in Margaret's eyes, then rolled down her cheeks. "I don't have nobody left," she whispered. "Nobody. Caleb was all."

"You have your mother," Silena said weakly.

Margaret gave her a disheartened look. "I never had Mama," she said. "Not really. Mama belongs to a lot of people."

"Well . . . you have me. I'm here for you, Margaret. You can turn to me anytime."

"Thank you, Silena," she whispered in a tone that lacked conviction. "But . . . Caleb was family. He was . . . he was my brother." The words came out on a rasp of breath, and she blinked back the tears in her eyes.

Silena stood quietly for a moment as Margaret struggled to stop her tears. She watched her walk to the window and look out to see Hitch putting the finishing touches on the woodpile.

"Don't seem like he's really gone, you know?" Margaret whispered. "Seems like if I keep lookin' at Hitch, purty soon Caleb'll come out from behind the barn and bolt into the house askin' what's to eat."

Silena thought of all the things she could tell her: that Caleb was here in spirit, keeping watch over his sister; that his soul was in a better place; that he was making a place for Margaret, and waiting for her there. But somehow those things seemed hollow and empty now. All she could do, instead, was offer a gentle touch . . . and quiet.

She walked up behind Margaret and set her hand on the girl's shoulders, and Margaret leaned her head against hers. For a long time they stood totally still, Margaret clutching Caleb's shirt, staring out at the place where Caleb should have been.

It wasn't until Hitch came to the door, perspiring and breathing heavily, that Margaret seemed to snap out of her reverie.

"The wood's cut," he said, wiping his feet on the mat and stepping inside. "I cut it small so you and your ma wouldn't have no trouble."

"Thank you, Hitch," Margaret said.

Silena waited for Margaret to offer him some coffee or ask him to wait for supper. But the girl seemed unable to speak.

"Hitch, come in and have supper, why don't you?" Silena asked, finally. "I have to get back to my father, and I don't want to leave Margaret alone."

Hitch shrugged. "Reckon I could. If ya got enough."

"I got plenty," Margaret said. "Mama prob'ly won't be home tonight, and Caleb . . ."

The words trailed off. Looking stricken at her mistake, Margaret focused her eyes on the floor.

"All right then," Silena said, gathering up her things and preparing to leave them alone. "It's all set. I'll check in on you later, Margaret."

"Yeah." The whispered word was lifeless and uncertain. When the door had closed, Margaret turned back to Hitch. "Guess she had to go," she said.

"No, she was just avoidin' me," Hitch said, suddenly not awkward anymore. He went to a chair, scraped it out from the table, and turning it backward, straddled it. "She's sweet on Sam, you know."

Margaret went to check the roast, which was hopelessly

overcooked since she hadn't checked on it in a while, and tossed him a look over her shoulder. "You think?"

"I think, all right," he said. "But she can't see that overblown piece of showmanship for what he really is. Just because he whisked her off her feet at the show, then came ridin' in here shootin' up the outlaws, she thinks he's some kinda hero. Well, what about me? I shot my share of them outlaws. How does she know that he shot all of 'em?"

"I don't think she does think that."

"Well, all I know is he has her hoodwinked. I don't stand a chance with her now."

Margaret dropped her gaze to the roast that Silena had started for her. She had no idea what was in it, so she reached for an onion and began chopping it to put it in.

Hitch got up out of the chair and went to the pot, took the knife out of her hand, and stabbed a small piece of meat. The look on his face as he tasted it made her want to cry.

"It's kinda burned a little," Margaret said meekly. "I'm not very good at this. Ma doesn't cook much, and Caleb and me mostly had to teach ourselves."

Hitch choked down the bite, struggling not to grimace. "You should get Silena to teach you. Miss Belle taught her to cook, you know. All Miss Belle's girls can cook up a storm."

Margaret refrained from telling him that Silena had given her an adequate head start on the meal, but that she herself hadn't paid proper attention to it. "Silena's been real busy," she said.

"You're tellin' me," he said, handing the knife back in surrender. "And that Hawkins fella never leaves her side. But he ain't so special. It's all talk's what it is. He's an actor, and I don't know why she can't see that it's all fake."

"I guess she likes him," Margaret said. "Folks can't always help who they like."

Hitch went back to the chair and, leaning on the table, crossed his hands under his chin and looked pensively off. "No, I reckon they cain't. Just wish I could do something to let her see that he ain't all that better than me."

"He's not, you know."

Hitch looked at Margaret and her wide, shy eyes. He frowned. "Not what?"

"He's not better than you. When I've seen you rounding up the cattle, you've done some pretty fancy riding. And that's for real, not show stuff. And you're just as good a shot as Sam, I'll bet. And you're better lookin'."

A slow grin dawned across Hitch's face, and he sat up straighter in his chair. "Yeah?"

Margaret blushed and quickly reached for the plates, though she doubted the wisdom in actually serving this meal. "Well, at least it seems that way to me."

He watched her as she served the dishes and brought them to the table.

"Wish Silena could see it," Hitch said. "But she don't. Never has, really. I don't even know why I keep tryin'."

Margaret tried not to let her spirits fall too far. "I don't blame you for likin' Silena. She's beautiful. She knows just the right way to act, how to dress, everything."

"But you're pretty, too."

Margaret's heart jolted, and she stopped and looked at him. "No, I'm not."

Hitch's grin was relaxed when he crossed his ankle over his knee, smugly looking up at her. "Of course you are, Margaret. You've got those big brown eyes, and all that hair."

"Ma says my eyes are too big," she whispered, unable

to look at him, now that he studied her so close. "She says my face is too small."

"I like your face," he said.

Again, her heart jumped. Finally, she met his eyes. "You do?"

"I think you're real pretty, Margaret," he said. "Not like your ma, either. Hers is all paint and stuff, but yours is real. You shouldn't compare yourself to Silena that way."

"And you shouldn't compare yourself to Sam."

He grinned, and she smiled back. For a moment neither of them said a word. "But for such a pretty girl," he said finally, "you still can't cook worth a damn. And if you think I'm gonna put another bite of this in my mouth, you're dead wrong."

Her smile faded, but when she saw that he was only teasing her, she giggled. "I'm sorry, Hitch."

"Don't be sorry," he said. "I'll just have to teach you a few things. Drivin' cattle, you have to learn to cook some. I can't promise that it's the best food you've ever had, but at least it won't kill nobody who eats it. Maybe I can salvage this yet."

She watched as he took the dishes and scraped them back into the pot. "You're gonna help me cook?" she asked.

He smiled. "I'll help you if you'll help me."

Margaret looked at him with confusion. "Help you with what?"

"With Silena. Help me think up some ways to make her fall for me instead of Sam."

Margaret's heart plummeted, and she wiped her trembling hands on her apron. "Well . . . I guess I could do that. I mean, I don't know what I could do, but–" Her voice broke off, and tears emerged in her eyes.

Alarmed by the disappointment on her face, Hitch

abandoned the pot and turned to face her. "I'm sorry, Margaret. I shouldn't have asked you that. You have a lot of other things on your mind."

Margaret wiped at the stray tear rolling down her face and nodded silently. Another tear fell right behind it.

"Hey." Hitch leaned against the stove and touched Margaret's chin, coaxing it toward him. When she looked up into his eyes, he slid his hand up her cheek. "You're real pretty when you cry, you know that?"

She gave a soft, tremulous laugh. "I couldn't be."

"You are, though," he said. "But you're real pretty when you aren't crying, too. Those big eyes, and your smile . . ." He wiped a thumb over her wet cheek, mesmerizing her, and again whispered, "Real pretty."

When he lowered his lips to hers, her body melted and flowed into a stream of restless longing. Abandoning the pot on the stove, she slid her arms around his neck and devoted herself to deepening the kiss.

As he moved his tongue against hers and slid his arms around her, Margaret felt, for the first time in her life, what it was to have something that was hers alone. Hitch might still be sweet on Silena, but he'd never kissed her that way. She was certain of it.

Somehow, it made him hers, whether he knew it or not. And, she vowed, she would just wait until he figured it out, too.

The time would come when he wanted more than a kiss, just as the men who liked her mother always did. When that day came, she thought, he would be hers alone. And unlike her mother, she would be exclusively his. She would make him happy.

Through whatever means it took, she would make him love her.

17

The lamp was burning in her father's store as the last of the daylight faded from sight, giving way to darkness. Silena made her way up the walk and cracked the door, reluctant to go in.

"Silena?"

She heard Sam from across the room, standing near the spices in a shadowy corner, and slowly, she stepped inside. The glass had all been swept up, and most of the debris from the floor had been discarded. The lamplight cast only a dim glow, but her eyes gravitated immediately to the spot on the floor.

The blood was gone, and in its place was only a damp circle that would dry by morning.

"How'd you do it?" she whispered.

"Just worked on it awhile," he said. "Just didn't give up."

She looked up at him, and their eyes met. He had bathed, shaved, and changed clothes since she'd seen him last. His hat was tossed onto a counter, revealing his shaggy hair in all its tousled glory, leaving his face more exposed than usual. She had to admit, she liked seeing him exposed like that.

"I really appreciate it, Sam," she said. "I couldn't have faced it myself."

"If it was my home, I couldn't have either," he said.

She stood still, not certain what to say next. The quiet in the aftermath of chaos was eerie, but smells, various and pungent, wafted together on the air. The scent of clove, which she had associated with Sam since she'd ridden his horse with him in Omaha, rippled stronger than the others, making her want to move toward him.

Instead, he shortened the distance between them, and when they stood face-to-face, he reached out and grazed her face with his thumb. "You look tired," he said.

"So do you."

He smiled. "Sheriffing takes a lot out of you."

"So does cleaning up messes that other people are responsible for."

"You weren't responsible for this," he corrected. "It was them. . . ."

Silena's alert eyes settled on him again as she tried not to think about the murderous gang. Finally, she backed away and sat down on a barrel of sugar against the wall.

"Pa woke up off and on last night," she said quietly. "He was hallucinating. Didn't know what he was saying."

Sam frowned and stepped closer. "What *did* he say?"

She looked down at her trembling hands. "That . . . that those outlaws came here for me . . . because he kidnapped me when I was born."

"Kidnapped?" The word came out as a soft question, lacking surprise or disbelief. That in itself made Silena focus her confused gaze on him.

"You know something, don't you, Sam? You've heard something about me that I don't know, haven't you?"

"No," he said, reaching for his hat and setting it back on his head. His face was instantly shadowed. "What else did he tell you?"

"Nothing," she said, still holding his gaze with hers. "When he woke again, he said he'd been hallucinating, that he hadn't meant any of it."

"Oh."

"Yes. Oh. And so I was right back where I started, only more confused, and more afraid. Last night, he said the colonel would send more men. That he wouldn't give up."

"We knew that," Sam said. "That's why I'm here."

Tears began to glisten in Silena's eyes, catching the light and the shadows at the same time. "But I have to know more than what I can surmise, or what everyone else has figured out, Sam. If I don't know, I think I might just go crazy. I might just lose my mind."

A big tear traveled down her face, leaving a silver streak on her cheekbone. Sam's face was enshrouded in shadows when he bent over her. Slowly, he reached out and wiped the tear away.

"Don't cry."

She moved her face against his hand and closed her eyes. Two more tears escaped.

"Come on, Silena," he said, stooping in front of her. "Please don't cry. I'll do whatever it takes to make you stop crying."

Her eyes opened, and she fixed her misty gaze on his. "Even tell me the truth?" she asked. "Would you go that far for me, Sam?"

"I've come pretty far already."

She didn't release him from that soft, tragic gaze, and he knew that he had no choice. Someone had to tell her something, and there wasn't anyone else, besides her father, who knew.

"Come here." He stood up. Taking her hands, he pulled her to her feet and looked down at her open, vulnerable face. Framing it with both hands, he studied it. "I want to help you," he whispered. "I want to tell you . . . but . . ."

"You're the only one who can help me, Sam," she whispered as more tears began to stream down her face. "I can't turn to anyone else. Give me a reason to trust you."

He swallowed. Slowly, she rose up on her toes, slid his hat off his head, revealing his face, half of it illuminated by the dim light.

"Please, Sam," she whispered. "I need you to tell me."

His lips took hers before she'd even gotten the words out, and she dropped his hat and slid her arms around him. His kiss was deep, longing, wet, and desperate, and her response was just as desperate.

The sense of goodness, of rightness, touched her soul. The feel of his arms around her, of his touch being only for her, of his possession stamped on her lips and her heart, was something rare and special to her. Jake loved her, but his moments of tenderness for her were few and far between. Sometimes her soul had hungered for affection. Now she didn't want to break the warm spell, didn't want to separate from the tenderness she had felt so seldom in her life.

But the lack of trust still pressed on her mind, making it impossible for her to surrender. She withdrew, her lips still grazing his. Closing her eyes, she whispered, "Please, Sam. Make me trust you."

He pulled back slightly, his eyes smoky with desire. "I don't want to hurt you," he whispered.

"The truth won't hurt me as much as the secrets."

He released her from his embrace, backed away, and picked up his hat from the floor. Slowly, he put it back on his head, letting the shadows swallow his face again.

He paced across the floor, staring at the wooden planks beneath his boots, letting the thudding of his heels shake the structure. Silena waited, holding her breath, afraid to move for fear he'd change his mind.

After a moment he went into the house, and she followed, watching, waiting. Slowly, he strode to the backdoor, opened it, and looked out onto the newly descended night.

"Come out with me," he whispered without looking at her.

Not arguing, she stepped outside with him, to that special place beneath the stars where her father always escaped with his secrets. The place where he always hid himself from her. She wondered if Sam planned to hide here, too.

He sat down on the ground, leaning back against the tree trunk, his legs bent at the knees. He took off his hat, and let it hang from his fingers as he draped his wrists over his knees. Slowly, Silena sat down on a bare patch of earth, facing him, her feet curled beneath her.

"Tell me, Sam," she whispered.

He took her hand, brought it to his lips, then kept holding it as he met her eyes. "I will," he said. "I'll tell you all I know."

"The kidnapping," she whispered. "Start with the kidnapping."

Sam looked down at her hand, fondling it as he began. "The story, as I understand it, is that Jim McCosky and Colonel Alexander Rafferty, everybody knows him just as the Colonel, got into a rift over the Colonel's treatment of some Indians who Jim had been trading with. Seems the Colonel killed a couple, and Jim vowed revenge."

Silena's frown deepened as the hazy picture of her father took form. "Go on."

"I should tell you right now," he said, "that Willy thinks some of this is hogwash, and so do I. I'm just telling you what I heard."

"I understand that," she said. "Jim vowed to get revenge. So what happened?"

"The rumor is that the Colonel's wife was having a baby, and when the Colonel left the house, Jim McCosky came and kidnapped his baby. And I can only assume that the baby was you."

The feeling of terror and despair rose up in her throat, and Silena found herself unable to speak. She had wanted the truth, yes, but the truth only unveiled so many more lies. She felt the blood draining from her face, felt her heart palpitating, felt her vision blurring.

Her hand suddenly felt cold, even in the confines of Sam's. She pulled it away and balled it into a fist on her lap.

"The story goes that the Colonel caught Jim stealing the baby and set out on a chase. Trying to get away from the Colonel, Jim and the child fell into the Platte River and supposedly drowned."

A moment of deadly silence followed as the words sank in. Swallowing, Silena asked, "What about my mother? What happened to her?"

"The story is . . . that she died a few days later. Grief, according to the Colonel."

Her eyes filled with tears, and she rose to her feet and turned away, unable to face what he had told her. Her life. A life that had no basis in truth. A life that had been built on a multitude of heinous lies.

She heard Sam get up, felt him stepping up behind

her, felt the warmth of him as he touched her arms and pulled her back against his chest. "Except we know at least some of that is a lie, Silena. You and your pa survived the river, got away, and started a new life here."

"He's not my pa," she said in a dull voice. "Until a few days ago, I didn't even know his real name."

"He's raised you like his own. He's sheltered you and nurtured you and loved you, hasn't he? He got shot trying to defend you. I don't know what part of the story isn't true, but I know that your average kidnapper doesn't devote the rest of his life to caring for his victim."

"You don't see, do you?" she asked, turning around and facing him with raging eyes. "You don't know what it's like, to find out that nothing you knew or trusted is true!"

"Yes, I do," he said. "Believe it or not, Silena, I've been there. I've had my life shattered a time or two."

"You don't even *live* a real life," she accused. "Your life is a show. How can you know about betrayal and deception?"

"I know about pain," he said, his voice rising. "I know what it's like to have your life pulled out from under you. I wasn't raised with Willy, you know. I didn't join him until I was twelve years old. Till then, I took care of my ma and my sister, Stella. And they were my whole life. They were all I knew and trusted."

"Did they lie to you? Did they betray you?" she shouted.

"No!" he returned. "I did that to myself. I pretended to be the head of the house, the big man who could take care of everything. But I was nothing more than a kid, and my mother died and I couldn't stop it. Then suddenly I was Willy's kid, trailing along behind Willy's troupe. And *I* betrayed me, when I let Stella die, too. I betrayed me when I let the two most important people in my life slip through my fingers. You still have yourself, Silena. That most important person in your life—yourself—hasn't betrayed you yet. You still have that."

"I don't even know what that is!" she shouted. "I don't even know what my real *name* is! Did my ma name me Silena? Did the Colonel? Is my last name Rivers, McCosky, or Rafferty? Who am I, Sam?"

"You're Silena Rivers," he said. "That's all I need to know."

"Well, it's not all *I* need to know!" She covered her mouth to muffle her sob of despair and tried to turn away. "It's not all I need!"

She started toward the house, then picked up her pace until she was running. Sam followed after her.

She burst into the house and found the Bible Sam had returned to the shelf after she'd flung it against the wall.

"See this?" she cried, waving the book at him. "This was a gift to my father . . . Jake . . . Jim . . . from my mother. From Eva. It had an inscription. 'No matter what, I'll always love you.' But it's gone. They took it, so it must mean something to the Colonel!"

Sam took the book. Closing it, he looked up at her. "Silena, I told you the story couldn't be all true. There's more that we don't know. You have to hold on to your faith in that. You have to believe that it's not all really as ugly as it sounds."

"If she loved him," Silena whispered, "then how . . . *why* would he steal her child? Why would he do that to *me*?"

"I don't know," he whispered. "But if she loved him, then maybe somehow he did it for her. Only Jake can tell us now. And until he's ready, we just have to trust him."

"Trust him? That's impossible."

"Silena, I'll say it again. Your pa loves you. I can see it from the things in your home. The special things he's done for you here. The little luxuries no one else in town has. When he was hallucinating while we were taking his leg, he said things about you, things that told me he loved you more than himself, things that made me realize that you're his in his mind."

"She was my mother," Silena cried, jerking the Bible back. "Because of him, I lost her forever, and now she's dead. She was my mother, and I don't know anything at all about her."

Sam watched as she ran her trembling fingers over the tear where the inscription had been, as if somehow it would help her to feel the woman's power. He wished he had something to give her, something that could ease the pain, something that could soothe the hurt. But he had nothing. At least, nothing real. But he'd always been good at lies. And he supposed that one lie to soothe the hurt of another wasn't so bad. Not if it made her feel better.

"I know a little about her," he said, "but I don't know if it'll help."

Silena's head snapped up. "What?"

"I know that she was a piano teacher, and she sang in the church choir. . . ."

"Really?" she asked, those tears in her eyes welling around her lashes. "I've always thought I could have played piano if someone had taught me. And I sing a little."

He smiled and told himself that what he was doing was harmless if it brought a smile to her lips. "She was also a good cook," he said. "Willy told me she was the best cook in town."

"Then Willy did know her?"

"A little."

A slight smile tipped the corners of her lips. "Did she entertain people a lot? Is that how they knew?"

"A lot," he said, realizing the lies were coming easier. "Willy said she was always entertaining."

Silena stepped close to Sam, looking up at him with hopeful eyes. "Do you know what she looked like, Sam?" she whispered. "Do you know if she was pretty?"

"I saw a photograph, a long time ago," he whispered, his voice dropping with the intensity of the lie. "She was beautiful." He reached up, touched Silena's silky blond hair, stroked it as he spoke. "She had long blond hair like yours, and the biggest, greenest eyes, and lips that looked soft and full and wet all the time. . . ." His mouth lowered to hers, but hovered above hers as he went on. "And she had a little mole on her left cheek, right here. . . ." He touched her cheek. "When I saw that picture, I thought she must have been the most beautiful woman I'd ever seen . . . but then I saw you. . . ."

He didn't know if it was gratitude or desire that made Silena melt so completely when he pulled her into his arms. He felt her hands moving around his neck, her body pressing close into his, and some primitive, barely controllable hunger sharpened inside him.

He could have her tonight, he thought without a doubt. He could reach down, unbutton her dress, slip it off her shoulders. He could slide his hand over her breasts, feel the softness against his palm, massage the nipples until they hardened against his fingertips.

He swallowed even as he kissed her and pulled back, looking for the yes in her eyes. Silena met his gaze with smoldering gratitude. With smoky emerald trust.

His eyes fell to the front of her dress as his hand pressed her hips closer against him. It would be so easy to stamp his possession on her. . . .

But that trust in her eyes caught his heart, and he told himself that she was too pure to taint, too sweet to shame, too confused to exploit on the basis of a lie. And if he took her in that bedroom and bolted the door, would he be locking the lies inside or out? Could he do it in good conscience, knowing what he had done to get her to this point?

The time would come, he vowed, but not now. Not yet.

He moved his hands from her hips, set them on her waist, and took a step back, until he could no longer feel the soft crush of her breasts against his chest.

For a moment she looked hurt at his withdrawal. Then relief dawned and she stepped back as well, touching her tousled hair and lowering her gaze to the floor. "It's . . . it's late," she whispered. "I should go to bed."

He swallowed. "Yeah. Me too, I guess."

"But . . . if you come back in the morning, I'll fix you breakfast. You probably haven't been eating right."

"I'll be back," he whispered.

Their eyes locked for an eternity as he questioned his sanity for not making love to her, as she questioned her own for wanting it so shamelessly. All it would have taken to shatter their resolve was one move . . . from either of them.

But neither of them moved.

Finally, Sam started toward the door. At the threshold, he turned back.

Her eyes were soft as feather clouds as she watched him. "Someday, Silena," he promised in a whisper.

Silena woke at various intervals during the night and contemplated with pleasure her scandalous yearning for the man who had given her the rare gift of details about her mother. When she woke for the final time at dawn, a sense of peace, of belonging, of trust washed over her.

Smiling, she tiptoed out of her bedroom into the kitchen, which Sam had restored to order yesterday. After lighting the lamp, she looked around, saw the can of coffee he had placed on the shelf above the stove, and began to make it. A soft tune played in her mind, and she hummed it as she cracked eggs into a frying pan.

Her mother was beautiful. A piano player. Socially accepted. Loved. Beautiful.

He had seen a picture, and her eyes were green. . . .

The nagging beginning of some foreboding thought stopped her cold. Staring at the wall, Silena went back through the things he had told her last night.

He had only seen a sepia-toned photograph. There would have been no colors. How could he have known her eyes were green?

Slowly dropping the spatula she held in her hand, she turned to the door he had gone through last night, staring beyond it as if it held answers. He couldn't have known the color of Eva's eyes if he had never seen her. He couldn't have known that from a picture. Had he made it up? And if so, how *much* of it was a lie? Just the part about her mother, or all of it? The colonel, the kidnapping, Jake's name? Was any part of it true?

Unbidden, that old feeling of panic rose inside her, and she realized that Sam was no more trustworthy than anyone else in her life. He, too, was a liar. But that was no surprise. She had known that the first day she met him.

Why then had she forgotten it last night?

A tear dropped to her cheek. Smearing it away, she went back into her bedroom, threw open the chifforobe, and withdrew some fresh clothes.

She heard the door to the store open and close, and Sam's steps thudding on the plank floor.

"Silena? I saw your light on."

Silena didn't answer. Instead, she closed the door and began dressing as fast as she could.

"Silena?" He was in the kitchen now, standing outside her bedroom door. "The eggs are burning."

She still didn't answer, for there was nothing to say. He had lied to her about the most sacred thing in her life. He had made her believe in something that didn't exist. He had mocked her.

She threw open the door and pushed past him.

"Silena, what is it? What did I do?"

Silena flung around at the door. The eggs began to smoke over the room, but she ignored them. "You lied to me!" she said. "Again, you lied to me!"

"About what?" he threw back.

"About my mother! You said her eyes were green! But you couldn't have known that, could you, Sam?"

Sam stood still for a moment, naked vulnerability on his unshaven face. "I was trying to give you something, Silena," he said quietly. "Something you needed."

"I didn't need more lies," she said. "I needed something . . . someone . . . I could count on."

"You can count on me."

"I can count on you to confuse me more!" she cried. "To make more of my life seem upside down! But nothing else. Not one thing else!"

Turning, she fled from the house. She didn't look back until she was past the saloon. But Sam had not come after her.

The middle C on the piano was silent among the untuned notes as Miss Lucy played "Bringing in the Sheaves," making the hymn sound offbeat and broken. The piano had caught a stray bullet while sitting in the saloon, but it wasn't until Sunday morning, when they had wheeled it down the ramp from the backdoor of Murdock's and up the hill to the schoolhouse that served as a church on Sunday mornings, that anyone had noticed it hadn't been repaired.

But it didn't matter to Silena; it only made the bizarre reality of her life seem more in tune with the events of the town. The congregation, seemingly unaware of the brokenness of their singing, as if by ignoring it they could deny the flat and dull notes, thereby making them nonexistent, continued through three verses.

Across the crowded church house, Silena saw Sam, standing among some of his newest admirers, people who didn't know he was a liar. Their eyes met, and she turned hers away and looked instead toward the broken window. Hitch, standing on the other side of Margaret, drew her attention with his stare, and she gave a mental groan.

As the parson got up and talked for the next forty-five minutes on the consequences of sin—those consequences being the bloodshed in the town—Silena's mind wandered back to the yearning she had experienced for Sam last night. Shamed, she made the self-confession that she would have given him all of herself last night, if he had taken it, regardless of what the preacher said about sin. She had trusted him, if only for a moment.

She was wiser now, she told herself. But those shattered illusions had sharp edges that cut into her heart, making her feel more alone than she'd ever felt in her life.

Sam sat in the church among his fellow worshipers and wondered if God would forgive him for all the lies he'd told. If He was as hard to please as Silena, he reckoned not.

He tried not to remember the other night, when she had responded so timidly in his arms. He tried not to think about how her skin would have felt beneath his hands. It was blasphemy. It was wrong.

But there she was, sitting so stiff and so pretty, so completely alone in the midst of all these people. And yet he was suddenly one of them, the overnight hero, the one everyone counted on. But they couldn't see into him, he thought. Not like Silena could.

He listened to the sermon about the consequences of sin for a while, and figured that if sin had such direct consequences, he'd be dead and buried by now. But God's retribution wasn't that immediate sometimes.

Sometimes it came in the way a woman turned away. Sometimes it came in loneliness. Sometimes it came in losing the joy in something you had worked so long to have.

Like this town. Suddenly it was his town, and they were his people. Suddenly he was a part of them, and they liked him. Moreover, they *needed* him, and he had a vital part to play in their safety.

It was something he'd dreamed of, but thought he'd never have. And now, through Silena's desperation, he had found it.

But he couldn't enjoy it. Because now there was something he wanted more.

The congregation broke up, and he waited, watching Silena, as the people slowly made their way out into the chilly November sunlight. And as the sunbeams fell on her bonnet and glanced off her hair, he thought, once again, that she was the most beautiful woman he'd ever seen.

But the reality of that only served to make him more miserable.

Silena pushed through the crowd of townspeople, who were still coldly ignoring her—those who didn't confront her openly about the trouble she'd brought to their town—and started down the hill toward her store.

"Silena."

She recognized Sam's voice and began to walk faster.

"Silena, wait. I have to talk to you."

He had caught up to her in a matter of steps, but she didn't look at him.

"Silena, please. I can't stand this. You have to know, I didn't lie about any of what I told you about your pa. At least, not that I know of. I told you just what I'd heard."

She stopped and looked up at him, her face reddening. "You lied about my mother."

"Yes, I lied about your mother." He tried to go on, stopped, and looked off into the distance. "But I did it because I saw all that darkness inside you, and I wanted to put a little light there. I wanted to give you something you could believe in."

"But you just gave me more reason not to believe in anything."

Sam saw several of the townspeople starting toward him, probably to offer him Sunday dinner or another pat on the back, so he took her arm and started walking with her. She jerked her arm away.

"Silena, I think it's awful that a beautiful girl like you doesn't know anything about her mother. I had just told you horrible things about your birth, and your father, and I just wanted to give you something good. Something sweet."

He stopped her, turned her to face him, forced her to look at him. "Silena, you trusted me that night. You were able to see past the stormy rumors about Jake and the Colonel, because you were focused on your mother. What I did worked. It softened the blow, and I'm glad I did it. I'm just so sorry you had to realize I made it up."

"It hurts to be caught in a lie, doesn't it, Sam? Makes it hard to feel good about yourself."

"I felt good about myself when you were kissing me that night, Silena. You felt good about yourself when your hands were sliding over me, when your hips were pressing against mine—"

"How dare you?" she whispered through clenched teeth.

"How dare I?" he repeated. "I dare because I didn't take you to bed like I wanted to. I didn't undress you like you wanted me to. I didn't make love to you, like we both wanted. Trust me for that, Silena, if nothing else."

Tears squeezed out of her eyes. Ignoring them, she turned away. "I can't talk about this," she muttered. "I'm going to see my father."

Sam stood still and watched her make her way down the hill toward town, her posture stiff and rigid and guarded. So different, he thought, from the happy-go-lucky young woman he had dazzled in Omaha. He thought of the sorrow in her expression now, the pale cast to her face, the shadows beneath her eyes, then recalled the laughter in those same eyes when he'd first met her, the way she had made Running Horse smile, the way she had played with the braves.

He shouldn't have humiliated her by throwing her passion back in her face, but it was too late to retrieve the words now.

Heaving a deep sigh, he started down the hill himself, realizing that he should have accepted one of the Sunday-dinner invitations that might have come his way at church. Now he was alone and Silena would never trust him again.

Approaching the sheriff's office, he looked up to see two familiar horses tethered to the post—Caleb's horse that Silena had left in Omaha, and Willy's horse, Lightning. A deep frown cut into his forehead. Straightening his hat and pulling it lower over his forehead, he started inside.

"'Bout time you showed up here, boy," his father said.

Sam bristled and prepared himself for the showdown with Willy.

* * *

Silena faced a showdown herself, for her father was sitting up in a wheelchair, sour-faced and mean-tempered, when she came in. Part of her wanted to hug him and take care of him, and tell him how glad she was to see him out of bed. But another part told her that she would be hugging a stranger, that she really didn't know him at all.

When he finished the soup that Miss Caldonia had prepared, grumbling about its taste as he ate, he shoved it away and turned to his daughter.

"You look mighty purty," he said. "Where you been?"

"Church, Pa," she said quietly.

He squinted at her, trying to discern why her mood was so somber, but she suspected he had a good idea.

"They aren't speaking to me, most of them," she said.

"Who ain't?"

"The town. They blame you and me for all the things that have happened. The other night, they even argued whether or not to run us out of town."

Jake's face tightened, and he leaned forward in his wheelchair, the pain on his face more pronounced as he did. "Run us out of town? Why?"

"Because it's obvious the outlaws are after us," she said, raising her voice. "Everybody knows it. And we all know they'll come again, as soon as the Colonel sends more."

The shutters over Jake's eyes slammed closed, and he sat straighter in his chair and looked down at the place where his leg should have been. "What do you know about the Colonel?"

"Enough," she said. She looked at him, her eyes searching, probing. "Pa, I don't know how much of what I know is true. I only know the rumors, the things that Sam told me. Things he heard from Willy."

Jake gave her a guarded look. "What things?"

She sighed and sat down across from him, setting her elbows on her knees. "He told me that when I was born, you kidnapped me from my ma. That the Colonel is my real father, and that you had had a quarrel with him."

Jake's face reddened, and he balled his hand into a fist. "That ain't true, Silena!"

"Yes, it is," she said. "I know it is, because you said it yourself when you were hallucinating."

His hand shook as he pointed a trembling finger at her. "I have raised you from the time you were born," he said, his eyes misting over. "I've took care of you, and fed and clothed you, and loved you—"

His voice broke off. He looked away, then looked back with an obvious effort. "I'm your father, Silena," he said. "No matter what else you hear, don't you never doubt that."

Tears trickled down her cheeks, but she didn't wipe them away. "I want to know the truth, Pa. I want to know what part of what Sam told me is true."

"None of it," he said, looking at her fully in the face. "Not one damn bit."

"You didn't kidnap me from the Colonel? My ma didn't die of grief?"

"Your ma was murdered!" he blurted, then cut himself off and began trying to turn the wheels of his chair so he could escape this scrutiny that he'd spent a lifetime avoiding.

She caught her breath and covered her mouth. "What do you mean? Who murdered her?"

He shook his head and struggled harder to move his chair. "No. I won't get into this. I *won't* get into this! A child ought not to know every ugly thing about her past."

"I'm not a child, Pa," she cried. "I'm a woman. I have to know."

He turned back to her and held her in his shaky gaze. "Silena, your ma loved you dearly, and I loved both of you. That's all you ever need to know."

"But they'll be back, Pa! How can I face that when I don't even know what they're after? Is it revenge? Is it retribution? Is it *me?*"

"They won't get you," he said. "I'll die before I'll let them take you."

Silena sprang out of her chair. "You can't stop them, Pa. You couldn't stop them last time, and you won't stop them next time. Sam was the only one who could stop them, and as soon as the newness wears off with his being the sheriff around here, he'll go back to Omaha and be the big star again. A man like him isn't going to hang around a one-horse town like Hayton indefinitely!"

"You have to make him," Jake said. "You have to convince him to stay. No matter what it takes."

Silena gaped at her father. "You can't be serious."

"He's our only hope," Jake said. "We need him. Caldonia thinks Sam is sweet on you. You have to use that."

"For what?" she asked, growing more furious by the moment.

"To make him stay. You got to reel him in, marry him, do whatever it takes—"

"I'm not marrying anybody for protection!" she cried. "I could protect myself if you'd only tell me what I'm up against."

"I'll tell you what you're up against," Jake said. "The meanest, slimiest son of a bitch that ever rode through these plains. And if the Colonel don't come hisself, he'll send more who are just as mean and just as slimy."

A chill of fear fled through her as she stared at the man she had always called her father.

"You go find Sam right now," he said, his breath coming heavy. "You cook him dumplin's or somethin'. That's your best. And smile. You got the prettiest smile in Hayton. Hell, prob'ly in all Nebraska."

"Pa, I'm hardly even speaking to him. He lied to me about some things, and I—"

"Then you *start* speakin' to him, girl! Quit worryin' so much about the lies you hear and start askin' yourself what could be important enough for people to tell you those lies! What could be dangerous enough."

She swallowed and backed away. "I . . . I've got a headache, Pa. I need to lie down."

"First you invite Sam to dinner," he shouted after her. "Do it before somebody who don't need him so much asks him."

Silena was out the front door before her father had finished shouting after her.

"So you're gonna give up bein' a livin' legend for a badge and a purty face?" Willy's question was laced with contempt.

Sam leaned back on the front of his desk and pulled his hat lower. "I wasn't a living legend, Willy. You were. I was just the hired help."

"You're my son!" Willy said, his eyebrows lifting. "That makes you a hell of a lot more than hired help."

Sam looked at his father across the room, at the sour look on his wizened face, and wondered how long he'd been sober. Not long, he guessed, for the man looked like he was teetering on the edge of pain. A thin sheen of perspiration glistened on his face, and his eyes squinted as if even the dim light filtering in through the broken windows hurt his eyes.

"Willy, they need me here."

"We need you there, too," Willy said. "*We're* family."

"But this is real life," Sam said. "This is a real danger. Not Indians shooting at me with blanks."

"No, boy, these are real bullets. And for real bullets, a town needs real heroes. Not showmen like us."

Sam's face reddened. "You haven't always been a showman, Willy. You used to be a hero."

"Yeah, well, heroism is short-lived. Unless you can bottle it and sell it to crowds, it ain't worth much."

"Well, maybe I'm not doing it for myself," Sam said. "Maybe I'm doing it for the town. Maybe I have more faith in my own abilities than you do."

Willy clenched his hand into a fist and hit the hard sod wall beside him. He swung around, his face full of rage. "Damn it, Sam, you're doin' this for that gal! Don't you know that you can get all the gals you want in Omaha? There's a cure for bein' horny, Sam, and you don't have to get killed for it!"

For the first time in his life, Sam grabbed his father by the collar and jerked him close. His eyes blazed as he stared at him. "Don't you ever say that to me again," he said. "Silena is not that kind of woman."

"They're all that kind," Willy spat. "Ever last one of 'em."

Outside, Silena waited beside the broken window, listening with eyes wide at the scene playing out inside. She had seen both Caleb and Willy's horses outside and then she'd heard the voices and stopped just out of sight.

Something crashed, and she stepped forward and peered inside. A chair had fallen over, but Sam still gripped Willy by the collar. He let him go, and Willy dropped back.

"If you say another word about Silena Rivers," Sam said in a quiet, breathless voice, "I'll take you apart."

Willy gaped at his son. "Sam, you're talkin' crazy. You're willin' to give up the show, your family, everythin' I've taught you for that girl? You're a star with me, Sam. People look up to you."

"People look up to me here. And not because I can shoot balls in the air or play a good game of cowboys and Indians. They look up to me for what I've really done . . . not what I claim to have done or what I pretend to do."

"But I didn't train you since you were twelve so you could park your ass in some nowhere town holdin' down a job that the barber used to have!"

"Why *did* you train me, Willy?" Sam asked. "So you'd have cheap help? Or because I was your son?"

Willy shook his head. "I trained you because I needed you. You belonged with me . . . in the show."

"Well, they need me more here, Willy. Just like Ma needed me, and Stella needed me, and whether you admit it or not, just like you need me. No matter what I did, I couldn't save Ma or Stella, and you won't *let* me save you. But by God, I can save Silena, and I can save this town. And as long as there's a breath left in me, that's just what I'm gonna do."

Through the window, in the shadows beyond, Silena saw the fury on Willy's face. She watched as he leaned over, got the sack he'd brought with him, and faced Sam with disgust on his rugged face. "I never woulda thought you were a fool, boy."

"A fool is a man who looks reality in the face and still thinks it's illusion," Sam said. "This ain't illusion, Willy."

Willy locked gazes with him for a long moment, his hard, leathered face tight and guarded. Finally, he turned and started for the door.

"Jim's down at Caldonia's," Sam said quietly. "Don't you want to see him before you go?"

"Got to get back."

Sam said nothing.

Willy left the office, went out to his horse, untied it, and mounted. And then he saw Silena, standing beside the window, watching him with wide, expectant, sad eyes. He tipped his hat slightly, then turned his horse around and started on his way.

Silena watched until Willy was out of sight, then went to the doorway and stepped inside. Sam was staring at the floor, his face full of pain and residual anger, and for a moment she thought perhaps she shouldn't disturb him.

But he saw her before she spoke.

Their eyes met, held, then withdrew.

"I heard some of that," she whispered. "I guess Willy wants you to come home."

Sam only nodded.

"I wouldn't blame you if you did," she said. Her voice grew hoarse, and she cleared her throat. "I wouldn't blame you at all, but . . ."

"But what?" He looked up at her, his eyes waiting, listening.

"But I hope you don't."

"Why?" he asked. "You hate me. You won't even talk to me. You treat me like I'm one of the outlaws."

"I don't hate you," she whispered. "I'm just . . ." She broke off into tears, and pinched the bridge of her nose with a trembling hand. "I heard what you said about my needing you, and your saving me."

She drew in a deep, cleansing breath, allowing it to fill her with the courage to say what she meant, without considering the cost. "The truth is, I really like knowing there's someone here watching out for me."

"Do you?" His eyes softened, and he unfolded his arms and took off his hat. "Do you really, Silena?"

"Yes." The word didn't come easily, or loudly.

"Then you want me to stay here?"

For a short eternity she stood motionless, struggling with the answer. When she spoke, it was on a shredded wisp of sound. "Yes."

He pushed off from the desk and took two steps, until he was face-to-face with her, looking down into those sad, green eyes. "Then you won't hate me?"

"I never hated you," she whispered. "It's just . . . all the lies."

Her hand came up to cover her face again, but he took her wrist and moved it away, making her look at him. "There won't be any more lies, Silena. I swear. No more lies, okay?"

He slid his hand down her arm and felt her trembling. Cradling her face, he tipped it up to his. "What is it, Silena? You're trembling."

"I . . . was so afraid."

"Of what?"

She sucked in a sob, trying to control her emotions. But they were bigger than she was. "When I saw Willy here . . . I thought . . ."

"That I would leave?"

"Despite all I've said," she whispered, "we do need you here." She looked up at him, met his eyes. "I don't want you to go, Sam."

He bent down and kissed a tear from her cheek, then moved his mouth to her temple, then to her chin.

His lips touched the corner of her mouth, and she breathed in a sigh. But even as she did she pressed a hand on his chest and stopped him from claiming her lips fully.

"What?"

"I don't . . . I don't like the way . . . you make me feel," she whispered.

"How do I make you feel?"

"Like I have no control. Like you're something that's happening to me, and I have no say in it."

He dropped his hands from her face, and smiled down at her. "You have a say, Silena."

She swallowed and backed slightly away. She looked out the broken window, turning her back to him. "What you said today . . . about my wanting you . . . it was true. I've never felt that way before."

"I know that," he said, so softly that she sensed the words more than heard them.

"And . . . I'm so ashamed."

He was standing behind her before she even knew he'd moved, and he set his hands on her shoulders and lowered his lips to her hair. "Don't be ashamed, Silena. You didn't do anything wrong. There's no shame in wanting. And for what it's worth, I've never felt quite that way, either."

She turned around, looking up at him with profound doubt in her eyes. "I don't believe you. You have women lined up."

"Yes," he said. "Sometimes I do. But I'm not talking about lust, Silena. I'm talking about what else I felt."

That unspoken emotion held their eyes in a mental embrace for longer than either of them intended. Silena searched Sam's eyes for the answer to some name for that feeling that, she suspected, had changed her life.

Had she fallen in love? Was that what she was talking about? And was he talking about the same thing?

The thought made her dizzy. Finally, she backed away and turned her eyes to the window again.

"We should . . . we should eat something," she said awkwardly. "My life has been such a mess lately, nothing's on schedule. And you . . . well, you probably don't have much here."

"If you're inviting me to eat with you, Silena, I'd be proud."

She smiled slightly, realizing that her face was turning warm. "All right."

He grinned. "All right."

The awkwardness was exhilarating, and Silena's heart fluttered as he touched her back and started to the door with her.

For days after Hitch's kiss, Margaret had dreamed of it, and how special she had felt in his arms, and how gently he had touched her. But now she wondered if it had been her imagination, for that morning in church he had acted as if he barely knew her, had avoided making eye contact at all cost, and had ridden home alone without a word, except to say that he would come by that afternoon to cut some more wood for Nell and her.

She stood in front of the brown-spotted mirror on her wall, evaluating her appearance, and decided it was no wonder that he wasn't more interested. She looked like a child, and an unkempt child at that. Her hair was too long and too thick, and she hadn't yet learned enough ways to fix it herself, without help from Silena. But Silena couldn't always be there. Margaret had asked her mother for help this morning, but Nell, who was sleeping late after a long night at the saloon, had muttered that men liked her hair down so they could run their fingers through it. Some part of Margaret supposed that no one would know better about what a man liked than her mother did.

The thought struck a spark inside her, and she looked at the straw mattress her mother had left more than an hour ago, since she had a "picnic" to go on with Murdock Smith, who closed the saloon for a few hours on Sunday afternoons, and couldn't wait until dark for the special favors Nell gave him. The bed was rumpled and unmade, and at the end of it lay three saloon dresses where Nell had dropped them. They were all satin and ruffles, dresses no one could be seen in at church, and Margaret wondered if it was blasphemous to wear them on Sunday at all. But her mother had worn one to her picnic, and she had looked nice when she'd left. Nell always looked pretty, and there wasn't a man in town who didn't notice.

That was what she needed now, Margaret thought. A little of her mother's magic. A little paint on her face. A dress that would make Hitch take notice. Some of the perfume one of the drummers had brought her from New Orleans. And her hair all long and streaming around her shoulders.

She unbuttoned her dress and stepped out of it, then folded it neatly and laid it on her bed. Sliding her chemise off over her head as well, since it came too high on her chest for her mother's frock, she tossed it on top of her discarded dress. She went to her mother's bed and picked up the prettiest of the three dresses there, a red one with black ruffles that rode low on the breast.

She had never tried it on before, for she'd never had any interest in looking like her mother. But now it held special appeal. Looking like Nell, acting like Nell, might give her a chance to feel Hitch's arms around her again. It might make him touch her face again. It might make him love her.

The dress slid over her head, then molded tightly

against the breasts she had inherited from Nell, breasts that, until now, had been a source of embarrassment to her. Now she saw them from Hitch's eyes, and was surprised at how smoothly the dress conformed to her shape.

The neckline cut low over those breasts, stopping just short of nipples that puckered at the feel of the fabric. Buttoning it, she looked in the mirror again and wondered if Hitch would be shocked when he came in. Would he smile at her the way men smiled at her mother? Would he take her in his arms, kiss her one more time? Would he look in her eyes and tell her how beautiful she was?

She heard a horse outside and raced to the window in time to see Hitch dismounting. He tethered his horse to a low tree limb, then started over to the woodpile, not even bothering to come in first. Her heart sank.

But the dress gave her courage. Not willing to let the chance pass, she opened the door. "Hitch?"

He glanced back over his shoulder, and his impression was transformed from cool, deliberate disinterest to surprise . . . and perhaps even embarrassment. She watched the color climb to his cheeks, watched him drop the ax, watched him stand up straight.

"Margaret? What are you wearin'?"

"It's a new dress," she said, wondering why her voice suddenly sounded hollow, distant. "Do you like it?"

He walked toward her, a suspicious frown on his face, and gave an exaggerated shrug. "I don't know. It's . . . it's different."

"Different?" she asked, disappointed. "That means you don't like it, I guess." Suddenly humiliated at her weak attempt to get his attention, she stepped back into the house. "I . . . I'll change then. I don't know what I was—"

"No!" His voice rose into a high squeak, and when

she turned back around, she saw that his face was even redder than before. "You don't have to do that on my account. It's just that . . . you look good in that. Real good. It took me by surprise."

Her eyes sparkled, and she smiled. "Come in for a minute, Hitch. Ma's not home, and I have coffee. . . ."

She could hear his breathing come heavier. His gaze fell to her breasts, then dashed back up to her face. "Where is she?"

"On a picnic somewhere," she said. "She won't be back for a while."

He swallowed, and his eyes fell to her breasts again. His face still raged red, but he nodded. "All right. For a minute. Then I have to cut the wood."

He came in. She closed the door behind him and, when she looked up, saw that he was watching her. His eyes traced the slope of her bare shoulders, then grazed her breasts again. "You look . . . real good, Margaret. I wouldn't want you to wear that in public, but . . ."

"I just wore it for you," she said boldly.

She stepped toward him, and suddenly he reached out and pulled her against him. Just as she had hoped, his mouth found hers. But the kiss was different this time . . . more urgent . . . more powerful.

His hands trembled as they glided over her bare shoulders, and then his mouth followed in their path. When his lips touched her throat, then the indention at the base of her neck, then her chest, a tiny chime of fear trilled inside her. But it was nothing like it had been when the outlaw touched her. This fear was different.

More than what was going to happen, she feared what wouldn't happen. What if he let her go and didn't touch her or hold her? What if he walked away and left her alone?

The alternative seemed much more appealing, for it meant being held and kissed and touched in a thousand different ways. And no matter how she tried to talk herself out of it, it seemed the best of all her choices.

When his hands groped to unfasten her buttons, and he opened the dress, revealing young breasts peaked and yearning, there was no more reasoning to sort through in her mind. There was only instinct, and longing, and desperation.

And when he took her to her bed, she told herself it meant he loved her. It would be different than it always was with Nell, she thought. Hitch wouldn't let her down.

They heard the wheels of Murdock's wagon before Margaret had managed to get all of her buttons refastened. It wasn't until she did up the last one that she realized she should have put on her own clothes before Nell came home. Wearing the saloon dress would alert her mother that something untoward had been going on. Whether that would stimulate pride or anger in her was something Margaret didn't care to find out.

"Your ma's home," Hitch said, buttoning his own shirt. "I gotta go."

"But . . . I was going to cook you supper."

"Can't stay," he said, his hands shaking as he peered out the window. "Oh, Lord. Murdock's with her."

"What's wrong?"

"He'll think we were . . . you know . . . they'll both think . . ."

Margaret was quiet as he ran around gathering his hat and slipping on his boots. "You don't have to run off," she said. "You really don't. Murdock doesn't ever come in."

"Can't stay," he said.

Without a good-bye, he burst out the door, headed for his horse.

"Hey, boy," Murdock said from his wagon as Nell began climbing out.

"I came to chop wood," Hitch blurted quickly.

"Thank you, Hitch." Nell looked around, but saw no evidence of his work. "Where'd you put it?"

"Uh . . ." He waved a hand in the direction of the outhouse. "Over there. I'll finish later."

He rode away before either of them had the chance to reply. When Nell turned back to Murdock, he had a grin on his face.

"Looks like the boy's feelin' a little guilty 'bout somethin'. Margaret ain't followin' in her ma's footsteps, is she?"

Nell turned and looked toward the house, where Margaret was busy changing into her own clothes before her mother could come in and see her dressed like a saloon whore. But it was too late, for already she felt like one.

Word about Hitch and Margaret reached Silena the next day when she reopened her store. Murdock Smith had waited until it was overrun with townspeople who'd waited longer than was comfortable for their supplies to drop the news that would send all the tongues wagging.

"Hitch Calhoun is breakin' in Nell's girl," the saloon owner said. "I reckon it's about time for me to start thinkin' about hirin' her to work at the saloon."

Silena hurried around the counter, her face burning. "What did you say?"

"I said little Margaret's growin' up. And it's time for some new blood in Hayton. Nell's gettin' too old."

Fire erupted in Silena's eyes, and she glared at him. "Margaret is not like her mother."

Murdock's laughter rose to the roof. "That ain't how it looked yesterday when I caught Hitch runnin' outta her house buttonin' his britches."

Stunned, Silena gaped at him. "I'm sure it wasn't

how it looked. Hitch and Margaret wouldn't do that. Margaret's only fifteen."

"Nell started younger," he said, laughing again. "And Margaret's more mature. At least she's filled out more than any fifteen-year-old oughta be."

Sam came in just as Silena thought of reaching out to slap the gossip out of Murdock's mouth. Seeing the murderous fire in her eyes, he stepped between them. "What's going on here?"

Murdock shrugged. "Just tellin' her about Hitch and Margaret rollin' in the hay."

"You're worse than an old maid!" Silena said, reaching around Sam to point at Murdock. "You're spreading lies about something that you don't even know—"

"*I* don't know what I'm talking about?" he asked, his laughter still barely contained. "Honey, I know when a man's been satisfied. I see 'em comin' down them stairs after they been with Nell. Hell, I been there myself. That boy got what he was after, and now there's a whole slew of men who'd like to take a turn. If I were to put her in the saloon, why, I bet I'd attract twice as many men. Three times, even."

Silena pushed Sam out of the way and reared back to slap Murdock, but Sam grabbed her wrist, stopping her. The other men in the store let out raucous laughs, and she sank back, although her eyes still sparked with anger.

"Sam, would you please ask these men to leave my store?" she asked in a barely controlled voice.

Sam looked around. "Come on, boys. You've made her mad. Why don't you come back later?"

"Damn it," Murdock said. "I came in here to get some stuff I've waited days for."

"Then get it and go," Sam said. He turned back to Silena, who still looked as if she could do the man serious harm. "I'll wait on him, Silena. Why don't you go to the back for a minute?"

Silena's nostrils flared and her eyes misted as she pivoted on her heel and busied herself straightening a counter. When Sam had finished with Murdock and the others who would, no doubt, spread the rumor to the next dozen people they saw, she waited for them to leave, then turned on Sam.

"Did you hear what he said about Margaret? Blatant lies!"

"There's nothing you can do about gossip," Sam told her, dropping his voice so as not to be overheard. "Just calm down. It's inevitable. People are probably gossiping about us, too."

Those misty tears sprang to full force, and she covered her mouth with her hand. "Oh, no."

"Don't worry about it. They have nothing better to do than to sit around fantasizing about what the young couples in town are doing. It's life, Silena. It happens that way."

"But with Margaret it's different," she said. "Margaret's mother is a saloon girl. Folks expect her to be one, too."

"Margaret will have to overcome that, Silena, but you can't go around beating up on anybody who ever says a bad word against her. And if you run everybody out of your store who ever spreads a rumor, you won't have anybody left."

Silena heaved a sigh and looked around at the people still milling around there. She wondered if she should tell Margaret what was going around about her, or if it would be better to keep quiet. And then, fleetingly, she wondered how much truth was in the rumor.

Angry at herself for believing even a hint of it, she set

back to work, telling herself that she'd learn what had really happened as soon as she had time to visit Margaret.

It was later that afternoon, three days after Willy's trip to Hayton, that Jessup, the manager of the Wild West show, rode into town. He found Sam still in Silena's store, standing by the stove in the center of the room with his foot propped on a stool, surrounded by men who had once come here on a regular basis just to shoot the breeze with Jake. Now it was Sam whose words they lingered on. He tried his best to keep the gossip from dwelling on Margaret and Hitch.

But Jessup caught his attention the moment he scurried in, for the urgency in his step was greater than that of the others who'd come in the store that day. Dropping his foot, he stood up straight. "Jessup! You looking for me?"

"They said you'd be here, Sam," Jessup said, dashing toward him. "I got to talk to you."

Sam slid his hat back slightly. "Who told you I'd be here? What are *you* doing here?"

"The folks who saw me goin' in the sheriff's office tole me. I come here to talk to you about Willy, Sam. It's real important."

Sam excused himself and started out of the store with Jessup, but he caught Silena watching him from behind the counter. He offered a smile and a slight wink, but the worry never left her face. Did she think that Jessup had come to take him home? he wondered. The thought that she really was concerned filled him with pleasure, and he fought the urge to go lay her fears to rest.

Instead, he followed Jessup out into the cold wind that had just blown up in the last couple of days, marking the first days of winter. Soon it would be snowing, he thought, and the Colonel's plans would have to wait. If they could just get to that point, Hayton could rest a little easier.

"What's wrong, Jessup?" he asked as they walked out onto the street. "Is Willy all right?"

Jessup turned back to Sam, his face tired and drawn, and Sam wondered if he'd slept lately. "Let's go to your office, Sam. I don't want nobody to overhear. The press gets wind of this . . ."

Sam laughed. "Jessup, Hayton doesn't have a press."

"Just the same."

They reached the sheriff's office, and Sam let Jessup precede him inside. The little man strode across the floor, then ran his hands nervously through his thinning hair.

"I'm at my wit's end, Sam. You got to do somethin' about Willy."

"What'd he do now?" Sam asked, settling into the chair behind his desk and slinging a booted ankle over his knee.

"What *ain't* he done? He's been on a drunk ever since he got back from seein' you. He's mad as hell at the world, and he's makin' everbody's life miserable."

Sam tapped a finger on the side of his boot. "It's not like it's the first time, Jessup. Everybody's used to Willy being drunk."

"Everybody's used to you takin' care of things when Willy's drunk, Sam. They're used to somebody bein' in control, and somebody knowin' how to handle Willy."

"You're in control," Sam said. "You can handle it."

"No, I cain't! Willy's out of control, Sam! He's dangerous! If you don't come back with me, now, today, I'm tellin' you, there won't be a Wild West show left."

Sam dropped his foot and sat up straighter in his chair. "What do you mean?"

"I mean that Running Horse and Lucy are plannin' to leave if you don't come back. Sam, they can't take it no more. He's wavin' his guns at ever'body who crosses him, he's treatin' the stars like cow shit, and he's a general menace to ever'body who's dependin' on him. You were the one stable factor in the show, Sam, and if you're gone, a lot of the troupers don't feel the need to stick around."

Sam sat back in his chair again and looked at the ceiling. "Why do Running Horse and Lucy want to leave?"

"They're fed up, Sam. Willy treats 'em like nobodies, and they've both worked a long time to be somebodies. Dr. Carver's Wild West has been sendin' 'em telegrams, tryin' to hire 'em over to their show. Adam Forepaugh, Carver's partner, is puttin' up more money than they ever heard of to get 'em to sign with 'em. They're thinkin' about it, Sam, and if they leave—"

"If they leave we've got nothing," Sam said as the reality of the disaster sank in. "Nothing except Willy."

"And Willy ain't worth a damn without you, Sam. You and I both know it."

Sam was quiet for a long moment, frowning at the desperate man with whom he'd spent so many of his years. Jessup was a worrier, no doubt, and he loved to overreact. But this was serious, and Sam couldn't take it lightly. Carver's troupe was almost as big a competitor with Willy's show as Buffalo Bill's was, and if he stole their biggest stars, they might as well just close the show down.

"Come on, Sam. I cain't handle this. You've got to come back. Please."

Sam rose to his feet, looming over the smaller man. Taking off his hat, he walked to the window, which had just been repaired the day before, and looked out across the street to the store where he had left Silena. The thought of leaving her made his stomach twist painfully, and yet he couldn't sit by and let his father destroy everything that meant something to him.

Making the decision, he turned back to Jessup and put his hat back on. "All right, Jessup. I'll go back with you today."

Silena was waiting at the door of her store when Sam strode out of the sheriff's office and across the street toward her. He was going to leave, she told herself as her heart lay aching in her chest. Jessup had come to talk him into going back, and from the look on Sam's face, she could tell that he had succeeded.

She tried to hide the emotion on her own face as he reached her, but she feared it still rippled on her voice. "You're going back, aren't you?"

Sam took her hand. "Let's go talk," he said. "In the back."

She struggled with stinging tears as he led her through the store into her house. When they reached the kitchen, he turned around, leaned back against the table, and looked down at her. Her incipient tears seemed to surprise him, and he touched her face, as though to smooth away her fears. Slowly, he kissed her.

"Don't go, Sam," she whispered, beginning to tremble as he slid his arms around her. "I'm scared."

"I'm going," he said, pulling back to look at her. "But you don't have to be scared. Because I'm taking you with me."

She caught a breath and stared up at him. "What?"

"I'm not leaving you here," he said. "I can't protect you if I'm not with you, but I have to go back. Willy needs me."

"But . . . I can't go to Omaha. I can't leave Pa here, and the store, and—"

"We won't be gone long," he said. "Just a day or two. You can close the store, and Jake will be fine. I don't expect anything to happen this soon. It'll take some time for word to get back to the Colonel that his people are all dead. He'll have to have time to round up more, and it's too soon. It's best to go now, and take care of my business there."

She backed away, shaking her head. "I don't know, Sam. I just don't know."

"It's not up to you." He grinned and took a step toward her, pulling her into him again. "I'm not asking, I'm telling. I'm going to Omaha, and you're going with me."

His commanding tone angered her, and she lifted her chin defiantly. "And if I say no?"

"If you say no, then I guess I'll have to throw you over my shoulder and tie you to the horse."

"You wouldn't."

"Want to see?"

She didn't say anything for a moment, and suddenly he bent over, grabbed her legs, and lifted her over his shoulder. She let out a scream, and he carried her into her bedroom and dropped her onto the bed.

Her face was flushed and laughing when he braced an arm on each side of her, his face inches from hers. "Now, are you going to get packed, or do I have to do it for you?"

The laughter left her eyes, and she looked seriously up at him. "Sam, what if you get there, and don't want to come back? What if they talk you into staying?"

"As long as you're with me, you can make sure that doesn't happen, can't you?"

She frowned up at him for a moment, her big eyes sad and confused. "There's a lot to do," she said. "I'll have to close the store, and Pa won't like it . . . and I'll have to pack."

He smiled and straightened. "I don't see any problem. You get packed, and I'll finish the customers in the store and go over to tell Jake where I'm taking you."

Silena sat up on the bed, a slight smile softening her face. "When do we leave?"

"An hour, if we're going to get there by dark," he said. "Be ready."

And before she could object again, Sam was out the door.

It was early afternoon when Jake asked Caldonia to wheel him outside for the first time so he might say good-bye to Silena. The thought of sending her off to Omaha, when he'd kept her so close and so protected all these years, was more than he could stand. But worse was the thought that if Sam left her here, Jake would not be able to protect her.

His eyes misted over as Silena bent down to kiss him good-bye. Moved by the look on his face, she touched his stubbled cheek. "Don't worry about me, Pa. We'll be back in a day or two."

"I'm not worried," he said gruffly, looking away to avoid making a spectacle of himself. "I'll just miss you, is all."

"You're worried," she said. "Like you were the last time I went."

"It ain't the same," he said, his voice hoarse. "This time you're with Sam, and I trust him to protect you."

Silena looked him fully in the face and smiled softly. "Then why do you look so sad?"

He reached up to touch a tendril of her hair. "Because I love you, girl," he said quietly.

She breathed in a sigh and stood up, a million conflicting emotions pulsing through her. If he wasn't her father, if he had, indeed, kidnapped her, if it had all been for revenge, why would he love her?

And yet he did, and she had always known it. Not at any time in her life had she ever doubted it.

"I love you, too, Pa," she whispered.

"You bring her back as fast as you can," Jake said to Sam.

Sam tipped his hat. "I will."

He helped Silena mount her horse, then mounted his own. She waved back to her father as they started away in Jessup's wake, and when Sam looked over at her, he saw one lone tear running down her face.

"What's the matter?" he asked across the cold breeze.

She shook her head. "He does love me," she said. "I know that."

"And you think that contradicts the rumors you've heard?"

"Well, don't you?" she asked.

Sam looked at her for a long moment. "Yeah, Silena. I do. The man loves you like any other father would love his daughter. Maybe even more. Love like that is rare, and when you have it, you shouldn't question it."

"But I have to question it," she said. "There are so many things I don't understand."

"Rumors are full of lies," he said, reaching across the space between them and taking her hand from the pommel. "I'll help you find the truth if I can, Silena. Maybe we can find out something more from Willy, if I ever get him sober."

"Maybe," she whispered.

He reached across and touched her face, then kicked his horse to a faster pace that would get them to Omaha before dark.

The Hayton Women's Church League had a new cause by that afternoon. Armed with their Bibles and their noses in the air, they paid a visit to the Calhoun house to talk to Hitch and his mother.

"We feel it's our duty to inform you of the gossip going all over town about your son, Anna," Lolita Phillips said as she took a cookie from the tray Anna Calhoun had brought out.

"What gossip?" she asked, looking troubled.

"About him and that . . . that woman's daughter. It was bad enough when there was only one in town, but now it looks like there'll be two, and—"

"Two what?" Hitch asked, cutting in, even though he had not yet sat down. He stepped forward out of the doorway where he'd been leaning.

"Two . . . ladies of the evening."

Anna Calhoun gasped and began to cough, and Hitch leaned over the sofa and peered at Lolita. "Margaret Plumer is not a 'lady of the evening.'"

"That's right," Evelyn Barlow spoke up. "Zane said he heard they did it in broad daylight."

Hitch flushed crimson. Standing back up, he glanced at his mother as he tried to control his racing heart. "Zane heard wrong."

"Well, of course we don't expect you to admit it in front of your ma, boy, but we're here to warn you. You're too young to be cavorting with someone of her caliber. We consider your family to be one of the best in Hayton, above reproach, and we hate to see you pull the name down."

Hitch ran both hands through his hair and turned away from the women. "I don't believe this."

"Sit down, Hitch!" His mother's voice was loud and angry. Unable to defy her, he sat down beside her.

"Is there any truth to this?"

Hitch shook his head. "No, Ma. None at all."

"Then why did Murdock see you runnin' outta there buttonin' your pants?" Evelyn asked.

"I was *not* buttonin' my pants!" Hitch shot back. "They were already buttoned! He made that up to make it sound good."

"Then you *had* been in there with Margaret?" his mother asked, astounded.

"No . . . yes . . . I was cutting wood for her and her ma. Caleb was my best friend, Ma, and they don't have nobody."

"Wood is customarily cut outside," Lolita pointed out. "Not inside. And Murdock was quick to point out that there wasn't much of a woodpile he could see."

Hitch's face mottled with anger, and he rose to his feet. "I've had enough," he said. "I don't have to listen to this."

"She's a whore," his mother said, her own face full of rage as she stood up to face him. "I don't want you associating with her anymore. If they run out of wood, let one of Nell's 'clients' help her. They don't need you."

"Margaret is not like Nell," he said, desperate for her to understand.

"If gossip like this is going around about her, then she's turning out *just* like her mother," Mrs. Calhoun said. "And so help me, if I hear of you going over there one more time, I'll wire for your father to come back from Kansas immediately and let him take care of it."

The threat hovered over Hitch like a lightning bolt without a target. Compressing his lips, he started for the door.

"Where are you going?"

"Out," he said through his teeth. Before she could object, he had slammed out of the house.

The compound where the Wild West troopers kept camp was quiet and lifeless as Sam and Silena rode in.

Sam stopped his horse and looked around at the tents where the stars and troopers stayed, but no one stirred.

"Something's wrong," he said quietly.

Silena looked over at him, saw the worry and apprehension on his face. "What?"

"It's too quiet," he said.

At that moment Jessup came running out of Willy's tent, motioning for Sam to stay quiet. He dismounted, helped Silena down, then braced himself for the blow.

"Willy's got his guns and he's been shootin' everything that moves."

"Anybody hurt?" Sam asked.

"Not yet. When I got back an hour ago, ever'body had left to go into Omaha. Runnin' Horse was still here, packin' a wagon. When I told him you were comin', he calmed down and went into town until you could do somethin' with Willy."

Sam tethered the horses to a post and started toward Willy's tent. "I'll go talk to him."

Silena's heart lurched. "Sam, no!"

He turned around. "Why not?"

"Didn't you hear him? He's got guns. He's shooting them. He's drunk, and he could—"

"Willy won't shoot me."

She started toward him, shaking her head. "Sam, you don't know that. If he's drunk . . ."

Sam stopped long enough to frame her face with his hands. "It'll be all right. I've done this a hundred times before. You just go with Jessup and wait until I get his guns from him."

He looked over her head to Jessup, who stood nervously waiting for Sam to move. "Take her to my tent, Jessup. I'll be there when I'm finished."

Silena tried to object, but Sam started away, and she knew better than to raise her voice.

Slowly, she followed Jessup to Sam's tent. The dimness within was a stark contrast to the sunlight blazing down, and letting her eyes adjust, she looked around her. Sam's bed was neatly made, untouched since he left, and his personal articles stood in a neat line on the folding table beside his bed. The scent of him lingered in the room, conjuring an instant image of him in her mind. An image of his holding her face in his hands, of his sweet, gentle kiss, of his telling her to trust him, that there would be no more lies.

"We need him here," Jessup said, his voice startling her. "We can't run this show without him."

She turned around and looked at the little man. He was staring at her with the slightest bit of contempt. "I know," she said.

"He belongs here," he went on. "This is his home."

She stood silent for a moment, not certain how to answer. "It looks a little temporary to me."

"Don't matter none," Jessup said. "It's still his home. This is his family. A man don't turn his back on that."

"Sam hasn't turned his back on anything," she said. "He's here, isn't he?"

"Yeah, but seems to me he's nursin' some misplaced sense of loyalty to folks he hardly even knows."

"Folks like me?" she asked.

"Folks who don't mind seein' him get killed for their own safety."

"No one in Hayton wants to see Sam get killed," she said. "Least of all me."

"Then make him come back. Make him come back here for good."

"I can't make Sam do anything," she said. "It wasn't

my idea for him to stay, and it wasn't my idea to make him sheriff. He doesn't listen to me."

"He went 'cause he was listenin' to you. You're the only reason he's stayin'."

"I don't think so." She sat down in the chair beside his small table and picked up a framed picture. It was of a young woman, a woman who looked a lot like him. Stella, she thought. His sister. The one he couldn't save. "I think he's staying because he likes it there . . . the sense of being needed, the sense of being respected."

"He's needed and respected here."

She looked up at Jessup. "I know he is. But that doesn't seem to be enough for him."

Jessup stepped forward and took the picture out of her hand, set it back on the table. "You've known him a couple of weeks, and you think you got him all figured out. I've known him for most of his life."

Tears welled up in Silena's eyes, and she took a deep breath. "I'm not making Sam do anything, Jessup. What he does is entirely up to him."

A gunshot rang out in the distance, and Silena jumped. "What was that?"

"Prob'ly Willy blowin' Sam's head off," Jessup said, picking a piece of lint off his sleeve.

Silena looked up at him. "Do you think—"

"He's all right," Jessup said. "He can handle Willy."

Silena sat back, holding her breath and waiting for the next gunshot.

The gun still smoked in Sam's hand, but at least it wasn't in Willy's anymore. It had gone off while he'd wrestled it from him, and now he stood facing his slobbering drunk father with disgust and contempt.

"Willy, you've got to pull yourself together. Folks are afraid to death of you. Running Horse has a wagon half-packed at his tepee, and Lucy's ready to sign with Carver's group."

"Carver's show ain't nothin'," Willy slurred. "Ain't got no names. Ain't got no talent."

"He's about to get ours, Willy!" Sam shouted.

"Whadda you care?" Willy asked. "You walked, yourself. You're off playin' sheriff to some fool town."

"I care or I wouldn't be here."

"Well, it's too late. Gimme my gun back."

Sam opened the chamber and emptied the cartridges into his palm. "Willy, I came back here for a reason. To get you sober enough that you can deal with the problems in the show all by yourself."

"I ain't dealin' with nothin'," Willy said, swatting a hand Sam's way. "They can all rot and burn in everlastin' hell for all I care."

"I'll tell them you said so," Sam said, gathering up the rest of Willy's guns. "But meanwhile, I'm going to make sure you don't send them there."

Willy sat down on his cot, not noticing Sam's work. "What're you doin' here, anyways? You tole me you wouldn't come."

"Jessup came for me. Said it was an emergency. Looks like he was right."

"Emergency," Willy scoffed. "It was a damn emergency when *I* came, but you wouldn't come then."

"I told you why."

"So how'd Jessup talk you into leavin' that gal?"

"I didn't leave her," Sam said. "I brought her with me."

"You did what?" Willy tried to get up, but staggered and fell back.

"She's in my tent, probably fearing for her life. Bringing her here around you drunk is probably worse than facing the Colonel's men."

"They'll be back there, you know. Ever'body knows you killed 'em all, and that'll stir the Colonel up when he hears. He won't let this go."

"I know that," Sam said. "I'm prepared."

"He'll kill you," Willy slurred.

"No, he won't." Sam shoved his father down onto the cot, then pulled off the boots, which smelled as if they'd been worn for three days straight. Lifting Willy's feet onto the bed, he said, "That's the most important thing you taught me, Willy. That feeling of being invincible."

"But that was a lie," Willy said. "You ain't invincible. And neither am I."

"It'll get me through, anyway."

"It'll get you dead's what it'll get you." The words came out on a tired sigh, and Willy closed his eyes.

"Go to sleep, old man," Sam said quietly. "And when you wake up, don't reach for any more liquor. I'm getting rid of it all."

"Leave my bottles be."

"Can't do that, Willy," Sam said. "You've got work to do when you're sober. Problems to solve."

"Why do you think I choose to stay drunk?"

Sam smiled slightly. As he left the tent he breathed a deep sigh of relief and braced himself for the mood Willy would be in when he woke in a few hours.

Willy slept until the next morning, then woke with a raging headache and a temper to match. Because they had heard that Sam had returned and had matters under control, the troupe members gravitated back to the camp during the night and by morning were lined up outside Sam's tent, ready to air complaints and elicit his help.

Silena sat next to him in his tent, quietly watching as he tackled each matter with concern and full attention. The respect each troupe member had for him was inspiring, and changed the way she looked at him. Despite the fact that he was a showman, there was no doubt that his sincerity and concern were real.

Willy's, on the other hand, was nonexistent as he swaggered into Sam's tent. "I wanna talk to you, boy."

Sam looked up at Willy with dull eyes. "How are you feeling, Willy?"

"Like buffalo shit, that's what. I need a drink."

"You can't have one," Sam said, coming to his feet as the two wranglers he'd been talking to scurried out of Willy's way and left the tent. "Too much to do."

Silena saw Willy eye her with disdain, and she cringed slightly. Slowly, she stood up. "I'll . . . I'll wait outside."

"No," Sam said. "I want you right here with me."

He took her hand and ran his thumb over her knuckle, reassuring her that she was safe from Willy's wrath, if not his mouth. She sat back down.

"Sit down, Willy. We have work to do."

"Not now," Willy barked. "I need some tonic for my headache. My hands are shakin'."

"I'm not surprised. Do you want something to eat?"

Willy made a face as if he'd throw up and shook his head. "No, no food. Just a drink."

"We have coffee right here," Sam said triumphantly, pouring Willy a cup.

"Coffee? That's all?"

"That's it," Sam said. "Coffee. And then when you feel awake enough, we're going to meet with Running Horse and Lucy and try to iron out some of these problems."

"Shit," Willy mumbled, frowning down at his coffee. "The last thing I need right now is to listen to their whinin'. If they don't like it here, they can leave anytime."

"And take half the troupe with them when they sign with Carver's show."

"His show won't last another season. Damn thing's so full of amateurs, the crowds don't even stay for the whole show."

"It'll be a hell of a lot better with our stars, Willy. Don't forget that."

Willy mumbled something incoherent and finished off his coffee, and Silena and Sam sat quietly, waiting for him to become alert enough to deal with some of his reality.

It was afternoon before Willy agreed to meet with Running Horse and Quick Shot Lucy, who had both finished packing their wagons and were more than ready to ride out at the next sunrise.

Silena sat next to Sam, quietly watching him mediate between his father—still ailing and ornery, though he was noticeably more sober than she'd ever seen him—and the two stars of the show. Jessup leaned against a table, a look of defeat in his gray eyes.

"What will it take to make you stay?" Sam asked. "Either of you."

Lucy, dressed in a fringed leather skirt and packing pistols on her hips, shook her head. "I already told you, Sam. Short of you comin' back here, nothin' could make me stay."

Silena looked at Sam with alarm in her eyes, but he squeezed her hand in reassurance. "You don't need me here," Sam said. "We're only talking about three shows a week during the winter. Willy and Jessup can handle anything that comes up."

"That's my condition," Lucy said. "Carver offered me a good hunk more to play for him. And I can guarantee you I wouldn't have to put up with none of the crap I have to put up with around here."

Willy bristled and leaned forward, bracing his elbows on his knees. "The crap flies both ways, gal."

"So do the bullets, Willy, and I'm tired o' dodgin' yours."

Sam stood up and stepped between them before Lucy could launch an attack on Willy. He'd seen her mad at her husband before, and it hadn't been pretty.

Running Horse sat stiff and motionless, glaring at them both.

The whole scene—Willy sitting down, chiding and daring Quick Shot Lucy, Lucy trying to get past Sam to swing at Willy, and the old Indian chief watching them all with vengeful eyes—suddenly struck Silena as dreadfully funny.

She looked down at her hands, desperately trying not to smile.

"What else would it take to make you stay, Lucy? More money? More time in the spotlight?" Sam asked.

"Hell, I'm carryin' the show as it is!" Lucy shouted. "And no amount of money would make it worth bein' under Willy Hawkins's tyranny another day!"

Sam swung desperately around to Running Horse. "What about you, Chief? What would it take?"

For a moment Silena wondered if the old chief had heard, for he didn't bat an eye as he stared at Willy, hunched over in the corner with a look of agony on his face. "If Willy stop drinking."

"What?" Willy sprang out of his chair, but his face

turned green at the effort, and he dropped back down. "Damn it, Runnin' Horse, you drink as much as I do."

"But not as often," Running Horse said. "When I drink, nobody gets hurt. When you drink, the whole compound takes cover."

Silena, once again, found her amusement edging up inside her. It wasn't funny, and if she laughed, the whole thing was liable to blow up. Sam caught her eye just as she summoned her greatest effort to hold her laughter back. Seeing the tilt to her mouth, the reddening of her face, the amused mist in her eyes, he almost smiled himself.

Willy stood up, more slowly this time, and leaned over to Running Horse, his face hot and defiant as he pointed his finger at the old chief. "I'll tell you one thing, Running Horse. I'll drink any damn time I please, and I don't need no damn Injun or no mealymouthed woman tellin' me I cain't."

Sudden silence fell over the room, and all amusement died from Silena's heart. For a moment she thought a gun would be drawn or a fist would fly.

Instead, Lucy looked at Willy, shrugged helplessly, and shook her head. "That's it, Sam. I've heard the last insult I'm gonna hear from that has-been. I'll be out of here by morning."

"Now, Lucy—" Sam's helpless plea was interrupted when Running Horse got to his feet. "Running Horse, where are you going?"

"To Springfield, where Carver's troupe is," he said. "Soon as I get my family ready. This 'damn Injun' is at the end of the line."

"Chief! You can't just—"

"Let 'em go, Sam!" Willy snapped. "Those crowds don't come to see 'em, anyway! It's me they come to see!"

"You fool!"

Jessup's words split the air with an explosion of rage. All eyes turned to the small man who'd been standing against the table. Now he leaned forward, his eyes shooting sparks of anger. "You can't hit nothin' anymore, Willy! You're too soppin' drunk all the time to do this show any good."

A collective gasp sounded over the room. Lucy and Running Horse stopped at the door, gaping at their manager.

"I don't hear nobody in the audience complainin' about my performances," Willy flung back. "My aim's better'n it's been in years."

"You wanna know how good your aim is, old man?" Jessup asked.

Sam took a deep breath and raised a hand to silence him. "Jessup, this isn't the time—"

"No, Sam, it *is* the time. It's long past the time!" Jessup walked toward Willy, his face intense with rage. "The bald truth, old man, is that if it weren't for Sam doin' your shootin' for you, we'd be stampeded with folks demandin' their money back."

Silence fell even heavier over the tent. Suddenly Silena realized that she was in the middle of a volatile battle, one that would leave casualties, one that would wound at least two people in the room.

Sam's face was stricken as he stared at his father. Willy gaped at him, a look of horror and disbelief wrinkling his face. "What did he say?"

Sam shook his head. "Willy, calm down—"

"No!" Willy shouted, and knocked over the table beside Sam's cot. His things fell off, scattering on the dirt floor. "What the hell did he mean, you've been doin' my shootin' for me?"

Sam looked around, seeking help, but none came.

Finally, he took a deep breath and answered quietly. "Sometimes, when you were drinking, Willy, when you were shaky, and you weren't hitting your targets . . . a few times . . . not very often . . ."

"You shot for me." The words came as a whispered revelation, and Willy looked as if he'd had the life knocked out of him. "You shot for me, and made me think it was me."

"I had no choice," Sam said through his teeth. "I did what had to be done."

Willy's trembling started with his hands, then went up his arms until his whole body shook. "You had no right! No right!"

"He had every right!" Jessup screamed. "We all had every right, because this is our show, too. We have big hunks of our lives invested in it, Willy, and Sam didn't want to see you throw it all away."

"*He's* the one who threw it away!" Willy shouted. "He's the one who ruined me!" He turned to his son, his finger flying high as he pointed it at him. "You get on your horse and you take your little girlfriend, and you can ride straight to hell."

Silena stood up. Sam grabbed her hand and pulled her behind him. "Willy, I didn't do it to hurt you."

"Get out!" Willy shouted. "Just get out."

"It's my tent," Sam said quietly.

"Everything in this compound is mine," Willy bit out. "Every damn inch of it. It's by my good grace that you have a penny to your name. All of you. Now get the hell out of my sight before I tear off your heads and spit down your necks!"

Sam stood stock-still for a moment, and Silena could feel the anger in his clenched hand as he held hers. Finally, he nodded for everyone to leave.

"I'm leavin'," Jessup said before he left the tent. "But I ain't comin' back, either. I've had enough."

"Good!" Willy spat. "You can ride straight to hell with the rest of 'em."

Slowly, they all left the tent, leaving Willy alone with himself . . . his worst enemy on earth.

"Jessup!" Sam pulled Silena along behind him as he chased after the small man storming away from the tent. He looked helplessly at Running Horse and Lucy cutting across the compound, then hurried to follow Jessup, instead. "Jessup, you can't quit! He needs you."

"Willy don't need nobody. Give him a bottle of gin and a gun and he's happier'n a clam."

"He can't run this show without you, Jessup!"

"Fine! Then you stay. I'm done."

Sam gave Silena a powerless look, and she realized suddenly just what the dilemma was that Sam faced. If the stars walked out, and if the manager quit, he was all Willy had left. And that would mean his making a choice all over again, a choice that wouldn't be easy for him.

She felt a new sense of purpose. Withdrawing her hand from Sam's, she stepped forward. "Jessup, I don't know you that well, but you seem so capable and so competent. There are a lot of people depending on you."

"Yeah, well, they cain't depend on me. Not when I

have to depend on the likes of him," he said, pointing toward Willy's tent. "I'm through, Sam. I expect my last week's salary, and then I'm gone."

"I'll give you a month's extra salary if you'll stay."

Jessup stopped and turned around slowly. "Sam, you cain't do that. Besides, it wouldn't be enough."

"Then make it twice that." When Jessup still didn't budge, Sam made a last desperate attempt. "Jessup, if you'll stay, I'll give you six times your monthly salary for a bonus . . . just between you and me. Out of my own pocket, Jessup."

Jessup eyed him suspiciously for a long moment. "You're only offerin' this so you won't have to stay. Don't think I don't know it."

"The town of Hayton needs me more than the Wild West show does, and that's where I want to be," Sam said. "But the show needs you, Jessup. Willy needs you. In the name of our friendship for all these years, Jessup, I'm asking you to stay."

They stared at each other for a moment that stretched into eternity before Jessup spoke. "Six times my monthly salary? That's a lot of money, Sam."

"You're worth more than that, Jessup, but it's all I have."

"You'd really do that?"

"I'll have the money within the hour," Sam said. "Come on, Jessup. Just promise me you won't walk. We can deal with Running Horse and Lucy leaving. We can always find new stars, but we can't do without you."

Jessup's chest seemed to swell with pride. He looked at the ground, slid his hands into his back pockets, and shrugged. "Well, I reckon I could wait awhile. Try to get things on a smoother footin' before I hit the road. Anyways, I'll have my work cut out for me tryin' to replace the stars."

"Then you'll stay?" Silena asked, a little too hopefully.

"Guess so. If Sam's willin' to do all that . . ." He swallowed, as if the whole offer had touched him in a place where he wasn't used to being touched. "The show means a lot to me, Sam. I wouldn't have wanted to leave it. But I cain't take much more crap."

"No one blames you," Sam said. "But you and I are the only two who can handle Willy."

He took Silena's hand again, gave it a meaningful squeeze, and started across the compound with her. "I'll get the money within the hour," he said, "but meanwhile I'm going to try one more time to calm down Lucy and the chief. Just stay away from Willy for a while. He'll be all right."

Sam's efforts to calm the two stars were in vain, and that night, after hours of talking and pleading and bribing, he finally reconciled himself to the fact that Lucy and the chief's minds were made up. Too much damage had been done, and they were leaving.

Defeated, but already coming up with ideas to recruit new stars, he took Silena to his tent, lit a small lantern on the table, and turned to look at her in the lamplight.

A warm wave of anticipation swirled over her, but his mood was quiet, somber. She wanted him to put thoughts of the show out of his mind, hold her, and give her his undivided attention just for the night.

The very thought of desiring such a thing sent a wave of guilt through her. She thought of Margaret, probably innocent of such thoughts, being gossiped about. If the town only knew of some of the thoughts Silena had entertained about Sam, the tongues would wag for sure.

But Sam made no move to come near her, and she

wondered how scandalous it would be to go to him and experience the burning sweetness he could offer her. The love that filtered through in everything he did, whether he professed it or not, and made her feel special . . . and less lonely.

"You can sleep here," he whispered. "I'll sleep on the ground outside the tent."

Her heart fell. "But it's cold out there."

He shrugged. "It's cold in here, too. I'll be fine."

She wet her lips, so that, like her eyes, they glistened in the lamplight. The urge to kiss her was almost more than Sam could bear, but he kept himself from it. The look on her face was too apprehensive, too innocent, too trusting, and the last time he had made love to her, she had made him feel as if he'd stolen something precious from her. Tonight, he wanted her to trust.

"Well . . . if you need me . . . I'll be right outside the door," he said.

He left her standing stock-still, staring at him with wonder and disappointment in her eyes, a look that almost drove him mad. He went outside, laid down a pallet on the dirt, and stretched out on it, his arms behind his head and his hat pulled low on his forehead.

His eyes strayed to the yellow glow of lamplight through the tent, and he saw her shadow moving across the floor. Slowly, he sat up, shoved his hat back, and watched as she began to peel her dress off.

His mouth went dry, and he pulled up his knees and braced his elbows on them as her shadow slowly undressed. He watched, mesmerized, as she unbuttoned her dress, then peeled the fabric back and slid her arms out of the sleeves. Her dress fell to the floor, and he watched her shadow step out of it, then bend to pick it up and lay it carefully over the chair.

Her silhouette looked bare already, but he watched further as she raised her arms and pulled her chemise over her head. Something about the change in the shadow, the separation of the silhouette of her breasts, told him her breasts were naked, and his mouth went dry. And then she stepped out of her pantaloons, leaving her small hips and legs completely bare. His breathing and his heart accelerated wildly.

He watched her shadow bend over again, fully naked, as she reached into her bag for her nightgown. She pulled it out and laid it on the bed. Before putting it on, she raised her arms, causing her breasts to flex even more, and pulled the pins from her hair. He watched as she arched her back and let the hair trail down to her shoulders, full and graceful and rich.

It was a shadow, he told himself, nothing more, but there was so much behind that shadow, so much that he wanted to reach for. So much that he wanted to take as his own.

It was like a madness, he thought, for each moment in her presence made him want her more. Her scent lingered in his mind, her taste tantalized his mouth, her feel mesmerized his body. He imagined how her bare skin would feel against his, how her body would fit beneath his, how he would feel inside her. . . .

He watched as her shadow drifted across the floor to the bed. She picked up the nightgown, but just before slipping it on, she blew out the light.

Something inside him snapped, making him feel physically unable to lie down and go to sleep. He needed to go for a walk, he thought, or take a swim. He needed to get his mind off her, but it was a bigger task than he was capable of.

The only other option was to go to her, and rely on the magic of the evening, the magic of his emotions, to guide him. He didn't want to hurt her, fill her with shame, or taint her in any way, but the cold reality of a night alone, after what he'd just seen, was more terrifiying than the thought of her turning him away.

Finally, not taking another moment to think, he followed his feelings. Standing up, he pulled back the flap of the tent.

Silena felt Sam's presence before she felt the rush of cold air from the open tent flap. She sat up slowly and squinted into the darkness. "Who is it?"

"Shhh," he whispered. "It's just me."

He came to the bed, knelt down beside it. Sliding his fingers into her hair, he coaxed her back down. "I just wanted to kiss you good night."

"You shouldn't be here," she whispered, pulling the sheet up over her gown. "I'm not decent."

His eyes swept down her chin, her neck, to her chest, barely revealed above her hands. "I know I shouldn't," he said. "But there's no one but us here, and I couldn't help myself."

His lips descended on hers, but just before they touched, she whispered, "Just a kiss."

"Just a kiss," he affirmed.

But the kiss was more than a kiss, for it reached into their souls and stirred the embers of all the passion that had smoldered between them since the first day they'd met. And in the midst of that kiss, something ignited, something deep within each of them, something that made it impossible to break away.

And yet he did.

She watched, mesmerized, as he stood up, gave her one last long, yearning look, and backed out of the tent.

Disappointment seeped through her as her heart

pounded out an urgent protest. She had wanted him to make love to her. She had wanted to feel his body moving next to hers. She had wanted to sleep wrapped in his arms. She had wanted to wake next to him and look in his eyes in daylight, knowing that they had made love and not being ashamed.

The thought was scandalous. It was wonderful. It was frightening. It was soul stirring.

Was it love that had made her want something so startling? Was it love that had made her heart and body ache with the same force?

Yes, she told herself, it was.

But she couldn't tell him, because she didn't know what it would mean, or how it would change her. She didn't know how it would save her . . . or destroy her.

As the night wore on, with Sam lying just outside her tent, a sadness fell over her, for she didn't know what life had in store for her . . . or for him. The uncertainty hung over her like a pall, and loving him only complicated things.

But it was a sweet complication, and she would deal with it somehow, she thought. For she wasn't ready to turn away from it yet.

Preparing for church when she knew the gossip she would face was almost too much for Margaret, but she determined to go, anyway. They were saying she was a whore, like her mother. Murdock Smith had offered her a job at the saloon. Men who had treated her like a child before were taking a second look and whispering lewd suggestions in her ear. And Hitch hadn't spoken to her in a week.

* * *

She wished Silena hadn't gone to Omaha, for she could have used a friend right now. But if Silena had known what Margaret had done, she wouldn't have approved, either. She might even want to cool off their friendship, just like Hitch had.

She stood in front of her mirror, surveying her image in Silena's hand-me-down dress and trying to decide if she looked conservative enough. There was no one to ask, for Nell was sleeping soundly in her bed.

She turned to Caleb's empty bed, and tears sprang to her eyes. If only he were here, she thought, she could talk to him about this. Of course, he'd probably want to kill Hitch for making love to her, not realizing that she had instigated it. . . .

"Oh, Caleb," she whispered. The tears fell over her lashes, and she wiped them away. "What am I gonna do? He won't even speak to me now. Everybody's talkin'. But I'm going to church this mornin', and I figure they'll see that God can forgive me. Won't they see that? Won't that make a difference?"

There was no answer, only cold loneliness, only the stark reality of her solitude. Wiping her tears, she checked her hair one last time and left the small house.

It was still early, so she decided to walk. The air was cold, colder than she'd expected, but her coat from last year was too small. There wasn't much chance of her getting a new one, unless Silena or someone outgrew one of their own. She supposed she could wear Caleb's, but not to church. She wanted to look respectable at church.

By the time she reached the schoolhouse, most of the congregation had arrived and were already inside. Passing among the wagons parked outside, she looked for Hitch's. It was near the church, indicating that he'd gotten there early. Could he have been there early for her? she wondered. Had he made a point of coming to talk to her?

But as she stepped into the schoolhouse and made her way up the aisle, a hush seemed to fall over the room. She sought out Hitch, sitting between his mother and Lolita Phillips, and he seemed to be the only one in the room not looking at her. Instead, he looked down at his hands in his lap, and his face reddened as she found a seat and slipped into it.

And as she stood with the congregation for the first hymn, Margaret realized that she hadn't reached her peak of loneliness, yet. For the loneliest lonely was when you were among a lot of people who looked upon you as the lowest form of human life. The loneliest lonely was when you figured they were probably right.

Silena rose and dressed before the first light of day filtered through the tent, then she and Sam ate and said their good-byes to the troupe members.

Finally, Sam did what he'd been dreading. He went alone into Willy's tent and found, to his surprise, that the old man was awake, slumped on his cot, his face in his hands.

"I came to say good-bye, Willy."

Willy didn't move, and for a moment Sam wondered if he was drunk again, sleeping sitting up.

"I don't know how long I'll be there," Sam tried again—"but things are taken care of here. Jessup's going to stay, and he'll start looking for some stars to replace the chief and Lucy. We thought of holding some contests, trying to recruit new talent. Meanwhile—"

"Who's gonna replace you?" Willy's words came out in a low monotone, surprising Sam with their calm sobriety.

"Any of the troupers could replace me. I'm not one of the biggest draws."

"Maybe you should be," Willy said. He looked up, his eyes as tired and red as Sam had ever seen them. "What if you were, boy? What if it was the Wild West show starring Willy and Sam Hawkins?"

Sam smiled slightly. "Wouldn't matter, Willy. It ain't the limelight I'm looking for anymore."

"That's what we're all lookin' for," Willy muttered. "You can get it here, or you can get it in Hayton. Might be a different kind, but it's the same thing."

Sam took off his hat, sat down next to his father on the cot, and ran his finger around the rim. "There are other things besides limelight, Willy."

Willy slid his rough hands down his face, then dropped them to his lap. He stared at them hard, and when he spoke again, his voice was hoarse. "I cain't believe you did my shootin' for me."

"It was the drinking, Willy. You stop drinking, and you'll be all right. But I can't do that for you."

Willy drew himself off the cot and took a few steps across the room, then turned back. "My hands shake, Sam. My eyes blur. I need to drink, sometimes."

"You're strong, Willy. You can stop it. The stories we told the press about me were lies, mostly, but a lot of what they said about you was true, Willy. The show is the success it is because of who you used to be. You were a hero, not afraid of anything. When I was a kid, I thought you could do just about anything. I didn't think you had a cowardly bone in you."

"And now?" Willy asked bitterly.

"And now I think you're just looking for a good reason to be a coward."

Willy's face reddened, and he leaned over toward Sam. "I ain't no coward. Never have been."

"Then pull yourself together, Willy. A lot of people

depend on you, and I won't be here to cover for you anymore." He stood up, still holding his hat, and looked at his father.

Willy turned away.

"Don't run anybody else off, Willy. You need these people."

"I don't need nobody."

Realizing the argument about who or what his father needed was futile, Sam shook his head and strode to the tent flap. He paused a moment, struggling to find an appropriate way of saying good-bye, but he came up empty. How did one say good-bye to a man who had berated and degraded him all of his life? How did one say good-bye to a man who had balanced for years on the precarious pedestal his son had held up for him? How did one say good-bye to a father who'd never known how to love?

There didn't seem to be a way, or a need, to utter the word. Accepting that, Sam decided to let it go unsaid.

Quietly, he left the tent.

The ride back to Hayton was tense and quiet, and Sam and Silena rode at a slower pace than they had on the trip over. Halfway between Omaha and Hayton, they came upon the cave where they had taken shelter from the storm. The place where they had first shared a kiss.

"Let's stop," Sam said quietly. "The horses need a drink."

Nodding, Silena slid off her horse and handed the reins to him. He led the horses to the creek running alongside the cave and turned back to her.

His hand closed around hers as he looked at her, and slowly, he pulled her into his embrace again. They walked back up to the cave, an unspoken pull drawing them there together.

Once they were inside, sheltered in the dimness, he turned around and pulled her into a crushing embrace. "I loved being with you these last two days," he whispered. "I loved spending so much time with you."

Her lips caught his, and he crushed her tighter, his tongue playing games in her mouth, games that stirred her yearning to life, games that drove her to distraction.

And then he let her go.

She stepped back, suddenly cold, and looked up at him with smoldering eyes. "Sam . . . I want you."

"Shhh," he whispered, touching one fingertip to her lips. "I want you, too, more than you'll ever know. But I want you to trust me more."

He pulled her against him again, holding her in a desperate clench that branded love deep in her heart. Then, releasing her, he took her hand and pulled her back into the light, down to the creek bed where the horses grazed.

Feeling flustered and still fevered, she had already started to mount her horse when Sam pulled her away.

"Ride with me," he whispered. "The way you did that first day we met."

Unable to speak, she allowed him to mount, then to hoist her up on the saddle in front of him. He put his arms around her and pulled her back against his chest, then kicked the horse lightly, tugging the other one along beside them.

"It'll take a long time to get there at this pace," she whispered.

He kissed her neck, licked up the column to her ear, making her roll her head back against his shoulder. "We've got plenty of time," he said.

His hands rose up her ribs, to the soft mounds of her

breasts, caressing her with warm touches. And as they rode, Silena learned that making love wasn't something that required shame or nakedness. Sometimes it was in the way a man touched a woman. Sometimes lovemaking was just a tender embrace that made one's body ache for a promise held just out of her reach. Sometimes passion was nothing more than a matter of trust.

They had ridden for miles before the question of trust erupted in her mind, demanding voice and clarity.

"Sam?" she asked on a whisper that mingled with the wind.

"Yeah." His voice was a deep rumble against her ear.

"Why didn't you want Willy to know you had done his shooting for him? It would have made him respect you more and stop treating you like a hired hand."

She heard him swallow, and his embrace loosened the slightest bit. "Sometimes there are more important things than the truth," he said. "Sometimes you have to think about how a person feels about himself . . . and what the truth might do to that."

"Is that why you lied to me about my mother?"

His embrace tightened again. "I wanted it to be true," he said. "I wanted to give you that. Even if I had to make it up."

"Just like you wanted to give Willy his pride."

"A little pride never hurt anybody."

"I guess neither did a little lie," she said.

And as they rode closer to Hayton Sam knew that he had been forgiven, at least on some small level. He had been redeemed. He had been understood.

And he couldn't remember the last time anyone had given him that.

* * *

It was obvious that the congregation, including the parson, were making concerted efforts not to speak to Margaret, as if she were unclean and not fit to sit among them in the house of God. A million mixed emotions whirled through Hitch's heart, but he couldn't make himself look at her. On the way back out to the wagon, three dowagers took Hitch aside and warned him that he would ruin his reputation if he kept seeing "that girl." He mumbled "Yes, ma'am" each time and picked up his pace toward his wagon. But four men waited for him there, with delighted underbreath comments about his "breaking in Nell's daughter." He controlled the urge to bloody their noses, for he knew that it would only make the gossip fly harder.

By the time he got his mother in the wagon and started to pull away, he saw Margaret walking alone down the hill from the church. She was cold, he thought, for she hugged her arms around her, and he saw her shivering against the wind. And when she turned to look at him, her face full of disappointment and shame, he saw the tears glistening on her face.

But his mother saw it as well. "Keep goin', Hitch," she ordered. "That girl needs to learn a lesson or two about where she's welcome."

"We were in church, Ma," Hitch said through his teeth. "Folks aren't supposed to judge each other in church."

"Nobody's judgin' her," she said. "They already know what kind of girl she is."

"Then what does that make me?" he snapped.

His mother's face took on a hard-edged glare. "A young boy seduced by evil. But if I have it in my power to stop it, it will not happen again."

Hitch cast one last look at Margaret, but she was almost out of sight. Feeling like a boy too afraid to stand up like a man, he slapped the reins on the horses and hurried home.

21

Margaret prayed beside Caleb's grave that afternoon. She prayed that God would forgive her for having her mother's nature. She prayed that Hitch would forgive her for the gossip she had brought upon them. And she prayed that, somehow, she would turn into a respectable young woman who acted properly and was accepted and liked.

But something told her that would never happen in Hayton, Nebraska.

She looked down at the mound of earth covering Caleb's grave. Grass had not yet begun to grow over it, and the flowers she had laid there after the burial were already dead. She didn't have the heart to move them.

"I love you, Caleb," she whispered as new tears ran down her face. "I wish you were here. I sure could use a friend."

But all she heard was the lonely sound of the wind sweeping over her, chilling her until her hands and feet ached with the bite of it. Finally, wiping her tears, she went back to the quiet house.

Her mother had gone out before Margaret even made it home from church. Margaret told herself she should eat, but the thought of food made her sick. She couldn't think of anything that would sit well on her stomach, and she told herself she needed to stop taking the town's rejection so hard. By now she should have learned to live with it.

She was tired, so tired. Deciding there was no reason not to, she crawled back into her bed and pulled the covers up. If sleep would come, she wouldn't have to face the heartache for a while. Eventually Silena would come home, and if her friend hadn't turned against her, too, she would help ease the loneliness.

Her eyes closed, and she felt herself drifting. . . .

She wasn't sure how long she had been lying there when she heard a wagon creaking in front of her house. Getting slowly out of bed, trying to shake off the grogginess, she went to the window.

It was Holl Brewster, one of her mother's regular customers at the saloon, who lived about ten miles out of town. He had been at church this morning, she recalled. Being already in town, he probably wanted a "favor" from Nell before he made the long ride back.

He strode to the door, purpose in every step. Dreading the confrontation, Margaret opened it.

"Ma ain't here, Mr. Brewster," she said. "I don't know when she'll be back."

His leer as his eyes swept her from head to toe told her that she shouldn't have opened the door. "I didn't come here for Nell," he said. He pushed into the house and closed the door behind him.

His gaze dropped to her breasts, appropriately covered with a high neckline today.

"Then . . . what? I . . . I don't have anything—"

"You have plenty," he said. Before she had the presence of mind to back away, he grabbed her arm and jerked her toward him. "Come here, and give me some of what you gave Hitch the other day. Folks are talkin' about it all over town."

"Get your hands off of me!" she cried, trying to pull away. But the more she struggled, the more anxious he became, and his grip grew tighter on her arms.

And as he groped at her clothes and struggled to get her to the bed, Margaret knew what it was to be helpless, with no one in the world who cared what was happening to her.

Hitch hadn't been able to eat a bite of his mother's Sunday dinner, even though Parson Evers and his wife had come to join them. He had sat lifeless at the table, nodding his head and trying to be polite, but the image of Margaret's tears as she'd walked home alone ate at his heart.

She wasn't a whore, any more than he was like the men who "befriended" Nell. She was a beautiful, lonely, sad young woman who cared more about him than she should have. And he had given her nothing but a bad reputation.

He excused himself from the table to go bring more firewood in for the fire, for the temperature was dropping rapidly. Pulling on his coat, he went outside, and recalled how Margaret had shivered walking home.

It wasn't fair. It wasn't right that a girl like Margaret should be born to a whore, and that everyone would assume that she was one, too. It wasn't right that everyone forgave him and overlooked what had happened, and turned their backs on her as if she didn't have the same shot at God they all had.

And it wasn't fair that he hadn't been back to see her since he'd made love to her. It wasn't fair that he'd succumbed to the pressure his mother and the church league had put on her.

He wasn't a boy, after all, who had to obey his elders. He was an adult, old enough to know what he wanted. Old enough to take responsibility for his own actions.

As the thoughts crystallized in his mind he realized how badly he wanted to see Margaret, dry those tears, and comfort her. He recognized the loneliness in his heart . . . not for just anybody, but for her.

And suddenly he realized that he hadn't thought about Silena in days. It was only Margaret who plagued his mind now.

He abandoned the firewood and went into the barn, to his horse's stall. He would go to see her whether his mother and the parson liked it or not.

He saddled the horse quickly and walked it out of earshot, so as not to alert his mother before he had time to get far enough away, then kicked it into a gallop.

Within minutes, Margaret's house came into view, and he saw the wagon parked out front. From the homemade wheel on the back left of the wagon, he recognized it as Holl Brewster's.

Margaret must not be home, he thought, if Nell was entertaining inside. Disappointed, he was turning away when he heard a muffled scream from the house.

A chill of fear burst through him. Leaping off his horse, he dashed to the door and opened it.

Margaret was fighting with all her might as Holl Brewster groped and grabbed and clawed. Hitch was on him in an instant, pulling him off her and flinging the man across the room to crash into a table. He didn't wait for Holl to get up to assault him again. Bending over, he picked the man up off the floor by his collar and steadied him while he reared back with one fist and crashed it through his face.

Holl dropped to the floor again, then scrambled back to his feet as blood began to run from his nose. "I didn't take nothin' that was yours, Hitch," he said. "There's plenty there for all of us."

Hitch rammed his fist into the man's stomach, making him double over, then crashed his other hand across the left side of his face. "Damn you, she's not a whore! Margaret Plumer is a lady, and don't you ever forget it!"

Holl lay on the floor and clutched his stomach, unable to get up. "I won't," he whispered. "I won't forget it. Just . . . let me go."

Hitch picked him up off the floor again and dragged him to the door. Throwing him out onto the small porch, he slammed the door behind him.

It was only then that he turned back to Margaret.

She sat balled on the bed, her face full of terror, shivering like an unswaddled babe in a snowstorm. Her clothes still seemed intact, for which he was grateful, and fleetingly, he realized that Holl's britches had still been buttoned as well.

He'd come in time, he thought, sitting down beside her and pulling Margaret into his arms. For once he'd done something right.

He held her as she wept against him, misery and agony and despair racking her small frame.

"That won't happen again," he whispered into her hair. "I won't let that ever happen to you again."

He felt her relaxing against him, yet clinging harder, and that was okay with him. He liked the way she needed him, and the reality of the emotions he felt for her.

"I love you, Hitch," she whispered, when her breathing had settled to an occasional hiccuping sob.

And as those words sank into his heart, filling it with their honey warmth, he realized that they didn't frighten him away.

"I love you, too," he said.

And he knew he meant it.

Word of Hitch and Margaret's continued affair spread along the Hayton grapevine, was whispered among the saloon crowd, then passed on at the general store. Silena heard it the morning after she got back from Omaha.

Mrs. Barlow had come calling to Margaret's house early one morning, hoping to lecture the girl on the wages of sin, and Hitch was there. It was obvious, she said, that he had been there since the night before, since she had seen him in the same clothes at the church social.

Lolita Phillips said that Hitch's ma was beside herself with worry, for her husband had been known to stray to Nell a time or two, and now she was losing her son to a whore.

And the parson had paid a visit to the Calhouns himself, to remind Hitch about the fires of hell. But Hitch had left the table before the parson had gotten into his lecture, and had headed off to Margaret's. The word was that he'd found her with Holl Brewster and, in a jealous rage, had beaten him to a pulp.

Realizing that Margaret needed a friend and a sounding board, and someone who would listen to her side, Silena determined to visit her the moment there was a lull in the store's business.

Not long after she'd heard about the fight, Sam

ambled across the street and found Silena working with a vengeance. Her hands trembled as she worked, and she looked ready to burst into tears.

"Are you all right?" he asked.

She nodded, but couldn't find her voice.

"What is it, Silena? Tell me."

She heaved in a deep breath and thought of telling him, but he'd never understand. How could she explain that Margaret was being bombarded with malicious gossip that could just as easily have been directed at her and Sam? "I . . . I can't."

He studied her for a moment, concern coloring his eyes. "Do you need a break? I could take over for a while so you could lie down or something."

"Yes . . ." she whispered, her eyes suddenly lighting up. "Yes, would you? The prices are marked."

"I know." He watched with concern as she flitted from the store to her house, as if she couldn't get out of his sight fast enough.

Quickly, he handled all of the customers in the store, and when they were gone, he went back into the house to see if she was all right. But Silena was gone.

A sense of panic rose inside him, and suddenly he feared that something had happened. Why hadn't he seen it before? Why hadn't he realized that something had upset her? Was it something to do with the outlaws? Was Jake sicker?

Before anyone else could come into the store, he turned the sign to "Closed," locked the front door behind him, and ran across to the sheriff's office for his horse, determined to find her if it took him the rest of the day.

* * *

Silena reached Margaret's house in record time and slid off her horse even before it had come to a stop. She saw Hitch out stacking wood and, fuming, stormed across the yard to him, hands on her hips.

Hitch looked up from the woodpile and frowned at Silena. "You look fit to be tied. What's wrong?"

"You, that's what," she bit out. "What have you been telling people about Margaret?"

"Nothing!" he said. "I ain't told nobody nothin'."

"Well, folks are sure getting a lot of ideas about her. The word is that you've passed a few around."

"That's a lie!" He turned away and took off his hat, ran his hand through his hair. She saw the bruises on his knuckles and instantly realized that the gossip about Holl Brewster was true. "I would never say anything bad about Margaret."

"Then why is the whole town buzzing about her? Why would you be so indiscreet that you'd let that happen?"

"I didn't *mean* to, damn it!" Hitch said, flinging around. "I just like to be with her, and I didn't plan any of it. Next thing I know, them fat biddies in town are yakking their fool heads off about us."

Silena could see that he was sincere, and she felt her anger cool a degree. "Look, I know that Margaret cares a lot about you. I don't want to see her get hurt anymore."

"Don't you think I feel the same way?" he asked.

"Then be careful with her. Don't give the town things to talk about."

"Yeah, well, I could say the same thing for you and Sam."

Silena's cheeks mottled, and she looked quietly up at him.

"Yeah, that's right," Hitch said. "I ain't blind. 'Course, the town is where Sam's concerned, and nobody'd ever think Silena Rivers would do anything unchristian. They might run her outta town, but they wouldn't think anything bad about her as they did."

She found herself unable to answer, unable to defend herself. It was all true. "Margaret has her mother hanging over her head," she said quietly. "She'll always have to fight that."

"You don't have to tell me," he said. "I know."

"Don't hurt her, Hitch. Please don't hurt her."

"I won't," he said, his eyes as serious as she'd ever seen them. "I swear it. You don't have to worry. I'm gonna take care of the gossip."

From a distance, they heard a horse galloping toward them, and as it came down the hill Silena realized it was Sam.

"It's your white knight," Hitch said sarcastically. "He does love to make an impression."

She ignored Hitch and watched as Sam approached them, breathing heavy as he slowed his horse. "Are you all right? You just disappeared, and I thought—"

"I'm fine," she said. "I just came to talk to Margaret."

She saw Sam eyeing Hitch, as if wondering what their intense conversation had been about, and for the first time it occurred to her that he might be jealous.

"I need to talk to her alone," she said. "I'll be back at the store when I'm finished. Would you please cover for me while I'm gone, Sam?"

Sam shook his head. "I don't like you being that far away from me in case trouble comes. I'll just wait out here with Hitch."

Silena saw the look of disdain on Hitch's face, but he didn't object. "All right," she said. "I'll try not to be long."

Leaving the two men together in their awkward quiet, she went to the door and knocked quietly, then went in. Margaret was standing over the stove, stirring a pot of stew that smelled better than anything she had previously been capable of cooking. Silena wondered if Hitch had started it for her.

Margaret turned around and smiled at Silena, but her face was pale and the shadows under her eyes showed that whatever had happened had taken its toll on her.

"Silena! You're back."

"I got back yesterday," she said, "and this morning when I opened the store, I started hearing things. Are you all right?"

Tears burst into Margaret's eyes. Abandoning the pot, she ran across the room and fell into Silena's arms. "Oh, Silena! It's wonderful! Hitch and I are getting married!"

The surprise of Margaret's announcement took some getting used to, but by the time Silena left her house that day, she was satisfied that both Hitch and Margaret knew what they were doing. It was gratifying to see Hitch's attention directed to Margaret rather than herself. She was glad they had found each other, for Hitch couldn't have picked a better time to come into Margaret's life. Just as Sam had come when Silena needed him most.

But Silena's new sense of security evaporated the next morning. She had just wheeled Jake across the street and into the store, where he was beginning to feel a part of things again, when she looked up to see Willy Hawkins standing in the doorway.

For a moment she didn't recognize him, for he was clean and fully sober for the first time since she'd met him. His eyes were sharp and alert as he looked past her toward Jake. Frowning, she took a step toward him. "Willy?"

Jake looked up with a start, and Silena instantly saw

the recognition there. His mouth fell open, and he made to get out of his chair, as though he'd forgotten that he had only one leg left to hold him.

"That you, McCosky?" Willy cracked out, and a slow smile stole across Jake's face.

"Well, I'll be damned."

Willy leaped forward and Jake grabbed his hand. Bending over, Willy pulled Jake into a harsh embrace.

"You ole son of a bitch," Willy said, standing upright again. "Look at you! You look like you been rode hard and put up wet. And where the hell is your leg?"

"Buried it so it couldn't walk away," Jake teased. "What on earth brings you here? You lookin' for Sam?"

Willy's smile faded. He pulled up a barrel, turned it upside down, and straddled it. "I came to see you," he said, his voice lowering. "I have some bad news."

Silena's face fell, and she stepped up behind her father. "What is it, Willy?"

"It's the Colonel," Willy said, fixing questioning eyes on Jake. "He's in Omaha."

Silena saw the blood drain from Jake's face. "He cain't be."

"He is, Jim. He rode in yesterday, roundin' up people to help him, wavin' money around like he'd robbed the national treasury. He's been askin' about you and Silena . . . and Sam. He knows what happened here, and he's bent on finishin' the job."

"The job? What job?"

Willy looked up at Silena, but he didn't answer her.

"What job?" she repeated, going around the chair to glare at her father. "Pa, is he talking about the job of killing you and taking me? Is that what he wants?"

Jake dropped his face in his hands. Furious, Silena spun around. "I'm getting Sam."

She dashed out of the store, and tore across the street to the sheriff's office. Bursting through the door, she called out, "Sam! Where are you?"

"Here. I'm here." He came out of the back room, his shirt half-buttoned. "What is it? What's wrong?"

"Willy's here," she said, trembling as he pulled her into his arms. "He says the Colonel's in Omaha."

"Oh, my God." He took her hand and ran across the street with her.

Willy didn't change expressions as Sam charged through the door, but Sam noticed immediately the degree of change in his father. "Willy, what are you doing here?"

"I came to warn an old friend about more danger comin' his way than he ever bargained for."

"Good," Sam said, pulling out his pistols and checking the chambers. "We appreciate the warning. Now we'll be ready."

"Ready?" Willy stood up, facing his son at last. "Sam, no fool will try to get ready when the Colonel is comin'. Best thing you can do is hide."

"Hide?" Sam gave his father a disgusted look. Squinting in disbelief, he asked, "Don't you know anything about me by now?"

"Yeah," Willy said. "I reckon I know that you're a stupid fool. What do you think'll happen when you're layin' dead in the street? You think folks'll write songs about you? Tell stories? Nobody'll even remember you two months from now. It ain't worth it, Sam."

"I don't have time for this," Sam said. "I have to round up the men in town and warn them. There's too much to do." He looked at his father, debating whether to ask. Finally, he forced himself. "Will you stay and help us, Willy? We could use your shooting."

"Hell, no, I won't stay," Willy said. "My days of bein' shot at are over. If I even look like I'm bein' shot, I better damn well get paid for it. No, I just came to warn you. I'll be leavin' shortly."

Not surprised, Sam nodded and left his father sitting beside Jake. At the door, he turned back. "Silena, I have to get word out, but I'll be back in a little while. I'm going to hide you, so you might want to get some things together."

Silena nodded, her eyes filling with tears, as he disappeared through the door.

When he was gone, she turned back to her father, her face raging with emotion. "Pa, it's getting dangerous here. You owe me an explanation."

Willy waited, watching the struggle on Jake's wrinkled face. But Jake made no move to answer.

Silena knelt in front of him, put her hands on his arms, and stared desperately up into his face. "Tell me the truth. Is the Colonel my father? Did you really kidnap me?"

"No!" He shook free of her and wheeled his chair back, trying to turn away, but she flung herself at him and stopped him. "I told you, *I'm* your father, and you're my daughter, and that's the way it is!"

"Then why is the Colonel after us?" she challenged.

"It's over somethin' else. Somethin' that has nothing to do with you."

"Was he married to my mother?" she shouted, her voice rising. "Was he married to Eva?"

"No . . . yes . . . you don't—"

"*Did* you kidnap me from her?" Her words came at a fever pitch.

"No, I didn't. I swear I didn't, Silena. It's nothing like that."

"Then what is it, Pa?" she asked as tears began to flow down her face. "What is it, if it isn't that? You told me it was, when you were feverish. You told me he was after you because you had kidnapped me."

"I was hallucinatin'," he said. "I don't even know what you're talkin' about."

"Damn you!" she screamed. "Why can't you just tell me the truth? Why can't anybody tell me the truth?"

"I *am* telling you the truth, Silena," Jake said, his eyes drilling into hers. "You have to believe me."

"I can't believe you," she cried. "You're a liar. You're all liars."

She ran from the store and locked herself in her room. But she knew that no lock would keep the forces of her mysterious past from catching up with her . . . one way or another.

Sam started back in less than an hour, his pistols loaded in his holster and a rifle in his hand. He found Willy and Jake crouched across from each other, engaged in quiet, solemn conversation. It occurred to him that Willy had never talked that seriously with him, but then he supposed it wouldn't have been natural. Willy was his father, but he'd never been his friend.

"Where's Silena?" he asked.

Jake didn't look up from the spot on the floor he was staring at. "In her room," he said. "You gotta hide her, Sam. I don't know how much good I'll be at protectin' her this time."

"I intend to," Sam said. "But you need to hide, too. This store isn't the best place for you to be as long as the Colonel's nearby."

"He won't have his men rounded up for a day or

two," Willy said. "Realistically, it could be a week before he's ready to make a move."

"Still, I'd feel better if Jake wasn't here. Why don't you wheel him back over to Caldonia's, Willy?"

Willy stood up, his bones creaking as he did. "All right, Jake. Let's go."

Sam watched him wheel Jake through the door, then he strode through the house, his bootheels shaking the floor. He found Silena's door closed, and when he knocked, there was no answer. "Silena? It's me."

She opened the door, and he saw that her eyes were raw and swollen, and that she was trembling. Instantly, she threw her arms around him.

"Hold me," she whispered. "Please, just hold me for a minute."

He set his rifle against the wall and slid his arms around her, holding her with the force and strength of a man who'd loved and lost before.

"What's the matter, baby?"

"Take me away from here," she cried. "Take me far away, where no one can find me. Where it doesn't matter whether I know the truth or not."

"Take you where?"

"Anywhere. Just away."

He pulled her back and looked down at her, realizing from the desperate, panicked expression on her face that she was serious. "There's nothing I'd like more than to take you away from here, Silena, but the fact is the town needs me. And we couldn't leave Jake. You can't run out on him now."

"Why not? Why can't I, when he can't even tell me the truth?"

"He will when he's able," Sam said. "If he's lying, it's for a reason. I haven't known him that long, but I know him well enough to know that. Besides, if you leave now, you'll never know the truth."

"So what? I've lived for seventeen years on nothing but lies. If I get far enough away, maybe I can start to believe all the lies."

"You'll never believe them," he said, "and you know it. But if you give me the chance to protect you, I'll help you find out the truth. And no matter how bad it hurts, I'll tell you. Can you trust me to do that?"

"No," she cried, breaking free of his arms and backing away. "I can't trust you. I can't trust anybody."

"You *can* trust me," he said, pulling her back into his arms. "You can, Silena. I'm only here because of you. You know that. If you run away now, you're no better than I was that first day, when you caught me trying to leave. But I stayed, Silena, because of you, and I'm not leaving you or the town to whatever the Colonel has planned."

He kissed her then, despite her struggle, despite her fury, despite her terror. As if she rechanneled that raging energy, she threw her arms around his neck, pressed her body against his, and slid her hands down to his hips. "Love me, Sam. Love me, please. Make me forget how afraid I am."

Control slipped away like a ribbon blown in the wind, and passion burned high as their hearts pounded and their hands explored.

An avalanche of charged emotion tumbled through them both as Sam unleashed the needs he'd held back, and as he took her to her bed he whispered words she hadn't expected to hear. "I do love you, Silena. I do love you."

She caught her breath, and he covered her mouth, their kiss growing more urgent, more orgasmic, more desperate. He laid her down on the bed, and quickly, awkwardly, urgently undressed her, then discarded his own clothes in a heated flurry.

Her fears vanished for the moment, and melted, instead, into something sweet and warm, something hungry and satisfying, something bigger than the uncertainty and the terror. They made love quickly, hungrily, taking, giving, exchanging. . . .

And when their release came, it was with heart flutters and misty skin and breathing that wouldn't be satisfied. And Silena had to face, at that moment, that she wanted it again . . . and again . . . and again . . .

No matter how scandalous it was, she was not ashamed. For she loved him. And she knew that he loved her.

For the first time in a long time, she felt safe, secure . . . and cherished. And she prayed that the moment wasn't the last of its kind.

Sam stayed with her that night, wrapping her in his arms as she slept. Beside the bed, he kept his rifle and six pistols—four of which had been hidden in hideaway holsters on his shoulders and in his boots—in case of a surprise attack before morning.

Looking at him in the pale moonlight falling through the window, Silena wondered how he slept at all, for she hadn't been able to surrender to the night. She snuggled closer, and he responded, moving his arm tighter across her back.

She thought of Sam's face when his father had said he would spend one night in Hayton so that he could catch up with his old friend, then leave before the Colonel could make it there. She could see that Sam missed that kind of camaraderie with his father, and that he almost envied Jake. And she hadn't missed Willy's subtle references to Sam's stupidity in facing the outlaws.

Now Silena wondered if Sam did, indeed, have the

skill to go up against a man who seemed to be something of a legend. But more importantly, she wondered why he should have to.

Because of her? If a man had kidnapped another man's child, wouldn't that man feel a vengeful anger that never cooled until the day he got his child back? Wouldn't that be enough for bloodshed and mayhem?

Doubt invaded her mind, and she told herself that the Colonel's actions were too extreme. There had to be more to it. Something that she didn't know.

Something she had no hope of finding out.

She slipped out of bed, and Sam stirred and opened his eyes slightly. "I'm okay," she whispered. "I'm just going into the kitchen."

He nodded and reached for a pistol, set his hand on it, and closed his eyes again.

She went into the kitchen and looked out the window, into the grove of trees where her father used to drink when he thought about her mother. There had always been love in his eyes—even pain—when her name crossed his lips. And yet rumor said he had destroyed her by taking the one thing important to her, causing her to die of grief.

It didn't add up.

She went into the store, cut across to the front window, and looked up the main street of Hayton. It was dark and quiet, for the saloon had closed early in anticipation of the gang who might ride in at any time. The town was preparing for more murder and rape, more destruction and devastation.

And it was all because of her.

Suddenly she felt a sense of tremendous responsibility. She couldn't let this happen. If anyone was going to stop it without more bullets being fired, without more terror and chaos, she was the one. Maybe if she just gave the Colonel what he wanted, what he had come so far to find, maybe he would leave Hayton alone.

The thought chilled her to the bone, and she hugged herself. Did she have the courage to go to Omaha before the Colonel came to her? Did she really have the bravery to find him and tell him who she was?

Yes, she told herself. She did have the courage. She also felt a desperate need to meet the Colonel, for it seemed now that only he could tell her the real truth. And if she went to him, his vendetta against Jake might be satisfied. Maybe then he would leave the town alone.

A new sense of purpose filled her. Quickly, but quietly, she began to move around the house, gathering the things she would need to take with her.

Before the first light of dawn woke Sam, she would be on her way to Omaha. And she would be close to finding the truth about her past, without one more drop of blood being shed.

Sam woke to an empty bed and sat up, looking around, angry at himself for falling so soundly asleep. He hadn't intended to do more than doze. Then he felt a keen loneliness, and he sat up and looked around the room. Silena's night clothes lay over the chair in the corner, and he realized she'd already dressed.

He got out of bed, slipped on his trousers and his holster, and peered out the curtain to the sun just barely beginning to rise over the plains. It was still early, he thought. It was doubtful that the Colonel would have rounded up enough men to come with him yet. He didn't really expect them for another day or two. Even if he was wrong and they started out today, they wouldn't be here before midmorning . . . unless they had camped outside town, waiting to make a surprise attack.

He went into the kitchen, hoping to see Silena waiting there for him, but there was no sign of her. "Silena?" He waited, heard nothing, and went into the store.

Light had begun to filter in through the windows, but no one was there. Jake and Willy had slept at Miss Caldonia's, since Jake was still under her care, and only his own footsteps echoed over the structure. "Silena? Where are you?"

As he realized that she wasn't here he began to panic. What if someone had come in and abducted her while he slept? What if she had been hurt?

Then another thought struck him, and he remembered her words of the day before. *Take me far away, where no one can find me. Where it doesn't matter whether I know the truth or not.* There had been panic in her eyes, and a distant glimmer of intention. Was she serious enough to leave alone?

Sucking in a deep breath, he ran back to the bedroom, dragged on his shirt, and grabbed his rifle from its place beside the bed. And then he saw the note.

She had laid it on the bedside table where he would see it as soon as he got the gun. Setting down his rifle, he sat down on the bed and opened it with trembling hands.

Sam,

By the time you see this, I hope I'll be halfway to Omaha.

Sam dropped the note and ran a shaky hand through his hair, trying to fight the dizzy wave of dread flowing over him. Beads of perspiration broke out over his lip, but he forced himself to read on.

I have to avoid any more bloodshed if I can. The only way is if I confront the Colonel myself. That way he won't come looking for me, and you and the others in Hayton won't have to risk your lives.

I'll also be able to learn the truth, at last. That's important to me, Sam. I can't run from it, so I'll run to it. It's the only way.

Please stay and guard the town in case my plan doesn't work. You're the only one they can depend on.

All my love,
Silena

Terror trembled through him. Wadding up the note, he threw it down and started out to the barn, where her horse was kept, hoping to God that she hadn't actually left yet. But even as he ran he knew that his hopes were in vain. Silena had made up her mind, and nothing, not even he, could stop her.

Jake heard the banging on the door downstairs and grabbed his gun from beside his bed, struggling to sit up. He heard Caldonia's frightened voice, and heavy feet running up the stairs. Holding his rifle poised with his finger over the trigger, he waited.

He let out a huge breath when Sam burst through the door.

"Damn it, boy, I almost shot you. I thought you was—"

"Silena's gone."

Jake squinted up at him. "What?"

"Silena. She lit out for Omaha before daybreak."

From the small cot along one side of the room, Willy stirred and sat up, coughing.

"Omaha!" Jake pulled out of bed, balancing on one foot, and grabbed the crutches leaning against the wall. "Damn it, why did you let her go? What's the matter with you?"

"I didn't know. She just got up and went. She left a note."

"A note? What did it say?"

Sam took Jake's rifle, checked to make sure it was loaded, then went to the pistols he had laid out beside his bed and began to check them. "It said that she wanted to see the Colonel to get to the truth."

Jake's face paled. "My God, Sam, you can't let her do that."

"I don't intend to," Sam said. Satisfied that the guns were properly loaded, he turned back to Jake. "I'm leaving right now. But you're going to have to fend for yourself if they come. My only worry is for her right now."

"I'll stay." Sam turned around to see Willy standing up now.

"Why, Willy? I thought you were bound and determined to get out of here before they came."

"Somebody's got to do it," Willy barked. "McCosky can't very well defend himself on one leg."

"Just hurry, Sam," Jake cut in, and Sam started to the door. "Every minute counts. You've got to get to her before she finds the Colonel. He'll kill her, Sam. I know he will."

Sam stopped and turned around. "What do you mean, he'll kill her? I thought he wanted her alive."

"He won't stop until he's bled every drop out of her, just to make me suffer, just like with Eva."

"Eva?" Sam took a step toward him. "Jake, what are you trying to say?"

"I'm tryin' to say, damn you, that the only reason I

took her in the first place was to save her life! Please don't let him take it now!"

He thrust forward and fell, caught himself, and scrambled up with Willy's help.

"All right," Sam said. "I'm going. And don't worry. I'll die myself before I'll let him touch her."

He dashed out and down the stairs, and was almost out the door when Willy stopped him.

"Son?"

Sam turned around and saw his father peering down the staircase. He had never heard Willy call him that, and something stirred in his heart.

"Don't cross the Colonel, son. Think of another way. He's a mean son of a bitch."

Sam cocked his pistol and started out the door. "So am I, Willy. So am I."

It hadn't occurred to Silena until she reached Omaha that it might not be as easy to find who she was looking for as it would in Hayton. She had never seen a big city before, for when she'd come for the show, she'd never actually entered the town. The activity in the streets, the number of people everywhere, the horses and carriages filling the roads, was more than she was prepared for.

For a while she rode helplessly through the town, wondering where she should stop to ask about the Colonel. She wondered how she would recognize him. Would he look like her, or would she instantly know him by some intuitive twist in her heart? She wondered what she would say when she approached him . . . or if there would be any need to say anything.

As the crowds around her swelled and she felt herself getting lost in them, she fantasized about her father—her real father, from whom she had been kidnapped—embracing her with tears in his eyes, touching her face, telling her that he'd looked for her all these years. She envisioned him telling her about her mother, wonderful things she could hold on to.

She fantasized about his loving her, and clearing up all the dark mysteries of her past. And in those fantasies, she ignored the violence he had already displayed, and put out of her mind his intention of murdering Jake and destroying her town.

She rode aimlessly along the street, gaping at the number of stores lining the walkway. Tobacco shops, shoe stores, women's dress shops, a store for undergarments . . .

The wonder of it all assaulted her, and she watched the people scurry by with purpose in their strides, people who knew where they were going, because they knew from where they had come.

The loud whistle of a train startled her, for she had never heard such a thing before. Following the sound, she prodded her horse into a trot. Rounding the row of buildings with their elaborate facades, she saw the train pulling to a halt.

A thrill shivered through her as she imagined all the places that train could take her, all the problems she could escape, all the dreams she could fulfill. . . .

But then she remembered the town of Hayton armed and waiting for an attack, and her purpose returned to her.

Near the train depot, she saw a hotel, tall and fancy, with elaborately dressed men and women going and coming through its beveled-glass doors. Perhaps the Colonel was staying there, she thought. Maybe they would know where she could find him.

She left her horse and went in, and waited her turn as businessmen in dusty suits signed in. Looking around, she felt small and out of place, as if everyone in the room could spot her as the country girl with a fraudulent past who'd never been to the city.

The desk clerk looked around the gentlemen signing the guest book and asked, "Can I help you, ma'am?"

"Yes." She stepped up to the counter, cleared her throat. "Um . . . I'm looking for a gentleman who may be staying here. His name is Colonel Alexander Rafferty.

As if she'd uttered the name of Lucifer himself, the man scowled and stiffened at once. "Yes, ma'am. He's stayin' here, all right."

"Oh, good." Tempering her smile, she tried not to look as hopeful as she felt. "Could you tell me his room number?"

"He ain't here."

Her heart sank again, and she let herself shrink back from the counter. "Oh."

"What you want with the Colonel, anyway?"

"It's personal business," she said, trying to look confident again. "Do you have any idea where he could be or when he might be back?"

"At one of the saloons, no doubt," the man said. "And if it's anything like it has been the last day or two, he won't be back till late. Which is just fine with me."

"One of the saloons?" she asked. "Which one?"

"Could be any of 'em," he said. "We have six on this street. He's been makin' the rounds."

Silena's eyes drifted toward the door, and she imagined going from saloon to saloon, asking for him. It wasn't something she'd counted on.

"Tell you what, ma'am," the clerk said. "If you want, you could rent a room, and I could tell you when he comes in."

She thought of the meager sum of money in her pocket and berated herself for not coming better prepared. "No. I need to find him now. I'll go to the saloons."

The man gave her a look of disbelief. "You goin' alone?"

She lifted her chin. "Yes. Is there any reason why I shouldn't?"

"Not unless you value your personal safety," he said. "The Colonel runs with a rough crowd."

Her heart sank further, and she thought of the men who'd tried to rape her, the same men who had killed Caleb and wounded Jake, and all but destroyed her town.

"Yes, I know." She took a deep breath, and tried to go on. "Is there anything you could tell me about him to help me recognize him? The color of his hair? His eyes? How tall he is?"

"He's got a big jagged scar on his left cheek," the man said, his face tightening. "And his hair's gray. And he's big enough to swallow two of you. Still want to go lookin' for him?"

Her face reddened, but she didn't let her expression change. "He won't hurt me."

"Are you sure?"

"Yes, I'm sure. Thank you for your help." A chill ran through her, but she fought it as she left the hotel.

This early in the morning, the saloons weren't filled to capacity, but the number of dirty cowboys standing at the bar or lounging at tables surprised Silena. She stepped into the first one, the Watering Hole, and scanned the faces for a jagged scar.

Several of the men looked up and leered at her, and a spiral of fear drilled through her. She backed toward the door, still searching, but no one there fit the Colonel's description.

Sucking in a breath, she left the stale-smelling room and hurried down the sidewalk toward the next saloon, which was only a few doors down, for the town seemed to sport more drinking houses than anything else. Silently, she prayed that she would find him soon so she wouldn't be forced to enter each one in turn.

She came upon one called Wheeler's Point and peered inside.

"Come on in, honey," a voice said from behind her.

She jumped and looked over her shoulder, and a filthy cowboy with sour breath stared down at her. His hand lit on her waist before she could move away.

"Get your hands off me," she said through her teeth. "I'm looking for someone."

His hand instantly fell away, but his leer only became more pronounced. "Well, if he ain't here, I'd be happy to step in."

She relaxed slightly, realizing that she was safe as long as he feared another man's jealousy. "Maybe you could help me," she said. "I'm looking for a man named Colonel Rafferty. I heard he was in one of the saloons."

The man's face went pale, and his leer vanished. "Damn it, woman. Why didn't you tell me it was him you was waitin' for? Tryin' to get me killed?" He looked around at the faces in the darkened room and nodded toward a table in the corner. "That's him, way back there."

He started to walk away, but Silena stopped him. "Wait. There are five men at that table. Which one?"

"The one with the scar, facin' us," he said. "He's wearin' a black kerchief. Now, if you don't mind, I don't think I'll let him see me talkin' to you. There's stories about the last time a man tried to cut in on one of the Colonel's women. He don't take well to it."

"I'm not one of his women," she said.

He shrugged and backed out of the doorway. "Just the same, I'm gone. Have fun, honey."

He left her standing there, and suddenly she felt as if

every eye in the room was upon her. Lifting her chin, she stepped fully into the saloon and focused her eyes on the back table.

He was sitting facing her, his back to the corner, and the others at his table were watching her with deadly hungry eyes, eyes that made her cold beneath their scrutiny. She could see his scar across his cheek even from a distance, a scar that boasted that he'd been in fights before, and that he wasn't afraid of risk.

Slowly, she started toward him.

A hush fell over the room as, one by one, everyone realized she was looking at the Colonel. Even the piano player slowed to a stop. The Colonel watched her come closer and closer, and when she reached his table, he didn't move a muscle.

Silena felt something between stark fear and deadly determination as she confronted him. "My name is Silena Rivers," she said, her voice trembling. "I understand you've been asking about me."

The Colonel rose slowly, sliding his chair back as he did. He was huge, she noted as he rose above her, and his face was bitter and aged. His eyes, a pale, pale shade of gray, studied her, not the way a father would look at a long-lost child, but the way a predator would assess his prey. A slow smile crawled across his face, and a shiver coursed through her veins, warning her that coming here might have been a mistake, that perhaps she should have stayed in Hayton and taken her chances.

But his first words changed everything.

"My God, girl," he said. "You look just like your mother."

And suddenly Silena felt she had done the right thing, and that everything would fall into place.

25

"Excuse me, boys." The Colonel's quiet command emptied the table quickly, and he nodded toward the chair across from him. "Sit down, Silena," he said. "I've waited years for this moment."

The words were not accompanied by a look that reinforced them, but Silena hung on them just the same. Slowly, she sat down, and he reclaimed his chair. "Why?" she asked. "Why have you been looking for me?"

The Colonel rubbed his stubbled jaw, his fingertips grazing the scar. "I thought you were dead. Saw McCosky fall into the Platte with you myself. Never dreamed he could have survived that."

She sat quietly, her heart pounding, for she knew the truth was about to surface. Everything she wanted—needed—to know was in reach. All she had to do was be patient.

"And then word got around to me that you'd been to Omaha askin' questions, and folks begun to put two and two together. Willy Hawkins had some theories that traveled the grapevine, and I became convinced that you were the baby that bastard stole from me."

Silena swallowed and leaned forward, her big eyes intent on seeing right to the heart of the ugliest truth she had ever encountered. "Tell me what he did. Why he did it. Tell me who I really am."

"He killed your ma," the man said, his face unchanging.

A burning heat scaled her cheeks. "No. He wouldn't have."

"Beat her to death," the man went on in a low, murderous voice through his teeth. "She died in my arms."

"No!" She caught her breath, sat back, and shook her head. "She . . . she died of grief . . . after he kidnapped me."

"That's what I told everybody," the Colonel said. "But that ain't the way it was."

Silena's heart took a violent plunge to her toes, and she sat still, staring at the man who held all her answers. "Why would he do that?"

"Revenge," the man said, throwing back the last of his whiskey and nodding to the bartender for another. "I killed some Indians McCosky was friends with. He swore to get even by taking the thing that meant the most to me. And he did. My firstborn child . . . and my wife."

"But he loved her," Silena said as tears came to her eyes. "I've never doubted that. And . . . and he loved me. He still does. He's spent the last seventeen years caring for me."

The Colonel sat forward and braced his elbows on the table, his eyes burning hers. "He beat her to death with the butt of his rifle, with you layin' in the bed next to her," he said. "Prettiest woman you'd ever seen, and I had to bury her with both eyes swelled shut."

One horrified tear dropped onto her cheek, followed

close by another. "Then . . . how did my pa . . . I mean, Jim . . . how did he get the ring? He told me it was hers . . . that he had given it to her. You know, the amethyst ring with the pearls . . . in the shape of a horseshoe?"

A look of hatred cast a shadow over the Colonel's face, and his mouth turned down in a scowl. "He stole it," he said.

"But the Bible . . . the inscription. She wrote the note."

"A forgery," he said. "Eva never wrote nothing to that man."

"But how could it be?" Her voice trembled, and her face twisted in disbelief. "Every time he looked at it, every time we discussed it, he got quiet and thoughtful, like he was thinking about her. I never doubted that he really loved her. Why would he get like that if it wasn't real?"

"Guilt," the man said. "He knew what he'd done."

The horror of it all was making her pulse race, and she searched her brain for more of the questions she had come here to ask. But the hateful revelations he'd already offered blurred them all. Nothing seemed to apply anymore.

"Tell me about her," she asked finally, her voice hoarse. "Did she . . . did she really look like me?"

"Spittin' image," he said. "Beautiful flowing blond hair, the greenest eyes you've ever looked into. A body that made a man do crazy things."

Silena blushed as his gaze seemed to drop below her neckline, and she shivered.

"I have a picture of her," he said.

Her eyes widened. "You do?"

"In my room," he said. "Back at the hotel. I want you to have it."

She caught her breath and nodded quickly. "Yes. I'd like that."

He reached in his pocket and pulled out some coins, tossed them down on the table, and stood up.

She sat still for a moment before she came to her feet. "Colonel? What . . . what are you going to do now? About my . . . about Jim? Now that I'm here, you won't have to go after him . . . will you?"

"The main thing was to find you," he said, and she told herself that wasn't an evasion. "You're my daughter. The only one I got."

"Then . . . why did you almost have me killed? Those men . . . they were terrible. They would have . . . hurt me . . . if my father . . . if he hadn't come in."

"I won't lie to you," the Colonel said, taking her hand and pulling her out of her seat. "I wanted Jake dead. But you I wanted alive. The morons weren't supposed to touch you."

"But you knew what kind of men they were," she said, planting her feet. "You would have let me be with them for days and days, knowing that they were murderers and rapists?"

His eyes took on a dull glare. "I was confused. Not thinkin' clearly. When I learned you were in Hayton, my only thought was to get you back."

"And to kill Jim McCosky."

He smiled sadly. "Revenge is a mighty potent thing."

Her heart sank, but she told herself she could talk him out of that revenge. He was her father, after all, and she was what he really wanted. And as he ushered her toward the door she told herself it would all be all right. The nightmare would be over soon, as soon as she had her mother's picture in her hand.

Beneath Sam's desperate prodding, Duke ran faster than he had ever run. Sam sat hunched in the saddle, his eyes focused ahead, praying that he wouldn't be too late.

But something in his heart told him he already was.

She was determined, he thought. Wildly so. And he had no doubt in his mind that she would have found the Colonel the first hour she was in Omaha. Either that, or he would have found her.

The wind was brisk, making his ears numb. He wondered if she had brought a coat, a change of clothes, a gun, and cursed the whim that had sent her to Omaha.

But he knew he was doing Silena an injustice. That wasn't really the way she did things. It wasn't a whim, but a lifelong yearning to know where she came from. And that was something that Sam could never give her.

Maybe that was good, for he doubted that her knowing her roots would make her life easier. Those roots were rotten, corrupt, and lodged in a place from which they should never be dug up. Some things were best left alone.

If the Colonel was, indeed, her father, he suspected that was one of them.

He kicked his horse harder in the flanks, and Duke made one last burst ahead. But the trip seemed longer than usual.

For the life of him, he hoped things weren't as bad as he imagined them to be.

The desk clerk at the hotel did a double take as the Colonel and Silena walked in, and he frowned and tried to catch Silena's eye, but she refused to look at him. She followed the Colonel up the stairs, down a long dark hall, and stood back as he put the key in the door.

When the door opened, the stench of sweat, cigar smoke, and whiskey wafted out of the room, but the Colonel strode in, dropped his key on a table near the door, and motioned for her to come in.

"I'll get the picture," he said. "And the other things I have of hers that I want to give you."

At the mention of her mother's belongings, all apprehension drained from her mind. In anticipation, she stepped into the room and looked around, taking in the arsenal of guns lying on the tables, the knives in holsters of their own, the boxes of cartridges stacked on the dresser. It was preparation for a war, she thought with a chill. The battleground was Hayton, and Jake would be the prize.

Behind her, she heard the door close. Slowly, she turned around and saw him locking it.

Dread pierced her.

"Why are you locking the door?"

He dropped the key into his pocket, and when he turned back to her, his eyes were deadly cold. "Don't want nobody to come in until we're done."

"Done with what?" she asked, beginning to tremble. "You were just going to show me the picture."

He didn't answer, but stood staring at her, his eyes hard and cold and emotionless.

"Where is it?" she asked. "Where's the picture?"

"There ain't no picture," he said.

Sudden terror struck her, and her heart tripped and hammered at a raging pace. "I trusted you. I believed what you said. . . . "

"That was your first mistake." He reached for her, but she shook him away. Running to the door, she banged on it and tried to turn the knob.

The Colonel grabbed her, and she felt a cold, sharp knife blade grazing against her throat. "Go ahead and scream," he said roughly against her ear. "I'll cut your throat and you'll never do it again."

"Why?" she asked. "*Why?*"

"I've waited seventeen years to get revenge on Jim McCosky," he said. "There are worse things I could do than kill you, but if it has to be, I'm willin'."

"No, please," she whispered. Tears ran down her face, and she sucked in a sob, trying desperately not to move. "Please."

He turned her to face him and shoved her against the wall. His mouth breathed a stench she hadn't smelled many times in her life, the smell of a man who'd slept all night with a bellyful of whiskey, then woken to take another drink. The blade made a soft sweep across her neck, reminding her how close her death could be.

"Take off your dress," he whispered against her ear.

Silena squeezed her eyes shut. "Please, no. Please don't do this. I'll leave quietly, and never say a word—"

"I'm gonna do it slow," he cut in, his lips sneering. "And then I'm gonna leave you bleedin' so you can tell him how bad it was. So he'll know without a doubt what it feels like to have somethin' of his tainted."

"Please." She closed her eyes, trying not to move, but he ran the tip of the knife to the center of her throat and cut the flesh until a perfect line of blood stung through.

She caught her breath to scream, but fear of that blade still poised at her throat silenced her.

"I said, take off your dress," he hissed again. "I want to watch you do it."

She looked up at him, her eyes full of fear and terror, but not defeat. "Kill me," she said. "Go ahead and kill me. I'd rather die than have you touch me."

As if the words broke some dam within him, the Colonel thrust the knife, and it landed beside her head in the door. Then he was ripping at her clothes, grabbing her flailing hands, throwing her down on the bed, and forcing his body between her kicking legs.

Something crashed. The door flew open, and a gun fired. The Colonel fell off her.

Silena sat up, screaming hysterically, and saw Sam coming toward her.

The Colonel reached for a gun and fired. She saw Sam's body flung backward by the impact, the blood splattering against the wall, his hand coming up, still clutching his pistol.

Before he hit the floor, Sam emptied the barrel of his six-shooter into the Colonel's body, until the man made no more move to fight back, until his lifeblood drained on the floor beneath him.

Still screaming, Silena flung herself down beside Sam and lifted his head into her lap. Blood soaked the front of his shirt. "Sam? Sam, are you all right?"

He could barely speak, but he muttered, "Yeah."

She sucked in a breath and looked over at the Colonel, who lay with his eyes staring straight ahead, his expression as evil in his death as it had been in life. "You . . . you killed him, Sam. You killed him."

He opened his eyes and looked up at her, and for a moment the clarity there convinced her everything would be all right. "I couldn't help it," he said. "You looked like you needed rescuing."

His eyes closed, and she felt the life sinking out of him. Holding him closer, she shouted for help. Several men who'd been within earshot but out of bullet range burst into the room, gathered Sam up, and began carrying him out.

"Please, hurry. He's bleeding so much."

No one answered, as if they had no time to be bothered with a woman's concerns. As they hurried him out of the hotel Silena didn't know whether he was dead or alive, and gathering all her strength, she followed them out.

By the time they got Sam to the hospital and the doctor saw him, he had lost more blood than most men could endure. He lay limp and lifeless beneath the doctor's hands, and Silena was told to leave the room as they dug for the bullet that had lodged too close to his heart. He could die before they were finished, she was told, and if he didn't, he'd likely die afterward from loss of blood.

She was frantic by the time the doctor let her back into the hospital room. "We got the bullet out," he said, "but we won't know if he's out of danger for a day or two."

"What does that mean?" Silena asked. "Could he still die?"

"I don't like to give false hope," the doctor said. "He's very weak, and he's still unconscious. We've stopped the bleeding, but he lost way too much."

"Can I stay with him?" she asked.

The doctor shook his head. "If I were you, ma'am, I'd

go on home. There's nothing you can do for him now."

"I can be here. You might as well give me permission, doctor, because I'm not leaving his side."

"Well, all right," he said. "If it's what you want."

She changed out of her torn dress, then sat next to Sam on the bed, stroking his forehead, talking to him, trying desperately to coax him back to consciousness. But he did not stir.

It was late afternoon when a soft knock sounded on the door, and Willy came in. Still sober, he looked like a man who hadn't slept in days. "Jessup wired me about the shooting," he said.

"Come in." She stood up, making room for Willy to see his son. Tears came to her eyes as he went to stand beside the bed. "He's going to be all right, you know," she said. "He has to be. He just has to be."

Willy stared down at his son's lifeless form, and after a moment Silena looked up at him. Willy had dropped his face into his hands, and his shoulders shook with the force of his regrets.

Silena touched his arm, the only gesture she felt comfortable offering.

"What did the doctor say?"

She issued a shaky sigh. "He said the bullet had hit close to the heart, and that the loss of blood might be too much for him. But it isn't, Willy. Sam's strong. He'll be fine. I just know he will. I won't rest until he opens his eyes."

Willy stared down at his son for another long moment and finally muttered, "Neither will I."

"Good," she whispered. "If he knows two of us are here fighting with him, maybe he'll fight harder."

Willy didn't say anything as he pulled up a chair close to the bed and sat down, waiting for his son to pull off the most heroic feat he'd ever performed. Crawling back from the abyss of death. Finding one more reason to live.

The first snow fell, soft and sweet, on the morning that Hitch came to pick up Margaret for the wedding he had decided would settle the town gossip once and for all. He had wanted to wait for Silena to stand up for Margaret, but the town talk was that Sam and Silena had both run out on Hayton when they'd heard the outlaws were coming back.

Something about the anticipation of more death and bloodshed had gotten Hitch to thinking, and he'd decided that there was no use in waiting for "the right time" to marry Margaret. He wanted to be married to her before he faced the outlaws again. If something happened to him in a gunfight, he didn't want Margaret left a marked woman because of him. Besides, if he made it legal, there wasn't a thing his mother, his father, Lolita Phillips, or anyone else in town could do to keep them apart.

She was dressed in her prettiest dress, one he'd seen often on Silena last year before she'd handed it down, and he decided the first thing he'd do for his new bride would be to take her on a shopping spree to buy some clothes of her own. Still, she looked beautiful, even bundled in Caleb's coat, and he smiled the proper smile of a groom-to-be as she came out to the wagon with him and let him help her in.

"Did you tell your ma?" he asked, sitting beside her and nicking the horses with the reins.

"No," Margaret said. "She ain't home from the saloon yet. It's still early."

"Do you want to wait?"

She shook her head. "No. I woulda wanted Caleb there.

He woulda been real happy. But Ma . . . I'd rather she found out later. Sure would like to have Silena with me, though, but I don't know where she is or when she's comin' back. Really, it's just us that matters."

He took her hand, and she clung to it, and he knew they were doing the right thing. They were quiet as they rode to the parsonage, where the seventy-year-old preacher—who'd been indignant that he'd left the table last Sunday—lived with his wife. He helped Margaret down, and together they went to the door.

Mrs. Evers opened the door in her robe and frowned at the young couple. "What on earth are you doin' here at this hour, Hitch?"

Hitch stepped inside, not letting go of Margaret's hand. "We need to see the parson, Mrs. Evers. It's important."

"Well, I'll see if he's up yet. He sleeps late sometimes."

They waited quietly as she disappeared into another room, and Hitch gave Margaret a grin and squeezed her hand. She suppressed a little giggle and looked at the floor.

The parson wore his trousers with his nightshirt hanging out over them, when he came into the small parlor. "Hitch Calhoun, what are you up to?"

Hitch took a deep breath. "Margaret and I would like for you to marry us."

"*Marry* you? Your ma know about this, boy?"

Hitch's smile faded, and he wilted a degree. "Well . . . no. We're elopin'. It's gonna be a surprise."

"It'll be a surprise, all right," the parson said. "One I don't want no part of."

Hitch looked at Margaret and saw that her eager expression had fallen as well. "What are you sayin', Parson?"

"I'm *sayin'* that I ain't gonna be responsible for a whim weddin'. I don't approve of what you're doin', boy, and I don't want to suffer your pa's wrath when he comes home and finds what you've done."

Hitch's jaw popped, and he swallowed. "I'm old enough to get married, Parson. So is Margaret. We know what we're doin'. We're in love."

"Hogwash!" the old man said, swatting his hand toward them. "You might be in heat, but you ain't in love, boy."

Margaret's face reddened, and Hitch saw tears welling in her eyes. He hadn't wanted to see her cry on her wedding day, he thought with a burst of anger. And he wasn't going to stand here and watch it happen.

"Fine," he said, starting to the door. "If you won't marry us, then we'll find somebody who will."

"I'm the only one in town can do it," the parson said.

"Well, there's other towns."

They left the parson gaping at them as Hitch dragged Margaret back out to the wagon.

They were almost a mile away when Margaret looked over at him with tears glistening on her face. "What are we gonna do, Hitch?"

"Don't worry," he said, taking her hand. "We're goin' to Omaha. And by dusk, you're gonna be Mrs. Hitch Calhoun."

Silena bathed Sam and tried to keep him cool as the day wore into night, and neither she nor Willy left his room for more than a moment at a time. They kept his lips wet and dropped chips of ice into his mouth to keep his tongue from drying.

As dawn crept quietly up over the horizon it was quiet in the room, except for the labored sound of Sam's breathing. Silena looked up at Willy with tears in her eyes. "I love him, you know."

Willy nodded. "I know. And I wouldn't be surprised if he loves you, too."

She stroked Sam's forehead, with no response. Rising fear assailed her—fear that she might never get the chance to tell Sam how she felt, fear that she'd never feel him hold her again. Fear that she'd have to return to her cold, dark world alone . . . a world where her past held only evil, where the truth still hid behind some dark shadow in her history.

Desperately, she looked up at Sam's father, determined to know his past if she couldn't know her own. "Tell me about Sam," she entreated. "Tell me about him when he was a boy."

"Sam was never a boy," Willy said. "He was born a man. Ran the family by hisself for years while I was gone. Did a good job, too. And that wasn't all he could do. He had brains. Sometimes made me feel downright stupid, even when he was no more'n ten."

"And then his mother died?"

Willy nodded. "I took him and my little girl, Stella, on the road with me." He looked over at his son and slowly shook his head. "Shoulda never done it."

"Why?"

"Because," he said as his own eyes glossed over. "It killed Stella, and her death nearly killed me and Sam both. Neither one of us has been the same since. At least, not until Sam met you. Then I started seein' that spark in his eye again, that purpose. But I didn't want him to leave. He was all I had left."

He looked at her, assessing whether to tell all, but the look of fascination in her eyes prodded him on. He'd never been one to waste an audience.

"You know, I didn't drink much before that. But Stella's death took somethin' from me. It's a powerful thing when your little girl dies. Does somethin' to you. Changes you."

"I guess having a sister die would be just as bad."

"Was," he acknowledged. "Sam was real tore up. Like he blamed hisself, 'cause he didn't save her. And I blamed myself. We just each had different ways o' showin' it. I drank, and he set out to save the world."

"At least a little part of it," she said quietly. "And he did, Willy. He saved Hayton . . . and today he saved me."

"I shoulda done better by him." The statement came out in a shaky, hoarse voice, and Willy braced his elbows on his knees and clasped his hands beneath his chin. "Damn it, I shoulda been a better father."

"I'm sure you did what you could."

"I didn't. I shoulda been more like Jake. I shoulda pulled out of the limelight and tended to my children instead of the show. Now look what I got. A show without no stars. I can't shoot worth a damn, and my son's layin' there dyin'. Hell of an end."

"It's not an end," she said adamantly. "It's not, Willy. Sam's going to be all right. We'll see to it."

"I stopped believin' in miracles long time ago, girl," Willy said. "But if you believe in 'em, you go right ahead and pray for one. Maybe you can give me a reason to believe again."

But as the day grew brighter Silena wondered if miracles did, indeed, still exist. Because none had come Sam's way, and she knew his time was running out.

When Hitch had suggested that he and Margaret get married in Omaha, Margaret envisioned them riding right in, finding Sam and Silena at the Wild West show compound, and heading as a foursome to the closest justice of the peace. The compound was practically deserted, however, and no one knew where Willy was.

But the troupe members they were able to find had heard a rumor—that Sam had been killed in a shoot-out with the Colonel.

Neither Margaret nor Hitch could speak as they rode from the compound into town. With stricken eyes, they searched the walks and faces for someone familiar who might tell them where their friends could be found, or even what had happened to them.

But there seemed no hope for finding Sam and Silena, and finally, as the sun began to set and the temperature began to drop way below freezing, Hitch made a decision. "We've gotta go on and get married, anyway, even without 'em. By now my ma has wired my pa in Kansas, and she's prob'ly sent out a search party. I don't want 'em to stop us."

Margaret's spirits sank, and she looked at Hitch with eyes that probed straight to his heart. "Are you sure, Hitch? You don't have to rush. I wanna be your wife, but there's no hurry."

"There is a hurry," he said. "I don't want 'em talkin' about you no more. And once the parson gets word out, why ever'body'll be talkin'. When we go back there, we'll go back married."

A slow smile stole across her face, and she reached up and kissed Hitch's cheek. "I'd like that, Hitch. It's just that . . . I wish we knew for sure about Sam."

"We'll find out before we go back," Hitch said. "And we'll spend the night here, in the hotel. But first we got to be man and wife, or it wouldn't be proper us stayin' together."

The idea sounded right to Margaret, so taking his hand, she let him lead her across the street to the justice of the peace.

The ceremony was sweet and memorable, for it was performed by a jolly, potbellied man with a bald spot on his head in the shape of a bowl. His wife, a stout woman who thought the two made a "precious couple," offered them tea cakes and hot cocoa before they left on their way.

It was dark when they left the justice of the peace, and out in the street, Hitch kissed his bride. Then, hand in hand, they found the loading house that the justice had directed them to.

They were standing in a short line to get a room, smiling like the newlyweds they were and gazing into each other's eyes, when Margaret caught sight of a sign hanging on the wall.

> WANTED: GUNSLINGERS & TRICK SHOOTERS. AUDITIONS HELD SATURDAY 10-2 FOR WILD WILLY'S WILD WEST SHOW. ONLY THE BEST NEED APPLY.

"Hitch, look!" she said, pointing at the sign. "They're lookin' for new people."

Hitch stepped closer to the sign and read the fine print, about the contests that would be staged and the number of people they were looking for. "I'll be doggone," he said. "You reckon I could get in?"

"Would you want to?"

Hitch turned back to his bride and touched her face. Suddenly his eyes turned serious. "All day I been thinkin' o' where I might get a job to keep from havin' to take you back to live in Hayton. Folks'll never accept you there, and as long as they treat you like Nell's daughter instead o' my wife, I'll never be happy there, either."

"You think the Wild West show is the answer?" she asked, astounded.

"I can shoot pretty well. Maybe not as good as Sam,

but I could learn. And I can rope and ride. I wouldn't be a star, maybe, but I could hold my own with most of them wranglers."

"Oh, Hitch!" Margaret threw her arms around his neck. "It sounds wonderful! I know you could get in! I just know it!"

"Maybe Sam could put in a word for me."

The words, uttered without thought, struck them both with full force. Margaret dropped her arms and stared up at Hitch.

"Oh God. I forgot about Sam . . . maybe it ain't . . ."

He slid his arms back around her and pulled her head against his chest. "We'll find out first thing in the mornin'," he whispered, "whether Sam is dead or alive."

Jake and Zane Barlow came into Omaha early the next morning with a wagonload of gifts and food for Sam from the people of Hayton. It was the first time in Silena's memory that Jake had ever left the small, secluded town, but now that Willy had wired that the Colonel was dead, he had no reason to fear travel.

She saw the wagon from the window in Sam's room, and quietly watched the man about whom she still felt so much confusion climb into his wheelchair. Willy met him in the street, shook his hand, and spoke to him in a low voice.

It was clear Willy was updating Jake on Sam's condition, but there wasn't much to tell. Sam still lay unconscious in a fever, unable to emerge from the cocoon of sleep that held him.

She reached over and touched his forehead, and shivered at the heat beneath her palm. She was losing him, she feared, and after all she'd been through, all the lies and deceptions and disappointments and shocks, she knew she couldn't endure this final loss.

She looked up and saw Jake in the doorway in his wheelchair, as Willy and Zane set him down. She met his eyes almost guiltily, as though she had been caught in her defiance once again.

"Hi, Pa," she whispered.

Willy and Zane tactfully left them alone. Tears burst into Jake's eyes, and he wheeled himself into the room and held his arms up to her. She leaned over and hugged him, loosely at first, but then his arms tightened in a death grip, and unleashing her sadness and misery, she clung to him as she had when she was a little girl and he was the master problem solver in her innocent life.

"Did he hurt you?" Jake's voice was ragged as he looked up at her, still holding her trembling hands.

She blinked her tears back and touched the razor-thin cut at her throat. "He would have. Sam stopped him."

Seeing the cut on her neck, Jake's face twisted. "That bastard did that to you?"

"It's okay," she whispered. "It could have been so much worse if Sam hadn't come."

Struggling to hold back his own tears, Jake dropped her hands and turned to Sam, as still as death on the bed. "Thank God he did."

"Yes, thank God."

She looked back at Jake, searching his eyes for something to believe in again. But it was hard, for every illusion she'd ever known had been hopelessly shattered. "He told me some things . . . about you . . . about Mama." Her voice broke, and she closed her eyes. "Pa, he told me you murdered her."

Jake's nostrils flared and his face reddened. "And what do you think? Do you believe him?"

As her incoherent emotions clarified themselves in her mind she shook her head. "No, I don't," she whispered finally. "I didn't believe it. You wouldn't have done that."

"I didn't," he said. Bracing his hands on the wheels of his chair, he looked up at her. "Sit down, Silena. We have to talk."

Slowly, Silena sat down, her eyes wide and waiting. The truth was a breath away, she thought, and Jake was finally ready to tell her. Her heart tightened with anticipation, but she swallowed and braced herself for what she had yearned for for so long.

"It was a long time ago," he said, wheeling himself to the window, the sound of his wooden wheels rumbling on the floor. "I was a scout for the cavalry. We were fighting to wipe out Indian resistance west of the Mississippi. And I wound up going through a little town in Kansas for a few days on my way home to Salina. It was her town."

He stopped, cleared his throat, rubbed his stubbled face, and went on. "Her name was Eva, and she was the most beautiful woman I had ever seen. Blond hair, green eyes, the most gorgeous smile . . . the kind that makes your heart do funny things in its chest when you see it." The twinkle in his eye was genuine, and Silena found no doubt in her heart that what he told her was true. He had loved her mother. She'd always known that.

"I fell in love the first time I laid eyes on her. It was in a dry-goods store, and she was buyin' fabric. She looked at me across a bolt of velvet, with those soft, bashful eyes, and asked me if I thought the color was too bright. I told her that it wasn't bright enough, if it was for her to wear. And she smiled."

Jake's smile was serene and rich with memories as he

stared out the window. "I decided right then and there that I wouldn't be leaving that town for a few days, and I asked her if she was married. She told me she had been married to a cavalry colonel who was recently killed. So I asked her if she'd mind if I called on her. Right then, she invited me to supper that night."

He heaved a deep sigh and tried to go on. His smile faded gently. "I saw right off that she was lonely, and needed some help, and I spent every minute I could with her. Couldn't stand to leave her house. Couldn't take bein' alone after I'd been with her. It was the first time I'd ever known somebody that I thought I couldn't live without. But when I asked her to marry me, she wouldn't. Said she wasn't ready, that it was too soon. And I was fool enough to respect that."

A deep, longing frown settled into his forehead, and he rubbed the wetness from his eyes.

"But you had an affair?" she asked softly.

"Yes," he said. "A deep, binding love affair. Those were some of the best days of my life. And when she told me she was with child, I—"

"With child?" Silena cut in, her eyes widening. "Me?"

"You," he said. "I told you, you're my child, Silena, not the Colonel's."

She let out a quick breath, and felt hope seeping back into her, warming the chill from her heart.

"I was delirious," Jake went on. "I thought surely she would marry me then. But when I pressed her, she finally told me the real reason she couldn't."

"She was already married?"

"She was already married," he confirmed. "To the Colonel. She had lied because she wanted it to be true. She hated him. He was cruel and ruthless, and she was scared to death of him. He was a powerful man in the cavalry, and when word came that he was on his way back, she told me she could never see me again."

He paused, wiped his eyes, then reached into his pocket for the black velvet pouch he'd put there that morning. His hands shook as he opened it and pulled out the ring that Silena had coveted for so long.

"I had given her this ring, had it made especially for her . . . but she gave it back before he came back, along with the Bible with the inscription." He paused, stared out the window, then brought his sorrow-filled eyes back to Silena. "I told her that I would take her away, that he'd never find us, but she knew he would. She wasn't willin' to take the chance."

"But didn't he realize she was pregnant when he came back?"

"He didn't realize it until he'd been home awhile, and then she told him it was his. He didn't know any different until she delivered three months early and you were obviously full term. Then he knew there had been somebody else, that he wasn't around when you were conceived."

The memory of the Colonel's description of her mother when he'd buried her came back to Silena, and a dreadful ache rose up in her heart. "What did he do to her?"

"He beat the truth out of her," Jake said, his voice cracking. Tears filled his eyes, and his mouth trembled. "He beat her to a pulp, until she gave him my name. And then he went lookin' for me."

Silena sat still, desperately struggling to keep the emotion from overwhelming her until she had heard everything. But her body trembled, and her heart pounded out a painful rhythm. Idly, her fingers rose to trace the cut on her neck. It was proof, had she needed it, that the Colonel had been capable of everything Jake said.

"What did you do?" she whispered.

"I had been watchin' the house since I'd heard you had been born," he said, his face twisting, "waitin' for the Colonel to leave so I could get just one look at my child. But when I went in and found her . . ."

The dam holding his emotions cracked. He doubled over and dropped his face in his hands. "She was bleedin', and her face was bruised and swollen. The whites of her eyes were bloody . . . and you were lyin' in her arms, cryin' your little heart out."

"And you took me?"

He slid his hands down his face, leaving it red and streaked with tears, and looked up at her. "I heard him comin', and I had to do somethin'. She died right in front of me; there was nothin' I could do. But before she died, she told me to take you . . . to hide you from him. And you were *mine*. . . ."

Tears ran in a river down her face, and she wiped them back with a trembling hand.

"He came back before I could leave, but I took you and ran out back, mounted my horse, and tried to get away before he saw us. But he heard you cryin' and set out after us."

"He thought we drowned in the river. Everybody did. Why?"

"I knew the river better than my own hand. I knew where we could go in to look like we'd drowned. But I jumped off the horse with you before we hit the water, and he shot at the horse until there wasn't much left. Thank God you didn't cry for a while, and he gave up, satisfied that we were both dead, and left.

"I didn't care what stories he told about how she died, or who took you. All I knew was that I had to get far away with you, and raise you the way Eva would have wanted you raised. I hired a wet nurse to come to

Hayton with us, and she took care of you until you were two. When she died, there were plenty others who couldn't wait to help out."

Silena breathed in a shaky sob. "All this time . . . I thought that evil man was my father. . . . Why didn't you tell me, Pa? Why didn't you tell me?"

"Because I didn't want you thinkin' bad things about your ma—havin' an affair while she was married, tellin' me to take you, bein' married to a man like that in the first place. And the less you knew, the less likely you were to say the wrong thing to the wrong person. It wasn't until you went to Omaha that word got out, and all it took was this ring."

She wiped her eyes again, her mouth distorting in misery. "I'm sorry, Pa. My curiosity has cost everyone so much."

"No, Silena. My silence has. You had every right to be curious. I shoulda trusted you more with the truth. I shoulda given you more reason to trust me. But it's hard, girl. It's hard rememberin' the way she died. It's hard picturin' her lyin' there beaten. It's hard knowin' how much I loved her—how much I still love her—and realizin' that I didn't do a damn thing to protect her from the Colonel."

Sobbing, Silena went to her father, knelt down in front of him. "You did what you could, Pa, and for seventeen years, you protected me from him. In my heart, I always knew you were my father. In my heart, I knew you didn't do the things they said you did."

He looked down at the ring, wiped his face again. "I put so much into designing this ring. I wanted it to be the only one of its kind. It was the horseshoe emblem that Willy and me had on the ranch we started."

He took Silena's hand, laid the ring into her palm, and closed her hand around it. "It's yours now, by all rights," he said. "There's no danger in wearin' it anymore."

"Thank you, Pa," she whispered. "Thank you." She slid the ring on, gazing at the symbol of the love between her parents with tears in her eyes. "But the Bible . . . they took the note, Pa. You don't have anything of her left."

He touched her face, and hot tears escaped his eyes. "I have you," he whispered. "That's the best thing she ever gave me."

She slid her arms around his neck, clinging to him again. "I love you, Pa."

"I love you, girl," he said, patting her back awkwardly. "And I'm so glad Sam took the Colonel down. I'm so glad it's all over." He looked up and saw Willy in the doorway, peering over at his son with worried eyes.

"Come in, Willy," Jake said. "We're done here. You can sit with Sam awhile."

Quietly, Willy came inside and leaned over the bed, looking at his son without touching him.

"You know, he saved my little girl," Jake said, wiping his eyes. "I owe him a lot for that. He's a real hero, just like the kind I remember from the old days."

Silena's eyes glazed over as she recalled the ride that first time Sam came with her to Hayton, forcibly and against his will. "Funny, when I brought him to Hayton, he was just a showman *pretending* to be a hero."

Jake nodded, as if he understood from a level beyond logic. "When I brought you to Hayton, I was just a hero tryin' to be a father."

Willy sat down on the bed next to his son and dropped his head into his palm. "And for the last third of my life, I've been a father tryin' not to be. Looks like we all wound up with what we wanted. Whether we really wanted it or not."

Silena went to stand behind Willy. Gently, she

touched his shoulders, massaged, and felt the knotted tightness in them. "It's not too late," she whispered.

With his rough, hard hand, he took hers and squeezed it. "Maybe not."

A slight movement on the bed startled them. Letting her hand go, Willy sat straighter. "He moved. I felt him move."

Silena stepped closer to Sam and, leaning over his head, heard him sigh. "Sam? Sam, can you hear me?"

His eyes opened a crack, and in a hoarse half whisper, he muttered, "What's goin' on?"

Silena sucked in a breath and threw her arms around him, with no regard for her tears falling on his face and neck and chest. "Oh, you're awake! You're awake!"

He lifted his hand and winced at the pain in his bandaged shoulder, then tried the other and circled her in a tight, though weak, embrace. "Are you all right?"

"Me?" she cried. "I'm wonderful. Just wonderful!"

"Then I'm feelin' kinda wonderful myself," he whispered.

He sought her mouth, found it, and kissed her, deep and long. When the kiss broke, they held each other still, their mouths pressed against each other's skin, breathing in the scent of one another. "I love you, Silena," he said.

"And I love you." She wept with the strength of emotion in those words, and quietly, Jake and Willy left them alone.

Hitch and Margaret found Jake and Zane at the Wild West show compound with Willy.

"I'm tellin' you, Sam crashed in and put the Colonel outta business once and for all," Jake said triumphantly. "It was damn near worth sacrificin' a leg to know that he ain't still walkin' around somewhere threatenin' ever' body who comes his way."

"We were so scared," Margaret said. "We couldn't find them anywhere. We got married anyway—"

"Married!" Jake frowned, looking from Hitch to Margaret, then back again. But after a moment the frown faded into a grin, and he reached out for Hitch's hand. "Congratulations, boy. I guess you know what you're doin'."

"Thank you, sir," Hitch said. "But my folks won't think so, and neither will most of the town. That's why I've decided to stay for the auditions on Saturday. See if I can get on with the show."

"*This* show?" Willy asked, looking him over with greater attention. "Can you shoot, boy?"

"I helped Sam pick off some of them outlaws," Hitch boasted. "You can ask him."

"I will," Willy said. "You can count on that. What else can you do?"

"Well . . . I can—"

Willy lifted a holster off his bed and tossed it to Hitch. "Put this on, boy, and we'll step outside. You can show us."

Hitch shot Margaret an uncomfortable look, but the enthusiasm on her face gave him more confidence than he would have had alone. He pulled the holster around his hips and buckled it on, feeling the heavy weight of a six-shooter on each hip.

"I do better with a rifle," he said, "but I ain't too bad with pistols."

Willy snorted and took Hitch to a target set up fifteen yards from where they stood.

"Let's see if you can hit that," he said, pointing to one glass bottle sitting on a fencepost.

Hitch drew, aimed, and fired. The bottle shattered.

Margaret squealed, but he shot her a quelling look.

"Ain't bad," Willy said. "A good shootist oughta be able to hit a target at fifteen yards. Means you got potential. But how are you with speed?"

"Ridin'?" Hitch asked.

"No, shootin'. How fast can you throw lead?"

Instead of answering, Hitch returned the gun to his holster, dropped his hands to his sides, opened and closed them to limber them up, and took a deep breath.

Then he drew both guns and unloaded all twelve cartridges within seconds.

Jake applauded from his wheel chair. "Where'd you learn to do that, Hitch?"

"Just messin' around at the ranch," he said.

Willy rubbed his jaw and shook his head. "Don't applaud, Jake. That was too slow. And he had to think too much about cockin' and firin'. It was awkward."

"Well, I never done trick shootin' before," Hitch said. "I'm a fast learner, though."

"Let's see if you are," Willy said. He took one of the pistols from the holster, reloaded the chamber with cartridges from the belt, and aimed.

"You have to twist your wrist down, like this," he said, demonstrating. "Grasp the handle this way, and your finger needs to point down at a forty-five-degree angle over the trigger. 'Course, your thumb's as important for cockin' the hammer fast as your trigger finger is.

"Takes practice," he said. "Hours a day. But before long, you can draw, cock, and shoot in one motion. That's the goal, boy. That's what I expect from my shooters, before I can ever train 'em how to do the fancy stuff."

Hitch's expression fell. "Then you're sayin' I ain't good enough?"

Willy crossed his arms and rubbed his jaw again. "We maybe could train you for somethin'," he said. "If you don't mind startin' at the bottom and workin' harder than you ever worked in your life."

Hitch's eyes reflected the grin creeping across his face. "When would I start?"

"You could start Saturday. We have three shows a week for the next four weeks, and then we're hirin' a train to take us to the East for the rest of the winter. You up to all that travel?"

"Yes, sir. It sounds good."

"What about your bride? It's a rough life for a young lady. Some ain't cut out for it."

"I'll love it!" Margaret said. "It's the best thing I could think of!"

For a moment Willy's face sobered as he remembered his daughter, about Margaret's size, with an ailing body and a broken spirit. "If I think for a minute that the show's gettin' to you, girl, I'll insist that you drop out. It ain't my intention to drag women or children around the country if they ain't right for it."

"I'll be fine," she said, struggling to rein in her enthusiasm. "Oh, Hitch, won't it be fun?"

With a loud whoop, Hitch threw his arms around her waist and swung her around. When he'd set her down, he turned back to Jake. "Where can we find Sam and Silena? We have a lot to tell 'em."

"Sam's still in the hospital," Jake said. "Jessup can tell you how to get there."

Hitch took Margaret's hand, and they rushed from Willy's tent. "Thanks, Mr. Hawkins. I won't let you down."

"Willy, boy. Everbody calls me Willy."

Jake and Willy watched as the young couple went off in search of Jessup. Willy smiled. "That boy reminds me a little of Sam when he was that age. Who knows? I've done miracles before. Maybe I can make him a star yet."

"Gonna take him under your wing, Willy?" Jake asked.

Willy laughed, for the first time since he could remember. "Hell, somebody needs to. He's about as green as a sapling."

"But saplings grow into trees," Jake pointed out.

Willy's smile faded. "They do at that. But we can make sure they have the chance to grow into mighty trees and don't get cut down before their time."

"I couldn'ta put it better myself," Jake said.

And the two old friends laughed together.

By the time Hitch and Margaret found Sam and Silena, Sam was sitting up in a chair, his arm in a sling, trying to eat the hospital meal that was the best incentive he could imagine for getting well.

Silena jumped when she saw Margaret in the open doorway. "Margaret! What are you doing here?"

"We . . . sorta had some business to take care of," Margaret said, hugging her.

Hitch stuck his head in beside her, and Silena gave them both a confused, suspicious look. "All right. What's going on?"

Hitch lifted Margaret's left hand and showed her the cigar band he had put there last night until he could afford a real ring. "We got married."

"*What?* When?"

"Last night," Margaret said. "Oh, Silena. I wanted you there with me, but Hitch wanted to go on and do it, and it seemed like the right thing. I hope you ain't mad."

"Mad?" Silena caught her breath and stared at both of her friends. "I can't believe this!"

Rallying, she opened her arms wide and hugged

them both. "But why . . . how? I mean, I thought you were going to wait awhile. Isn't this all of a sudden?"

"Leave them alone, Silena," Sam said, reaching out to shake Hitch's hand. "When you're really in love, what's the use in waiting?"

Silena met Sam's eyes as she tried to decipher the meaning of his words. His eyes were serious, probing, and her heart did a tiny flip in her chest.

"Are you all right?" Hitch asked Sam, cutting into their silent exchange.

"I'm fine," Sam said, realizing those were the first truly kind words the young man had ever uttered to him. "Just a shoulder wound, like yours. Nothing to worry about."

"It was *not* a shoulder wound," Silena corrected. "The bullet was about an inch from his heart. It could have been bad."

"Wasn't, though," Sam said, taking her hand and pulling her to his chair. "I'll be back to normal in a couple of days. Just in time for the wedding."

"No," Silena corrected. "They're *already* married. We missed the wedding."

"I'm not talking about their wedding."

Silena looked down at him, confused. "Whose, then?"

"Mine," he said, a grin igniting in his eyes. "And yours."

Silena stared at him for a short stretch of time, before she fell to her knees in front of him and looked up into his eyes. "Really, Sam?"

"If you'll say yes," he whispered.

Tears burst into her eyes, and she stared at him, speechless.

"Go ahead, Silena," Margaret prodded. "Say it!"

"Well . . . yes! Of course I'll marry you!" She threw her arms around his neck, and he embraced her with his good arm, holding her until he thought he might break her.

"Oh, my gosh. There's so much to do. So many things to take care of!" she cried.

"We'll let the troupers help," Sam said. "We can get married on the compound, before we leave Omaha. It'll be my last great performance before I move on for good. Would that be all right with you?"

Silena's smile grew from her heart, and she wiped her tears and nodded. "Yes, that's fine with me, Sam. That's just fine with me."

The wedding took place in the center ring of the Wild West show, with the entire troupe in full dress, and Willy riding Lightning, sober and fully dressed in white. Sam did no trick shooting or stunt riding for the fans who turned out, however, for he'd made it clear to everyone who knew him that he was trading in his fame and notoriety for a wedding ring and a sheriff's badge.

Margaret and Hitch sat in the bleachers, among the Hayton crowd, for Hitch had not yet joined the troupe, though he'd been hired to start that week. Margaret's arm was hooked through his, and his hand was placed lovingly over hers, not hiding from anyone the fact that he was proud to have her as his bride.

Jake gave Silena away, dressed in clothes he'd purchased from an Omaha tailor and hobbling on a crutch. Before he handed her to Sam, he shook his hand. "You're the only man I've ever met who can do a better job protectin' Silena than I could," he said. "Make her happy, son."

"I will," Sam said, taking her hand and hooking it through his arm.

Silena smiled with a peace and serenity she had never known in her life, for now she knew who she was and where she came from, and just how much love was associated with the myriad lies in her life, the lies that only now contained truths that reached to the roots of her existence.

For through all the pain and turmoil, all the mystery and confusion, Silena had learned that sometimes, when people aren't as they appear or wish to be, they have the capacity to become so.

The preacher pronounced them husband and wife before the troupe and a thousand fans, and a cheer went up over the whole arena. Then, mounting his horse, Sam performed the final stunt of his career.

Once again, he swept Silena off her feet and into his saddle and, amid cheers and whistles from the fans, left the arena with his bride.

They had ridden for several minutes when Sam reached down and kissed the tender flesh just at the juncture of her neck and shoulder. "You look so beautiful today, Mrs. Hawkins. So beautiful."

"I feel beautiful today," she whispered. "And madly in love."

He let the horse slow and nuzzled her neck some more. "Tell me, Mrs. Hawkins. What was it that made you decide to marry me?"

She thought for a moment, and a slow grin skittered across her face. "You just looked like somebody who needed rescuing."

Sam laughed and pulled her back against him as the horse broke into a gallop, and together, they rode off for their new home, in Hayton, where life was predictable and secure, but where there would never again be a dull moment.

MARIANNE WILLMAN
YESTERDAY'S SHADOWS

WINTER TAPESTRY